Mixing business with pleasure!

The Elliotts:
Secret Affairs

Three glitzy and glamour romances from three
beloved Mills & Boon authors!

G000320406

The Elliotts:
Secret Affairs

SUSAN CROSBY

HEIDI BETTS

CHARLENE SANDS

First published in Great Britain 2011
by Mills & Boon, an imprint of Harlequin (UK) Limited,
Eton House, 18-24 Paradise Road, Richmond, Surrey TW9 1SR

THE ELLIOTTS: SECRET AFFAIRS
© by Harlequin Enterprises II B.V./S.à.r.l 2011

The Forbidden Twin, Mr and Mistress and *Heiress Beware* were first
published in Great Britain by Harlequin (UK) Limited in separate,
single volumes.

The Forbidden Twin © Harlequin Books S.A. 2006
Mr and Mistress © Harlequin Books S.A. 2006
Heiress Beware © Harlequin Books S.A. 2006

ISBN: 978 0 263 88345 9

05-0511

Printed and bound in Spain
by Blackprint CPI, Barcelona

THE FORBIDDEN TWIN

BY
SUSAN CROSBY

THE FORBIDDEN WAY

Susan Crosby believes in the value of setting goals, but also in the magic of making wishes. A longtime reader of romance novels, Susan earned a B.A. in English while raising her sons. She lives in the central valley of California, the land of wine grapes, asparagus and almonds. Her checkered past includes jobs as a synchronized swimming instructor, personnel interviewer at a toy factory and trucking company manager, but her current occupation as a writer is her all-time favorite.

Susan enjoys writing about people who take a chance on love, sometimes against all odds. She loves warm, strong heroes; good-hearted, self-reliant heroines…and happy endings.

Susan loves to hear from readers. You can visit her at her website, www.susancrosby.com.

For Mabel, a woman of grace and humour.
Mum knew best.

One

Early March

John Harlan clutched a two-carat, brilliant-cut diamond engagement ring in one hand and a Glenfiddich on the rocks in the other, his third in the past hour. Cold had settled in his bones, his heart, his soul. It probably didn't help that he hadn't turned on the heat or even a lamp since night fell hours ago. Only the lights of New York City through his huge picture window illuminated his living room, making a hazy silhouette of the bottle of scotch on the coffee table. What more did he need to see than that, anyway?

A few hours ago his fiancée—former fiancée—had gently placed the diamond ring in his palm. He hadn't let go since.

John had thought he knew and understood Summer Elliott. She was goal-oriented and orderly, like him, and together they were dynamic, a power couple with great lineage and an amazing future. At twenty-nine, he was at a perfect age for marriage, and at a perfect point in his career at his advertising agency. Everything according to schedule.

She'd ended all possibility of a future together that afternoon.

He hadn't seen it coming.

They'd dated for months, long enough to know the relationship worked. They'd gotten engaged less than three weeks ago, on Valentine's Day, appropriately, romantically. And now, while he'd been in Chicago working with a new client this past week, she'd found herself another man—a rock star, of all people. Calm, sedate Summer Elliott, the woman whose personality matched his, had found herself a rock star.

John downed his scotch, relished the burn and was contemplating another when the doorbell rang. He didn't move. The bell rang again. He picked up the bottle and poured, the ice from the previous drink almost melted. Knuckles rapped on the door, and a female voice called his name.

Summer? No. She wouldn't come here.

Curious, however, he set the glass on the table and stood, taking a moment to shove his fingers through his hair and to find his balance. Although it was uncharacteristic of him to have more than a glass or two of wine in an evening, he wasn't drunk. At least he didn't think so, maybe just slightly off-kilter.

He opened his door and did a double take at the sight

of Summer standing at the elevator ten feet away, her back to him.

"What are you doing?" he asked, squinting against the light and stepping into the hall just as the elevator pinged, indicating its arrival on the fifteenth floor, his floor.

She spun to face him but said nothing. He registered that she looked different in her short red dress, but couldn't put his finger on exactly why. Her scintillating light auburn air caught the light, the soft, natural curl caressing her shoulders and drifting down her back. Her light green eyes were focused directly on him, her expression open and caring. Caring? Why should she care? She'd dumped him. Unceremoniously. Emotionlessly.

Which pretty much defined their relationship. Emotionless. Sexless. A partnership with a future based on a solid friendship and healthy respect for each other, if without passion. But he'd loved her and believed she'd loved him. He'd always figured the passion part would fall into place at some point, and had respected her wishes to save herself for the marriage bed.

Had she realized her mistake in breaking it off with him? Was that why she was here?

Why wasn't she talking? She'd come to see him, after all.

"Are you here to apologize?" he asked. Did he *want* her to apologize?

"Made a mistake," she said so low he could barely hear her. She walked toward him, her hand outstretched. "A big mistake." Her fingertips grazed his chest, then she pulled back as if burned, curling her fingers into a fist that she pressed against her heart.

His gut tightened. Her touch had been light, but lethal

to his equilibrium. Hope tried to shove hours of hurt out of the way. The hurt resisted giving way…until she reached out again and was suddenly kissing him—kissing the hell out of him. Caught off guard by her new, surreal level of passion, he kissed her back until she moaned, even as a cautionary voice in his head shouted at him not to forgive the woman who'd never slept with *him,* her fiancé, yet who'd given herself to a man she'd just met.

When she pressed her hips to his and moved against him, he was grateful he hadn't had that fourth drink and could still think clearly enough to know what to do next. Resisting wasn't an option, even though he'd spent months doing exactly that. Not this time, however. Not this time.

He scooped her into his arms, carried her to his bed and laid her on the comforter, deciding that the reason she looked different was that she'd come dressed to seduce him—something she'd never done before.

An unexpected warmth spread through him at the thought that she'd made that kind of effort for him.

"This is out of the blue," he said, turning the words into a question, wanting to trust her motives, but afraid to. What did it say about him if he so easily forgave her?

"I never expected to make love with you."

He frowned. "What do you mean?"

"Just that."

It wasn't an answer, but apparently it was all he was going to get. Had the bad-boy rock star already dumped her? Did it matter? Yes. But…*but* John wanted to show her what she'd been missing as he'd reined himself in all those months, honoring her self-imposed pledge of chastity. His ego even demanded it.

He turned on a bedside lamp, pulled off his tie and un-buttoned his shirt, his movements jerky. She wasn't telling him to stop. She was really going through with it?

He shrugged off his shirt and tossed it aside, reached for his belt buckle and pulled his belt out of the loops, letting it drop to the floor, noticing her spiky red high heels there, as well, a vivid reminder of the strangeness of the evening. He'd never seen her wear heels that high, which put her equal in height to him.

Equal. Was that the point? To make them equals? She'd suddenly become aggressive, not merely assertive?

His jaw tightened painfully as he searched her face, seeking answers to questions he didn't ask because he wasn't sure he wanted the answers. Not only did she not tell him to stop, she didn't even flinch and instead studied his every move, not a hint of virginal shyness in her eyes. He toed off his shoes, slipped his trousers down and off, along with his socks.

His briefs were black and tight, had gone tighter in the past few minutes. She made a leisurely inspection of him that was more exciting than any kiss or touch he could remember. She swallowed and lifted her eyes to meet his again. Her nipples pressed against her dress. His heart thundered; his fists clenched.

If he took off the briefs, would she run? She'd kept him at arm's length for months and months, yet after she'd slept with another man, she wanted *him* now? What kind of sense did that make? Comparison? It was totally out of character for her.

And if he slept with her now, would it be in forgive-ness…or out of revenge? He wasn't sure if he even wanted to find out, but an irrational force made him continue, even knowing he might be shot down or stopped. Or humiliated.

Except she'd said she'd made a mistake….

He pushed off the briefs. She rose to her knees and reached out to touch him, her fingertips gliding down him like warm, silky water. He sucked in a breath, knelt on the bed and peeled her formfitting dress over her head, discovering a red lacy bra and matching thong underneath. He pushed the satin straps down her arms, the weight of her breasts taking the fabric temptingly lower, the lace hanging up on her nipples. Her lemony scent drifted up to him.

His mouth went dry. He'd imagined Summer as a white-bra-and-panties woman….

He lifted his gaze to hers as he laid his palms on her breasts, feeling the smooth, warm firmness of her flesh, the heels of his hands grazing her hard nipples. She was so different from what he'd expected. So sexy. So willing. So…

So not Summer.

"Scarlet?" he managed to ask, taking his hands away, sure of her identity even as he asked the question. No wonder she was different. Not Summer, but her identical twin sister. Scarlet had a wild reputation, but he never would've guessed she would pretend to be her sister. What purpose did it serve? She'd always been standoffish with him, as if she didn't like him.

She sat back, confusion in her eyes. "Have you ever seen Summer wear a dress like that?"

He could tell her he was three-quarters drunk, but it would seem like an insult. "I thought she'd come to seduce me."

Scarlet's lack of answer could mean anything. He wouldn't try to second-guess her.

Mistaken identities aside, he was acutely aware that his arousal hadn't suffered at the recognition of Summer's twin. If anything, the shock of the revelation excited him even more, though he didn't stop to determine why—didn't want to determine why, except he'd endured a long abstinence.

"What are you doing here?" he asked, tired of waiting, frustrated by her actions and his own wayward thoughts.

She rose to her knees again and set her hands on his chest. For several endless seconds their gazes locked. "Does it matter?"

Not at the moment, but soon it would probably matter a lot. Her words about never expecting to make love with him echoed in his head. "You hadn't intended to make love? Then what—"

"Maybe you shouldn't be thinking so hard," she said, drawing him closer.

Her touch erased all thoughts, banished all doubts, and he let go of his curiosity and kissed her instead. He forgot about Summer and opened himself up to Scarlet....

Scarlet, who made incredibly sexy, needy sounds that vibrated from her throat, whose hands wandered over his body as he sought her in the same way. He flicked open her bra, tossed it aside, captured a nipple between his lips, then tongued the hard contours before drawing it into his mouth and savoring as she arched her back, her fingernails digging into him to keep her balance. He took as much care with her other breast, but need pounded him relentlessly, especially when she wrapped her hand around him as he throbbed and ached.

He jerked back, trying to slow down. This was probably the stupidest thing he'd done in his life, but he couldn't stop— Yes, he could. He just didn't want to.

He set his hands on her waist to help her stand, then he eased her thong down her legs. Grasping his head, she leaned over to kiss him, kissed him as he'd never been kissed before, with lips and teeth and tongue, until he couldn't wait another second. He shoved her onto her back and moved her thighs apart. He watched as he entered her, clenched his teeth at the hot tightness that enveloped him, felt her contract, heard her long, low moan that quickly escalated in volume and tempo. He squeezed his eyes shut, holding back, waiting for her, then he exploded inside her. Sensation bombarded him, starting deep and low then racing through his body, even into his mind, blocking everything but feeling, hot, overwhelming feeling. It was good. She was good. Incredible....

He resisted the return of logic and sanity, which came regardless of his wishes. He rolled onto his back and stared at the ceiling. She lay silent beside him. Silent and still. He couldn't even hear her breathe. Her perfume mingled with the earthy smell of sex. He wouldn't soon forget it.

He would *never* forget it.

He turned toward her—

The mattress jiggled as she rolled away from him and off the bed. She gathered up her clothes and hurried to his bathroom, shutting the door.

Shutting him out.

Scarlet tried to let her mind go blank as she dressed inside John's elegant bathroom. She focused on the black fixtures and brushed-nickel faucets. She avoided the mirror as long as she could, then she had to look.

Mascara smudges under her eyes made her skin look paler and her eyes darker than usual. She dampened a tissue and cleaned off the smudges, then finger-combed her hair, stalling, not wanting to face him again.

What had she done?

She'd only come to tell him she thought Summer had made a huge mistake in ending their engagement. Then somehow they were kissing. Scarlet had told him the truth. She'd never expected to kiss him—ever—much less make love with him. She may have cultivated a reputation for outrageousness in the past, but this was over the top, even for her.

The problem was, Scarlet had been in love with John forever, feelings she'd had to keep to herself when she realized he and Summer had discovered an affinity for each other—then they'd realized they were in love just about the time when Scarlet was going to tell Summer how she felt about John herself.

Scarlet had envied the way John had treated Summer, the way he looked into her eyes when she talked, the way he touched her whenever he was near, a sweep of a hand down her back or the surprisingly sexy brush of her curls with his fingers. But it was his consideration of Summer that had made Scarlet the most envious— how much time he spent with her. How they never seemed to run out of things to say, their discussions deep and long. How he always called to say good-night and good-morning.

Scarlet had never had a man treat her like that.

Well, consider the source.

She closed her eyes for a moment, not wanting to dwell on her own shortcomings.

She'd ignored those tender feelings she'd had for John for a long time, had avoided ever having a private discussion with him, fearing he might see how she felt. She'd thought she had those feelings well under control, had made herself stop thinking about him in a romantic light when her sister had gotten serious with him, but seeing him tonight, seeing his pain, had made her realize she hadn't stopped caring, that she'd only shoved everything aside because of Summer.

And now Scarlet needed to kill those feelings once and for all. She and John couldn't have a relationship. Propriety would be reason enough, never mind that he wouldn't want to have anything to do with her beyond this night, since it would keep him in proximity with Summer, as well. This was a once-in-a-lifetime opportunity. Over and done. Relegated to the memory book.

She brushed her hands down her dress then opened the bathroom door. He was still lying in bed, his hands tucked under his head, the sheet pulled up to his waist.

She hunted down her shoes, put them on, wobbling some because she was shaking.

He threw back the covers, climbed out of bed and set his hands on her shoulders. "Take it easy, okay? Nothing—"

"You could at least cover up," she said, wincing at her snippy tone.

After a moment he grinned, revealing heart-tugging dimples. She stopped a sigh from escaping. He was one fine-looking man, with those intense dark brown eyes and sandy brown hair. Who would've guessed that hidden under his boring business suits was such a remarkable body, strong, muscular and toned. Tempting.

"You're leaving, I guess," he said.

"Of course I'm leaving. Do you think I'm an idiot?" She closed her eyes. "Scratch that question." Her behavior already gave her idiocy away.

He looked at her curiously, then grabbed his briefs and donned them. "Why did this happen, Scarlet?"

She searched for a reason he would believe. The only thing that came to mind was what Summer had confided earlier that day when she'd told Scarlet that she was ending her engagement with John—that even though she'd loved him, there had been a complete lack of chemistry between them. For months she'd thought she was just sublimating her passion, so that she could avoid sleeping with him until their wedding night. One hour with rock star Zeke Woodlow had changed all that.

But Scarlet couldn't believe that Summer had been talking about the same man who'd just made love to *her*. Lack of chemistry? Not a chance. The man Scarlet had just made love to took passion to a whole new level.

"Cat got your tongue?" John asked.

All she could do was give him a weak smile.

"Why did this happen?" he repeated.

"Because we got carried away?"

"I know why I would, but why would you?"

She couldn't tell him she loved him, so what could she say? After a few seconds, she felt him touch her cheek. The tenderness of the gesture almost made her throw herself into his arms.

"I figure you know I never slept with your sister."

She nodded. "She was wrong, though. You are a passionate man."

His mouth quirked. "Maybe it's just you. Maybe you brought that out in me." He brushed her hair behind an ear, then rubbed her earlobe. "How about helping me hone my skills? I never want to disappoint another woman."

"This is no time to joke. You don't need lessons, and we have no future together. What happened shouldn't have happened, and I'm sorry."

He narrowed his gaze. "Sorry? For what?"

"I know you must be hurt and angry, and you probably even want revenge, but please, please, don't tell anyone what happened," she said, then walked away before he could say or do anything to stop her. She was confused, not sure why she had done what she'd done, or what she could do about it now. She needed to get away and think. She grabbed her purse off the living-room floor and raced out the door, then hurried down a flight of stairs just to get away fast. She picked up the elevator on the next floor.

The doorman called good-night as she left the building. She stepped into the cold, damp evening and realized she'd forgotten her coat. She couldn't go back for it.

She couldn't go home, either, to her grandparents' town house where she and Summer shared the top floor. Summer probably wasn't even home, might even be with Zeke, but Scarlet didn't want to take the chance. She would get a hotel room for the night, order a bottle of wine, take a hot bath and figure out where she'd gone wrong.

Except that it hadn't felt wrong—not when she was in John's arms. It had felt so…right. He wasn't her sister's fiancé anymore. She hadn't violated any codes of ethics, sibling or otherwise. She and Summer had made a pact when they were eight years old that they would never pretend to be the other, and while she'd gone to John's apartment as herself, she knew fairly soon that he'd thought she was her sister and she hadn't corrected his mistake until it was almost past the point of no return. If he hadn't realized it on his own, she would've told him, though—wouldn't she?

Yes, of course. Probably.

So…a bath, some wine and some reflection. She would put John Harlan out of her mind once and for all.

And by morning she would be fine.

Just fine.

Two

Early April

Scarlet glared at her watch. A quarter past noon. She checked her cell phone, making sure it was turned on. It was. No missed calls. No voice-mail messages. Irritation whipped through her. It was unlike Summer to keep her waiting, especially for fifteen minutes. But then, Summer had lost her predictability. She'd even gotten herself engaged to Zeke Woodlow less than a month after ending her engagement to—

Scarlet went no further with the thought. At least there was a sparkle in Summer's eyes and a lightness in her step that hadn't been there before. A totally different kind of aura surrounded her, and for that Scarlet thanked Zeke.

He'd just better not ever hurt her….

Pasting on a smile, Scarlet returned a wave to a fellow employee then stabbed a piece of avocado in her Cobb salad. Seated in the company cafeteria, she was grateful she'd been able to grab a booth. She hated eating alone in public—Summer knew that. And it was especially bad here where noise bounced off the walls and the steel tabletops, the modern decor not helping to absorb sound, not letting a person think clearly. Plus, the entire twenty-five-story Park Avenue building was owned by EPH—Elliott Publication Holdings, her family's business. Or rather, businesses, their many magazines, so that a lot of people could pick her out of a crowd. Plus she was an Elliott, one who'd already caused enough talk.

She should've told Summer to meet her at the deli down the block.

"Who are you waiting for?"

Scarlet looked up to find Finola Elliott, editor in chief of *Charisma* magazine and Scarlet's boss for the past two years—and for twenty-five years, her aunt Finny.

"Summer. She's late."

"That's unlike her."

"I know."

Fin lowered her voice. "Are you okay?"

Surprised, Scarlet focused on her aunt instead of the cafeteria entrance. "Sure. Why?"

"You've seemed tense lately."

"I'm fine," she said, resisting the temptation to make a similar comment to Fin, who was under a great deal of stress since her father, Scarlet's grandfather, had issued a challenge regarding who was to fill his shoes when he retired at the end of the year—a challenge which had only added to the long-standing tension existing between Fin and her parents. The fact that Fin was eating in the company cafeteria instead of the executive dining room indicated her discomfort, as well.

"I'd ask you to join us, Fin, but Summer called this meeting. Here she is now."

"No problem," Fin said as Summer hugged her then slipped into the booth. "I'm meeting Bridget. See you later."

"Sorry I'm late," Summer said, her eyes shimmering. "Cute outfit. Can I borrow it?"

Scarlet smiled. Even though Summer had made sweeping changes recently, her wardrobe still wouldn't include anything like the purple-and-red minidress that Scarlet had designed and made this past week. "My closet is your closet," Scarlet said.

Summer laughed.

Scarlet could usually anticipate what her sister would say, but not this time. Not for the past few weeks, actually. She only knew that Summer was revved about something. "What's up?"

She linked her fingers together and set her hands on the table. "I'm taking a leave of absence from *The Buzz.*"

Shock heated Scarlet from the inside out. "Why?"

"I want to go with Zeke on his international tour."

"For how long?"

"A month."

Scarlet could barely find words. "We've never been apart for more than a week."

"Life is changing, Scar. *We're* changing."

"Separating." *I used to be able to read your mind. We used to finish each other's sentences.*

"It was bound to happen someday." Understanding *and* determination rang in Summer's voice.

"I can't believe you're giving up your dream job, and an imminent promotion, for a…man."

"Not just any man, but Zeke. The man I love." Her calm voice was offset by a stubborn glint in her eye. "The man I'm going to marry."

"When do you leave?"

"Tomorrow."

"So soon?" Scarlet felt more vulnerable than ever. Her link to life as she knew it was breaking. It had been hard enough this past month not to confide in Summer about her night with John Harlan, especially when Summer had asked her where she'd been all night.

"Don't be jealous," Summer said, laying her hand on Scarlet's.

"Jealous? I—" She stopped. Maybe she was, a little. She'd been wanting to try her hand at fashion design but hadn't had the nerve to quit her job as assistant fashion editor for *Charisma*. "Granddad will accuse you of being ungrateful," she said to her sister instead, reminding herself of that fact, as well—the main reason why she hadn't quit her job herself.

"That's what I'm afraid of. But Zeke has tried to convince me otherwise. Loyalty matters more than anything to Granddad, but I need to do this. I want to do this. I'm *going* to do this."

And everyone thought Summer was the meek twin. "Have you told him?"

"I'm telling you first. I'll tell Shane after lunch. Then Gram and Granddad."

Shane—Uncle Shane—was Fin's twin and the editor

in chief of *The Buzz,* EPH's showbiz magazine, where Summer worked as a copy editor, and was about to be promoted to reporter. Scarlet didn't envy Summer telling Shane or, worse, Granddad.

"I'm going to miss you like crazy," Scarlet said, nearly crushing Summer's hand.

"Me, too," she whispered, her eyes instantly bright. "I'll call lots. I promise. Maybe you could meet us somewhere on the tour for a weekend."

"Three's a crowd." Scarlet made an effort to keep things as normal as possible. She dug into her salad again. "Want some?"

"Butterflies," Summer said, patting her stomach.

Scarlet nodded. "What I said about my closet being your closet is true, you know. If you'd like to take some of my stuff on the tour, you can."

"Zeke likes me as I am."

So had John, Scarlet thought. Summer was so much easier to be with—not anywhere near as demanding of equality or independence as Scarlet. At least, not openly.

"There you go again," Summer said, tapping the table next to Scarlet's salad bowl.

"What?"

"You've been zoning out for, I don't know, about a month now."

"Have I?"

"Yes. Right after you spent the night away from home and wouldn't tell me where you'd been. Seems to me you've been keeping a secret, and that's a first for us, too."

Scarlet wanted so much to talk to Summer about John, about that night, but that was impossible. There was no one she could talk to, except the man himself, maybe, but he hadn't contacted her at all, and she both resented and appreciated his self-control. Except for having her coat delivered to her office the next day, without a note, they hadn't existed for each other.

Except that her body hungered in a way it never had.

"Can we spend the evening together?" Scarlet asked, changing the subject altogether, then noting the hurt in her sister's eyes. But Scarlet couldn't confide. Nothing would ever change that. Some secrets would be taken to the grave.

"You'll help me pack?"

"Sure."

"I don't know what time I'll be home. I'm taking the helicopter to The Tides to tell the Grands."

"I'll wait up. We'll have margaritas. You'll need one." Scarlet added teasingly, "Better you than me this time."

Summer grinned. "I know. The shoe's finally on the other foot. For years you've made it your goal to irritate Granddad with your men of choice, and I've always tried to get you to stop doing that. The Grands have taken their role as guardians seriously since Mom and Dad died. I guess after fifteen years in that role it's hard to change. And of course, Granddad still cares about image."

"He cares too much about image." And Scarlet thought, they hadn't really been her "men of choice," but men she'd chosen specifically to irritate her overbearing grandfather. Men came and went. Very few had been lovers. Most were just friends.

Then there was John. She missed him. How had that happened? But she couldn't reach out to him—she, who'd never been known for her patience, had controlled her impulse to contact him, made easier by the fact that he'd left town, or so the rumor went. In mourning for losing Summer?

"I need to get going," Summer said. "I'll call you when I'm headed home, as long as Granddad lets me take the copter back. If not, it's a long ride from the Hamptons."

"I'll go up the elevator with you," Scarlet said, not wanting to stay in the booth alone.

They waited at the doors. Scarlet would get off at the seventeenth floor, Summer one higher.

Scarlet swept her into a big hug as the elevator rose with silent speed. "Promise you won't change."

"Can't."

Scarlet pulled back and brushed her sister's hair from her face. "Is it wonderful, being in love?"

"Zeke is an amazing man."

The simple statement, layered with tenderness, almost made Scarlet cry. She wanted that for herself—a partner, an amazing partner. One who cared for her more than anyone, who thought *she* was amazing. Someone who was hers, and hers alone, as she would be his alone.

"I love you," Scarlet said as the elevator door opened.

"Me, too, you."

Scarlet stepped out of the elevator and headed for her cubicle, past the dazzling sign with the company slogan—*Charisma, Fashion for the Body*. The bright turquoise color scheme and edgy, bold patterns seemed to shout at her. Everything was topsy-turvy. She needed a little peace.

She would find none in her cubicle, which was filled with photos and swatches and drawings—colorful and eye-catching, not soothing. She grabbed her sketch pad and flipped to a blank page. She drew almost without thought—a wedding gown for Summer, with a long veil and train, something fairy-tale princesslike, a fantasy dress, layered with organza, scattered with a few pearls and crystals, but nothing flashy, just enough to catch the light. Elegant, like Summer.

Scarlet turned the page and sketched another wedding dress—strapless, formfitting, no train, no veil, just a few flowers threaded in the bride's long, light auburn hair—hers.

She stared at it, her pencil poised over the pad, then tore off the page, crumpled it into a ball and tossed it in the trash can. Turning to her computer, she opened a work file. She wasn't the Cinderella type. She would skip the grand ceremony, the stress of the spectacle and have something simple instead, if she ever married. Married was married. It didn't matter how it happened.

Her phone rang. Her one o'clock appointment had arrived. She stood, hesitated, then pulled the wadded-up design from her trash can. Her hands shaking slightly, she smoothed out the wrinkles and tucked it back into the pad behind Summer's design.

It was a good design, she thought, something she should redo and put in her portfolio—that was the reason she'd retrieved it. She didn't throw away good work.

Liar. The word bounced in her head, as much in accusation as relief, but above all, honest, a trait that seemed in short supply these days.

Three

At 9:00 p.m., two days later, John stood in front of the Elliott town house near 90th and Amsterdam. The gray stone building sported stately white trim and a playful red front door. He put his hand on the ivy-covered, black wrought-iron gate meant to keep out passersby. He knew of another entrance, however, a private entrance that would take him to the third, and top, floor—Summer and Scarlet's living quarters, comprised of a bedroom suite for each and a communal living room.

The home's owners, Patrick and Maeve Elliott, patriarch and matriarch of the Elliott clan, spent most of their time these days at The Tides, their estate in the Hamptons. Summer and Scarlet were raised there by their grandparents after their parents' deaths in a plane crash. Now the girls lived mostly in the city, occasionally going home to The Tides on weekends.

John's family owned an estate neighboring the Elliotts' in the Hamptons, yet they'd had little contact through the years. John was four years older than the twins. He'd headed to college when they were just entering high school. A couple of years after Summer and Scarlet graduated from college, he'd met them as adults and became an occasional companion to Summer, their relationship escalating from there. No big romance, just an increasing presence and steadily growing relationship.

This last month away from New York had given him perspective. He and Summer had never been suited for each other. They were too much alike, both with their five-year plans, career focuses and even-keeled personalities.

She'd changed, apparently. He'd read in some Hollywood gossip column that she'd accompanied Zeke Woodlow on tour to Europe. Amazing. Who would've guessed that such an adventurous spirit lived inside her?

Over and done, he reminded himself. Now he needed to see Scarlet. The month's separation had allowed him to acknowledge the absurdity of anything happening beyond their one stolen night, but he knew they would run into each other now and then, so they needed to settle things between them.

He hadn't called her, although many times he'd picked up to the phone to do so. Nor had she called him. And as bold and direct as she was, the fact that she hadn't made contact spoke volumes. It had been a one-night stand for both of them.

He reached for his cell phone to alert her he was there, then didn't make the call. He knew he should—

it was unlike him not to be courteous. He had no idea if she was even at home, or alone, but he wanted to catch her off guard and see her real reaction to him, not something manufactured while waiting for him to climb the stairs, so he punched in the security code to enter the half-underground four-car garage, slipped inside the door and strode past the indoor pool and up the staircase to Scarlet's floor.

Nerves played havoc with his equilibrium. The thought caught him by surprise, keeping him from ringing her bell immediately. Maybe he should've worn a suit, shown her—and himself—that he meant business. Instead he'd pulled on a sweater, khakis and loafers, as casual as he owned. At the last minute he'd slapped on some aftershave, something with a citrus base that reminded him of Scarlet's perfume, which had lingered on his skin for days, it seemed, showers not ridding his memory of the fragrance. He'd gotten hard every night in bed just thinking about it, about her, about the way she'd admired and touched him, about the way she kissed, and moved, and—

Hell, things were stirring *now.*

He rang the bell, needing to get the conversation over with so that he could move on with his life. After a few seconds, a shadow darkened the peephole, then came a few long, dragged-out seconds of anticipation. Maybe she wouldn't even open the door, or acknowledge she was home….

The doorknob turned; the door opened slowly.

The living room lights were off. Behind her the open door to her bedroom spilled enough light to cast her in silhouette. He saw only her outline, her hair around her shoulders, a floor-length robe. Her perfume reached his nose, drifted through him, arousing him the rest of the way.

"John?"

How he'd ever confused her voice with her sister's the other time was beyond him. Scarlet's was silky, sultry...sexy.

"Are you alone, Scarlet?"

"Yes." She gestured toward the living room. "Come in."

He looked around, as if seeing it for the first time. He'd been there often with Summer, yet everything seemed different. He saw Scarlet's modern influence now instead of Summer's more homey leanings, the eclectic mix of antiques and minimalist furnishings effective and dramatic.

"Have a seat," she said, indicating the couch in front of the picture window overlooking the street. She pulled her robe around her a little more, tightened the sash, switched on a lamp, then sat at the opposite end of the couch.

Her breasts were unrestrained; her nipples jutted against the fabric. He could hardly keep his eyes off her. He knew she was waiting for him to start the conversation, to let her know why he'd come. He wasn't sure of his reasons anymore.

"How have you been?" he asked finally, starting slowly, gauging her reaction to him being there without an invitation.

"Fine. And you?"

"Okay." *Inane. Say something important, something honest.*

She smoothed the fabric along her thighs. He wanted to do that, too, then lay his head in her lap.

"Where did you go?" she asked.

"L.A. My partners and I are expanding the markets for some new clients, growing the firm. It seemed like a good time to go."

"So your decision was because of business, not because of—"

She didn't finish the sentence. Would she have said "Summer" or herself?

She angled toward him a little, which created a gap in the robe, allowing him a glimpse of the upper swell of her lush breast. He really needed to stop fixating on her body.

"Business," he said. Which was not entirely true. He'd manufactured some business that needed one of the partners' attention, then had volunteered to go. His ad agency was already hugely successful, but there was always room to expand.

"I see."

A long silence followed.

"Why are you here, John?"

He finally remembered the reason. "I just wanted to make sure you were okay with…what happened. I don't want things to be awkward between us, since we're bound to run into each other now and then."

"I think picturing you naked will remove any sense of awkwardness for me."

Her eyes took on some sparkle. He was glad to see it.

"It's vivid for me, too," he said.

"It was good, John, but emotionally charged. We need to remember that. Make it real, instead of…"

"Surreal."

"Exactly. A fantasy, nothing more."

"And a one-time thing." He added the tiniest inflection at the end, turning the phrase into a question if she chose to hear it that way.

"Absolutely." Definite. Certain. No question.

He looked away. He had his answer. "Okay. I'm glad we cleared that up."

"Me, too."

He shifted a little. "I didn't use protection."

"We both got carried away. But there's no problem."

"Good. Great." He stood. "I'll go, then."

He heard her follow him. The air seemed thick. Breathing took effort. He turned when he reached the door, wishing he could read her mind.

"Is there something else you want?" she asked, reaching toward him then pulling back.

"You," he answered, catching her hand, tugging her toward him. "I want you."

"John…." There was hunger in her voice, need in her eyes.

Then they were in each other's arms, kissing, moaning, hands wandering, bodies pressing. She tipped her head back as he dragged his mouth down her neck, her robe separating, revealing her naked body, warm and dewy, as if she'd just stepped out of the bath.

"You're all I've thought about," he said just before drawing a nipple into his mouth, cupping the most feminine part of her with his hand. "You. This."

"Me, too." Her voice was deep, breathy. "Come with me."

He went willingly into her bedroom. Lights were on full. Sketches were everywhere—tacked on corkboard on the wall, scattered over the floor, even on the bed, an unmade jumble of linens. She swept the papers away.

They drifted to the floor, as did her pale blue robe, pooling around her feet, making her look like a goddess rising from the sea.

He jerked his sweater over his head, got rid of his shoes and socks. He touched his belt. She brushed his hands away and undid it, all the while looking at his face. Her color was high, her cheekbones sharp, her eyes a deeper green. Her lips were swollen from kissing, and parted slightly. He felt his slacks drop to the floor and kicked them away. Then she hooked his briefs and tugged. As she knelt to remove them, her hair brushed his abdomen, then his thighs, his shins.

He dug his fingers into her scalp, pulled her hair into his fists, squeezed his eyes shut. A month of fantasies became reality. Hell, not just a month, a lifetime, but a month of specific fantasies about one particular woman.

When her exploration became more daring, he pulled her up, moved her back and made her stretch out on the bed. He wanted to drag it out, make it last, but he lost all sense of control and finesse. He plunged into her. She arched into him. His body blasted apart in a long series of hot, explosive, rhythmic sensations. She clenched him from inside and climaxed with him, her face contorted, her mouth open. Then their movements slowed...stopped. He rolled over, taking her along. She stretched out on top of him and he wrapped her close.

For a long time, neither spoke.

Scarlet had spent the better part of the past month—months, really—convincing herself that she didn't love John, that she'd merely been infatuated because he was so different, attentive to Summer in ways that no man had been attentive to her. She'd been envious, that was all, and had created a fantasy about him. Now she was back at square one. Because she did love him.

Now, how could she keep him in her life long enough for those feelings to run their course? Obviously absence hadn't helped. And obviously they couldn't go public. People would assume that John and Summer had slept together, so the idea of Scarlet sleeping with her sister's ex-fiancé was— She couldn't even come up with the right words.

Appearances were important, especially for John, personally and professionally. And while Scarlet had a reputation, such a liaison with John would be beyond her usual outrageousness. How could they get past that? Not to mention him coming in contact with Summer.

And also not to mention she was probably a kind of substitute for her sister, a way to end his curiosity about her. Why else would he have come on this strong? He would certainly want closure; *she* would, in his shoes. Since he'd missed out on a physical relationship with Summer, having one with Scarlet *could* give him closure. Of sorts.

The thought that she and Summer might be interchangeable in his mind made her a little sick to her stomach. But maybe he wasn't thinking that way at all. Maybe she was just imagining it.

So, now what? It seemed to Scarlet they needed to let the attraction burn in a controlled environment or it might be a bank of embers forever, taking on too much importance as time passed, always waiting to flare.

She had an idea....

"Do you still want lessons?" she asked, burrowing against him, not wanting to see his face.

His arms tightened around her, and he drew a long breath, as if she'd awakened him. "Lessons?"

"Last time you asked for help honing your skills."

"You said I didn't need lessons."

"Not in bed. But you could learn something about being more romantic if you want to woo a woman into bed…in the regular way."

After a long, drawn-out moment of silence, he rolled to his side with her, then propped himself on an elbow to look her in the eyes. His were filled with humor. His dimples deepened. "Woo?"

She shoved his shoulder as he laughed, apparently at her use of such an old-fashioned term. "You have to admit you could use lessons."

His smile faded some. "I admit it. Instinct doesn't seem to be serving me well. Except—" he slid a hand down her back and pulled her closer "—where you're concerned."

"Only in regards to sex, then." She knew he didn't return her feelings.

"No stronger instinct, is there?"

She shrugged.

He stroked her hair, tucked it behind her ear. "So, you'd be willing to advise me on how to properly *woo* a woman? What would that entail?"

Lots of time together. Lots of touching. Lots of— "Lessons," she said instead.

"Homework?"

She hadn't thought about that. He would have to experiment on other women, to see if the lessons worked.

That would never do. "You'll practice on me. If you can make *me* fall under your spell, then you know it can work on any woman."

"She says humbly."

"I'm not being egotistical. I'm just immune to the games of most men."

"What happens if you do fall under my spell?"

She had no answer for that. She'd dug a ditch she couldn't climb out of, however.

"Seems to me this is a game with potentially disastrous outcomes," he said.

"Or fun ones." She laid a hand along his face. "It's very selfish, I suppose, to want this."

"But if we're both in agreement, what's the harm?"

"We're adults, after all."

He said nothing for a few seconds, then seemed to relax. "When would we start?"

"Sometime when we're dressed."

He grinned. "In the meantime…" He hooked a leg over hers, bringing her closer then kissing her until she forgot everything but the feel of his mouth. "Will this be part of the wooing?" he asked, dragging his lips along her jaw.

Huh? Oh. He was talking to her.

She didn't answer immediately. She understood that he was trying to figure out what the parameters of their relationship were going to be. She wanted more than sex, but she knew that was all she could have. Too much stood in their way, especially how quickly they got together after the breakup. Should she settle for only sex? Would the desire fizzle in time?

"I'm enjoying this as much as you are," she said

truthfully, testing his own expectations. "Although we both know—"

He put a hand over her mouth. "We do. And we don't need to talk about it."

She moved his hand away. "I wouldn't have guessed that you were an avoider of truth."

"It's my superhero role. That's why you never see me in tights and a cape, and only in suits."

"Oh, *that's* why. I did wonder."

"When do we start Woo University? Tomorrow?"

So, they weren't going to define their relationship yet. Maybe that was a good thing for now. "Why wait?" she asked.

"I'm not done registering for class yet." He rolled on top of her, bent to kiss her. "Haven't finished uploading from my hard drive."

She laughed. Who would've thought the man could be so playful? "You're not what I expected."

"In what way?"

"In every way. You always seem so serious."

"You'd never seen me naked."

She smiled. "I guess it does make a difference."

He nuzzled her neck. "You're not what you seemed, either."

Her body tingled from the feel of his warm breath against her skin. "How?"

"Less bold."

"I thought I'd been plenty bold."

"Sexually, you have been."

"What other way is there?"

He didn't answer. The hand that had been roaming over her body stilled. "Do you really want to spend our time analyzing this?" he asked, pulling away, locking gazes.

No. It was a time to enjoy him, to make memories. He would change her life—she knew that without a doubt—but her obsession could finally end and she could move on, once and for all. Her relationship with her sister would never have to be tested, nor would Scarlet give the publicity hounds something to sniff out. If Summer could change, so could she.

"No," she said, looping her arms around his shoulders and pulling him down to kiss him. "No analysis necessary. Although I do plan to study your moves."

"As a mentor?"

She smiled slowly. "As a woman."

"Nothing like putting on the pressure."

His words may have indicated a lack of self-confidence but his actions didn't. He knew exactly what to touch, and how, and when. She couldn't remember being aroused so skillfully. But was that all there was—skill? Was his heart engaged even the slightest?

He cupped her face. She opened her eyes, sensing a question coming.

"You don't seem to be in the moment," he said.

"I am completely in the moment," she replied honestly, although his interpretation was probably different from her own. All her desires, all her fears raced through her mind. She wanted to ignore them. They refused to go away.

His silence lasted several long seconds. He started to pull away. She wrapped him close, drew him down… and gave him no more reason to wonder.

Four

John picked up his office telephone the next day, started to punch in a number, then stopped. His first homework assignment was to ask Scarlet for a date in the way he usually asked a woman out. He had to think about it. When he was seeing Summer they'd talked every day and decided together what they would do. He'd never *wooed* her, since they'd just sort of fallen into the relationship gradually. It had been a long time since he'd asked out a woman.

He ran a hand down his face, then dialed Scarlet's work number, feeling like a novice at this dating game instead of a twenty-nine-year-old veteran.

"Scarlet Elliott," she answered, all businesslike.

Which turned him on. He pictured her as she was last night, leaning against her headboard, her hair tangled, face flushed, the sheet tucked over her chest but drifting bit by bit while they talked, until he'd tugged it away and gathered her close.

"Hel-lo?" she singsonged.

He ignored his body's stirrings. "Good morning."

A pause, then, "Who's calling?"

"The man who heated up your sheets last night."

"Stop that," she said in almost a whisper. "You're supposed to have just met me and are asking for a date."

Role-playing? He considered that for a moment. It might be fun—for a day or so. "Not my fault. My mentor didn't give me a syllabus for my first Woo U class."

He heard her laugh briefly.

"Start over." She hung up before he had a chance to say a word.

John sat back in surprise then began to laugh. He redialed.

"Scarlet Elliott."

"Good morning, Ms. Elliott. This is John Harlan of Suskind, Engle and Harlan. We met at the *Charisma* open house over the holidays."

She sighed. "If you have to add the name of your firm, you didn't make much of an impression in the first place. Start over." She hung up.

He was tempted not to call her back, but after a minute, he did.

"Scarlet Elliott."

"Good morning, Ms. Elliott. This is John Harlan. We met at the *Charisma* open house over the holidays."

"I remember. You defended the existence of Santa Claus quite well."

He smiled. "Someone told me your name was Virginia."

"Friend or foe?" she asked.

"Someone who wanted me to embarrass myself, apparently, by calling you by the wrong name."

"You didn't. Embarrass yourself."

Was there double meaning in her remark? "That's good to hear." He was aware she wasn't calling him by name, probably so that no one could overhear her. "I'd like to get to know you better. I was wondering if you would have dinner with me."

"When?"

"Saturday night." This was too easy. How long could he draw out the lessons? He'd have to play dumb just to drag it out.

A long pause ensued. "This is Friday," she said coolly.

"Would you rather go out tonight?"

Dead silence.

He brushed a speck of dust from his slacks. Something told him he'd just messed up his first assignment, big-time. "Scarlet?"

"You don't think it's a little insulting to ask me out the day before? You don't think I would have other plans already?"

"We only started this class today," he countered. "If we'd started on Monday, I would've asked you then." Although he'd would've asked her for Tuesday, but he wasn't about to tell her that. "Do you have plans for Saturday night?"

"Yes, I do."

He wasn't sure what to say. Should he ask her for the following Saturday?

"Start over," she said, then hung up.

He decided to make her wait. When he finally redialed fifteen minutes later, he got her voice mail.

"Ms. Elliott," he said, starting from the beginning. "This is John Harlan. We met at the *Charisma* open house over the holidays. I was wondering if you'd like to have dinner with me a week from Saturday. Here's my private line." He recited his phone number. "I look forward to hearing from you."

He'd barely hung up when his private line rang.

"It's a good thing I came into your life," Scarlet said. "Has that method worked in the past?" She said *method* as if it were something that stank.

"What method?"

"Leave a message for a woman asking her on a first date?"

She sounded either shocked or disgusted.

"I asked for more than a week from now."

"You asked her answering machine."

He massaged the bridge of his nose and closed his eyes. "Which is apparently the wrong thing to do. I'll start over," he said, hanging up before she could. Normally he would've been frustrated by that kind of game by now, but he found it stimulating. She challenged him. The trick would be to challenge her in return.

He lifted the receiver, then hesitated. She would be expecting him to call back.

"Not this time, Ms. Elliott," he said as he flipped through his Rolodex. He wanted an A on his first homework assignment.

She'd gotten him thinking outside his normal box. He wanted her to see what he'd already learned.

* * *

"Somebody likes you," a woman said as she rounded Scarlet's cubicle.

She smelled the flowers before she even looked up from her computer and spotted the bouquet, not something neat and tidy like a dozen roses, but an exotic bundle of baby orchids in a variety of deep colors. Her heart did a little dance at the sight. She hadn't been sent flowers in a long, long time. Even so, she resisted the temptation to bury her face in the blossoms as the vase was set down in front of her by Jessie Clayton, the vivacious twenty-three-year-old intern assigned to work with her.

"Shall I read the card?" Jessie asked, green eyes sparkling behind trendy glasses as she snagged the tiny envelope and held it over Scarlet's head.

"I write your performance reviews."

Jessie laughed and handed Scarlet the card. "I don't suppose you're going to read it out loud."

"Good guess."

Alone, Scarlet held the envelope to her lips for several seconds before opening it. Inside was a phone number. No flowery sentiment. No invitation to dinner. Just a phone number.

She smiled, slowly. Score one for John.

She picked up the phone and dialed.

"John Harlan."

She heard expectation in his voice, maybe because he was trying to cover it. "Nice move."

"Who's calling?"

She grinned. "Let me start over." She hung up and redialed. After he answered, she said, "The flowers are exquisite. Thank you."

"So you remember me?"

She slipped into the role. "Of course. We met at the *Charisma* open house over the holidays."

"You were wearing a green dress the color of your eyes," he said.

Her breath caught, even though they were talking about an imaginary occasion. He made it sound real, as if he'd seen and admired her in that dress. "You were wearing a suit and tie," she countered.

"Lucky guess. I hope you're wondering why I sent the flowers."

"I'm curious, yes."

"I'd like to get to know you. Would you have dinner with me? Maybe a week from Saturday?"

"I'd love to."

"May I pick you up, say, at eight o'clock?"

"That would be perfect."

"I'll call you during the week to reconfirm."

"Okay."

He said goodbye and hung up, and she was left wondering if he meant they wouldn't talk to each other or see each other until he picked her up. Was that how far the role-playing would go? Or would they have a separate life, continuing what they'd started?

For now she would let him lead the relationship. She would go to The Tides for the weekend to visit Gram and Granddad, as planned; attend the Spring Fling at the country club; and make herself unavailable to John, letting absence do its work.

Which was crazy, since nothing long-term could come of this relationship, anyway. But for the month that Summer would be out of town, Scarlet would indulge herself with the man who should be most forbidden to her and make herself a memory.

Five

Since the tragic day when Scarlet and Summer were orphaned, Scarlet had never spent an entire weekend at The Tides without her sister. It was strange now to be in her own bedroom and know that Summer wasn't just a few feet away in hers, or sharing a room as they got ready for a special occasion. The tomblike quiet was eerie.

Scarlet took a final look in the mirror and gave herself the okay sign, something Summer would've done. Once upon a time, Gram would have come in to share in the fun, too, but her arthritis prevented her from climbing the stairs easily anymore. She and Granddad had moved downstairs. Why they hadn't installed an elevator was a mystery to Scarlet.

Her heels tapped softly as she descended the long marble staircase to the first floor. She looked forward to the evening, even though she was dateless. She would know many of the guests, however, and would surely be asked to dance.

She was glad she hadn't told John where she was going. He might have decided to show up, and she wasn't sure she could pretend not to notice him.

Scarlet headed toward the back of the house to the living room, beyond which was her grandparents' suite. As Scarlet neared, her grandmother came out her bedroom door, carrying herself with the grace of a queen, a far cry from the seamstress she'd been when Patrick had first met her in Ireland and swept her off her feet, bringing her to his home in America. Her face barely showed age or tragedy, even at seventy-five and having suffered the loss of several children through miscarriage or death.

"Aren't you enchanting, *colleen,*" she said as Scarlet hugged her. "And dressed to stop lungs from pulling in air, I'm thinking. Your own creation?"

"Brand-new." Scarlet did a quick pirouette, showing off the snug violet-and-fuchsia sheath with the flounce that would swirl just above her knees when she danced. Three-inch heels brought her to six feet in height. She loved the additional height, which gave her a sense of power. "You're looking beautiful yourself, Gram."

Maeve wore a simple lavender beaded gown on her petite frame. Her makeup was applied deftly, a few freckles visible on her gorgeous Irish skin. She'd worn her white-and-auburn hair in an elegant updo for as long as Scarlet could remember, and it was no different now. As usual, too, a gold locket hung around her neck, rumored to hold a picture of her daughter Anna, her secondborn, who had died of cancer when she was seven. Scarlet wondered if the locket also contained a picture of her thirdborn, Stephen, Scarlet and Summer's father.

"Looking to turn a few heads, are you?" Patrick Elliott boomed from behind them.

In her heels Scarlet met her grandfather eye to eye, yet another reason she liked wearing them.

At seventy-seven Patrick was still a sight to behold. His fit body, thick gray hair and blue eyes continued to draw glances from women thirty years younger. "I'm hoping to, yes," Scarlet said.

"I was talking to your grandmother, missy." He tempered the comment with a slight smile at Scarlet, which turned tender when he looked at his wife and kissed her cheek. "You look lovely, *cushla macree.*"

Pulse of my heart. Scarlet had heard him call her grandmother that forever, had always found it hard to believe that this adoring husband was the same dictator who'd raised her and Summer. And as a businessman, he was ruthless—even, or more accurately *especially,* with his children, who ran four of his various enterprises.

"Are you taking your own car?" Patrick asked Scarlet. "I'm sure you'll want to stay longer than your grandmother and I."

"I'll ride with you. If I'm not ready to come home when you are, I'll get someone to drop me off."

"We'll send Frederick back for you," Gram said.

"Thanks, but it won't be necessary." Scarlet recognized she was being stubborn out of habit. Her grandparents' driver would be happy to make a second trip to pick her up. Still, she found it hard to alter the long-established adversarial relationship with her grandfather. "I'll make my own way."

"Make sure your escort hasn't been drinking." He put his hand under Maeve's arm as they moved toward the door.

Scarlet brought up the rear, irritated that her grandfather assumed a man would bring her home. "I'll make him take a Breathalyzer."

Maeve chuckled, which stopped Patrick from countering with something equally sarcastic. "So alike, you two," Maeve said.

"Alike? Us?" Scarlet wasn't as stunned as she pretended.

"Yes, *colleen.* But enough of this. It's a night to celebrate the arrival of spring. New beginnings. Let's have no more battles of wit, no matter how clever the words."

"Fine by me," Scarlet said.

Patrick said nothing, which was answer enough. He would do whatever Maeve asked of him.

Scarlet stopped short of heaving a sigh. She and Granddad had butted heads forever, with Gram and Summer interceding when possible. Her grandfather had never liked any of her boyfriends, even during her first tender explorations into the dating world, and so she had begun to bring home guys she was sure he would despise—men without much motivation or ambition, men whose main interest in life was having fun, not working. Nothing turned off Patrick Elliott more than a man without a solid work ethic, especially since he had built his own empire from nothing.

Scarlet was tired of the game, though, and tired of being at odds with her grandfather, especially now. He must be feeling less invincible these days or else he wouldn't have given his children the challenge that the next CEO of Elliott Publication Holdings would be the person who produced for their magazine the biggest individual financial success by year's end. His surprise announcement at a New Year's party that he would be retiring, and the game he'd begun by pitting the Elliott children against each other, had turned all their lives upside down—a typical Patrick Elliott move.

During the twenty-minute limo ride to the country club, the conversation turned to safe topics, setting a new, peaceful tone for the evening. The club ballroom was decorated for the Spring Fling as it always was, with spring-flower arrangements and tiny white lights everywhere, nothing overly original or creative. A sumptuous buffet would be laid out, bars set up in convenient places, with dancing to come later, a twenty-piece band providing music. Scarlet loved its predictability.

"You look like an exotic bloom," Gram said as they waved and nodded to friends and acquaintances. "Your talent for design is staggering."

"I learned from the best." Scarlet put an arm around her grandmother, remembering fondly the hours and hours they'd spent sewing.

"That's a fine compliment, indeed, but I never had the vision, just the practical skill. I always expected you'd go into that field instead of the magazine, especially with your degree in design." Her sideways glance probed.

"I've got time. And the magazine's a useful place to learn more," Scarlet said evasively, wondering if Granddad had overheard. He didn't indicate outwardly that he had; in fact, he seemed focused on something across the room. She followed his gaze, spying the couple she'd most wanted to avoid.

She leaned closer to her grandmother. "Bill and Greta Harlan are here. Have you seen them since Summer called off the engagement?"

"I called Greta. As you know, we weren't great friends before John and Summer decided to marry. If you're wondering whether everyone will be civil, the answer is yes. Especially here. Now then, be off and enjoy yourself."

"I'll join you for supper later."

"You're not to feel obligated. Have fun, *colleen*. I don't think you're having enough fun these days."

"I miss Summer."

"And you're a mite envious, perhaps?"

"Not at all." Scarlet waited for lightning to strike her at the lie, but the world stayed normal. She did envy that Summer could be public with her relationship—and with a man she could count on and keep, whereas Scarlet was setting herself up for heartbreak, one she could never talk about or get sympathy for when it ended. But she wasn't jealous of her sister's happiness.

Scarlet wandered around the festive room, stopping to talk, admiring baby pictures thrust in her face from old friends settling down. She'd attended a record number of weddings in the past few years.

Gram was right. She wasn't having enough fun. Maybe it was because Summer wasn't there, and she was Scarlet's best friend. Maybe because Scarlet lived in Manhattan most of the time, and the country club now seemed too laid-back and...rigid, even though that seemed contradictory. Rules, rules, rules. She'd grown up with them, ignored them, gotten into trouble when she did. There were fewer rules in the city, more action, more options.

After dinner the dancing began. She watched her grandparents take the floor for the first slow dance, their steps perfectly matched after so many years of dancing together. Scarlet smiled as she watched them—until she spotted John walking onto the dance floor.

The lightning she'd expected before struck her, although for entirely different reasons. Everything inside her came feverishly to life. He was the best-looking man in the room. And she'd made love with him. And he'd wanted her, bad.

Okay, so she *was* glad he'd shown up. Admitting she had a problem was half the battle, she thought, being honest with herself. Then she saw a petite blonde step into his arms. Who was she? They waltzed together like long-time partners, their steps perfectly attuned, his hand resting at the small of her back, his gaze on her. He said something and the blonde laughed. Scarlet hated her.

The music went upbeat, and her grandparents left the dance floor, but John and his partner didn't. Scarlet tapped her toe. Was he trying to make her jealous?

"Hey, Scarlet."

She focused on the man who'd approached invisibly through her green haze. "Mitch, hi. Long time."

Mitchell Devereaux was as handsome as he was shallow, which was a lot.

"Yeah. Wanna dance?"

She certainly didn't want to sit on the sidelines,

watching. She would ignore John and have fun, as Gram had ordered.

Scarlet didn't leave the dance floor after that, changing partners with each new song, dancing her heart out and keeping a casual eye on John, who also didn't sit out a dance until the music slowed again, although he finally changed partners. Over her own dancing partner's shoulder she watched John stroll away, get a drink from the bar then prop a shoulder against a pillar and scan the dance floor, stopping on her, catching her looking at him.

He lifted his glass slightly, his gaze intense. She could hardly believe she knew what he looked like naked, what his skin felt like, tasted like. How he kissed as if he were being sent to war, and how he made love as if she were the only woman on earth.

The song ended. She made an excuse to leave the dance floor and headed toward him, pulled by a force stronger than her own willpower. Discreetly she pointed to a side door. He pushed away from the pillar and headed there. She followed at a distance, but as she passed through the door she saw her grandfather, apparently already on the patio, approach him.

Almost caught, Scarlet darted behind a pillar topped by a plant large enough to hide her.

"I never expected it from you, John," Patrick said.

"Expected what?"

"Retaliation."

"It's business, Patrick. Nothing more."

Scarlet wished she could see them, analyze their body language. All she could do was listen. Granddad's voice cut through the darkness, sharp and lethal. John seemed unaffected.

"Gills and Marsh have bought ad space in *Charisma* since the magazine debuted," Patrick said. "Crystal Crème soda has been with *The Buzz* for five years."

"A lot of my clients have decided to experiment with other forms of advertising, to see what gets them the most bang for their buck. Product placement in movies and on television guarantees a bigger, wider audience, not only in initial viewing but in DVDs and reruns."

"With the target demographics?"

"We're choosing each situation carefully."

The sound of crickets filled a long silence.

"You must be angry with my granddaughter," Patrick finally said.

"I'm over it."

"I don't think you are."

Scarlet leaned closer, as her grandfather's voice had gone low and cool.

"What makes you say that?" John asked.

"The way you were watching Scarlet a few minutes ago…. That wasn't the expression of someone who was 'over it.'"

"You're wrong. But even if I hadn't stopped caring about Summer, I wouldn't take it out on my clients— or Scarlet. Or you."

Another silence ensued. John didn't take the bait. Scarlet was grateful her grandfather hadn't realized John's expression was one of lust, not anger.

"Don't know what got into that girl," Patrick said at last. "She always had such a good head on her shoulders. Now she's run off with that…that singer. Left her job."

Exasperation coated the words. John still said nothing.

"I'm going to keep a close eye on all your accounts, John. Might have to do a little wooing of my own."

Scarlet smiled at the word and figured John had, too.

"They pay me for sound advice," John said.

"We'll see how sound it is."

"It's a new day in advertising, Patrick. Time for changes."

"Maybe." He took a couple of steps then stopped.

Scarlet had to duck a little.

"I should've called you and apologized," Patrick said. "Thought about it. Just didn't do it."

"No need to, but thanks. It was between Summer and me."

"So it was. Good night."

"Good night, sir."

Scarlet eased farther around the pillar so her grandfather wouldn't see her as he passed by.

"You can come out," John said after a few seconds. "He's inside."

She moseyed over. "That was close."

"I'm surprised you risked being seen with me in the first place, Scarlet."

"That wouldn't be a scandal, just a reason for people to talk a little. Are you enjoying yourself?"

"Not particularly."

"You could've asked me to dance, you know."

He straightened. "You had a partner for every dance. I shouldn't cut in, should I?"

"Maybe."

His gaze intensified. "Consider this tonight's Woo U lesson. Yes or no?"

"Each situation has to be judged individually."

"I judged. I chose not to."

"Okay." Because he was right and there was nothing more to say, she changed the subject, twining her fingers so that she wouldn't touch him, though she *really* wanted to. "*Was* it strictly business, John? What my grandfather asked you about?"

"Yes."

"You would've done the same thing, switched the business, if you and Summer were still engaged?"

He hesitated no longer than a breath, and his gaze never wavered. "Yes."

She wondered if he'd paused because he had to justify his answer to himself first.

"Wanna blow this joint?" he asked, surprising her.

"More than I can tell you. But impossible, as you know, at least together. I'd better go." She started to turn.

"Scarlet?"

His husky voice would've stopped her, no matter what he said next. "What?"

"I was jealous of every guy you danced with tonight, every guy who touched you and got to be so close to you."

Desire flooded her body…rushing…pounding…pulsating. His gaze drifted down her. Her nipples drew taut. She wasn't used to having a man want her so passionately, so…violently. It fascinated her, both that he wanted her that much and that she liked his Neanderthal reaction. She'd never tolerated jealousy before, but the flare of heat low in her body told her *his* jealousy meant something.

"You don't think I felt the same?" she asked. "I have to go." She wouldn't risk staying any longer with him, having someone see their attraction instead of just acquaintances having a conversation, or whatever defined the parameters of their relationship now in the public eye.

He said nothing. He was good at that.

She didn't see him return to the dance, and was torn between gratitude and disappointment as Mitch again invited her to dance. She saw her grandparents come onto the floor, as well, as Glenn Miller's "Moonlight Serenade" played, Gram's favorite.

A few seconds later, John tapped Mitch's shoulder. Mitch looked at Scarlet. "You don't have to."

"It's fine." Her heart thundered as John's arms came around her. Several inches of space separated their bodies.

"What are you doing?" she whispered, pasting on a smile.

"Passing another Woo U course."

"I can't believe you did that."

"Then you don't know me."

She didn't. She loved him, but she didn't know him. Not really. But everything she learned about him only deepened her feelings.

"Scarlet, there's no reason we can't be civilized in the world's eyes. So, there'll be a little talk. It'd mostly be about me and that I must still be pining for Summer."

"Are you?"

"No."

It was one of the most awkward moments of her life. She glanced at her grandparents. Gram lifted her brows. Granddad kept a carefully blank expression.

And yet through all the awkwardness, all the awareness of eyes focused on them, all the annoyance at being the center of attention when she'd tried so hard to stop doing that, she loved that he'd done it. Loved that he was that self-confident and daring. She never would've guessed it of him.

At the end of the dance the club manager approached Scarlet. "You have a phone call, Miss Elliott."

"From whom?"

"I wouldn't know. If you'll follow me, please."

She excused herself from John, grateful that the potentially awkward moment of moving off the dance floor and away from each other had been solved by a mysterious phone call.

She and the manager went down a long hallway to a door marked Conference Room. He opened the door then walked away. Scarlet peered in. A phone sat on the conference table but no light blinked. Uneasy, she took a step back.

"Careful," came a whisper in her ear. John. He moved her inside the room, shut the door and locked it, the sound echoing like a prelude to gothic seduction.

He slid a hand along the wall beside her, then the lights went out, plunging them into darkness. Music drifted faintly through the closed door.

"You dance like you make love," he said, dragging a finger along her jaw, across her mouth.

"How's that?" Breathless, she parted her lips.

"Primal. Like a creature of the earth. With passion and abandon." He slipped his arms around her waist. "Dance with me. A real dance."

"Dance" was a relative term. They barely moved. It was just an excuse to align their bodies, and since in her heels she was as tall as he, their bodies aligned perfectly.

"You're quiet," Scarlet murmured after a while.

"Some of us are capable of it."

She nipped his earlobe, and he laughed softly. She'd needed this moment alone with him. Needed to touch him. The music stopped, but they kept moving, pressed together, their clothing the only barrier, and even that wasn't much. He curved his hands over her rear and lifted her slightly, changing the point of contact. Perfume and aftershave mingled with the urgent scent of desire. His need was evident in the tautness of his body and the hard ridge pressed to her abdomen. His breath felt hot and unsteady against her temple.

Scarlet tried to resist. She couldn't abandon herself to him, all too aware of where they were and the possibility of discovery. She wouldn't do that to her grandparents or Summer. Or herself.

But she had a hard time not letting go, giving in, enjoying....

His hand slipped over her breast just as his mouth took hers in a long, hot kiss, a merging of breath and need and unchecked lust. They were always in such a hurry with each other.

He moved her back until her thighs hit the table. She realized what he intended and pushed at his chest.

"We can't do this here."

He trailed her low V neckline with his tongue, leaving a damp, shivery trail. "I'm familiar with the long list of rules this club has," he said. "Nowhere does it say there can't be sex in the conference room. In fact, I would hazard a guess that this room has seen plenty of action."

"Stop." She slipped away from him and found her way to the door, then fumbled for the light switch, turning it on. "I mean it. We can't do this here." She blamed herself for letting things get out of hand. The speed at which they'd landed in bed before this— twice—would have led any man to think he could have what he wanted, whenever he wanted it.

He shoved his hands through his hair. "You're hard to figure out," he said, then blew out a breath.

"I know. I'm sorry." *But I love you, and that's why I took those chances the other times. I needed a memory of you.*

"You don't really live up to your reputation, do you?" he said, half sitting on the table, his arms crossed.

"Do you want me to?"

After a few long seconds he shook his head.

She thought about her grandfather, how much she'd disappointed him. As a teenager she'd desperately wanted his attention, and he'd been totally focused on his business, but his disapproval of her dates meant he would at least communicate with her, if only to berate her. She was such a cliché, she thought.

"I always found the 'wild-child' tales interesting," John continued, "because there was no hard evidence you were easy, just speculation, based on who you dated—and maybe how you dress in look-at-me outfits and move like a whirlwind, as if you always know where you're going and who you are, which is very sexy. I'd say you pretty much made everyone wonder."

"I'm not the one who arranged this tryst."

"I didn't mean to offend you, Scarlet. I thought you would want it as much as I did."

"Believe it or not, sometimes I think about other people before my own needs."

His gaze locked with hers. He studied her for a long,

quiet moment, then he nodded slowly and stood. He ran a hand down her arm as he passed by.

"Good night," he said. "Thank you for the dance."

After the door closed quietly behind him she stood motionless, waiting for her world to return to normal.

She'd misread him, pure and simple. And maybe he'd misread her. It was her manufactured reputation that had driven him to take such a chance as to want to have sex with her on a conference room table with hundreds of people—her grandparents included—nearby.

Maybe he got a rush out of such clandestine moments.

She didn't. She'd only gotten a rush out of *him.*

So where did that leave them now?

Six

On the Wednesday after the country club incident, John arrived a few minutes early for a three o'clock meeting with Finola Elliott at *Charisma* magazine. He wasn't made to wait in the lobby but was escorted immediately to Fin's office by an auburn-haired young woman named Jessie, who kept up a running commentary as they wove through the maze of cubicles. He learned she'd been raised in Colorado, was an unpaid intern and a roommate of a *Charisma* proofreader, Lanie Sinclair. And by the way Jessie eyed him curiously, he guessed she knew he'd been engaged to Summer.

He wished he could ask her which cubicle was Scarlet's. If he could just look into her eyes, he'd know where things stood between them. They hadn't spoken since the disaster at the club. In three days they were supposed to go on their first Woo U date.

Or were they?

Maybe his lesson had been only in how to ask a woman out, not the actual follow-through. Another question he needed answered.

Who would break the stalemate? Or had they already burned out? He wasn't ready to end it. He wanted the whole month until Summer returned. Every last minute. And he wanted some of that in bed.

John wasn't taken into Fin's office but to the conference room attached to it. Several people were seated at the oval mahogany table—the editor in chief, Fin; her executive editor, Cade McMann; Bridget Elliott, the photo editor…and Scarlet.

He'd never been to a meeting with Scarlet in attendance before. Why would an assistant fashion editor be there?

John shook hands with Fin, Cade and Bridget. He met Scarlet's gaze directly and nodded. She raised her brows. No clue there as to how she felt.

"I'm not going to beat around the bush, John," Fin said. "I'm sure you've heard about the competition my father instituted."

"I'm aware of the details." Having just seen Maeve over the weekend, John realized how much Fin looked like her mother, although she had Patrick's head—and drive—for business.

"I intend to win." She leaned toward him, her body rigid. "But I can't if you keep pulling ad revenue from my profits."

"I'm responding to what my clients' needs are, Fin."

"We came up with an idea we'd like to toss out at you. Go ahead, Scarlet."

Scarlet picked up a remote control. She gave him a quick look, all business, which might have worked had she been wearing a gray, pin-striped, baggy suit and her hair in a bun. Maybe. As it was, her shiny hair curled softly over her shoulders, and she wore a deep purple dress that clung to every shapely inch of her. His mind wandered....

She brought up an image on the big-screen monitor on the wall. "Picture this as a feature article. We might call it 'Trends,' or something like that," Scarlet said. "Ten to twelve photos of the hottest trends for each season, as we generally do. But this is an example of how we would incorporate your clients' products."

A hip blond model was seated at a bar in what looked to be a neighborhood pub. She wore an outfit meant to draw the magazine reader's eye, but in her hand was a bottle of Crystal Crème soda. The juxtaposition of a soft drink being served at a bar would make the reader pay even more attention, he decided. Very clever.

"Product placement," Scarlet said unnecessarily. "Here are a few more."

Images flashed across the screen, each photo the superb quality that *Charisma* was known for, and each including a product of one of his clients, generally a food or drink item, easily integrated into the scene.

Cade pushed a folder toward John. "Price guides. You'll find it cheaper than a full-page ad, of course, but a fair price, we think, for the value."

Scarlet handed him a manila envelope. "Here's a CD of each sample so you can pitch your clients with visuals. These are mock-ups, obviously. We'd have to work closely together, matching our focus for the article with your product for the layout. Some products will lend themselves easily, but some won't. Some of these products have never been advertised in *Charisma,* like Crystal Crème. We think it opens a lot of new doors."

"You know that once you start down this path, you won't be able to go back," John said, skimming the price sheets. "And you'll be accused of selling out."

"We've talked it over," Cade answered. "Analyzed it. Had a few hearty debates, too. It's no different from a television program or movie showcasing products."

"It's not as if it's something new in the business," John said. "But it *is* new for you. Something you've resisted because of the ethics involved."

"It's a new day," Scarlet said. "A time for change."

She'd parroted what she'd overheard him say to Patrick the past weekend.

"We ask one thing, John," Fin said. "We want an exclusive. You don't go to the other EPH magazines—or anyone else—asking for the same thing. Let us run with it first."

John nodded. "Unless they ask. I can't pass up reasonable business, either, Fin. And I want an exclusive, as well. You don't offer this opportunity to anyone else for a few months, either."

"Fair enough," Fin said. "I've asked Scarlet to be your liaison on this project. Does that work for you?"

He didn't dare look at Scarlet. "Sure."

"She came up with a list of your clients whose products might be suitable for us."

"That's very competent of her."

A momentary silence hung over the room, then Fin

said coolly, "We're pleased we found a way to keep your business at *Charisma*."

"So am I." And now he and Scarlet would work together as well as play together, if that was what they could call it. But this business relationship would extend beyond the month.

"If you have time to stay and talk with her now, we would appreciate it."

"I do."

"Good." Finola rose, as did Cade and Bridget. "We'll be in touch."

The room emptied except for Scarlet and John, who sat across the wide table from each other.

"Your concept?" he asked her.

"Does it matter?"

"Just curious. I couldn't figure out why an assistant fashion editor was in on an ad meeting. If you came up with the idea, it makes sense that you would be here. Seems to me, though, that you'd like to take credit for something so daring for *Charisma*."

Scarlet sat back in her chair, her arms crossed. "Fin's a great boss. She's turned us into a team where credit *and* blame are shared."

"I've known her for a few years. This is the most on edge I've seen her."

"The competition." Scarlet shrugged. "Everyone's feeling the pressure."

"You think she should be the one to win? The one to become CEO of EPH, over your uncles?"

"I don't work for them." She smiled sweetly. "Here's the list." She skated it across the table.

He caught it, stood and walked around the table, not

taking his eyes off her. She watched him, as well. He sat beside her, close enough that her perfume drifted across the space between them. Her signature scent aroused him instantly.

"Are we still on for Saturday night?" he asked.

The door opened. Jessie shouldered her way in, carrying a tray with bottled water and glasses of ice. "Cade said I should sit in on your meeting."

"Great," Scarlet said with a little too much enthusiasm.

Saved by the intern. John could see the thought flash through Scarlet's mind.

And because he wasn't going to take no for an answer, he decided to be creative himself.

John had been right about one thing, Scarlet thought a half hour later as they left the conference room and headed to her cubicle. She *did* want credit for her idea to keep his business at *Charisma*. Not for the glory— she was a team player—but she wished her grandfather knew what she'd come up with. She wanted him to see that she was valuable to the magazine, not just an Elliott being given a position because of the family name.

As long as she was being honest with herself, she admitted she wanted John to know, too, because she needed him to acknowledge her abilities. It was unlike her to crave approval. What did that say about her? A sign of a new maturity...or insecurity? She wished Summer was home so they could talk about it, at least the part about Granddad. But their phone conversations, frequent but short, never allowed time for deep discussion, plus Summer was living a dream. Scarlet didn't want to wake her with reality yet.

Scarlet knew John was right behind her as they reached her cubicle, but his footsteps were almost silent. Sneaky. He was sneaky in a lot of ways. Good ways, interesting ways, like his card with the flowers that had only his phone number printed on it. Like luring her to the conference room at the Spring Fling. Like disguising his incredible body with boring suits. Outwardly he needed some flair to match what he was inside, which was fascinating.

The orchids he'd sent were still fresh, the vase overflowing with the wondrous blooms. She saw his gaze land on them.

She thumbed through a stack of papers on her desk, pulling out the one she wanted to give him.

"Thanks," he said. He stuffed the sheet into his briefcase. "I'll be in touch as I meet with each client."

He left. Just like that. Without finalizing plans for Saturday night, even though he'd asked her before.

An assortment of possibilities about how she could do him bodily harm ran through her head. Had he forgotten or was he playing a game with her? Maybe he was unhappy that they would be working together on the same project for an indefinite period of time.

Any other man might—

She stopped. Sat down. Set her elbows on her desk and rested her chin in her hands. John wasn't like any other man. And that was the problem.

She was used to leading a relationship, had thought *she* was letting *him* lead. But the fact of the matter was, he wasn't...leadable.

At five o'clock she headed to the elevator bank, grateful she wasn't an executive, whose work hours often stretched long into the night, even more so since Granddad had fired the starting gun on the competition. She was worried about Aunt Finny, who was way too tense, and determined to win, and was spending far too much time in the office these days.

"Scarlet!" Jessie ran up to her at the elevator, holding tight to a red helium-filled balloon. "This just came. There wasn't a card, but the delivery guy said it was for you."

Scarlet spied a piece of paper inside the balloon. She had no doubt who'd sent it.

But what did the note say?

"Thanks," she said to Jessie, leaving her curiosity unsatisfied as Scarlet stepped into the waiting elevator. "See you tomorrow."

She strode down Park Avenue, the string wrapped securely around her hand, the balloon hovering just above her head. She smiled as she walked. People smiled back. It was a drizzly spring day, but it was beautiful.

The man learned fast, she thought. He could've talked to her while they were in her cubicle, or called her after he'd returned to his office. Instead he sent her a balloon. How imaginative. Maybe it held a little apology for last Saturday night, as well as a reminder of the upcoming Saturday night.

She hailed a cab, lucky to find one unoccupied. Then at the town house she swung open the gate and headed for the door to the underground pool and garage to get to her private entrance. The sound of someone knocking on a window caught her attention. She spied her grandmother waving at her, motioning her to come through the front door.

Gram rarely came into the city anymore unless she was going on a shopping binge, in which case she made arrangements to shop with Scarlet in tow. They always made a day of it.

Curious why Gram hadn't alerted Scarlet that she was coming, Scarlet climbed the front stairs and walked into the entry, where a grand piano held center stage. When someone played, the sound reverberated through the entire three-story house.

"What are you doing here?" she asked her grandmother as they hugged.

"We have tickets for the opera. We came early so that Patrick could go into the office." She smiled at the balloon. "It's a special occasion, then, is it?"

"What? Oh, someone was passing them out. They're advertising something."

Maeve's brows lifted. "And you carried it all the way home?"

Scarlet shrugged, trying to look innocent. "It suited my mood."

"Why don't you pop it and see what's inside?"

"I, um, don't really care what's inside. I'd like to enjoy the balloon for a while."

Gram's eyes held a secret smile. "If you don't want to share the note, just say so, *colleen*. I respect your privacy."

Then for no fathomable reason the balloon popped on its own and the note went flying, landing faceup at Maeve's feet. Scarlet grabbed it before her grandmother could bend down, then held it up to read.

I look forward to Saturday night. Pick you up at eight.

Scarlet somehow managed not to sigh her relief at the

G-rated note, unsure whether her grandmother had had time to read it or not.

"So, you have a date tonight, then," Gram said, her eyes twinkling.

Scarlet looked at the note again. "No. Saturday."

Maeve pointed to it. "I think you've got a different message on the other side."

With dread Scarlet turned the note over. *Tonight. Nine. Be prepared for some lessons of your own.*

Gram laughed, softly at first, then with utter amusement at Scarlet's embarrassment.

"A healthy love life is a good thing. Is it anyone I know, then?"

Scarlet's face heated to broil. "Gram, please."

"Someone your granddad would approve of, for a change?"

She wished she could answer yes. Wished it with all her heart. But no one would be happy with her choice of John Harlan. No one.

Her grandmother patted her on the arm. "I won't tell Patrick, if that's your worry."

"I'm just not ready to talk about it."

"Sure, then, I'll leave it alone for now. Oh. We'll be taking the helicopter back to The Tides tonight, so you don't have to be worrying about us seeing your young man in the morning."

Like there was any way she would let John come over tonight, knowing that Patrick could change his mind and be there in the morning.

"Have a wonderful time at the opera," she said to her impish grandmother.

"I don't suppose you'll be visiting us this weekend?"

Scarlet laughed. "Good night." She headed to the indoor staircase, appreciating, as she always did, the calm, tasteful decor of the town house, decorated so similarly to The Tides. Maeve Elliott knew how to bring peace to a place—and a person.

When she reached her floor, she went straight into her room and dialed John's number.

"You got my balloon?" he asked, his voice full of sexy promise.

"My grandmother got your balloon."

"What?"

Good. At least she'd shocked him in return. "I was reading your lovely note about Saturday, while she was reading your more direct note on the other side."

The sharp, succinct curse that came next made her relax, although she didn't know why.

"What did she say?" he asked.

"That you could spend the night."

A long pause, then, "I beg your pardon?"

"You didn't sign your name to the note, so she doesn't know it's you specifically, but she made it clear that my young man could spend the night. She and Granddad are taking the copter home tonight."

A pause ensued. "I'm not willing to risk that," he said.

"Neither am I."

"Are you disappointed?"

She waited a couple of beats to answer him, not because she didn't know the answer but because she wasn't sure she wanted him to know exactly how disappointed she was.

"I'm going to take that as a yes. Saturday night is still a go, though, right?"

"Of course."

"Scarlet? About Saturday night… Is that to be a Woo U date, like a real first date?"

"You mean with no fringe benefits?"

"I'm just trying to know what to expect. Having two different—and opposite—relationships doesn't make things simple."

"It's a first date," she said. "We've already straightened out a few errors you've made in the past. Let's see if anything else needs fixing."

"All right."

She couldn't tell if he was disappointed, but she could guess. She didn't know how well she could stick to her own rules herself. She was still revved up from Saturday night at the country club. Just sitting next to him at the meeting today had made her wish they could find a dark corner somewhere and put an end to the aching need.

"Good night, John," she said as cheerfully as possible.

"'Night."

Scarlet changed into casual pants and a top, grabbed a leftover chicken Caesar salad from the refrigerator, then settled on the sofa with her sketch pad. She'd been unusually creative lately, ideas flowing so easily that she had already filled one pad and was halfway through another, in barely a month's time.

A psychologist would say she was sublimating— diverting her forbidden desire for John into a socially acceptable substitute, like designing an entire clothing line. After more than an hour she set aside her pad and wandered to the living-room window. People walked along the sidewalk, going to or coming home from dinner, probably. Singles moved along in haste. Couples strolled.

When was the last time she'd been on a date? Gone out to dinner with someone other than Summer or a girl-friend? Sometime during the past year she'd given up trying to irritate her grandfather by dating men he wouldn't approve of. She'd been asked out during that time, but had made excuses not to go.

Looking back, she realized she'd stopped dating when John and Summer had started getting serious, and Scarlet had begun falling in love with John. She'd spent a lot of time at home, sewing. Summer had been worried about her, had often invited her to come along with her and John. Scarlet had made so many excuses she'd run out of creative ideas.

The irony, of course, was that her grandfather would approve of John—if he hadn't once been engaged to Summer. Patrick wouldn't tolerate scandal. He'd even forced Aunt Finny at age fifteen to give up her baby born out of wedlock, in order to save public face. Scarlet figured Fin was fighting so hard to win Patrick's corpo-rate game because she'd harbored so much resentment for him these twenty-plus years since having her baby taken away.

Scarlet didn't want to become like Fin. She wanted to make peace with Patrick. But there was no way she could make peace by pursuing John for anything beyond this month of stolen nights. People would talk too much, especially this soon after the breakup.

She wished she were brave enough to end the rela-tionship now, but she wasn't. Only a couple more weeks, then the choice would be taken from her.

The phone rang, slicing into her thoughts, for which she was grateful.

"What do you think about using Une Nuit as a locale for a shoot?" John asked without saying hello. "Models seated at a table, looking at a menu, the name of the restaurant right there for the world to see."

"I think it could be considered a conflict of interest, since my cousin Bryan owns the place. Is he a client of yours now?"

"Brand-new."

"I thought Bryan liked to fly low under the radar. And last I heard he had reservations booked until the twelfth of never."

"I can't tell you what his plans are."

"Can't or don't know?"

"Take your pick."

She smiled. She liked a man who could keep confidences. "So, you're spending the evening working?"

"It was that or stand in a cold shower all night."

She burrowed into the sofa cushions, tucking the phone closer. "Were you serious in your note about having something to teach me?"

"That's for me to know and you to find out."

How in the world had Summer given up this man? Scarlet wondered for the thousandth time. He was quick-witted, funny, smart and sexy. What more could a woman want?

"Want to reschedule tonight's plan for Friday?" he asked.

"Can't. I have a meet and greet at Michael Thor's new studio," Scarlet said.

"It can't last all night."

"I promised Jessie I'd take her by Une Nuit afterward. I'm really sorry."

A beat passed. "So, that leaves us back at our Saturday night Woo U date," he said.

"Good thing you asked early," she said pertly, glad when he laughed. "John?"

"What?"

"I've been thinking." She waited for him to come back with some clever insult, but there was only silence. Maybe he heard the tension in her voice. "I'm not sure we should be doing more than just the Woo U stuff."

"Meaning?"

"We were lucky my grandparents didn't catch us tonight. Maybe that's a sign we shouldn't spend all that much time together."

"You believe in signs? Omens? Fate?" he asked.

"When it's convenient...or logical."

"Before we make such a big decision, why don't we sleep on it? We'll talk about it on Saturday. After the date ends."

Because she wanted to avoid the discussion herself, she said, "Works for me. Good night, John."

"Sweet dreams, Scarlet."

The way he said the words turned her to mush. She knew he had to be disappointed in her decision, yet he'd said his own good-night with tenderness in his voice, not impatience or irritation. Personally, she would've been irritated if he'd come to the same determination that she had.

She liked that she kept learning something new about him.

After a minute she glanced at the clock. She could change her mind right now—grab a cab and surprise him. He was at home and alone. He would satisfy her deprived needs....

Instead she took a warm bath and went to bed, in search of those elusive sweet dreams.

John printed the results of his evening at the computer, stacked the papers and put them in his briefcase. He started to pour himself a Glenfiddich, hesitated then went ahead and splashed some in a glass. The smooth, pricey scotch could've easily reminded him of the day Summer broke their engagement, but instead he chose to associate it with his first night with Scarlet.

He carried the glass with him to look out his window. It had started to rain sometime in the past hour. He turned off all the lights and stood, sipping and watching and remembering. The way she'd watched him undress. Her red bra and thong. The incredible sounds she made, flattering and arousing. Then the way she rushed away, leaving her coat behind. He'd sat on his bed, holding it to his nose, breathing in her scent for a long time after she was gone.

He hadn't expected to ever see her again, at least not like that. He'd been wrong.

And somehow he'd gotten himself into a position where they would spend hours together on Saturday without hope of ending up in bed. Maybe never sleep together again.

He really wondered whether he'd fried a whole lot of brain cells since he'd first slept with her. He knew he was infatuated, because she was rarely out of his mind. Even now he'd gone hard just thinking about her, a condition he hadn't experienced with this much uncontrolled regularity since he was a teenager.

It couldn't be more than lust. He refused to have his

heart broken by another Elliott woman. Or even have his life turned upside down.

But he wanted her....

To hell with it. He set his empty glass on the bar, grabbed his coat and keys and went out the door. He could sneak out of her house long before anyone was up to see him, convince her not to give up the sexual relationship.

But when the elevator doors opened he stared at the empty car until the doors closed. He returned to his apartment. His huge, quiet apartment. And went to bed alone.

Seven

Une Nuit buzzed no matter what night of the week, but this was Friday, and the crowd was different on Friday. Younger, even hipper, if that was possible. A visual sea of beautiful people dressed in New York's color of choice—black—enjoying the daring French/Asian fusion cuisine that was always being written up in the media, thus keeping the very trendy restaurant *the* place to be.

With Jessie in tow, Scarlet wove through the bar crowd at the front of the restaurant, looking for her cousin Bryan. While he might join them at dinner briefly, he generally wandered around the rest of the time, a hands-on owner.

She'd almost reached the maître d's podium when she came across Stash Martin, a wickedly handsome

Frenchman in his early thirties. As manager of Une Nuit, he was as much a fixture as Bryan.

"Scarlet, welcome," he said. They exchanged kisses on both cheeks.

"Crazy," she said, grinning, looking around.

"But quite typical. If you are looking for Bryan, he is not here. He is out of town. Again."

"Where does he go?" she asked rhetorically then introduced Stash to Jessie, who was wide-eyed at the scene. Bryan had always been an adventurer, even as he seemed to love his restaurant. He came and went a lot, but his business thrived because he had a staff he could count on.

"You would like a table, eh?" Stash asked.

"Any family members here?"

"Not a one. The Elliott table is free."

"What do you think?" Scarlet asked Jessie. "Table or the bar? How hungry are you?"

"Not very. The bar is fine."

"Wait here a moment," Stash said, then he approached the maître d'.

Scarlet had talked Jessie into borrowing an outfit from the closet of designer clothing at the magazine, but she hadn't been able to talk Jessie into letting her hair loose from the braid she always wore. The black leather pants and turtleneck did give her a different look, a fashionable one. Even Scarlet, usually a standout because of the colorful outfits she often wore, was wearing black—a miniskirt, boots and belted leather jacket. Her hair was pulled up into an untidy knot. She considered the look as just another aspect of her personality.

Stash returned then pointed to a couple sitting at the very center of the long, black lacquered bar. "Stand behind them. They'll be called in to dinner as soon as you make your way over there."

Scarlet flashed him a smile. "You're the best."

He lifted Scarlet's hand to kiss, and she fluttered her lashes playfully.

"When are you going to sleep with me and get me out of your system, *ma chérie?*" he asked, as he always did.

"Soon," she answered, as she always did.

A few minutes later she and Jessie were seated at the bar, waiting for their drinks.

"I've never seen anything like this," Jessie said in awe. "It's like a movie. Red and black and sexy. And I love the copper-topped tables."

"Maybe we'll order something to eat later, so that you can taste how incredible their food is." She smiled at the bartender when he placed an apple martini in front of her, then lifted her glass to Jessie. "To adventures in the big city."

"I wish I could afford more of them. Someday. When I have a paying job. Every penny of my savings is budgeted. Thanks so much for this treat."

"Keep performing well at *Charisma,* and you could be offered a paying job at the end of your internship." She sipped her drink then looked around, making eye contact with a man at the end of the bar, who toasted her. She smiled but looked away, then realized she shouldn't put up roadblocks, since Jessie might be interested. She decided to give him another chance, but Jessie's words stopped her.

"There's that man from the ad agency, John Harlan."

Surprise pelted Scarlet from all sides. "Where?"

"At a table behind you, in the corner."

She wasn't sure she wanted to turn around. If he was with a woman, she didn't want to know.

"He's looking right at you. I think he knows I'm telling you he's there," Jessie said in an emphatic whisper.

"Hmm." She took a long sip of her drink. He was courteous and would probably approach them at some point, especially since he and Jessie had taken note of each other. Scarlet would wait for him to initiate contact. Until then she could ignore the possibilities of whom he was with.

Maybe that blonde from the country club dance. She never had asked who that was.

"Is it true he was engaged to your sister?" Jessie asked.

Scarlet sighed. "They were engaged on Valentine's Day, but Summer called it off a couple of weeks later, just about the time you were hired."

"It must be weird for him, seeing you. Working with you, her identical twin."

Tell me about it. She'd wondered at the beginning if she was only a substitute for her sister, a way to get Summer out of his mind, but she didn't think that was true now. They had their own relationship. And while it was fun at times, she was always aware of the impending and necessary conclusion. They couldn't even just date and see where things might go. Even if Summer—and their grandfather—could somehow accept it, because of Scarlet's reputation, many people might assume that Scarlet had interfered somehow, even before Zeke Woodlow had appeared on the scene. It wasn't worth the grief.

Or was it?

The man from the end of the bar approached, saving Scarlet from coming up with an answer. Late twenties,

Scarlet decided. A little taller than she, blond and blue-eyed. He didn't look overly sophisticated or jaded, which meant he might work as a flirtation for the still-naive Jessie. Diverting her attention from watching John was a good idea.

"I'll bet you're sisters," the man said.

Scarlet met Jessie's gaze. She looked startled, but Scarlet smiled. "Coworkers," she said.

"I'm Rich."

"Money doesn't matter to me," Jessie said sincerely.

Scarlet grinned. "I think he means his name is Rich. That's Jessie. I'm Scarlet."

"I know who you are," Rich said to Scarlet, his hand resting on the back of her bar stool, almost touching her. "I saw your picture in the newspaper with Zeke Woodlow."

Scarlet angled closer to the bar. "That was an impersonator," she said, trying to make light of it. It had actually been Summer, dressed in Scarlet's clothes, made to look like a groupie. Scarlet held up her empty glass to the bartender.

"I'll get that," Rich said to the man.

"No, thank you." She decided she didn't want this guy around, after all. She caught Stash's eye, then tipped her head slightly toward Rich. Stash headed her way.

"Mon petit choux," he said, nudging Rich out of the way to kiss her, a little longer than was necessary for the ruse, Scarlet thought, wondering what John was thinking of the scene. "I apologize for keeping you waiting, *ma chérie,*" Stash continued, nuzzling her neck.

"Don't do it again." She leaned into him as he slipped an arm around her shoulders.

Rich was resourceful, however, and undeterred. He turned his attention on Jessie. "May I buy you a drink, um, Jenny?"

Jessie used her little straw to swirl her ice, then she slipped the straw in her mouth and pulled it out slowly, getting his attention. "You know, Rich, I believe my daddy would get a kick out of you."

He looked ready to swagger. "He would?"

"In fact, he has a saying that would fit you to a T. He'd say, 'That poor Rich. He's got nothin' under his hat but hair.'"

Scarlet had to set her drink down before the contents sloshed over the sides. Jessie's handling of Rich showed she wasn't quite as naive as she sometimes seemed.

"Bitch," he said, low and furious. "You—"

Stash moved but was blocked by John, who snatched the glass out of Rich's hand and thumped it on the bar next to Scarlet's. "Time to find a new watering hole, partner," John said, clamping a hand on his shoulder.

Rich glowered, but he left without comment, just a surly look.

"Are you okay?" John asked Jessie.

"I'm fine. Actually, it was kinda fun." She grinned.

Scarlet waited for him to turn his attention on her, but he said good-night and left. She watched him walk out the door, cross in front of the window and disappear. Only then did she look toward the corner where he'd been seated. Three women sat there.

"He had been alone," Stash whispered in her ear.

Scarlet tried to calm her nerves. She didn't know what to think about John. Was he mad? Jealous of Stash? Hurt?

She decided to change her outward mood since even Stash had picked up on something he shouldn't. "Thanks for the rescue. But, *mon petit choux?*"

"My little cabbage." His eyes twinkled. Jessie laughed.

"I know what it means."

"It is an endearment." He lifted a loose strand of hair over her ear. "Perhaps you ladies have had enough excitement and would like to have dinner now. I have kept the table for you."

Scarlet decided if she didn't take some time to think about John and how to handle what had just happened, she would probably do the wrong thing—like go after him. "I've worked up an appetite. How about you?" she asked Jessie.

"I could use a big ol' rib eye myself. There's nothing like dispatching a preening bull to give me an appetite."

Scarlet smiled. She was glad they'd gone out together. Glad she'd gotten to know Jessie better. "Would your father really have said something like that?"

"Oh, yeah. He's full of 'em."

"What does he do?" Stash asked as they reached their table.

"He's a cattle rancher."

"Do you rope and ride?"

"About as easily as breathing," she said.

His brows raised. "I have never before met a cowgirl." He asked a passing server to bring two menus.

"I'm going to use the restroom first," Jessie said to Scarlet then headed toward the back of the restaurant.

Scarlet hoped Stash wasn't going to comment on John's behavior, but she should've realized she wouldn't be that lucky.

"So. Your sister's fiancé."

"Ex-fiancé."

"And you."

"No. Just in the same place at the same time."

"T'es menteuse, toi."

"I'm not a liar." Technically, they weren't together. They were just enjoying each other's company briefly.

"He did not take his eyes off you from the moment he saw you."

She wished she had a menu to hide behind. "I have no control over John's actions."

He only smiled. "Bryan would want me to tell you your meal is on the house."

"He's my favorite cousin," Scarlet said sweetly.

Stash grinned and walked away.

Much later Scarlet and Jessie shared a cab home. Scarlet lived only a few blocks from Une Nuit and was dropped off first. Jessie continued on after thanking Scarlet profusely for the amazing night.

Scarlet headed up her stairs, questions running through her head. Should she call John? *Was* he angry? Was it better just to leave it alone for now?

She turned the landing of the third floor and spotted John leaning against the wall by her door. She slowed, studying his face, trying to guess his mood. She wanted to see him flash those dimples, but she didn't think there was much chance of that. He looked...single-minded.

He didn't move an inch when she approached. Her shoulder brushed his chest as she put her key in the lock. "What would you have done if I'd brought someone up with me?" she asked mildly, her heart pounding.

"Discouraged him from going inside."

Scarlet opened the door and went in, leaving the door open but not inviting him. He came inside and shut the door.

She tossed her purse on an entry table then crossed her arms. "What do you want, John?"

"You know the answer to that."

"Short of *that*, what else?" The game, the words, excited her. She sensed he knew it, too.

"You ignored me."

"You ignored me, too," she said. It had confused her, angered her, that he'd spoken to Jessie at the bar but not her.

"You were cozy with Stash. I didn't want to interfere."

"Stash and I flirt with each other. It's nothing."

"I'm not telling you what to do or not to do. We don't have an exclusive relationship."

That hurt. Even if it lasted only the month, she'd thought it was exclusive.

"Well, fine, then. Because I don't explain myself to anyone." She turned away, not having a clue what to do next, just that she couldn't look at him.

"Look," he said, coming closer, touching her shoulder. She pulled away.

"This is not going the way I envisioned," he said, frustration in his voice. "I just wanted to clear the air before tomorrow night. I don't think I could have even a pretend date with you with tonight hanging over us."

"What is 'tonight' to you? Why are you angry?"

"You think it was easy watching you flirt with that jerk at the bar, then again with Stash? And you knew I was there. I know Jessie told you. Were you trying to make me jealous?"

She spun around. "The jerk came up on his own," she said, breaking her own rule about not explaining herself. "I sort of encouraged him because I thought he might work for Jessie. Then he showed his true, sleazy colors and I beckoned Stash to come over. I flirted with Stash so that there wouldn't be a scene, but the jerk was also stupid and things got out of hand, anyway. Stash is a friend. That's *all*."

"You could've beckoned *me*," John said quietly.

He was hurt? That was what his problem was? She closed her eyes for a moment. Since he was being honest with her, she could do the same. "I hadn't turned around at the bar. I didn't know if you were on a date. I didn't want to know."

"I would've come to your rescue regardless."

"Your date would've been unhappy about that."

He set his hands on her shoulders. "Why would I have taken a date to Une Nuit? You told me you were going to be there. Why would I do that to you?" He didn't wait for answer. "What kind of man do you usually go out with that you would think me capable of such rudeness?"

"Obviously a different kind of man. I'm working on changing that, however."

She saw him relax.

"I don't intentionally hurt people, Scarlet. I *am* civilized."

Maybe on the surface he was. He'd been raised well, raised to be civilized. But at moments like tonight and during their private tryst in the country club conference room, he wasn't completely civilized. She liked that about him. She loved that about him. She'd fallen in love months ago with the kind man who'd been so good to Summer, but now she'd fallen deeply, hopelessly in love with this fascinating man who was more primal than she'd expected, more intriguing, more complex. She liked that he'd been waiting for her when she got home, wanting to clear the air, even if the answers to his questions weren't what he wanted to hear. She liked that he faced things head-on.

She laid her hands on his chest and looked him in the eyes. Words didn't come, however. After the longest thirty seconds of her life, he lifted his hands and pulled out her hair clip, letting her hair fall around her face, then combed it with his fingers. He cupped her head, moved toward her. She suddenly wished she'd kicked off her shoes so that she could rise up on tiptoe to meet him. The idea made her smile.

"What?" he asked.

"You make me feel so…female."

One side of his mouth lifted. "Is that a good thing?"

"No one has made me feel like that before."

"Again, is that a good thing?"

"Yes."

"How have you felt before?"

"I don't know. Equal. Or sometimes even dominant." She didn't want to tell him more, didn't want to give him ammunition for teasing her. She just knew she felt different with him.

"You've been plenty dominant with me." He was still holding her head, keeping her close. His breath dusted her face. His beautiful dark brown eyes were filled with tenderness and need.

She smiled wider. "Not in comparison."

"Ah." He brushed his lips over hers once, twice, once more. "You make me feel different, too."

His mouth finally settled on hers, his tongue seeking hers. She wound her arms around him.

So much for resisting each other.

With a sigh she gave in to her needs, not attempting to stop the urgent sounds that rose from within her, which seemed to arouse him more. He pulled her close, slid a hand over her rear, tugging her against him, letting her feel his need. She moved her hips against him, and his kisses turned almost violent. He fisted her hair and tipped her head back, ran his tongue down her neck, his fingers frantically opening the belts and buckles on her jacket then shoving the jacket off her, hearing it land with a quiet thud. She was starved for him, had never wanted like this before, as if she could die if she didn't have him inside her immediately.

He fumbled with her zipper, then her skirt joined her jacket, leaving her in a sheer black bra, thong and boots. Her nipples were so hard, they hurt.

He took a step back to unbutton his shirt, dragged the tails free.

"When I'm ninety I will remember this," he said, low and harsh.

She hooked her hand in his waistband and brought him closer, wanting him, needing him. She knelt before him, pressed her mouth to his fly, his hard need flattering and exciting. She reached for his belt buckle—

The phone rang.

"The answering machine will get it," she murmured, placing both hands on him, watching his head fall back as she traced the length and breadth of him through the fabric.

Second ring.

He dragged her up, flicked open her bra and sent it flying.

Third ring.

He cupped her breasts, thumbed her nipples, sucked one into his mouth.

Fourth ring.

"We're not home. Leave a message," came Scarlet's own voice from the nearby machine.

"Hi, it's me!"

Summer.

John became like a statue.

"You must be out having fun. Maybe I'll call your cell after this. Haven't talked to you for a couple of days, and I'm missing you. Although not too much," she added with a laugh. "Scar, I can't tell you how happy I am. How incredible Zeke is. You've got to fall madly, passionately in love. You do. It's…it's indescribable."

John straightened, stepped away. He shoved his shirt into his pants. His eyes met Scarlet's. She felt naked, clear to her soul. She couldn't read his thoughts. He guarded his expression.

"Zeke, stop. I'm talking to my sister."

In the background came the rumble of a deep voice, but the words weren't clear.

John scooped up Scarlet's jacket. She turned around, letting him help her put it on. She tugged the edges together before she faced him again.

"I guess I won't call you on your cell, after all. I have something else—" Summer laughed "—to do at the moment. I'll catch you later. Bye. I miss you."

Scarlet didn't know what to say. She couldn't joke

about it—it wasn't the least bit funny. And making light of it wouldn't sit well with either of them.

As a reminder of the predetermined parameters of their risky relationship, it had a powerful effect. Resistance was the key. This time they needed to try harder.

Maybe her disappointment and fears were in her eyes, though, because John laid a hand tenderly along her face. She covered it with her own.

"Tomorrow night?" he asked.

She nodded. She wasn't going to miss any opportunity to see him, be with him.

He left with no kiss, no hug. Just a long, thorough, final look at her in her jacket, thong and boots.

For the first time in her life, she wished she didn't have a sister.

Eight

Saturday refused to pass by with any kind of speed. Scarlet picked out what she would wear on her Woo U date, pressed it, chose jewelry, then looked at the clock. Noon. She had hours and hours to fill. Normally she would spend her free time sewing, but not now. She was too keyed up, plus today was glorious, clear and crisp. She decided to walk the three miles to the EPH building and work out in the company gym.

At the gym Scarlet pushed herself until every muscle burned, then she showered, wrapped up in a towel and settled in the sauna. She wished she could say that she'd been able to block John from her thoughts, but she kept seeing the look on his face—or the nonlook—as Summer talked to the answering machine, and how quickly he'd left.

Not that she would've wanted to make love after that, either, but—

No *but*. There was nothing either of them could've done differently. Fate had intervened. For a moment— just a moment—she'd even thought they might have a chance for a future together.

The sauna door opened, and Fin came in. She was entitled to use the private executive section but hadn't chosen to. The four siblings being put through the wringer for the CEO job were straining to keep their familial ties, but it was more of a competition now than a family unit.

"Good workout?" Fin asked as she sat a few feet from Scarlet.

"I pushed myself hard. I needed it. Hadn't been here for a couple of weeks. I'm sure I'll pay for it tomorrow, though."

"I just had a massage from Magda. See if you can catch her before she leaves."

Scarlet stuck her head out the door, caught an employee passing by and made her request then sat again.

"I'm glad to see you taking care of yourself," Scarlet said to her aunt. "I worry about you. Everyone's worried about you."

"It's only a year out of my life. I'll manage. After I win, I'll take some time off." She leaned her head back and closed her eyes.

"Did you go home last night or sleep on the couch in your office?"

"Office," she said lazily. "Everything going okay with the new project?"

"Everything's great."

"It's comfortable working with John?"

"It's fine." Scarlet didn't want to get into it with Fin. "It's business."

"And how's the new intern working out?"

"Good. Jessie's got the eye, Fin. I think you should seriously consider keeping her on. She'll land someplace. Might as well be with us rather than with a competitor."

The door opened. "Ms. Elliott, Magda says if you can come now, she can give you forty-five minutes."

"Tell her I'll be right there, please."

She scooted close to her aunt and tapped her arm, making her open her eyes. "We all want you to win, Aunt Finny. But we all want you healthy when you do."

"I'll be fine. Go."

Scarlet made sure an attendant knew not to let Fin stay in there for more than fifteen minutes. She would undoubtedly sleep, and could easily end up in the sauna for hours without anyone knowing.

An hour later, exercised, steamed and massaged, Scarlet headed for the elevator, feeling utterly relaxed. She would go shoe shopping, she decided. It would help her pass the time.

"Ms. Elliott," said a gym attendant, running to catch up and sounding frantic as Scarlet waited for the elevator. "Your grandfather would like to see you."

To her credit, Scarlet didn't groan, but thanked the young man and hit the up button. If she hadn't taken time to indulge herself with a massage she would've been long gone by now. She sighed at her bad timing.

Scarlet had been to the twenty-third floor surprisingly few times in her life, and not at all since she'd been working at *Charisma*. Her grandfather's office was furnished in an old European style, like The Tides and the

Manhattan town house, with antiques that he and Gram had collected on their travels. The familiarity should've helped to make her feel comfortable, but it never had, not when the man himself was present.

Had Gram told him about the note in the balloon? She'd said she wouldn't, but…

Mrs. Bitton, his assistant/watchdog, wasn't at her desk, and the door to his inner office was open. She peeked in.

He was on the phone and waved her in.

"I will be there in time," he said gently into the telephone. "And I'm not working too hard, *cushla macree*. In fact, Scarlet just stopped by, so I'm going to visit with her for a while, then I'll head home."

Scarlet shook her head at his ability to twist things for his own purposes. As if she would just stop by on her own. Ha!

She wandered to the opposite wall to study a painting of her grandmother as a young bride. Most of the Elliott women took after her in one way or another. In this pose, Scarlet could see Fin's heritage directly.

"Prettiest woman on earth," her grandfather said, coming up beside her.

"Inside and out," Scarlet said.

"Why she's put up with me all these years only God knows."

Her instinct was to agree with him. Because of that, she didn't.

"No comment, missy?"

She smiled and shrugged. He invited her to sit in one of the wingback chairs in front of his desk. Surprisingly, he sat in the other instead of taking his position of authority behind the desk.

Hmm. He must not want to intimidate her this time. What was going on?

"Would you like something to drink?" he asked.

Curiouser and curiouser. "I'm fine, thanks. What's up, Granddad?"

"Are you dating anyone in particular these days?"

She went on full alert. "Why?"

"Just making conversation."

"Since when?" The words slipped out before she could stop them. She regretted being sarcastic, but his question worried her. Did he know about John? No. He would've been direct if he knew.

His lips compressed. "Can't I be interested in your life?"

"So, you're just making conversation? You really don't care if or who I'm dating, right?"

"Of course I do." He shifted in his chair, obviously uncomfortable.

"What if I told you I was dating, oh, say, John Harlan?" Was she stupid or brave to test him? she wondered.

"I would know you were just being obstinate about answering."

"Why?"

"You would never betray your sister like that."

Betray. Of all the reasons she'd come up with for why she couldn't see John beyond this month, it had never entered her mind that she would be betraying Summer. Summer had given up John. Period. Scarlet hadn't stolen him. But Granddad would see it as a betrayal, probably because it would be like shoving Summer's nose in her mistake, a reminder of how much she'd hurt another human being.

"Nor would John go out with you," he added. "Don't even joke about such a thing. Although I was surprised to see you dance with him."

Scarlet couldn't find words to reply.

"Okay, I can take a hint," he said after a few seconds. "No personal questions. I called you up here because I've been hearing good things about the job you're doing. Competent and creative, that's what people are saying. I wanted you to know I'm proud of you."

Scarlet was stunned into further silence. She couldn't remember her grandfather ever doling out compliments to her. "Thank you," she managed to say, fighting back the sting of tears.

"I'm looking to you now, Scarlet. Summer has gone off to live in sin with that rock star. Even if she does come back to work, she'll probably have babies soon. I think you'll stick around. You're not one to romanticize."

He shocked her anew, this time in a way that ticked her off. Did he think he was complimenting her by saying such a thing? "Meaning?" she asked.

"I think you're part of the future of EPH. Like your aunt, you'll devote yourself to your work."

Considering that Fin was driving herself to an early grave, Scarlet didn't consider her aunt's devotion something to strive for.

Then there was the other issue, how Scarlet wanted to be a designer, not an editor. How long would she have to pay family dues before she could do what she wanted? How much did she owe her grandfather for raising her after her parents had died?

"You're not usually so reluctant to argue with me, missy."

"Maybe I'm growing up."

"That's a welcome possibility."

She kept her expression serious. "It couldn't be because you're getting feeble, and I'm being careful not to cause you to have a heart attack or something."

His fists landed on his thighs. "Feeble?" he roared.

She drew a deep breath, exhaled slowly. Now this was the Granddad she knew and understood. She decided to take advantage of his bluster to kiss his cheek and leave while she had the upper hand. "Let's do this again sometime, Gramps."

She heard him chuckle as she walked through the door. It made her smile—until she got into the elevator and remembered his comment about betraying Summer. Summer wouldn't see it as a betrayal, but she would surely be uncomfortable. Adults made choices in life. Scarlet could choose to make things easy on her sister or difficult.

Without question, Scarlet would always make things easy for Summer—even to the point of denying herself love and passion, something Summer had found, and wanted Scarlet to find.

But probably not with John Harlan.

John knocked on Scarlet's door at precisely eight o'clock. He was nervous—seventeen-years-old, first-prom-date nervous. Which was stupid, since he'd already slept with her. How could he be tense about seeing her, making conversation now?

Because he had to act like he *hadn't* slept with her. Hadn't seen her incredible body in its natural state. Hadn't seen her face as an orgasm overtook her. Hadn't felt her hands and mouth all over him, hot and curious....

Okay. That line of thought had to be stopped right now, or else when she opened her front door she would see a bulge in his pants and he'd get his hand slapped with a ruler or something. The thought made him smile. Sister Scarlet. *There* was an image.

He saw the doorknob turn and tried to get himself into character. First date... First date.

"Hello, John," she said, looking soft and sweet in her buttoned-to-the-neck, electric-blue dress, her hair piled on top of her head but still looking touchable.

"Hi." He handed her a single white rose wrapped in green florist's paper and tied with a satin ribbon. He watched her bury her nose in it and smile. She looked nervous, too, he decided. It relaxed him.

"Thank you," she said. "It's lovely."

"Are you ready to go?" he asked.

"Let me put this in water and get my wrap. Come in."

He almost told her not to bother putting the rose in water, then decided not to spoil the surprise he had for her later.

She was Scarlet but not Scarlet, he thought, as she disappeared into her tiny kitchen. Her dress wasn't as daring as she generally wore, except that long line of buttons begged to be undone. Her jewelry was understated, and not as musical as usual. A couple of bangle bracelets that made a little noise, diamond studs instead of intertwining hoops in her ears, but that was all.

"I'm ready," she said, slipping a silvery wrap around her shoulders.

Should he tell her she looked beautiful? Was that kind of compliment encouraged at this point? Man, he felt like a kid.

"You changed your perfume," he said instead. It wasn't her usual citrusy scent, but tempting nonetheless. He couldn't put a name to the fragrance. Not flowery. Not powdery. He'd smelled them all in his years of dating. Scarlet's was just arousing.

She smiled. He guessed it was a good thing, noticing a detail like that.

He rested his fingertips lightly against her lower back as they left her apartment. It was going to drive him crazy not being able to touch her more than that all night. But he planned to kiss her good-night at her door later, a decent kiss, not a polite, end-of-evening peck. He didn't care if it messed up the Woo U curriculum at that point.

While in the car, they didn't speak beyond routine chitchat about the traffic and weather. The awkwardness of knowing what they did about each other, and pretending not to, tied his tongue. Hers, too, he guessed.

He pulled into his underground parking garage, a luxury he paid a huge premium for.

"This is your apartment building," she said, sitting up straighter.

"Yes. I hope you like paella."

After a long, uncomfortable pause she gave him a tentative smile. "It's one of my favorites."

They rode the elevator in a silence that wasn't completely awkward, but unusual for them. He opened his apartment door and took in the scene, trying to see it through her eyes—the table set for a romantic dinner for two. The fireplace ready to light. Candles waiting to be lit. The scent of paella lingering, being kept warm in the kitchen.

"What a wonderful view," she said as if seeing it for the first time. She moved to the window.

It gave him time to turn on the stereo, set to play a classical guitar CD to match the dinner theme. He lit the candles, then the fire. He went into the kitchen to pour them some wine. By the time he returned she'd moved to the fireplace.

"Thank you," she said, accepting a glass.

He touched the rim of his glass to hers. "To the lady in blue. Welcome to my home."

She didn't make eye contact as she sipped. What was going on? Something was obviously wrong, but what?

"Have a seat." He indicated the couch facing the fire. "How was your day?" he asked when they were settled.

"Busy. I walked to the office so I could use the gym. Talked to Fin and my grandfather there for a little while. Went shopping. How about you?"

He'd spent the entire day getting ready for this date, worrying about things he'd never worried about before. "I spent the day awaiting the night."

Everything about her relaxed—her expression, her shoulders, her spine. Had she just been nervous? She couldn't possibly be more nervous than he.

Still the evening dragged. Where was the vibrant Scarlet he knew? Oh, she smiled, even laughed, and touched his hand across the dinner table with her fingertips, but their conversation was less than dazzling. He plied her with work anecdotes and celebrity stories, but she kept her distance. He told her that the vase of eleven roses on the table was for her, to add to the one he'd given her earlier. She thanked him sweetly.

He had no idea how to fix what seemed to be wrong.

When she excused herself to use the bathroom he pushed back from the table, moved to a cabinet and poured two brandies. To hell with Woo U. He wanted Scarlet back.

He heard a slight noise and turned. Scarlet stood a few feet from him—and it was definitely Scarlet. There was fire in her eyes, a flush of color in her face. She'd taken down her hair. She looked like every fantasy he'd ever had of her.

He started to pass her a snifter of brandy, but she held up a hand.

"I'm sorry, but this just isn't working, John."

Nine

Scarlet saw him retreat, his expression distant and self-protective. She hurried to assure him.

"No. Wait." She blew out a breath. "I shouldn't have said it that way. I meant that this...dating thing isn't working for me."

She'd tried all evening to just be his date, but she knew too much about him, wanted him too much. Loved him. And what was she doing, turning him into a better date for other women, anyway? How ridiculous was that?

He set the glasses on the table and took her hands. "Why didn't you say so earlier? I thought I'd really screwed something up."

"Well, actually, you had, but that wasn't the problem."

His brows drew together. "What'd I do wrong?"

"You brought me to your apartment on a first date."

"Where was I supposed to take you? We can't be seen in public."

"You could've gotten creative. You could've thought of someplace to go, something to do where no one would know us. We're not *that* recognizable."

"You're right," he said after a moment. "Bringing you here, especially when we already had memories here…"

"Exactly." She laid her hand against his chest and looked into his eyes. "But that's minor. Truly. Let's be honest. The real issue is that we both know that Woo U was only a ploy to keep us in proximity, an excuse and nothing more so that we could…"

"Sleep together."

She nodded. "We only have two more weeks until… Until. I don't want to waste that time going on 'dates.'"

He scooped her into his arms. She knew where his bedroom was, knew he was headed there. She kicked off her shoes along the way. He said nothing. Maybe he couldn't. She wasn't sure she could, either, she wanted him so much.

It had been nine days since they'd slept together. During that time they'd aroused each other to fever pitch twice—last night and at the country club the week before. This wasn't going to be slow or tender, and she didn't care. Except that sometime she wanted slow and tender.

He didn't wait for her to undress, didn't undress himself. In the bathroom she'd taken off her underwear. When he discovered that, he shoved his pants and briefs out of the way, and drove into her, filling her so suddenly and completely that she cried out.

"I'm sorry. I didn't—"

"It's fine. It's good," she interrupted in a rush. "I was more than ready. You feel wonderful. Incredible." She arched toward him as he moved, finding a strong, hard rhythm. Demand became need. Need didn't want to wait another second. Was that her making that noise? His mouth covered hers, open, wet. He changed the angle of the kiss, groaned into her mouth. She grabbed his hair as the climax hit her, no gentle buildup but a thunderous explosion, matched by him in sound and intensity. Life stood still. Life went on. Life suddenly had direction.

The two other times they'd been together were good. This was phenomenal.

This would never be matched by anyone, anywhere, anytime. She wasn't given to exaggeration, so she believed her own prophecy.

She wrapped her arms around him as he sprawled over her, taking off some of his weight with his elbows, but mostly lying on her like a warm, heavy quilt.

"That was quick," he said, his mouth near her ear.

"And good."

"And good," he agreed, rolling to his side, keeping her in his arms.

She snuggled close, savored the way he stroked her hair. The pent-up tension dissipated. He felt like home.

"Hungry?" he asked.

"Not yet."

"Want to sleep?"

"Hmm." She burrowed closer.

"Let's get undressed first."

She left her eyes closed as he unbuttoned her dress and slipped it off her. She didn't even have the energy to watch him undress. He pulled a quilt over them, wrapped her in his arms, ran his hands up and down her back, then over her rear, along her thighs. When he gently stroked her breasts, she wriggled.

"Relax," he whispered as her nipples puckered. "I just want to touch you. Go to sleep."

She laughed drowsily. "Sure."

He propped himself on an elbow, continuing his exploration. She opened her eyes.

"Spend the night, Scarlet."

"Okay."

His hand stilled for a moment, then journeyed on. A while later, his generosity accepted and enjoyed, she fell asleep in his arms.

He could get used to this, John decided, sitting next to Scarlet. They'd dozed for half an hour, showered together, then decided to have ice cream by candlelight in the kitchen. She was dressed in his robe. He'd pulled on boxers and a T-shirt.

"I would've guessed you didn't even own a T-shirt," she said, spoon in hand. Candlelight flickered across her face. "You look younger."

"Since when is twenty-nine old?"

"Since you dress like you're fifty."

"I do?" He set down his bowl. "In what way?"

"Your suits are boring. And your shirts. And your ties."

He felt too relaxed to take offense. "I think anything compared to your clothing probably seems boring."

"It's an observation, not a comparison."

"I've never felt a need to keep up with the trends."

"You should. You're supposed to be selling cutting

edge, whether it's products or people. You should look like it."

He'd never considered that. "What should I do?"

Even though she didn't rub her hands together, it seemed like she did. "Let me help you choose some new things."

"Put myself in your hands?" The image that came to mind had nothing to do with clothes, but rather the lack of them.

She set down her bowl carefully then moved over to straddle his lap. He was learning just how complicated she was. He'd always expected her to be a sensual, sexual woman, although he'd based that opinion on her reputation more than anything tangible. But he saw shyness at times, too, which surprised him.

This wasn't one of those moments. When it came to sex, she was bold and demanding, but not domineering. A partner in every sense.

"What are you thinking about?" she asked, planting little kisses all along his jaw. "You're so serious."

"Everything that should be at attention is at attention," he countered, with a smile. He had no interest in starting a conversation at the moment.

She dragged her fingers down his cheeks. "I don't get to see these dimples often enough."

"When a clock is ticking on a relationship, there's not much to laugh at." He surprised himself admitting such a thing out loud.

She kissed him, tenderly, chastely. "Let's go to bed."

They blew out the candles, set their bowls in the sink, turned out the lights. In his bedroom they got naked, slipped under the covers and held each other close.

"This is just about sex, John," she said finally. "We can't have more than that."

"I know."

After they made love, she fell asleep. He studied his ceiling for hours, as if the answers to his problems might be written there.

All he saw was that it looked very much as if an Elliott woman would break his heart, after all.

In the morning, her head on a pillow next to John's, Scarlet watched him sleep, his hair mussed, his beard shadowy. She'd slept until nine, not waking once. She couldn't remember a night when she'd slept so well.

Her eyes stung. Anything in life she'd wanted badly enough, she'd gotten, had worked hard enough to get. But no matter what she did in this relationship, she couldn't win.

Betray. Her grandfather's word echoed in her mind.

She eased out of bed, donned John's robe and headed to the kitchen. She hunted for coffee and filters, then fixed a whole pot, not knowing how much he drank in the morning, or if he drank it at all.

At the front door she looked out the peephole to make sure the coast was clear, then grabbed the Sunday *Times* from the hallway. She finished up the dishes from the night before and checked out his refrigerator for possible breakfast food, finding eggs, cheese and English muffins.

At about ten o'clock she heard water run in the bathroom. Curled up on the sofa, she was enjoying her second cup of coffee and the *Times* travel section. A few minutes later he emerged, unshaven but with his hair combed. He'd put on the T-shirt and boxers from the night before. She'd been afraid he would come out in khakis and a preppy sweater or something, dressed for the day.

He stopped in the doorway. A slow smile came over him. "Good morning. How'd you sleep?"

"On my side, mostly."

His smile widened.

"I slept really well," she said, moving her legs so that he could sit beside her, facing her. "And you?"

She offered her mug. He took it, then leaned over and kissed her, deeper than a peck but not an invitation to more. He sipped from the mug, resting his hand on her thigh, rubbing it through the fabric.

"I slept great, thanks. So, what do you usually do on Sundays?"

"If I'm at The Tides I go to church with Gram and Granddad. If I'm in town, I'm pretty lazy. Read the paper. Go for a walk. Have a late breakfast somewhere. Do some sketching and sewing. How about you?" There was so much she had yet to discover about him. She knew his body. She knew his scent, his touch, his laugh. But nothing about his routines, his likes and dislikes. His passions.

"I don't think any two Sundays are the same for me. I play racquetball sometimes, or golf, depending on the season. Visit my parents sometimes. Work at home or even in the office occasionally. Go for a drive. Would you like to go for a drive?"

She wished she could say yes. "Probably not a good idea, John."

His hesitation was barely noticeable. "Right. Well, breakfast, then. I'm pretty sure I have the makings for omelets."

"Do you cook?"

"A little. You?"

"Salads and eggs. And I reheat brilliantly."

"Took a master course in that, did you?"

She recognized the conversation for what it was—avoidance. They were painted into a corner. Don't get too close, learn too much, enjoy too thoroughly. Sex and inane conversation were apparently all they could have. They had to otherwise resist.

"Maybe I should shower," she said. "Then we can fix breakfast together. Then I'll go home."

We can't spend the whole day with each other. The words hung over them as if in neon lights.

"How about we shower together?" he asked, standing, holding out a hand.

Later, she argued against him driving her home. She could take a cab. He didn't think she should be seen wearing what was obviously an evening dress at noon. On the drive to her house he held her hand. She didn't pull away.

"Can we get together during the week?" he asked as they neared her house.

"Definitely. Let's talk later and compare calendars. It'd have to be at your place," she added. "Granddad seems to like being unpredictable these days. I never know when he's coming to town."

"Okay."

They had shared a long goodbye kiss before leaving his apartment, yet she hungered for another.

"Did you expect it would be this complicated?" he asked when they pulled up around the corner from her house.

She nodded. "I'm pretty realistic about most things in life."

"Are you having regrets, Scarlet?"

"None." *Yet.*

"Can I ask a favor of you?"

Her heart fluttered a little.

"If I can arrange a private consultation with my tailor, would you come along and help me choose some new things for my wardrobe?"

"Will you promise not to argue about my choices?"

"No."

She laughed. "Well, okay. That's fair."

"I'll call you later."

The long day loomed before her. She almost wished she'd taken the chance and gone on a drive with him. "Have a good day," she said, then looked around, not seeing anyone she knew. She opened the door.

He just watched her, apparently as tongue-tied as she by the necessarily banal conversation, then he drove off. She walked around the corner. Someone was sitting on her doorstep. She could see fabric through the railings but that was all. Then the person stood, not looking in her direction, as if giving up.

"Aunt Finny." Relieved it wasn't…well, almost anyone else, she waited as Fin met her on the sidewalk.

"I wish I looked that good without makeup," Fin said.

"Oh, right, like you're some old crone. You're only thirteen years older than me."

"That's a lot of years in prime-woman age. I hope you had a good night?"

Scarlet grinned. "I'm relaxed."

"Ah. Lucky you."

"Come inside," Scarlet said, heading to her private entrance. "What are you doing here?"

"Taking your advice. I went for a walk in the park. I've been calling you off and on to see if you wanted to have brunch with me."

"Why didn't you call my cell?"

"I did. It's turned off."

"Oh. Sorry." Probably not turned off but a dead battery, Scarlet decided. "Well, I had a late breakfast, but I'll be happy to keep you company. Did you see Granddad yesterday? He called me up to his office."

"I got the same order, but I had a message sent to him that I'd already left."

"I should've thought of that," Scarlet said, unlocking her apartment door. "I'm trying to figure out who's talking to him about me."

"What do you mean?"

"He said he'd been hearing good things about me. Called me creative and competent. How does he know that?"

Fin frowned. "I haven't talked to him about you."

"You think we have a mole? Someone who reports to him about the goings-on at *Charisma?*"

"Maybe."

Scarlet started to press the message button on her answering machine, then decided against it. Later, maybe. In private. She'd learned her lesson there. "Who could it be? And why is it necessary? Granddad has access to all financial information. Since he's only worried about fiscal profit to declare the winner of this contest, why would he need someone reporting behind the scenes?"

"A very good question." Fin paced the living room.

"I'm going to change. Make yourself at home." Scarlet hurried. She changed into jeans, a T-shirt and a leather jacket, then pulled her hair into a ponytail, added a little mascara and lipstick and was done. She could smell John's soap on her skin, and her body ached comfortably. One area where the man had above average creativity—and flexibility—was in bed. The aftereffects lingered.

"Do you want to go to Une Nuit?" Scarlet asked Fin as they left the house.

"I don't want to go to any family-run operation."

Scarlet smiled. "Hot dog and soda in the park?"

"Sure. Why not?"

A few hours later Scarlet dragged herself home. They'd listed every employee, trying to come up with the name of the snitch. She wished she hadn't said anything to Fin, who didn't need something else to obsess about.

Scarlet made a promise to herself that she would never let her job consume her life as Fin had—easy for Scarlet to say, she supposed, at this point. Maybe when things ended with John, she would dive into her work, too, and not come up for air for a long time.

She hit the message button as she passed by the answering machine, listened from her bedroom to a message from Summer saying she would call Scarlet's cell, four hang-ups, then one from her grandfather.

"Your grandmother and I are coming to the city for the week. She thought I needed to warn you, for some reason."

Scarlet could almost see him rolling his eyes.

"So, here's your warning, missy. We'll be arriving around four. Plan on dinner with us."

Another command performance. Scarlet looked at her watch. Almost four. She needed to call John, let him know….

Why? How would it matter to him?

You just want to talk to him.

Right. And wrong. She had a legitimate reason. They needed to coordinate schedules and see when she could help him with his wardrobe. And she'd expected to spend the night with him at least once. Now they needed a new plan. She couldn't stay away overnight with her grandparents there.

With that rationale in her head she picked up her phone. His number was still on the speed dial.

She hesitated. Why hadn't Summer removed his number? Would a psychiatrist say she was keeping her options open in case things didn't work out with Zeke? Even though she and Zeke were engaged, she'd been engaged before, to John, and that hadn't worked. Maybe Summer was having a life crisis—

Scarlet shook her head. Summer was different with Zeke. Openly happy. Relaxed. Excited. All the things she hadn't been with John, or even before John. Nothing was going to change there, even if Summer changed her mind. And John wouldn't want her back, anyway. Would he? No. Of course not.

She dialed his number, got his machine, but didn't leave a message. She didn't know his cell number.

The intercom buzzed from downstairs. Her grandparents had arrived.

Time to put on a happy face.

Ten

A few days later John stood by while Scarlet pulled item after item from his closet to make room for his just-delivered new clothes and shoes—although he suspected her reason had more to do with removing the temptation of his ever wearing his old stuff again. His new tux and five suits wouldn't be ready for a couple of weeks, but everything else they'd bought could be put away—shirts, ties, jeans, leather jacket, T-shirts, boots, shoes, other casual clothing.

His credit card statement now seemed in line with the national debt, but he had to admit he liked the new look, not flashy but up-to-date.

Not that he hadn't argued with her, starting with her wanting him to use a friend she'd gone to design school with instead of the tailor he'd used all his life, his father's tailor. Somehow—he still wasn't exactly sure how—she'd convinced him to give her guy a try, then decisions were made all around him for a while before he asserted himself with veto privileges and started offering his own opinions. He was happy with the end result, particularly after he finished trying on clothes, when Scarlet locked the dressing room door and they made love, their need to be quiet somehow intensifying everything—scents, sights, the silken feel of her skin, the force of his orgasm.

Or maybe it was the four walls of mirrors that had done that, especially as she'd stripped for him, and he'd had a view of her everywhere he looked, and from every angle.

He went hard at the memory.

"When do you have to be back at work?" he asked her now, coming up behind her in the closet, his hands on her hips, keeping her rear snugly against him.

"Same as usual. One-thirty."

It was the third time this week they'd met at his apartment at noon, and it was only Thursday. They'd also had two meetings at her office about product placements, plus that evening at the tailor's before she had to go home to have dinner with her grandparents. She had to attend the symphony with them tonight, then they were returning to The Tides tomorrow, just in time for the weekend.

Tick tock. His time with Scarlet was slipping away.

They didn't talk about the inevitable end anymore, apparently deciding separately not to bring it up. Sometime soon they would have to, though. Only twelve days until Summer's return.

He'd had lunch delivered before he and Scarlet arrived—corned-beef sandwiches and coleslaw. They sat at his kitchen counter to eat.

Scarlet held a dill pickle aloft. "Make sure you bag your old clothes and leave them with your doorman tomorrow. They'll be picked up around ten o'clock."

He was grateful he didn't have his new suits yet so he didn't have to donate his old ones. They were good suits, with life left.

"And when your new suits are ready, you'll give your old ones away," she added, using her pickle as a pointer.

"Who appointed you queen of my closet?"

She grinned. "Trust me. Once you've worn the new suits and gotten a hundred compliments in five days, you won't miss the old ones a bit."

"If you say so." He had no intention of getting rid of them, but she didn't have to know that. He was taking back a few of the things she'd tossed onto his closet floor today, too.

"Do you have plans for the weekend?" he asked. They rarely planned ahead, usually not even a day, as if they were afraid to. Afraid that they would plan then something would prevent it, which would be worse than not making plans at all.

"I have to make an appearance at JoJo Dawson's party Friday night," she said, "which starts at eight. How about you?"

"I have to be seen at Shari Alexander's opening at the Liz Barnard Gallery."

She frowned. "I didn't get an invitation to that."

"Maybe because at the last opening, you stole Liz's boyfriend."

She met his gaze directly then studied her sandwich for a few seconds as she held it near her face. "I didn't know he was hers. He sure didn't act like he belonged to anyone.

Not to mention he's twenty years younger than she is. Anyway, I wasn't doing anything but flirting a little, *after* he made moves on me. Besides, he was too fussy."

"Fussy?"

"And full of himself."

He wasn't sure what she meant, except they weren't compliments. "I take it I'm not fussy."

She almost snorted. "Hardly."

He wanted her to explain what she meant, but left it alone. They only had a few minutes left before they had to return to their offices. "Want to get together after our respective appearances tomorrow night?"

"Sure." She picked up their plates and carried them to the sink.

He stuck his hand in his pocket, toying with the item he'd dropped in there earlier. After a few seconds, he pulled it out and passed it to her. "In case you're done before I am tomorrow night."

She stared at the gleaming object while she dried her hands, which seemed to take an extraordinarily long time. Then she folded the towel precisely into thirds and hung it on the oven door handle.

"It's a key, Scarlet, not a branding iron."

She took it from him without comment as she edged around him, heading toward the living room. He would love to know what was going on in that head of hers.

"I'll see you tomorrow night," he said as she opened the front door. He wanted her to come back and kiss him goodbye. He stuffed his hands in his pockets, waiting.

She stopped at the door. Her expression seemed to say she wanted to give back the key. A key was symbolic of a relationship deepening in trust and intent, a sign there was a future. It wasn't true here, which obviously confused her, and apparently upset her.

"It's just a key," he repeated to her. "I'm trying to make things more convenient for both of us."

"You keep on thinking that, John, if it makes it easier for you," she said, then she left, closing the door quietly.

So, he really didn't have a clue about how her mind worked. She hadn't been focusing on the same issue at all.

But she was wrong about one thing.

Nothing was making this relationship easier. Absolutely nothing.

Although Scarlet had been taken—dragged—to the symphony and the opera since childhood, she'd never developed an ear for it, nor could she easily distinguish one composer from another. Except for Wagner, that is, especially his *Tristan und Isolde*. Selections from it were on the program tonight.

Still, she would've rather been at a jazz festival or enjoying the pounding beat of a rock concert.

Just before the lights went down she spotted her aunt Finny sitting a few rows ahead with Georges Caron, a French designer old enough to be her father. From their vantage point her real father and mother had a perfect view of their emotionally estranged daughter. Scarlet didn't catch her grandfather looking, but Gram's gaze returned again and again. Scarlet wondered if Fin would ever forgive her parents for forcing her to give up her baby long ago. She'd rarely spoken to them through the years, *Charisma* having become her baby.

On the other hand, Scarlet was glad to see Fin out and about, a rarity for her. Undoubtedly it was a work night for her, an attempt to woo Georges Caron into giving *Charisma* exclusive coverage of his next collection or something. At least it got her out of the office.

Woo. The word stuck in Scarlet's head, along with the other dilemmas crammed in there like a Pandora's box. John had given her a key to his apartment. He was falling for her, beyond sex, beyond their stated intent at the beginning of their relationship. She knew she had to give him up at the end of the month, because of Summer and family image and other things that separately didn't matter a whole lot, but together made it impossible for them to be together.

So...her big dilemma now was whether to end things early with him, before he got hurt, too. She would suffer at the loss of him, but she'd gone into the relationship with her eyes open to that potential. He hadn't. He'd thought it would be a purely sexual relationship, that his heart wouldn't be in danger. She sensed that was changing. Maybe he wasn't in love with her, but he liked her a lot. They had become friends as well as lovers.

It was a dangerous situation for both of them. How had he put it at the beginning—a game with potentially disastrous outcomes? She'd been led by her heart. His mind had presented a more realistic view of the future— then, anyway.

Could she give him up before she had to?

Applause erupted around her as the lights came up. Intermission already?

Georges stopped beside her grandfather's aisle seat and chatted for a moment. Fin stood behind him, expressionless. She wouldn't make eye contact with Gram. Scarlet hated that most.

The Frenchman moved on. It appeared Fin would, too, then she stopped next to her father and in a low voice said, "If there's something you want to know, just ask me. Don't recruit spies."

"I don't know what you mean," he said calmly.

"Liar," Fin fired back before she went to catch up with her escort.

Gram's hands were clenched. Scarlet laid a hand on hers, but her grandmother couldn't even smile.

"Want to attempt the line at the ladies' room, Gram?"

She shook her head. "I see an old friend. I'll go off and visit for a few minutes. Stretch the kinks out, then."

After she left, her grandfather turned to Scarlet. "Do you know what Finola was talking about?"

"Yes. Don't you?"

He looked away, saying nothing. Scarlet didn't know whether he was telling the truth or bluffing.

Scarlet wished John was beside her, holding her hand, defusing the situation. He was diplomatic. He would know how to change the mood. She was too emotionally involved and didn't dare get into it. Instead no one spoke the rest of the evening beyond necessary, polite words.

When she climbed into bed later, she eyed her phone. She knew John's number by heart now. She wanted to hear his voice, but needed to come up with a reason to call….

Food. Food was always a safe topic. She would ask him if she should pick up something to eat tomorrow on her way to his place. He would have appetizers at the gallery, but not dinner, and she wasn't planning to stay for dinner at JoJo's, just to have a drink and show her face.

She dialed. The phone rang four times, then his answering machine picked up. She didn't wait for the beep, but hung up. She glanced at the clock—almost midnight—and tossed the phone out of reach.

Neither of them ever questioned what the other had done on nights when they weren't together, but this was the first time she'd called and not found him at home.

Jealousy reared up. She tamped it down. He'd said they didn't have an exclusive arrangement, but she didn't buy it. He wasn't a player. But she was curious about why he wasn't home yet.

Of course, she had no business calling him at midnight on a work night, when most people were sleeping, and especially to ask a question she could talk to him about the next day. He would see through her ploy. It didn't matter. She didn't care. Let him think what he would.

The phone rang. She leaped across the bed to grab it.

"Hey!" Summer said. "Where've you been all night? I've been calling for hours."

Scarlet settled into her pillows, the phone tucked between her shoulder and ear as she adjusted the bedding. Her disappointment that it wasn't John disappeared. "At the symphony with the Grands. What's up?"

"I just wanted to let you know that we're coming home a day early. The twenty-eighth instead of the twenty-ninth."

One less night. "How come?"

"I'm homesick."

"Really?"

Summer laughed. "No. Well, kind of. Zeke's got a meeting in New York on the twenty-ninth. This is not for public broadcast yet, but he's going to do the music and lyrics for a rock musical."

"Good for him!"

"We think so, too, especially since it means we'd get to live close to home."

"You're going to live together?" Scarlet had assumed they would, but having it confirmed—

"Well, yes. What did you think?"

"Are you coming back to work?" She recalled her grandfather assuming Summer wouldn't return to the job, and had wondered, herself.

"I don't know yet. I'm still figuring things out. Scar?"

"What?"

"You've seemed really distracted every time I've talked to you. This whole month. Longer than that, even. What's going on?"

"Nothing worth talking about."

Static crackled in the silence. "When I get home, we'll catch up. When I can see your face, I'll know whether there's something I should know."

She was right, of course. Nothing Scarlet could say or do would prevent Summer from seeing into her soul—her broken heart at that point, since her relationship with John would have ended.

"Are you planning your wedding yet?" Scarlet asked, changing the subject.

"Not yet. We don't feel we need to hurry. Maybe at Christmas."

"You'll want the fairy tale, I think. It takes time to plan."

"You'll design my dress, won't you?"

Scarlet smiled. "I already have."

Summer's voice softened. "I love you."

"I love you, too," Scarlet managed to say before her throat swelled shut.

"See you soon."

"Okay. 'Bye."

Scarlet could never do anything to alienate her sister. Watching Fin tonight with Gram and Granddad settled that in Scarlet's mind. Family came first. Always and forever.

There would be another man to love someday, she told herself as she turned off her bedside lamp.

Then she lay there in the dark, alone, denying herself the luxury of tears.

Eleven

As director of sales for *Snap*, the celebrity-watcher magazine of the EPH empire, Cullen Elliott had worked closely with John for several years. Almost the same age, they also had a friendship unrelated to the business, having known each other longer than John had known Summer and Scarlet. The men golfed together. Challenged each other. Wagered with each other, too. John liked Cullen and was glad the friendship hadn't been strained when the engagement ended.

"I can't believe you beat me by thirteen strokes," Cullen muttered as they rode the elevator to John's apartment late Saturday afternoon after a long day golfing. "*How* long has it been since you played?"

John smiled leisurely. "I told you. The last time you and I played. October, I think."

"You didn't squeeze in a round or two while you were in L.A. last month?"

"Nope. But conditions weren't the best today."

"Don't be condescending."

John grinned as they exited the elevator and walked down the hall. Usually a prankster, Cullen had seemed to be forcing jokes all day, so John hesitated before he spoke again, not knowing whether he should discuss what he'd observed.

"You did seem off your game," he said finally. "And distracted. Woman trouble?"

"Women," Cullen scoffed. "Sometimes I wonder if they're worth the effort."

"Amen."

"Although I don't ever question it when I'm in bed with one."

John laughed. As he opened the door, an incredible scent rushed at him. Garlic. Basil. Something Italian.

Cullen sniffed the air, making appreciative sounds. "I hope I'm staying for dinner."

Scarlet must be there.

"Sorry, Cullen," John said, upping his normal volume. "Private party."

He heard a soft scampering sound and talked over it, hoping Cullen hadn't noticed. "I'll get that book you wanted."

"Don't I get to meet the chef?"

"I'll check." He walked into the kitchen and looked around. A pot of red sauce simmered on the stove, the source of the mouthwatering aroma. A salad was half prepared. And a pair of spiky black heels lay jumbled on the floor.

He heard a noise from the pantry and headed there, opened the door—

"What are you doing with my cousin?" Scarlet asked in a fierce whisper.

She was wearing a French maid's costume.

John's shock instantly became laughter.

"It isn't funny," she said through clenched teeth.

"From my vantage point it is." He grabbed and kissed her. "I'll get rid of him. Cool your jets, sweetheart."

He shut the pantry door in her face.

"She left a note. Went to the store," John said to Cullen as he passed through the living room on his way to his office. He grabbed a book from his desk. "Here you go. No hurry getting it back to me."

"Feels like someone's shoving a boot against my ass," Cullen said with a grin, heading to the front door.

"What can I say?" The maid costume stayed emblazoned in his mind. The short, short skirt, revealing long, gorgeous legs in fishnet stockings. The low-cut, lace-edged top, exposing inviting mounds he wanted to bury his face in. He could untie her frilly white apron, strip her to whatever fancy lingerie she wore under—

"I'm glad to see you've moved on, you know, since Summer."

John came to attention. "I've become a fatalist."

"Everything happens for a reason?"

"Something like that."

Cullen stared out the window for a few seconds. "Have you stopped loving her?"

I don't think I ever did love her. He didn't say the words aloud, but their truth hit him like a thousand-watt lightbulb. "As you said, I've moved on."

"Mind over matter?"

The way Cullen pushed the conversation, John recognized there *was* something going on with him. "You need to talk, Cullen?" They couldn't now, not with Scarlet trapped in the pantry, but… "We could get together for drinks one day this week."

"Maybe. I'll give you a call." He left.

John returned to the kitchen and opened the pantry door. "Your master awaits."

She eyed him coolly. "My master?"

"If you're the maid, that makes me the master, right?" John admired her in full light. He'd never known a woman with so many dimensions. And he'd never known one so playful, so willing to get into a role just for the fun of it.

He was tempted now to untie the lacy cap on her head and let her hair down. He reached for the dangling ribbons—

"Why didn't you tell me you were golfing with Cullen?"

He lowered his arm, stuffed his hands into his pockets. Obviously she wasn't into her role yet. "I didn't want to wake you this morning. You looked so peaceful."

"You could've told me last night before we went to sleep."

"I could've."

"But?"

"My relationship with Cullen is separate. I don't relate him with your family, even though he is. Why didn't you tell me you were coming over early tonight?"

"I didn't know until after you left your message on my cell, saying to keep the night open for you." She shrugged. "And I wanted to surprise you."

"Which you did." He trailed his fingers down her face, gently, caressingly. "Can I go out and come back in? Start over?"

"First you have to put on your costume."

"Costume?" He hadn't minded the other games, but he'd never had to wear a costume before, either.

"It's on your bed."

"What exactly am I?"

"You're a nineteenth-century duke visiting my master."

"Did I time-travel forward or did you time-travel back?" he asked, pointing to her modern costume.

She ignored his question. "Do you know how men of your stature were treated in the merry old days?"

"With more respect than today?"

His comment earned him raised eyebrows instead of a laugh, then she hooked a finger behind his belt and pulled him toward her. "When a titled man visited, the lady of the house was often sent to assist him in bathing."

"I was born in the wrong century."

Her smile was slow and sultry. "When there wasn't a lady of the house, often a maid was sent."

No joke came to mind. "You're going to…bathe me?"

She dragged his shirt from his waistband and slid her hands up his chest. "I'm going to feed you, then undress you, then bathe you, then have my way with you. And you have to promise not to tell my master, or I could lose my position."

He closed his eyes and enjoyed the feathery touch of her fingers against his skin, although he was more than a little stunned that she had willingly assumed such a subservient role. Another layer of her. Another fascinating layer.

"I think you should go change now, your grace," she whispered. "You can wait in the parlor. I'll bring you some ale to sip while I finish supper."

He'd rather hang out in the kitchen with her, but he acknowledged that anticipation was an appealing part of the game. He expected to stay aroused until she chose to do something about it.

He just hoped his costume wasn't too dorky.

The following Friday, Cade McMann, *Charisma*'s executive editor, stepped into Scarlet's cubicle just as she was about to head to a meeting. Noting Cade's distant expression, she said nothing, especially since he'd come to her. Usually he summoned her to his office.

"You seem to have more influence with Fin than anyone," he said in a low, brusque voice.

"As her niece, not as her employee."

"I don't care which role you assume—whatever works, as far as I'm concerned—but she slept in her office again last night. Obviously I want her to win the contest as much as she does. I stand to win, too. But there's no reason for her to sacrifice everything to it. Someone has to convince her of that."

"If you can't settle her down, Cade, I don't think anyone can."

"I've tried. Short of sending an armed escort to her office to take her home each night, there's nothing I can do. She's the boss. But I'm worried about her."

"So am I." She tapped a finger to her lips. "Maybe I should talk to Uncle Shane."

"They may be twins, Scarlet, but they *are* in competition."

He was right. "Back to square one."

"Just talk to her, please. Better yet, kidnap her for the weekend. Take her to a spa."

This would be her last weekend with John. Summer would be home on Monday. "I can't this weekend, but I'll try to arrange it for the following one."

"Good. Thanks." He turned to leave and bumped into Jessie.

"I'm so sorry," she said, her eyes widening.

Cade frowned.

Looking a little flustered, she turned to Scarlet. "John Harlan is in the conference room."

"Thanks, Jessie."

She hurried away after muttering another "sorry" to Cade.

"She's always hovering," he said, watching her leave.

Scarlet picked up a file folder and stood. "What do you mean?"

"Just that. And she's too eager to please. She volunteers for everything."

"The way our internship program is set up, she's allowed to float from department to department if help is needed, or if she wants to be involved in a particular project. She just has to clear it through me."

"Is she good?"

"She's a natural. As if she's had years of experience instead of just having graduated."

"People said that about *you*."

"They did?" She smiled, pleased. She didn't want to tell the boss to get out of the way, but she did have a meeting to attend. She held up the file. "Is that all for now?"

"Yeah. Thanks."

She was the last to arrive at the conference room, which was populated by most of *Charisma*'s department heads. She was not in charge of the project, so the discussion was being led by the managing editor and the art director.

Scarlet slipped into a chair. John, flanked by members of his own staff, sat across the table. She met his gaze briefly, saw a smile flicker in his eyes, then she tried to focus on the meeting. An hour and a lot of discussion later, the meeting ended. She had no official reason to approach him, plus he wasn't alone, anyway.

She'd been waiting all day for him to call and make plans for their last weekend together. He'd had a lunch meeting, so they hadn't even met at his apartment as they often did. But Summer would be home on Monday. That fact had to be faced.

Scarlet lingered near the conference room in hopes of catching him for a second, but his employees were on his heels and he only got to say a quick goodbye, then he was gone.

Fin was in her office, hunched in front of her computer. Scarlet considered going in and talking to her about getting away next weekend, but decided it didn't matter when she did that, since Fin probably had no plans to interfere with anyway. Scarlet would need next weekend away even more than Fin. A time to mourn.

She returned to her cubicle. It was almost four o'clock. She and John were bad about making plans, but this was ridiculous. It was their last—

She spotted an envelope on her keyboard, her name printed on it. She opened it, unfolded a sheet of ivory-colored parchment. The note was handwritten:

Good afternoon, Ms. Elliott,

Your mission, should you choose to accept it, will begin at 6:00 p.m. You will be picked up from your home and taken to a secret location, where you will be wined, dined and sublimed until Sunday evening. Bring only the basics; no finery required. Lingerie optional but not preferred.

This paper is encoded with a special substance that can read your mind. If you decide not to accept this mission, this note will self-destruct in ten seconds.

10...9...8...7...6...5...4...3...2...1...

See you at 6:00.

Scarlet smiled. A weekend. A whole weekend...
To say goodbye.

Twelve

"I know it's unusual to come to the beach this time of year," John said, following Scarlet as she stepped onto a weathered porch. The surf pounded softly. Clouds hid the moon. Distant houses were the only points of light, like earthbound stars.

"It's perfect," she said, leaning her elbows on the rail. "How'd you find it?"

He rested a hand on either side of her, spooning their bodies, sheltering her from the breeze. "Belongs to a client. He's offered it a number of times."

It was late. They hadn't rushed to get there, had even indulged in a leisurely dinner at a roadside diner about an hour out of the city as they drove up the sound toward Rhode Island. They'd lingered in the small, homey restaurant—their first and probably only restaurant appearance as a couple—keeping watch on the parking lot, checking out the new arrivals, even as it seemed an unlikely concern.

After dinner they made the decision not to talk about anything serious while they were at the cottage. Maybe on the drive back, but not now.

Scarlet straightened, forcing him to, and leaned against him, nestling in his arms.

"I haven't been to the ocean in so long, except for The Tides," she said with a sigh.

Until now they'd always been in a hurry, as if someone or something would tear them apart at any moment. For two days, however, they could relax and enjoy each other's company. It was probably a big mistake to end their relationship with a trip to paradise, but he felt entitled to the grand finale. It had been about sex these past weeks—intense, driven sex, with a few quiet or playful moments now and then. That kind of intensity was good in the beginning, but now…?

Now he wasn't guessing anymore. He'd come to believe that Summer hadn't broken his heart at all. Maybe he'd assumed it went with the territory of broken engagements, that he should have been brokenhearted. He *had* been surprised, disappointed and a little humiliated when she called off the engagement, but he'd recovered too quickly for her to have been the love of his life.

But *this* Elliott woman—this one was the heartbreaker.

"Congratulations, John."

He pressed a kiss to her temple. Her hair blew against his skin. "On what?"

"On graduating from Woo U, with honors." She turned to face him and looped her arms around his neck.

He'd been inspired to do the weekend up right, just now realizing he'd been arranging a honeymoon.

And a farewell.

"I think it requires a valedictorian's speech," she said, her eyes sparkling.

He kissed her slowly, gently, thoroughly, savoring the warmth of her mouth, the softness of her lips, the searching brush of her tongue. It was a luxury not to rush, to know no one could arrive unexpectedly or recognize them out walking tomorrow. They could pretend they were a normal couple for once—except they would wear ball caps and sunglasses as a precaution.

"Ah, the ol' actions-speak-louder-than-words speech," she said, snuggling against him, shivering.

"A month in the making. Let's go inside."

The house was typical of seaside cottages, with a nautical theme and blue-and-white decor. Seashells decorated lamp bases and a mirror frame. Interesting glass containers held more, here in the living room, and everywhere, even the bathrooms. The master bedroom's French doors allowed a view of the ocean from the bed. The bathroom held a claw-footed tub with showerhead, and a wraparound curtain on a track.

"Would you like to take a bath?" he asked, still holding her hand.

"Sure."

"Go ahead. I have things to do."

She patted his chest, smiling. "I may have to change your grad status to magna cum laude."

"That would seem to require a more elevated speech."

"Oh, definitely. One that lasts for hours."

"I'll see what I can do."

She laid her hands against his face and kissed him. When she backed away, her eyes weren't smiling anymore but shimmering with something else he could only guess at....

That she didn't want to give up this relationship, either.

Scarlet had debated about what nightgown to bring. Although he'd said in his note that lingerie was optional but not preferable, she'd considered bringing none, then decided that she wanted to tease him with something red and lacy, a reminder. She'd chosen a long gown, which covered her, yet didn't. She'd never felt so voluptuous, her skin warm and damp from the bath, her breasts barely contained by the gown's deep neckline.

Silk brushed her body like a lover's caress as she returned to the living room. Candles were lit; the fire crackled. He'd plunged a bottle of champagne into a condensation-beaded silver bucket and draped a white towel around the neck. Two crystal flutes sat beside it, as well as bowls of strawberries and whipped cream. Quiet jazz played in the background. Pillows were piled on a quilt laid out in front of the sofa. A vase of yellow daisies topped the coffee table, which he'd moved aside. She recalled the white daisies in the master bedroom. He'd set a perfect scene.

How was she supposed to give him up after this? Maybe this last-hurrah weekend was a big mistake. Maybe they should've just kept everything simple. Focused only on the sex. Gotten that out of their systems.

Too late now.

"Did you do all this?" she asked as he came toward her.

He nodded. "I had the refrigerator stocked, too." He cupped her shoulders. "You've never looked more beautiful. And that's saying something."

"You're looking pretty good yourself." She admired his black silk pajama bottoms, and the flesh otherwise revealed. And the sexy mouth. And the gorgeous brown eyes.

Even though the house seemed relatively isolated, he'd drawn the curtains, and she was glad.

"What's wrong?" he asked.

She shook her head. She couldn't ask him if they were making a mistake. She didn't want anything to ruin their time together. "We agreed we wouldn't talk about anything serious."

"Then you need to wipe that serious look off your face."

He was right. She owed him that, anyway. He'd kept his part of the bargain. So she smiled and stepped close and kissed his chest. She felt him inhale, slow and deep.

Guilt settled on her shoulders. She'd started them on this path by going to him. Whatever pain they endured was *her* fault.

"This reminds me of the first time," he said quietly, breaking into her thoughts. "You wore red then, too."

She liked that he remembered. "And you wore black." She slipped a hand down his stomach, his abdomen....

He sucked in air, captured her hand. "I don't want to hurry tonight. Tonight's about romance."

"And memories."

He was quiet a few long seconds. "Let's sit by the fire."

They fed each other strawberries dipped in the whipped cream, and sipped champagne, and touched each other with feathery strokes as the fire provided heat and mood. Words swirled in Scarlet's head, but none she could utter out loud. They were too serious. Too full of what-ifs. Too sad. She had to let the thoughts go, let him fill her world, this world.

He didn't seem in the mood to talk, either. When they weren't kissing, they stared at the fire, hands clasped. But desperation finally seeped in. She toyed with the drawstring on his pajama bottoms, loosened the band and slipped her hand inside. He stretched out and closed his eyes.

She tugged on the fabric, dragged it down and off him, flattened her hands on his shins and kept moving, along his thighs, over his abdomen, up his chest then back down. He arched his hips. She held her champagne flute aloft and dripped the cold liquid over him. He lurched up. At the same time she took him in her mouth, warming him, tasting the champagne…and him. He lay back down, making sounds of need as her tongue sought and savored.

Every muscle was taut. Nothing about him was relaxed. She loved that she made him that way, and that he let her take her time. He made her stop now and then, drew quick breaths for a few seconds, then gave her freedom again for a while. He was a wonder of taste and texture. Heat rose from him. Control slipped away minute by minute, touch by touch, breath by breath.

He stopped her. Moved out of range. Dragged himself up and leaned against the couch. She wished she could sculpt. She would recreate that beautiful, chiseled body still full of need. His muscles were bunched, tendons visible.

She moved closer, laid a hand on his thigh. "Let me finish."

He smiled slightly and shook his head. "I like this feeling. I want it to last. C'mere."

He dove his hands into her hair, pulled her close and kissed her, but it was such a little word for what that kiss was, all open mouth and inquisitive tongue and nipping teeth and hot breath.

"Stand up," he said, low and fierce.

She rose.

"Strip for me."

She let the music guide her. Without hesitation or shyness she moved, turning in a circle, her hips swaying, then finally letting one strap fall down her arm, then the other. Gravity pulled the gown to the floor. She stepped out of it then over his outstretched legs. He grabbed her ankles, applied pressure until she moved her legs farther apart, found her with his mouth and fingers, taking long strokes with his tongue, his fingertips igniting fires, tickling, teasing, letting her need rise, pulling away to let it ebb, then returning again and again.

When her legs started shaking, he pulled her down. She took him inside her, clenched around him. She closed her eyes and arched her back as he drew one aching nipple in his mouth, then the other, cradling her breasts in his strong hands. He was fast losing control, though, she could tell. And so was she. She ended up on her back, somehow, in a maneuver she barely knew happened, and welcomed his thrusts, responded with her own, called out her pleasure, heard his rise above hers. The duet their bodies performed reached crescendo, stayed there, stayed there, stayed there, then slowly, slowly faded.

The beauty of it all made her throat burn and her eyes well up. She wrapped her arms around him, imprisoning him, and refused to let go. They had been well matched physically, sexually, from the beginning. But not like this. Nothing close to this. This was what came when everything was right.

I love you. She said the words to him over and over in her head.

"Fire's dying," he said after a while.

Not mine for you. "We could just go to bed," she said.

"You go ahead. I'll put out the candles and take care of the food."

"We can do it together."

Naked, they moved around the room, eyeing each other, flirting silently. She tried to picture him in fifty years, his hair silver, his smile still wicked. A father. A grandfather. The image came easily. Too easily.

They turned out the lights, walked hand in hand to the bedroom and climbed under a downy quilt. His hands roamed her body, warming her, exciting her when she should've been satisfied.

"Thank you for this weekend," she said, her lips brushing his neck.

"You took the words out of my mouth."

Later she felt him drift into sleep, his body heavy against hers. Only then did she allow herself the luxury of a few tears.

Even so, she had no regrets—except for how it all had to turn out.

* * *

"We have to talk about it," Scarlet said as they drove across the bridge into New York City on Sunday night.

She was right. John wasn't usually one to duck a situation, but he'd been diverting the conversation whenever she even hinted that they should discuss the future—or lack thereof—during the drive home.

They would make love one more time. That was all he knew for sure.

Last night they'd gone to bed and only slept, something a normal couple might do but they never had, because they hadn't had time for such a normalcy. He figured tonight would more than make up for it, sexually. Emotionally, last night couldn't be matched. It had felt good to just sleep together, to wake up in each other's arms and linger in bed.

"So, talk," he said now.

"Summer comes home tomorrow. We agreed to end the relationship when she returned."

"I'm trying to remember the reasons why."

"You know why."

"I know in the beginning we said it was about sex. We figured a month of sleeping together would take care of that." He gave her a quick glance. "It hasn't. Or at least not for me."

"Meaning?"

"I don't want to stop seeing you. Why can't we still meet at my place whenever we can manage it?"

"For sex?" Her voice was strained.

"Not just that." He reached over to wrap a hand around hers.

"It's hopeless, John. We can't ever go public, so why drag out the inevitable any longer?"

"Why not?"

"Because it's too risky. Every time we're together is a chance for exposure. And I'm tired of all the hiding. The sex has been great, but as long as we continue with it, I won't date anyone else. That's who I am. And I'm tired of going places alone. I want a partner. More than ever now, I want a partner."

She shifted toward him, her expression fierce. "Last week when I went with my grandparents to the symphony, Fin was there. They didn't speak to each other, except for Fin to tell Granddad off. It was horrible. My grandmother was so hurt. I've been an observer of their estrangement for years, but never like that. That total public snub. I won't do anything that hurts anyone in my family. I couldn't live with myself if I did."

"How would our relationship hurt your family?"

"It could hurt Summer deeply. Don't you think people might think I had something to do with your breakup if we're seen together this soon after? I'm the one with the reputation, after all. It could seem like I'm rubbing Summer's nose in her mistake—a reminder of how she hurt you. It would be embarrassing for her. I would never, ever hurt her like that, or betray her like that."

"Then maybe you shouldn't have slept with me in the first place."

A few long seconds passed. "I know you're upset, so I'm going to forgive the fact you just put the blame all on me. I was the instigator, I admit, but we both agreed to the terms," she said tightly. "I'm upset, too. But we've been lucky not to be caught. We need to end it before our luck turns bad."

She was right. He'd argued the point because he wanted her to come up with a way for things to be different. An impossible wish.

During the drive they'd agreed she should spend the night with him. It meant her getting up very early in the morning to go home and change clothes for work, but it seemed the best course of action, the path of least possibility of discovery.

He pulled into his parking garage. They got their suitcases from the trunk and headed to the elevator. They hardly took their eyes off each other. He saw in her everything he felt—expectation, need, gratitude and…desperation. In the elevator she went into his arms, pressed her face into his neck then leaned back to look right at him.

He kissed her without restraint, without hope. The doors whooshed open. He would've picked her up and carried her, except their luggage would've gone down in the elevator without them.

He opened his eyes, took a step back…and spotted Summer standing in the open doorway.

Thirteen

Scarlet's world took on a dizzying slant. Her sister stared in horror, in shock, in disbelief. The doors started to close. John slammed his arm against them, keeping them open, then grabbed both suitcases and set them in the hall as Scarlet forced herself out of the elevator.

"Summer," Scarlet pleaded, her hands outstretched. "I can explain."

Summer's face was ghostly pale. She looked back and forth between John and Scarlet. "Did you just spend the night together?" Her voice registered an octave higher than usual.

"Yes, but—"

"Let's go inside," John said, interrupting.

Summer shook her head, took several steps back. "This is the secret you've been keeping from me?

Him?" She looked around wildly. "Was he the reason you didn't come home that night? *The same day I gave him back his ring?*"

"Please let me explain."

Summer held up her hands, warding off the words, then punched the down button. The elevator doors opened immediately and she stepped inside. "And to think I came home a day early because I missed you so much," she said to Scarlet. "And I came here tonight to apologize to you," she said to John, "for treating you so badly."

The doors closed and Scarlet's heart shattered.

"Come inside," John said.

"No."

"She won't be going home. You know that. You won't find her tonight."

"I can't be with you," she said. "I have to go."

"All right." He spoke gently but firmly. "I'll put my suitcase in my apartment, then I'll drive you."

"I'll get a cab." She pressed the down button again and again. "C'mon, c'mon."

"I'll drive you."

"I can't talk to you right now."

"You're mad at *me* for this?"

"No. Yes." She closed her eyes, put a fist against her chest, over her heart. "Both of us. We were stupid to take such a chance just to satisfy physical needs. Stupid, stupid, stupid."

He grabbed her shoulders. "It wasn't just physical for me. Except in the beginning."

What could she say? She didn't want him to know she loved him. She'd kept it secret all this time. She could keep it secret until it died a natural death. She owed Summer that much. "It *was* for me."

"I don't believe you."

"That's *your* problem." She needed to find Summer. To explain. To beg forgiveness. When the elevator opened, she grabbed her suitcase. He followed with his.

"Go away."

"I'm taking you home."

She stopped talking to him. Didn't speak all the way home. Got out of his car and shut the door without saying a word. Words couldn't solve this disaster.

Her apartment seemed cavernous. She looked into Summer's room, saw her luggage still unpacked.

She sat on her sister's bed, brushed her hands back and forth over the spread, then dragged a pillow into her arms and squeezed.

Everything hurt—her head, her eyes, her throat. A cannonball had made a target of her stomach. Her heart pounded a painful rhythm that she could hear in her ears and feel everywhere else.

All these years—all these damned years—they'd never let a man come between them. Some had tried to play games with them, but they'd been open and honest with each other, had avoided misunderstandings and arguments because of that directness.

As soon as she'd realized John was interested in Summer, Scarlet had avoided him, so much so that Summer had asked if she even liked him. At least she had been able to answer honestly that she liked him just fine but that three was a crowd. Still, Scarlet had fallen in love even though she'd fought it every step of the way. Shoved it into a box until that night at his apartment—that amazing night that she'd never dared to hope would happen.

She pushed Summer's pillow against her face and screamed into it. Why had she gone to see him that night? Why had she let herself believe it would be okay to console him, to offer a friendly face? She'd known. In her heart, she'd known nothing good would come of her seeing him alone.

And then she'd convinced herself she only wanted some good memories. Instead she'd hurt the person she loved most in the world, the one who loved her the most, too. Her sister, her best friend.

And it all could've been avoided if she hadn't been so selfish.

Scarlet looked around the bedroom, decorated so differently from her own. Summer's stamp was here— more feminine than Scarlet's. More homey. Her love of antiques reflected their grandmother's.

Will you ever be back?

Will you ever forgive me?

She swiped her wet cheeks with her hands then picked up Summer's bedside phone and dialed her cell number, knowing her sister wouldn't answer it. She waited for the beep.

"Summer—" her throat closed up for a couple of seconds "—there's more to this situation than what you're thinking. I'm not trying to excuse what I did, only to tell you why it happened. Please, I beg of you. If you won't see me in person, at least call me. I...I love you."

She cradled the phone carefully, tossed back her hair and went to her own bedroom, closing the door on the empty room. She wouldn't sleep, she already knew that, so she grabbed her sketch pad and curled up in her armchair, but it was as if the creative forces in her body had imploded, leaving only rubble.

She tossed aside the pad, dragged her hands down her face and leaned her head against the back of her chair. The phone rang. She jumped up, answered it in the middle of the second ring.

"Summer?"

"No, it's me." John.

Scarlet sank onto her bed.

"I figured you'd still be up," he said. "Want to talk?"

"What is there to say?"

"You need to give her time to adjust to the idea."

"If the situation was reversed, I wouldn't adjust."

"Summer will."

"Meaning Summer is a better person than I am." Like she hadn't always known that.

"I didn't say that. You would adjust, too, but it might take you longer."

Scarlet thought she heard a smile in his voice. How could he be smiling?

"But she's in love and happy," he continued. "And she loves you. It's going to be fine. No one else knows, and she won't tell anyone. Except Zeke, probably. You'll get past it."

"How can you be so sure? Why are you so calm about this?" Tears sprang to her eyes.

"I don't think it's worth getting worked up about."

"Not worth—" Scarlet couldn't finish the sentence. "Well, that's easy for you to say, John." Not worth it? "I can't talk to you anymore."

She hung up then curled into a ball on the bed. She'd

regretted some of her actions before—small regrets, like immature choices she'd made or her constant attempts to annoy her grandfather.

But all of them together didn't add up to this.

"Are you in mourning?" Jessie asked Scarlet the next day at work. "I've never seen you wear all black to work before."

Without having slept, Scarlet had gone into the office early, straight into her cubicle, and hadn't emerged.

"Did you need something?" Scarlet asked.

"Touchy," Jessie said, her brows raised. "This came for you. You've sure made somebody happy, to get so many presents." She set a Tiffany's box on Scarlet's desk then strolled off.

Scarlet had no interest in opening a gift from John. She set the box in her desk drawer and went back to work, wishing the time would fly and the lunch hour would come.

At some point during the night she'd realized there *was* someone she could talk to—her cousin Bryan, the only person she was certain could take secrets to his grave. He'd had plenty of opportunities as they grew up to tell on her for things she'd done, misadventures he'd somehow ferreted out, but he never had.

She planned to head to Une Nuit at lunchtime and talk to him, had already called to make sure he would be there. Not only would he keep her confidences, she could count on him for good advice.

All morning long she reached for the desk-drawer handle then jerked her hand away and focused on work again. Every time footsteps approached her cubicle she hoped it was Summer. Scarlet had called her office, thinking maybe she'd come back to work today, but her voice-mail message still said she was out of town.

Finally it was time to leave for Une Nuit. Gray skies and a cool spring shower dampened her hair and matched her mood as she grabbed a cab. When she walked into the restaurant her cell phone rang. She didn't want to step back out into the rain to talk, but she didn't want to miss a call from Summer, either, so she answered it.

"Hey. I hope I caught you in time." Not Summer but Bryan. It could only be bad news.

"In time for what?" She looked around, saw Stash, who headed toward her. "I'm standing inside Une Nuit."

"Damn. I'm sorry, Scarlet. I had to leave. I'm on my way to the airport."

"Something that couldn't have waited until after you saw me?" She was on the verge of panic. She'd needed to talk to someone, and Bryan was her only hope. "What could be so important it can't wait for an hour?"

A few beats passed, then he said, "I got a good line on a saffron plantation in Turkey."

Scarlet sighed. "Okay, I got it. It's none of my business."

"I'll call as soon as I get home, I promise. Or talk to me now, while I'm driving."

Stash stood patiently in front of her.

"I can't. It's too complicated. And too personal."

"I'll make it up to you. I'll call you from the road, if I have time. In the meantime, have lunch on me."

Like she could eat. "Sure. Thanks."

"Later, Scar." He hung up.

She tucked the phone in her pocket, exchanged greetings with Stash, then looked around blindly, wondering what to do next.

"You do not look well," Stash said, concern in his eyes.

"I'm okay. Just not sure what to do, since Bryan's gone." Eating alone was not an option. *Eating* wasn't even an option this time.

"Your cousin Cullen is in the Elliott booth. You could join him." He touched her arm. "At least have some soup. Ginger carrot, one of your favorites."

She nodded, too tired to make conversation. She hoped Cullen was in a talkative mood. She wouldn't mind just listening, being distracted.

"Can I join you?" she asked Cullen, forcing a smile.

"Um." He looked past her, then at her again. "I'm expecting—"

"Me."

From behind her, Scarlet heard John's voice, even imagined that she could feel his body heat.

"So? Three for lunch, eh?" Stash asked cheerfully.

"No." Scarlet stumbled back a step, bumped into John.

Cullen's cell phone rang. He opened the phone then frowned at whatever number was displayed on the screen. He said hello tentatively.

"I…I won't interrupt your plans," she said over her shoulder, feeling John's hand on her back, keeping her steady. She just wanted to fall into his arms. She wanted to be held, and comforted and taken care of and soothed. She'd never wanted that before, never needed to be treated like such a…girl. She even forgot Summer for a moment. She wanted John.

"What?" Cullen asked, his voice rising. "How is she?"

Scarlet focused on Cullen, on the alarm in his voice.

"Where'd they take her?…I'll be there as soon as I can." He snapped his phone shut and stood. "I can't stay."

"What's wrong?" Scarlet asked. Cullen was always in a good mood. Nothing ever seemed to faze him—until now. "Who's hurt?"

"No one you know." He dropped his napkin onto the table. His gaze sought John. "Sorry. I appreciate you coming, but I need to get to Las Vegas."

"No problem. Anything I can do?"

"I'll let you know. Thanks."

He didn't even say goodbye.

John, Scarlet and Stash watched Cullen jog out of the restaurant.

"I wonder if he and Bryan will run into each other at the airport," Scarlet said, feeling sorry for Cullen without knowing why. She'd just never seen him as upset as that.

"Join me for lunch," John said to Scarlet.

She shook her head.

Stash made a quiet retreat.

"We need to talk," John said.

"I can't." She took a few steps, then returned, getting close enough so that others around them couldn't hear her. "And don't send me any more presents."

He looked surprised. "I didn't send you a present."

Then who had? Summer? Scarlet needed to get back to the office. Open the box.

"Goodbye, John," she said, hoping he heard the finality in her voice.

If he said anything, she didn't hear it. She made her way back to her office, pulled out the box, yanked off the ribbon, lifted the lid. Nestled inside was a hinged jeweler's box, which creaked a little as she opened it. Inside was a beautiful gold choker in a modern serpentine design with red enamel accents.

She scrambled to find the card, found it tucked underneath the necklace.

> Just a little something to show you how proud I am for what you're doing—with your life and your work.
> Love, Granddad

Scarlet put her head on her desk and cried.

Fourteen

Summer stood framed in the hotel doorway, looking only slightly more rested than Scarlet had two days ago at Une Nuit. John was prepared to prevent Summer from shutting the door in his face, but she crossed her arms instead and glared at him.

"How did you find me?" she asked, belligerence coating her words.

It was the first time John thought the sisters seemed alike, the first time he'd seen real fire in Summer.

"May I come in?" he said, not answering her question. He'd pulled strings and greased palms to track down Zeke's Waldorf-Astoria suite.

"I don't think we have anything to say to one another," she said.

"Yeah, we do. It's not like you to jump to conclusions."

"Oh? I have concluded that you and my sister slept together the night we broke our engagement, and have continued a relationship ever since. Is there some other conclusion?"

"The night *you* broke our engagement," he said quietly.

Her face flushed. She started to close the door.

He stopped it. "Look, Summer, I didn't come here to rehash the past—our past—but because I'm worried about Scarlet. I would prefer not to have this conversation in the hall, but if I need to yell it through your closed door, I will. I figure if there were security people in your suite, they would've been all over me by now, so let's just be civilized and talk in private."

After a few moments she stepped back in silent invitation. The enormous suite provided an unparalleled view. He waited for her to be seated, then sat across from her. "Where's Zeke?"

"Out."

"You know, you're acting pretty self-righteous for someone who slept with another man while you were engaged."

"It isn't anything I'm proud of, and you know it. And I also didn't carry on for two months in secret. I told you right away. I also tried to explain. As soon as I met Zeke... You know all this, John."

"You know why Scarlet couldn't tell you about us."

"And you're looking for what from me? Acceptance? Approval?"

"I don't give a damn how you feel about me. I don't want anything for myself." He leaned toward her. "But you need to talk to your sister. She's falling apart. She's not sleeping. She looks...haunted."

Summer pushed herself out of her chair and walked stiffly to the window, but not before he saw concern in her eyes.

"Do you plan to continue your relationship with her?" she asked.

"All I want is for you to reconcile with her."

"Do you love her or were you using her to get back at me?"

He came up beside her. What he felt for Scarlet was more real and powerful than what he'd felt for Summer, but he wouldn't tell her that. "I've learned a lot about myself recently," he said instead, "and I've come to understand what must have happened to you when you met Zeke. I now know I wasn't as engaged emotionally as I should have been or I probably wouldn't have been content with your insistence on abstinence before the wedding."

"And my sister more than made up for that. A good substitute, was she?"

"None of this had anything to do with you." It ticked him off that Summer wasn't seeing the whole picture, but he didn't rise to the bait, knowing it was the only way for her to understand what was happening—that Scarlet needed her. "You learned a few truths yourself when you met Zeke. Do you regret anything?"

She shook her head.

"You caused a small scandal," he reminded her. He didn't need to detail what happened, but it sat there between them, still a little raw. She'd not only ended their engagement in less than three weeks, she'd taken up with a rock star, publicly, happily. It had been a lot for John to swallow.

"You don't think this would be scandalous, John? For

you and my sister to be together? Don't you know how that would look?"

"I'm only interested in getting the two of you back on speaking terms. Nothing else."

"She has hurt our grandfather so many times with things she's done. Not big hurts, mind you, but things done just to irritate him. This would be huge. He might not ever forgive her. And just when they're finally starting to get along."

"There is no reason for Patrick to ever know."

She went completely still. "It's over between you?"

"Yes." Scarlet would never have anything to do with him again. He knew that without a doubt.

Summer was quiet for a long time. John had nothing more to say.

"Does she love you?" she asked. "Does she know what you're willing to sacrifice?"

He slipped his hand in his pocket and fingered his house key, which she'd returned to him by messenger that morning. In the box was a tiny piece of paper. She'd written on it, "Goodbye."

"There's no sacrifice," he said. "It's done. If I can look past what you did, surely you can look past what she did. We were going to end it that night, before you came home. You should've never found out. She was insistent, even though I wanted to continue. She was afraid that someone would catch us, and she would never do that to you."

"I'll think about it," she said after a little while.

But John knew she would go see Scarlet and they would make up. Maybe their relationship would change some, but it had been changing anyway since Summer's engagement to Zeke. John hadn't fully understood the bond between twins before, but he did now. That sibling relationship was like no other.

The distinctive sound of a key card preceded the hotel door opening. Zeke Woodlow came in, saw them together and headed toward them. He put his arm around Summer then extended a hand to John.

"I hope you had better luck than I did convincing her to see her sister," Zeke said.

Any small irritation he'd harbored for the man dissolved. John liked his directness, as well as his obvious love for Summer. "I tried."

"She can be stubborn."

John refrained from saying, "She can?" He'd never seen her stubborn, or pushy, or demanding—all those things he enjoyed about Scarlet. "Those Elliott women," John said instead.

Zeke smiled.

John focused on Summer. "I wish you only the best."

"Thank you," she replied. "That means a lot."

John walked out the door and went home to his empty apartment, where every nook and cranny held a memory of Scarlet Elliott.

Scarlet pushed her sewing machine foot pedal to full speed. She was making new drapes for her bedroom, something that would suit the house from the outside but blend with the contemporary interior. This was the fourth and final panel. In the past few days she'd worked at *Charisma* all day then sewed at night until she fell asleep with her head on the sewing machine table.

As for food—what was that? Toast and tea was about all she could stomach.

She came to the end of the eight-foot-long seam, shoved the pressure-foot lever into reverse, then stopped and snipped off the excess thread, the motion automatic, mindless.

The ensuing silence was horrific. Her CDs must have played out. She rolled her head, trying to relieve the ache in her shoulders, then stood, intending to start up the music again.

Summer was standing just inside the doorway.

Hope gathered strength inside Scarlet, a whirlwind of optimism, a powerful need.

"I came to hear what you have to say," Summer said. "But you have to tell me everything. Don't hold back because you might hurt my feelings." She turned around. "Let's go sit in the living room."

They sat at opposite ends of the sofa. Scarlet didn't know whether Summer was calm or detached, but there was definitely a wall between them, one they'd never had before.

Scarlet didn't know where to start, then finally started with the most critical fact. "I've loved John for about a year now."

A shocked silence blared in the room as if coming from a loudspeaker.

"You have?" Summer finally said.

Scarlet nodded. "I'm not proud of it or happy about it."

"No, I don't suppose you are. But it explains a lot."

"You thought I disliked—" Scarlet began at the same time her sister said, "I thought you disliked—"

They smiled a little at each other. "We haven't done

that in a long time," Summer said. "So, you love him. How did you feel when I told you I'd broken off the engagement?"

"Upset. And confused."

"Why?"

"I thought you were acting without thinking things through, and that you were hurting him unnecessarily."

"You didn't think that now he would be available for you?"

Scarlet shook her head vehemently. "It didn't occur to me. He was in love with you. I never, ever let myself think I had a chance to have him. And I also thought you were just infatuated with Zeke—and the newness of sex. Then when you said you'd never really felt any desire for John, I was angry, too, because you'd been cheating him of yourself, not giving him everything. And he deserved everything."

Summer retreated a little. "You're right. So, actually, you should've been relieved."

"I only knew that he must be hurting. I went to see him that night. To tell him I thought you'd made a huge mistake in ending the engagement, then suddenly we were kissing. And then more." She stopped, breathless, then continued more calmly. "It was my dream come true. I took advantage of it, knowing I would only have the one night. I knew we couldn't have a future."

"Yet it continued."

"Not right away. Not until after you left the country and he returned from L.A. It just grabbed hold of us, Summer. We didn't seem to have any control over it. Like you with Zeke."

"I understand that."

"We decided to take the month you would be gone. It…it was supposed to be a physical relationship only."

Summer's eyes widened. "You never told him you loved him?"

"No. And because we couldn't go out in public, the relationship was more…intense, I think. There were no diversions, no normal dates. We were going to end it the night you showed up."

She nodded. "Now what?"

"Now, nothing."

"You aren't going to see him anymore?"

"No."

Summer went to stand by the window. Scarlet waited. "Why not?" Summer asked eventually.

"You know why. Because we still can't go public."

"Why not?"

"Because there will be a scandal when that happens, and another scandal when it ends. I'm not putting the family through that." *Granddad just told me how proud he was.*

"Why do you think it would end?"

She'd returned his key. He hadn't called her or come to her to try to give it back. If he loved her, he would fight for her. "I just know."

"You know, Scar, if you'd just been honest with me from the beginning, we could've avoided all this."

"That's not true. You know it's not true. You would've been just as hurt and angry—maybe even more so. You would've hated both of us, John *and* me."

"I meant way back, when you first fell in love."

Scarlet joined her sister at the window. "How could I tell you? What was I supposed to say? He preferred you."

Summer pressed her fingers to her eyelids. "Maybe you're right. And maybe you're right about not telling me after the first night you shared. I certainly would have thought that John was using you to exact revenge on me."

"He wasn't."

"I realize that now." Summer stared at the street. A long time passed, more than a minute. "I think you should go after what you want," she said at last, her voice wavering just a little.

Scarlet felt her jaw drop. "You're kidding."

"No."

"How can I do that? What would everyone say? The Grands—"

"They always liked John."

"How do I explain it? People will talk. I'll need to have answers."

"The four of us will go out together. Be seen. Let them talk. Who cares?" Summer's whole attitude changed, from her posture to her voice. She exuded strength and certainty.

Hope returned to Scarlet with a vengeance, but practicalities still got in the way. "I can't do the public thing unless John and I have a future together. A long future."

"So find that out first and go from there."

"I can't believe how generous you're being. If the situation were reversed—"

"You would do the same thing."

Scarlet put a tentative hand on her sister's shoulder. "It was so hard keeping this a secret from you."

"Don't do it again." Summer's eyes welled. "I know a lot has changed for us, but nothing can destroy our bond unless we let it. Regardless, Zeke is a part of my life now."

"I know that, Summer. I do. I think I felt left behind. Maybe a little jealous. You were so in love and so happy. And I envied you leaving your job, even if it was only for a month. It was only for a month, right?"

"I don't know yet. I doubt it, though. I'm finally going to do it, Scar. I'm going to make a career as a photographer."

There were no more questions, no more revelations. They went into each other's arms and held tight.

"I love you so—"

"I love you more than—"

They laughed shakily.

"So, why don't you show me your design for my wedding dress," Summer said after wiping Scarlet's tears away.

"Have you set a date?"

"We're talking about one. But I'm willing to wait until it can be a double wedding."

More hope wove its way through Scarlet. A different kind of hope. One with John as the focus. "You'll want the big, splashy wedding, Summer. I won't."

"Yes, you will." Summer's smile was all-knowing.

"It's never been my dream."

"Until you fell in love." She hugged Scarlet. "Show me my dress. And yours."

She found the sketch of Summer's dress and brought it out to her. Scarlet didn't want to jinx anything by pulling out the sketch of her own dress—the wadded-up paper she'd rescued from her trash can at work with her impetuous design. She hadn't redrawn it on clean paper. Nothing was certain yet.

"Oh!" Summer traced the lines of the gown with her

fingertips as if the fabric were in her hands. "It's exquisite. And exactly what I want."

"I know."

Summer shoved her, and they laughed.

"I'll hire someone to sew on the beads and crystals, but I want to make it for you," Scarlet said.

Summer nodded, tears in her eyes. She grabbed Scarlet in another big hug.

"Can you stay tonight?" Scarlet asked.

"Don't you want to go see John?"

"Not tonight. Tonight I want to be with you." She stepped back and smiled. "And sleep."

"I'll call Zeke and let him know."

Scarlet wondered if they would ever have another night like this, just the two of them. Probably not.

The thought colored the rest of the evening, giving everything they said and did a bittersweet edge. Who could have predicted they would undergo so many changes in just a couple of months?

Where would they be a year from now? Would they even be in the same country? When Summer and Zeke decided to have children, would Scarlet even get to know them or would they always be on the road?

She pictured her sister pregnant, smiling serenely. Summer would take motherhood in stride.

As for herself, Scarlet couldn't bring up the picture as readily. Maybe because her future wasn't as settled as Summer's.

But that was all about to change.

Fifteen

The Elliott helicopter swooped over The Tides, preparing to land. Scarlet took in the vista from above—the enormous turn-of-the-century home rising near a bluff overlooking the ever-changing Atlantic. The elegant circular drive, so often filled with cars. Her grandmother's glorious rose garden and perfectly manicured lawn, fragrant and inviting. Many a game of hide-and-go-seek had been played in that garden and countless touch football games on the lawn.

Hand-carved stone stairs led down the bluff to a private beach where Scarlet and Summer had whiled away warm July days and hot August nights as they talked about boys and life and their parents, desperately trying to keep them alive as their memories threatened to fade.

Scarlet's relationship with The Tides was complicated. A haven but occasionally a jail. Gram the peace-keeper; Granddad the warden. Summer the diplomat, and Scarlet the rebel...until this past year, when she'd stopped waging war with her grandfather. It had felt good, too. Incredibly good.

She gathered her courage as the helicopter set down gently, then she thanked the pilot and battled the wind generated by the blades as she ducked to race across the helipad.

For the first time ever Scarlet had ditched work.

She ran into the breezeway and entered the house from the side entrance. Heading straight into a powder room tucked under the staircase, she brushed her hair, straightened her clothes then went in search of her grandparents, who were expecting her and had surely heard the helicopter arrive.

Her stomach hurt from stress and anticipation as she walked through the house, expecting to find them in the solarium enjoying the morning sun. They sat on a love seat, heads close together, speaking quietly. Maeve touched Patrick's face lovingly. He laid a hand over hers. Their tenderness after fifty-seven years of marriage was enviable.

Scarlet closed her eyes; drew a slow, deep breath; let it out just as slowly then walked into the room. "Good morning," she said, bending to kiss each of them. "Thank you for sending the chopper," she said to her grandfather.

"It sounded urgent."

"Have you not slept in a month, then?" her grandmother asked, concern creasing her face.

"I'm okay." Scarlet thrust a box at Patrick. "I can't keep this. It's beautiful, Granddad, and exactly the kind of necklace I would wear, but I don't deserve it. I don't deserve what it represents, what you said in your note. You won't be proud of me once you hear what I came to tell you."

He frowned. "You've caused no gossip since that hoodlum a year ago. And I've been assured that you've become invaluable to *Charisma*."

"Just because he rode a motorcycle doesn't make him a hood—" Scarlet stopped the automatic argument. She couldn't lose her temper now. "It doesn't have anything to do with my job," she continued, forcing herself into control, then remembering he had a snitch in place at the magazine. "Who's your source there, anyway? Fin hates being checked up on."

"Fin's paranoid."

"Patrick," Maeve chided.

"Well, she is. I don't check up on her. I've no need to. I can see the numbers any time I choose. I asked Cade how Scarlet was doing. At least he speaks to me. Finola chooses not to."

With good reason, Scarlet thought.

"Sit down, missy. Tell us what's on your mind."

She pulled up a chair, grateful to sit. "I've been seeing John Harlan."

Her grandmother's eyes opened wider, but that was her only outward reaction. Her grandfather's expression darkened, the calm before the storm.

"Seeing him? What does that mean?" he asked coolly.

"Dating him."

"Sleeping with him?"

"Yes." Okay. The worst was out now.

"For how long?"

"A month." She decided they didn't need to know

about the stolen night, the first night a month earlier. That could only hurt all those involved.

"Does your sister know?"

Scarlet nodded. "She wouldn't have, but she came home a day early and saw us together. We were going to end it that night."

Her grandfather shoved himself up. Scarlet stood, an ingrained response. She wasn't wearing heels this time, so she couldn't meet him eye to eye. He seemed to tower over her.

"I thought you'd grown up finally. How could you do that to your sister? Betray her like that?"

He'd used the word before—betray. Even though Summer had forgiven her, it still stung, especially since she'd worked so hard to change. *Had* changed.

"I couldn't help myself," she said quietly. "It's no excuse. I know there'll be penance to pay."

"Couldn't help yourself?" he roared. "Animals can't help themselves. The weak can't help themselves. You're a strong woman who knows the difference between right and wrong. This is wrong, missy."

"I know."

He walked away.

"I'm sorry," Scarlet said. "I know I've disappointed you. Both of you." She dared a look at her grandmother. "I didn't mean to hurt Summer. She's the last person on earth I'd ever hurt."

"But you did, *colleen*," her grandmother said.

She could bear being a disappointment to her grandfather—that was nothing new—but not Gram. Scarlet wanted to stare at the floor. Instead she kept her head up.

"Why are you telling us?" he asked.

Scarlet hated that she'd put that tone in his voice that said she'd failed him, had fallen short of his expectations. "Because I'm in love with him."

"You mean you have every intention of going public with this? Humiliating your sister?"

"Summer is fine with it. As for going public, I don't know for sure. I just wanted you to know, in case."

"Does he love you?" Gram asked.

"He hasn't said so."

"Are you looking for my blessing?" Granddad asked, as if dumbfounded. "You think I would—"

"Quit prowling," Maeve said, interrupting. "Sit yourself down. You're not helping."

"I should help this?" he queried righteously, but he sat anyway. "I should make her comfortable?"

"Yes, I do believe you should, dearie."

Scarlet was grateful to sit again. "I didn't have anything to do with their breakup."

"Of course you didn't," her grandmother said, patting her hand.

Scarlet grabbed it as an anchor. "I do want your blessing, Granddad. I don't know what will happen. Maybe all this would have been unnecessary. But I can't even begin to hope things can work out with John unless I know you accept it."

"Give my blessing, you mean."

She nodded.

"And if I won't?"

She met his gaze directly. "I won't see him anymore."

He sat back, his brows raised. "You would give him up?"

"I'm not the girl I was. I've grown up. I appreciate

all you did for Summer and me after Mom and Dad died. I'm sorry it took so long for me to show you."

The room held no clock to tick during the long silence that followed, but the sound seemed to reverberate inside Scarlet's head, anyway, a time bomb determining her future—she hoped. John still had to have his say.

"You have our blessing," he said at last.

As if a nuclear blast hit her, she fell into her grandmother's waiting arms, wishing she could control the relief that spilled out in huge, gulping sobs, but finally just giving in to the overwhelming emotions. She felt her grandfather pat her back a few times.

"You'll make yourself sick," he said, obviously uncomfortable with Scarlet's tears when he was accustomed to arguments.

He stuck a handkerchief in her hand. She grabbed hold of his hand, too, then shifted from her grandmother's arms into his. "Thank you," she whispered shakily. "Thank you so much. I'll try to handle it in a way you can be proud of."

"I am proud, missy. I've always been proud. You've got a good bit of myself in you. It's why we butt heads. I expect you'll go far in the company, maybe even run it someday."

Scarlet used his handkerchief to dry her cheeks and blow her nose, stalling. She tried to smile. They had, after all, taken Summer's request for a leave of absence well. "About that…"

He raised his brows.

"No matter what happens with John, my plan is to stay on at *Charisma* until the end of the year—when Fin wins the contest," she added pointedly. "And then I'm going to try my hand at designing full-time."

"You couldn't have saved that bit of news for another time?"

"Might as well put everything on the table at one time. Deal with it and move on."

"That sounds suspiciously like a motto of your own," Maeve said to him.

He smiled, then shrugged.

"You'll be wanting to take the helicopter back right away, *colleen*."

"Yes, Gram. Thank you." She stood.

Patrick stood as well, and passed the jewelry box back to her. "I haven't been more proud of you than now, Scarlet. Wear it with pride. My pride. You've become your own person. It needs recognition. No more tears," he added in mock horror.

She laughed. Then she left to find the man she loved.

Sixteen

Late that afternoon John closed his office door, shutting out the normal workplace noise, which seemed suddenly chaotic. He'd been sure he would hear from Scarlet as soon as Summer forgave her—or whatever they did to make things right again. He'd certainly expected their reconciliation by now. He didn't know what to make of Scarlet's silence.

He checked the time. She would still be at work, but just barely. He dialed her number, got her voice mail, waited for the beep. "It's John." Did he really have to identify himself? "Give me a call when you have a minute. Thanks."

If she didn't call back before he left the office he'd try her home phone, then her cell. He needed to know what was going on with her, wanted to tell her a few things, too.

His private line rang. He let it ring twice, his hand on the receiver. "John Harlan."

"Hi, it's me."

Scarlet. Message received. He dragged a hand down his face and relaxed into the chair.

"Thanks for calling." He held back from bombarding her with questions because he wanted to see her in person, to know for himself how she felt. He needed to talk her into meeting him somewhere. "Did you and Summer settle things?"

"Yes."

He waited, but she didn't add anything. "Well… good."

"John? We need to talk."

"I agree. That's why I called you."

"You—" A pause, then, "When?"

"Just now. Isn't that why you're calling?" he asked.

"No. I wanted to let you know I'm sending you an envelope by messenger. You can read what's inside and think it over and get back to me."

"Why don't we just meet?" he asked.

"Everything will be clear when you get the message."

At this point in their relationship she'd decided to play a game? Why wouldn't she just talk to him? "All right, Scarlet. I'll get back to you."

"One way or the other, please?"

He wasn't sure what she meant but figured it would work itself out. "Okay."

"See you later," she said, almost turning it into a question, but not waiting for an answer before she hung up.

He called the doorman in his apartment building to

say he was expecting a delivery and to call him as soon as it arrived. Someone rapped sharply on his office door, then opened it without waiting to be invited.

"Got a minute, son? We need to talk."

John stood to greet his father, aware of how ominous those words sounded, echoing his own to Scarlet. It was not the best day in his life.

Scarlet shook out her hands to help calm her nerves then strode lightly across the sumptuous hotel suite to the door. She viewed the room from the entry. The small fortune she'd paid for one night in the two-room suite at the Ritz-Carlton was worth it. A table for two was already set by a window overlooking Central Park. She'd arranged for a memorable meal from the hotel's award-winning restaurant, Atelier, everything from beluga caviar, to bluefin-tuna-and-artichoke salad, to herb-crusted rack of lamb with spinach-and-ricotta gnocchi, to the decadent final touch—warm molten chocolate cake with caramel ice cream.

It was a meal meant for a celebration. She'd even met with the master sommelier to choose wines for each course.

Now all she needed was John.

She paced the room, caught a glimpse of her reflection in a window in her fitted black sheath, black-satin-and-rhinestone high heels and her mother's pearl-and-diamond necklace and matching earrings. She'd never worn them before, had saved them for a special occasion. She couldn't imagine an occasion more special.

The mantel clock struck six. Any moment now, he would arrive.

She was scared and anxious and exhilarated.

She wandered around the room, moved dinner plates half an inch then back again, straightened perfectly aligned silverware, picked up a wineglass, held it to the light then set it down again in precisely the same spot.

She walked some more, stopped at a window. A siren blared, an everyday sound that pierced the quiet hotel room then stopped nearby.

In the sudden silence the clock chimed the quarter hour.

She went into the bedroom to find her watch, double-checking that the clock was right. It was.

Six-thirty came. Anxiety played hide-and-seek in her head.

Six forty-five. Worry joined the game.

The phone rang. She almost came out of her skin. He was delayed, that was all, and calling to say so.

"Hello?" She heard herself, breathless and hopeful.

"Miss Elliott?"

Not John. "Yes."

"Were you ready for room service?"

"I need a little more time." She'd arranged to call them when she was ready but had told them it would probably be about 6:15 p.m. "I'll get back to you as soon as I can."

"Of course, ma'am. Good evening."

Scarlet blew out a breath. Where was John? She had left nothing to chance, had even called to alert him about the envelope. Yet now she was left staring at the hotel door, willing him to knock on it, but only silence echoed back.

Seven o'clock came. Eight. She dimmed the lights and curled up on the sofa.

He wasn't coming. Apparently he'd thought about what she said in the note and made his decision. Except that he'd told her he would call, one way or the other, and he hadn't, and he was usually a man of his word. Maybe she had been too pushy, her expectations too high.

But he'd called her, too, wanting to talk. He'd said so. What did it all mean?

At 9:35 p.m. she cancelled room service and turned a chair to the window. Headlights dotted the nightscape as a steady stream of traffic passed below her. They blurred into ribbons of light, red one direction, white the other. Horns honked. Life went on.

But not hers.

Why didn't he want her? Was she too much trouble? Maybe she'd been too bold, undermining him as a man. Maybe he thought she was high maintenance, someone who brought too much drama into a life.

Okay, perhaps she'd stirred his life up a bit, but she wasn't exactly a drama queen. She hadn't changed him. He was still the cool, calm person he'd always been.

Maybe that was the crux of the problem. She was too intense. He was too calm.

Fire and ice. Good for a sexual relationship, but not for life.

She looked blindly around the room, aching disappointment drifting around her. How could he just blow her off like that? Okay, so she hadn't exactly encouraged him since Summer had discovered them, had actually discouraged him. But he was big on courtesy. He should have at least let her know he wasn't coming. He'd said he would. He was a promise keeper.

Unless he was hurt?

She laughed at the idea, the sound brittle, and wished she'd ordered the champagne to be delivered anyway, so she could toast her fertile imagination. She'd seen *An Affair to Remember* too many times, that was all. And she'd heard the siren earlier. It had stopped right in front of the hotel, hadn't it? Had it been an ambulance?

"Right, Scarlet. He was looking up at the hotel and was hit by a car on his way to meet you."

Frustrated, she walked to the window again and looked out, resting her forehead against the cold pane. She just wanted—needed—a reason for why he wasn't there, that was all. Because her imagination put him in an ER somewhere, bleeding, barely conscious, calling her name, since in some way it was preferable to him ignoring her.

And that was her wake-up call. She grabbed her things, then left for home, wanting nothing more than to curl up in her own bed, and never see the Ritz-Carlton again.

In her car she rolled down her car window, felt the chilly air against her cheeks as she drove, trying to erase the memory of the night. The short drive seemed infinite yet instantaneous.

She reached the town house, hit the garage door opener and saw the spot where she usually parked her car, gaping and empty—a glaring reminder of the state of her life.

Some welcome home.

John clutched a Glenfiddich on the rocks in one hand, his first of the night, and a ring in the other, not missing the irony of the déjà vu moment and wishing he was as close to drunk as the other time.

A small scraping sound made him turn toward the

front door. Something flat and white lay there. He slipped the ring into his pocket, walked over, picked up the envelope. Finally, Scarlet's envelope had arrived. Instinct made him open the door, because the doorman would've called first.

A woman stood at the elevator, her back to him. There was no mistaking her this time.

"Scarlet?"

She spun around. "I thought—" She hesitated, looking confused. "Your car is gone."

"It's in the shop." He waited for her to approach, but she didn't, which confused him.

The elevator door opened. She looked into the empty cavern then didn't step inside. The doors closed quietly.

He opened the envelope and pulled out a piece of paper. "Obviously we don't want the same things," she'd written. "Goodbye."

That was it? The big mystery in the envelope? She'd already said goodbye, when she'd returned his apartment key. So what did this goodbye mean? She'd changed her mind, but had changed it again now?

"Come in," he said.

"I'm comfortable here."

Leave it to Scarlet to make everything a challenge. She kept him on his toes, and fascinated.

John held up the paper. "I don't understand. What do you want that I don't?"

She pushed back her shoulders as if gearing for a fight. "I had *wanted* to continue our relationship."

"Continue in what way?"

"As we had. Just spending time together."

As they had? "In private?" he asked, bewildered.

"Snatches of time during the week when we can find it? Maybe an overnight on Saturdays? An occasional week-end away?"

"Yes."

He studied her. It wasn't what he'd expected. He'd thought she would either cut him off altogether as a sac-rifice to her relationship with Summer or demand more of him. At the least he'd figured she wanted the one last time in bed they'd missed out on when Summer had sur-prised them.

"Nooners?" he asked, stepping into the hall.

She flinched. "Everything the same as it was the past month," she said. "Except this time with everyone's blessings, which they gave."

"Even Patrick?"

"I think he's mellowing."

John didn't have time to consider the implications of that. "No," he said.

Silence stretched out for days, it seemed.

Finally, she jabbed the down button.

A door across the hallway opened, and his neighbor looked out, eyeing the both of them.

"Sorry, Keith," John said to the man, taking quick strides to get to Scarlet before the elevator arrived and she was swallowed up by it. His neighbor shut his door.

In a low voice he told Scarlet, "I'm not interested in that proposition, tempting as it sounds on a base level."

"I figured that out already. *No* has no alternate mean-ing. This conversation is over."

"Not even close. But unless you want my neighbors to hear the rest of it, I suggest you come inside." He put his hand on her arm, urging her toward his apartment.

"There's nothing more to say."

"There's a helluva lot more to say."

After a moment she went along, although jerking free of his grasp. She walked directly to his couch then didn't sit.

"May I take your coat?"

"I won't be here long." She crossed her arms.

"I'm missing a piece of the communication puzzle, Scarlet. You act as if I should've known what you wanted."

"If you'd shown up at the hotel, you *would* know."

"What hotel?"

She looked at him as if he'd lost his mind. "The Ritz-Carlton, of course."

"Of course," he repeated without any understanding. "I was supposed to be there, I gather."

She narrowed her gaze. "It was in the envelope."

He glanced at her note. Had she lost her mind?

"Not that envelope," she said. "The other one."

"This is the only one I've received."

"But…it was delivered five minutes after we talked. The courier confirmed it."

He stared at her, baffled. "At my office?"

"I told you it was coming." Frustration coated her words and stiffened her body.

"My father dropped by. He needed to talk to me about some family business, so we went to the bar next door. I called my doorman and told him to contact me when—" He paused. "I assumed you would send it *here*."

"I didn't."

He'd gone crazy sitting at the bar with his father, waiting for a call. "Sit down, please. Can I get you something to drink?"

She shook her head then perched on the sofa, her hands clenched on her knees. John sat in a chair opposite from her. He wasn't alone in his loss for words. A comedy of errors, he thought, but not funny at all.

"You're wearing one of your new suits," she said after a moment. "It looks nice."

Avoidance. She was trying to regroup. What was in that envelope, anyway? "You were right. I got compliments."

"Why are you still dressed up?"

He ignored her question. "What was in the other envelope, Scarlet?"

"A key card for a room at the Ritz."

"And when I didn't show up, you thought I'd left you high and dry? Do you know me at all?"

She looked out the window. "I didn't know what to think," she said into the quiet.

"Why didn't you call?"

"Because if you were intentionally ignoring me, I didn't want the humiliation."

"So you came in person instead?" He smiled at her, not quite following her logic but appreciating how much her emotions were involved.

She stood abruptly. "This isn't going anywhere. Let's just call it a day. A month. Goodbye, John." She headed toward the door.

"When I said *no* earlier," he said, following her, "I meant I wasn't interested in keeping the status quo."

She continued toward the door.

"What I *am* interested in," he said, "is a full-time, publicly acknowledged relationship."

Her steps slowed.

"I love you, Scarlet."

She stopped and turned around, her gaze meeting his, her expression one of guarded surprise. He caught up with her and slipped his arms around her, but still she didn't speak.

"This is the part where you say you love me, too." His heart thudded. He was taking a leap of faith, based on everything he'd seen in her eyes this past month, heard in her voice, felt in her touch. Still, he wouldn't know until she said—

"I fell in love with you a year ago," she said, her voice just a whisper, as if she were afraid to admit it.

"A year ago? But—"

She put a hand over his mouth. "As it turns out, you're not the man I thought I fell in love with."

A year ago. She fell in love with me a year ago. The unbelievable words kept repeating in his head. Then it hit him that she was speaking in the past tense. "Meaning what?" he asked.

She toyed with his lapels. "You were an ideal, and I loved the ideal without really knowing the man. I hadn't seen below the surface until this month. Now you're real. And now my love is real, too."

The world righted itself. He pulled her closer, needing to hold her, needing her arms around him, squeezing tight. She pressed her face against his neck.

"Do you want to know when I started falling in love with you?" he asked, loving the feel of her breath against his skin, warm and unsteady, hinting at intense emotions. "At the country club. In the conference room. When you stopped me from making love with you on the table. That hadn't been my goal when I got you in there. All I wanted was a kiss, but things escalated. You do that to me."

He stroked her hair, enjoying the soft sound of pleasure she made as she snuggled closer. "There is much more to you than I'd guessed, and I want to know it all. I want *you*."

He kissed her, long and lingeringly, putting everything into the kiss that he felt, feeling everything back from her. Then he framed her face with his hands, keeping her close.

"I want you to marry me, Scarlet. Will you marry me?"

She smiled; her eyes welled. "Yes," she said, then repeated it in a stronger voice. "Although one little problem does stand in the way. Summer wants to have a big, splashy wedding. Those take a while to arrange."

"What do Summer's plans have to do with us?"

"She'd like to have a double wedding."

It didn't surprise him. The twin bond was a powerful force. It did surprise him that they'd discussed it already. "And you? What would you like?"

"I want to marry you, period."

"But you'd like to do the spectacle with your sister. The Cinderella thing."

"I promise it won't be a three-ring circus. It'll be tasteful and classy and—"

He kissed her, this time without restraint and with the intent of getting her to think about something else— him. Them. Now.

He lifted her into his arms and carried her to his bedroom, as he'd done the first night she'd knocked on his door. In his pocket was the ring, nothing as simple as a diamond. She was a complex woman who needed a different kind of engagement ring, something untraditional, something with flair.

He'd chosen it yesterday, had tried not to think about what he would do if she said no. He would've fought for her, though. Fought hard.

He wouldn't give her the ring tonight. Tonight he would give her himself, and let himself just enjoy her. Tomorrow, though, he would find a creative way to present the ring to her. His magna cum laude graduation from Woo U wouldn't go to waste.

"I love you," she said, reaching for him.

There was so much yet to say and do and discover. But it started and ended with one truth. "I love you, too," he said. "Forever."

* * * * *

MR AND MISTRESS

BY
HEIDI BETTS

Heidi Betts, an avid romance reader since junior high school, knew early on that she wanted to write these wonderful stories of love and adventure. It wasn't until her freshman year of college, however, when she spent the entire night reading a romance novel instead of studying for finals, that she decided to take the road less traveled and follow her dream. In addition to reading, writing and romance, she is the founder of her local Romance Writers of America chapter and has a tendency to take injured and homeless animals of every species into her central Pennsylvania home.

Heidi loves to hear from readers. You can write to her at PO Box 99, Kylertown, PA 16847, USA (an SASE is appreciated but not necessary) or e-mail heidi@ heidibetts.com. And be sure to visit www.heidibetts.com for news and information about upcoming books.

For Jackie Stephens-thanks for your help with the
research for this book, and for all the
great e-mail chats!
And always, for Daddy.

One

"Hello?"

"I'm in town. Thought I might come over."

His voice reached through the telephone wire and slid down her spine like warm maple syrup on a cold winter's day, into every nook and cranny of Misty Vale's traitorous body.

"All right," she replied softly. "I'll be waiting."

She hung up and quickly began moving around the room, straightening magazines and throw pillows, dimming the lights before heading for her bedroom. Shedding her skintight bike shorts and sports bra, she slipped into a new black teddy she knew Cullen would love.

If it weren't for him, she probably wouldn't own

half as many pieces of fancy lingerie. But he liked the sheer, sexy stuff, and she liked wearing it for him.

She quickly pulled her long, wavy hair out of its ponytail holder and ran a brush through to fluff it up.

A second later, the doorbell rang. She hurried across the room, glancing around one last time to be sure everything was in order. And then her hand was on the chain, releasing it. On the knob, turning it.

"Hi."

He was leaning against the jamb, black hair glistening in the porch light, blue eyes sparkling with barely banked desire. She swallowed hard, wishing she knew how to settle the butterflies flitting around in her belly.

"Hi. Come on in," she said, stepping back to allow him entrance.

She closed the door and refastened the security chain, then turned to find him watching her like a hawk might watch a mouse just before swooping down and carrying it away.

He was dressed for business in charcoal gray slacks and a white dress shirt, both of which were slightly wrinkled from a long day of meetings and travel. His tie was silk, with pastel swirls that reminded her of a painting she'd seen once in an art gallery. It was pulled away from his neck and hung limply from the collar with the top two buttons undone. The jacket that matched his slacks was folded over one arm.

He looked tired, and as much as she wanted to

drag him straight to the bedroom, she thought he might need to relax a bit first.

"Do you want anything?" she asked, tipping her head in the direction of the kitchen at his back. "A glass of wine? Something to eat, maybe?"

With the flick of his wrist, his jacket fell to the floor and he was striding forward, his gaze focused intently on her face.

"Later," he growled in a low voice that sent every cell of her being into erotic overdrive. His arms wrapped around her and a second later, his mouth hovered above hers. "Right now all I want is you."

As always, his kiss scorched, setting her afire from head to toe. She buried her fingers in the hair at the nape of his neck, caressing his scalp. His lips moved over hers, sucking, biting. His tongue delved inside to lick and stroke.

Her breasts swelled beneath the satin material of her teddy, pressing against his solid, muscled chest. His hands ran along her spine, over her waist, and finally cupped her buttocks, pulling her into the evidence of his arousal. Misty moaned, holding him tighter and hitching a leg up to hook on the jut of his hip.

Tearing his mouth away, he breathed heavily against her cheek. "Bedroom. Now."

"Yes."

Bending slightly, he lifted her into his arms and strode with purpose across the living room. He knew the layout of her apartment as well as she did. Not surprising, since he'd bought the building for her three years ago, after an accident on stage had damaged her knee and ended her career as a showgirl on the Las Vegas Strip. Her dance studio was downstairs, and she lived above.

Cullen lived in New York, working hard for *Snap*—one of his family's many successful magazine ventures—but he visited Nevada as often as possible. And whenever he was in town, he spent the night with her...in her bed.

She lived for those nights. Waited for them, craved them, even though everything inside her told her it was wrong.

He was five years her junior, his family—the Elliotts—one of the wealthiest and most prominent in New York. They couldn't have been more different if they'd been born in opposite hemispheres.

But from the moment she'd seen him, standing backstage after one of her nightly performances, there had been something about him. Something that drew her, kept her connected to him no matter how many times she told herself they should call off their blazing red-hot affair.

Reaching the edge of the bed, Cullen laid her on the mattress and followed her down, covering her body with his own.

"I love this," he said, fingering the black fabric that barely covered her from chest to thigh. "But it has to go. I want you naked."

"You're the boss," she told him with a small smile.

One side of his mouth quirked up in sensual

amusement as his fingers slipped beneath the teddy's spaghetti straps, sliding them over her shoulders and down her arms. She moved to allow him to uncover her breasts and pull the garment down past her hips and thighs.

His beautiful blue eyes seared through her like laser beams. He openly admired her breasts, her belly, the triangular area between her legs hidden behind a swatch of black lace.

Rising up from the bed, she helped him remove the lingerie completely. He tossed it aside, returning his attention to her bare, curvaceous form.

She wiggled anxiously, wanting to touch him. Wanting him to touch her.

"You're overdressed," she told him, grabbing the end of his tie and giving it a tug. The action brought him several inches closer, until their noses nearly touched.

His chest rose and fell with his harsh breathing and she took a moment to run her hands over the wide planes of his pectoral muscles before her fingers moved up to the knot at his throat.

She loosened the tie, taking her time pulling the length of silk free of his pristine white collar. Then she went to work on the buttons of his shirt, slipping them through their holes one by one. When she reached the bottom, she tugged the tails out of the waistband of his slacks, revealing his smooth, tanned chest and six-pack abs.

She swallowed, overwhelmed by the sheer perfection of Cullen's toned build. He'd mentioned once that he worked out several times a week in the company gym of Elliott Publication Holdings (EPH).

And she reaped the benefits.

Pushing the soft cotton off his shoulders, she pitched the shirt in the direction of her discarded negligee. Next came his belt, unbuckled and pulled through the loops of his pants. When her painted, manicured nails dipped behind the button at his waist, he sucked in a breath, sending his stomach rippling.

"I hope you're enjoying yourself," he said through gritted teeth, "because I fully intend to repay the favor."

"Uh-oh. I'm in real trouble, then, because I *am* enjoying myself. Very much."

She flicked the button of his trousers open with her thumb, creating even more space for her fingers to delve and explore. The heat of his body—so close to the throbbing, insistent center of him—enveloped her, soaking through her skin and down into her soul.

With the backs of her fingers brushing over the sprinkling of hair leading downward from his navel, Misty used the heel of her hand to push the zipper down. Slowly, the individual snicks echoed through the room.

Cullen held his breath, the sensations she was creating were almost too much to bear. Each click of the zipper teeth separating seemed to reverberate through his bones, his teeth, his rigid, straining shaft.

He'd been half-hard all day, anticipating the moment when he could tie up his *Snap* business in

Vegas and sneak away to make love to Misty. The things she was doing to him now didn't help matters, either. His blood was boiling, his head pounding. Much more, and he thought he might implode.

She was amazing. Every time they were together, it was like fireworks on the Fourth of July. Hot, vibrant, spectacular. He was surprised they hadn't set the sheets on fire years ago.

If he told anyone, even his brother, how Misty made him feel in bed, they would have given him one of those sly, knowing looks and said, "Sure. She used to be a showgirl. What do you expect?"

But it was more than that, because as explosive as they were in the bedroom, they worked just as well out of it. He wanted to make love to her as often as his schedule and physical endurance would allow, but he was equally happy to sit on the sofa with her and watch a movie or pick at day-old Chinese takeout.

That's what no one would have understood. What he didn't particularly understand himself.

The zipper reached its end and Misty dipped her entire hand into his pants, into his briefs to circle his pulsating length. His diaphragm seized, and his nostrils flared as he fought to pull air into his lungs. She stroked him, squeezed him, teased him until he wanted to scream.

"Enough." Before he lost it to her fingers instead of inside her where he most wanted to be, he grabbed her wrist and extracted her hand from his trousers.

In a few jerky moves, he kicked off his shoes, socks, pants and underwear.

Once he was naked, he climbed onto the bed, pushing her to her back as he straddled her thighs. Bracing his weight on his arms, he leaned forward and took her mouth the way he'd fantasized all through the long flight from New York.

She responded as she always did—passionately, with her whole heart and soul. Her arms wrapped around his neck and he sank down on top of her, luxuriating in the feel of her soft breasts pillowed against his chest.

Shifting beneath him, she somehow maneuvered so that his legs were no longer bracketing her. Instead, hers were now locked at the small of his back. He could feel her heels digging into his buttocks the same as her nails were digging into his shoulders.

He liked it. Maybe too much. Although, with Misty, it didn't seem to be a case of too much, but never enough.

Tugging at her bottom lip with his teeth, he broke their earth-shattering kiss and blazed a hot, damp trail down her body. He skimmed the slope of her throat, the rise of one breast, stopping to explore the tight bud of her nipple. He circled the areola with his tongue, then closed his mouth over the tip and began to suckle.

Misty writhed beneath him, making those sexy little mewling sounds in her throat that drove him crazy.

All day, he'd imagined the things he would do to her once he could break away and get to her apartment…the things she would do to him. But now that he was here with her, both of them naked and mindless and desperate, he didn't think he had the patience for any of them. He was hard and throbbing and simply wanted to sink himself inside her, then stay that way forever.

Lifting his head, he gazed down at her, chest heaving, blood rushing through his veins like a forest fire.

"I can't wait," he grated. "I'm sorry. I'll make it up to you, I promise."

And then he was thrusting inside her, buried to the hilt. Their gasps mingled as sensations washed over them, the friction almost too much to bear.

"Cullen," Misty panted, her fingers raking across his back, sure to leave marks. "Wait. We didn't use protection."

For a second, her words didn't make sense. He could barely hear her over the rushing in his ears. She felt amazing, so warm and wet and tight around him. Better than ever, if that was even possible.

Then suddenly what she was trying to tell him sank in.

He'd forgotten the condom. Dammit.

He pulled out immediately, shaking his head in disbelief. "I'm sorry, Misty. I don't know what's wrong with me. I've never been that careless before, I swear."

She smiled gently, wiggling out from under, then turned over and shimmied across the lavender coverlet toward the nightstand. "It's all right. I'm sure we caught the mistake in time. I don't think there's any need to worry."

He didn't reply, but hoped to hell she was right. It wasn't like him to forget something as important and ingrained as protection.

His eyes remained glued to her bare back, bottom and legs while she opened the top drawer of the bedside table, rooting around for a loose foil packet.

Such a close call should have cooled his ardor. Should have, but didn't. His mouth was still dry with wanting her.

She came back, crawling the few feet to the end of the bed, the shiny square held up between two fingers. "Got it," she said, her grin widening triumphantly.

Tearing one edge open with her teeth, she removed the latex circle and tossed away the empty wrapper. His eyes were riveted to her slim fingers as she held the condom lightly in both hands and slid it competently—mind-numbingly—down his rigid length.

He held his breath the entire time, afraid that if he moved, if he didn't hold completely, absolutely still, he would lose control and embarrass himself. His abdomen was concave with the effort not to inhale, his arms and legs shaking with the desire to reach out, topple her to the bed and simply take her. Ravish her.

She brought out the animal in him, no question. With any other woman, he would have tried to temper his response, hold back his natural instincts. But with Misty, he could do anything and know she was right there with him. Her passions matched his own, and she was daring enough to try anything once.

"Two seconds," he rasped, clenching his fists to keep from grabbing her.

Her brows drew together in confusion.

"That's how long you've got before I lose my patience and take over."

"Uh-oh. I guess I'd better make the most of the time I have left."

Rather than backing off, she drifted closer until they were thigh to thigh, chest to chest. She placed an openmouthed kiss on his chin, nipping lightly with her teeth as her lips slid away.

"One," she murmured.

Her fingers wrapped around the base of his erection and she gave a little squeeze, sending pleasure skyrocketing through every cell and nerve ending of his body.

"Two."

Before she could count to three or do anything else that threatened to send him over the edge, he grasped her wrists, lifted them above her head and leaned forward, toppling them both to the mattress. They bounced slightly, and Cullen found Misty's brief giggle infectious.

Still grinning, he crushed his mouth down on hers, at the same time running his palms down her body, over her arms, breasts, waist, hips. When he reached her thighs, he nudged them apart and settled more securely, hovering just above her feminine warmth.

With a single forward thrust, he sank inside, then froze, waiting for the ripple effect of the nearly knee buckling sensations to subside. His heart pounded hard in his chest, threatening to break through his rib cage.

Beneath him, Misty squirmed and moaned, raking her nails across his back and tilting her hips in an effort to drive him even deeper. He didn't think it was possible, but he was happy to let her try.

Bending her knees, she hugged his waist with her legs, and he began to move. At first his strokes were long and slow, as he took his time to enjoy the clasping heat of her moist sheath. But after only a minute or two, he knew he wouldn't last and began to increase his pace.

"Yes. Cullen, yes."

Misty's soft voice, mewling in his ear, sent flames licking through his bloodstream, heading straight for his groin.

"Misty." He breathed her name like a prayer, nipping at the tender spot between her neck and shoulder.

She cried out, arching her back and clenching around him as the waves of orgasm washed over her. He pumped his hips. Harder, once. Faster, twice. Stars burst behind his closed eyelids and he gave a guttural groan as everything inside him exploded.

"I should go."

Cullen's chest rumbled with the softly spoken words, jostling her awake just as she'd begun to drift off. She lay snuggled in his arms, her head on his shoulder, one arm draped across his stomach.

Stifling a sigh, she pushed away from him and sat up, keeping the sheet clutched above her breasts. She tucked a strand of hair behind her ear as she watched him sit up on the edge of the bed, then move around the room retrieving his clothes.

This was the part of their time together that she liked the least—when Cullen had to leave. He didn't always come over just to sleep with her and then take off. Sometimes he spent the night and they would have breakfast together in the morning. Once in a while, he even stayed for a few days and they would do normal everyday things together like watch television or take a walk in the park.

But no matter how long they were together, she hated to see him go. It made her heart hurt and emphasized the charade that was their relationship.

They were having an affair, that was all. They were never going to end up together, with a house and kids and a minivan in the driveway.

For one thing, she wasn't the minivan type. She was an ex-showgirl with bigger dreams and better taste. If she hadn't fallen on stage and ruined her knee three years ago, she would still be dancing in one of the flashy casinos on the Las Vegas Strip.

For another, Cullen wasn't the marrying type. He was twenty-seven to her thirty-two, but even if he weren't five years younger, he came from one of the wealthiest families in Manhattan. The likelihood of his wanting to spend the rest of his life with a woman like her—of his family ever *allowing* such a thing—was slim to not-a-chance-in-hell.

But the simple facts of the situation didn't keep her mind from making the occasional trip down fantasy lane, imagining what it might be like if she weren't an ex-showgirl/dance instructor and he weren't a high-powered magazine executive. If they were normal, everyday people who had met in some normal, everyday way.

She didn't spend long wishing for things that could never be, though. She was happy with her life, and happy with what she and Cullen had, even if she knew it wouldn't last.

For now, it was enough.

And she could certainly do worse…had done worse, considering some of the real treats she'd dated in the past. Compared to them, Cullen was a veritable Prince Charming.

In a tailored Italian business suit.

Dressed now, he stood at the end of the bed with his hands in his pockets. Scooting out from under the covers, Misty grabbed her silk robe from a hook on the back of the closet door and shrugged it on, looping the belt loosely at her waist.

"I'll walk you out."

He gave an almost imperceptible nod and they moved together through the living room area to the front door. She released the locks and turned the knob, but before she could open the door, Cullen stopped her with a hand on her wrist. When she lifted her head to meet his gaze, his eyes were smoldering.

Leaning in, he slid a hand under her hair to cradle her neck and kissed her until her bare toes curled. A full minute later, he pulled away and she clutched at the door to keep from melting into the carpet at their feet.

"If I didn't have to get back to New York by morning," he murmured softly, rubbing her bottom lip with the pad of his thumb, "I'd drag you back to bed and keep you there for a week."

"If you didn't have to be back in New York by morning," she whispered in return, "I'd let you."

One corner of his mouth lifted in a subtle grin and his arm dropped to his side as he stepped through the doorway, onto the landing above the stairwell that led to the alley at the back of her dance studio.

"I'll call you."

She nodded, then stood at the top of the stairs as she always did to watch him walk away.

Two

Four months later—late April

The music from the studio sound system, mixed with the staccato beat of her students' feet on the hardwood floor, pounded through Misty's head, making her wonder if she'd manage to stay on her feet.

For months now, she'd been fighting dizziness, nausea and a laundry list of other symptoms associated with the early stages of pregnancy. She'd thought, with the first trimester out of the way, that she might start to feel better. Instead, she felt worse.

Today was especially bad. She'd barely been able to get out of bed, and ever since had been fighting waves of lightheadedness and the need to lie down.

But she had classes to teach, and if she missed even one, her plan to become self-sufficient and support herself on the income from her dance studio would be in jeopardy.

Three years ago Cullen had bought this building in Henderson, just outside Las Vegas, for her and had it completely refurbished, turning the downstairs into a studio large enough to teach both children and adults.

As much as she'd hated taking his charity, he'd insisted, and the condition of her knee at the time hadn't given her much choice. It was either accept Cullen's generosity or risk being homeless in a matter of weeks.

But she'd promised him—and herself—that she would pay him back. Every cent, once the studio became profitable.

Unfortunately, that had yet to happen. What she made on her classes went for the little things like food and electricity, but Cullen was still paying for the general upkeep of the building and business.

She hated that, hated feeling like a kept woman, a mistress, even though that was exactly what she was.

It wasn't her affair with him that made her uneasy, but the fact that he was supporting her financially. It felt too much like he was leaving money on the night-stand for services rendered.

She didn't have much choice, though, did she? The only way to get out from under the debt she owed Cullen was to make a success of the studio, and with a baby on the way, that was suddenly more important than ever. Especially since Cullen had no idea he was going to be a father in five more months.

Resting a hand over her slightly distended abdomen, she swallowed past the dizziness that seemed to be with her twenty-four/seven these days, along with the sense of guilt she felt more often than not at keeping her pregnancy a secret from Cullen.

It was better this way, she reminded herself. If Cullen knew about the baby, he would want to do the right thing. He would insist they get married, even though it was the last thing he really wanted.

He'd been raised to always be responsible and protect the family name. When his father had gotten his mother pregnant right out of high school, his grandfather had insisted they marry to give the child a name and keep from tarnishing the family's sterling reputation.

Misty didn't want to put Cullen in that position, didn't want to force him into a situation he would hate and later resent her for.

No, it was better this way. She'd been avoiding him for months, ever since the home pregnancy test—and later a blood test at the doctor's office— had confirmed her suspicions.

If only she could avoid him a while longer, until the studio began to operate on its own funds, everything would be all right. She would be able to begin paying him back all the money he'd invested in her, and he would eventually come to realize that his unanswered and unreturned calls meant she didn't want to see him anymore.

She hated to break things off with him so abruptly, but it was best for everyone.

He'd been good to her. Better, she'd often thought, than a girl like she deserved. Because of that, and because she really did care for him, she refused to saddle him with a wife and a child he probably didn't want and had never planned for.

Misty pushed herself away from the mirrored wall where she'd been standing—leaning, more like—as the music drew to an end and the dancers' steps slowed. She was only half paying attention, she realized, but at least she'd been watching closely enough to know the routine had gone off with barely a hitch. This was her adult class, so they caught on more quickly than the children.

"Good job, guys," she told them, clapping her hands together in approval. "Now this next time through, I'd like you to add…"

Her words trailed off as the room started to spin around her. She'd only taken one step toward the line of women who were awaiting her instructions, but her heart was beating as if she'd run a mile. Her mouth went suddenly dry and her skull felt ready to explode.

And then the floor seemed to tilt upward, closing in. Her vision narrowed into a tiny pinpoint of darkness, and she knew she was in trouble a tenth of a second before the world went dark.

* * *

Cullen sat in the Elliott family booth at his brother's restaurant. Une Nuit was Bryan's pride and joy. Located on Ninth Avenue, between Eighty-Sixth and Eighty-Seventh Streets in New York City, the trendy, very popular establishment specialized in French/Asian fusion cuisine and was often praised in reviews and articles alike for its daring menu. The low red lighting set a seductive cast to the black suede and copper décor.

At the moment, Cullen was sipping a cup of coffee—some fancy French creation Bryan was apparently trying out this week—and waiting for John Harlan to arrive for lunch.

They'd been friends forever, and after a game of golf on Saturday where John beat him by thirteen humiliating strokes, Cullen had started to think he might be willing to confide in his friend about the recent troubles he'd been having with Misty.

He wasn't sure he was ready to tell anyone about her, but since she wasn't answering his calls, and his feet were itching to fly out there and discover for himself what the hell was going on, he thought a little advice from a friend might not be out of the question.

If it hadn't been for this damn competition his grandfather, Patrick Elliott, had set up between his sons to decide who would take over as CEO of EPH upon his retirement, he likely would have flown out long before now. But he'd been so swamped with work, he'd barely gotten out of the office at all the past few months, let alone found enough time for a trip to Vegas.

"Can I join you?"

He turned his head, surprised to find his cousin Scarlet standing beside his booth. She was dressed in one of her usual outlandish outfits, but just like all the others, the bright colors and stylish design suited her flamboyant personality.

"Mmm." He looked past her, then back into her pale green eyes. "I'm expecting—"

"Me."

Harlan appeared, almost out of nowhere, and Cullen would have had to be blind not to notice the sudden nervousness emanating from his cousin's slender form.

"So, three for lunch, eh?" Stash, the restaurant's manager, asked in his cheerful French accent.

"No." Scarlet stumbled back a step, bumping into John. John caught her by the elbows, keeping hold of her a moment longer than Cullen would have expected for mere acquaintances.

Before he could ask or even speculate as to what was going on between his cousin and John Harlan, his cell phone rang. He glanced at the caller ID screen, his stomach turning over at the number on the lighted display.

It was Misty, calling from the dance studio phone.

He'd been trying for months to reach her. He'd left dozens of messages, but she'd never called him back.

It was just an affair. One he'd intended to break off years ago. But having Misty avoid him, suspect-

ing she was doing so in the hopes of breaking things
off with him…

He didn't like it. And for some reason, it made him
even more desperate to talk to her, see her.

He flipped his phone open before the second chirp
ended. "Hello?"

"Mr. Elliott?" a voice questioned tentatively from
the other end of the line.

It wasn't Misty, after all. But how would someone
else, someone from Misty's studio, get his private
mobile number?

With a frown, he said, "Yes."

"Umm…"

The woman, whoever she was, sounded even
more nervous than before.

"My name is Kendra. I'm one of Misty's dance
students."

"Yes," he said again, still confused.

"Well, umm…there's been a bit of an accident,
and your number was the first on her speed dial. We
didn't know who else to call."

"What?" His voice rose and he sat up straighter
in the black suede booth, leaning forward on the copper-topped table. His brain was stuck on the word
accident, barely processing anything else the woman
said. "What happened?"

"She collapsed during our class, and—"

"How is she?" he demanded.

"I'm not sure. We called an ambulance, but—"

"Where'd they take her?"

"St. Rose Dominican Hospital."

With a sharp nod meant more for himself than anyone else, he barked, "I'll be there as soon as I can. If you learn anything more, call me immediately at this number, do you understand?"

Once the woman agreed, he said a curt goodbye, snapped his phone shut and rose from the booth all in one swift motion.

"I can't stay."

"What's wrong?" Scarlet asked. "Who's hurt?"

"No one you know." No one his family even knew about.

Meeting John's gaze, he apologized to the man for wasting his time. "Sorry. I appreciate your coming, but I need to get to Las Vegas."

"No problem. Anything I can do?"

"I'll let you know," Cullen replied through tight lips, already heading for the door. "Thanks."

Due in large part to the Elliott family jet and the pilot's awareness of Cullen's desperation to reach Henderson, Nevada, as quickly as possible, he arrived at the hospital just over five hours later.

He burst through the emergency room doors and made a beeline for the nurses' station, demanding an update on Misty's condition and to be taken to her. The nurse on duty—apparently used to frantic and distraught loved ones—looked up Misty's name on the computer, then gave him a room number and pointed him toward the elevators.

He took it as a good sign that she'd been moved from the emergency room to a regular room. And the nurse hadn't mentioned anything about the Intensive Care Unit.

Then again, wouldn't it have been better for Misty to have been treated and released?

His nerves jangled as he rode the elevator up to the third floor, his pulse racing in fear. He stepped out the minute the doors slid open and grabbed a passing nurse.

"Misty Vale," he demanded. "I'm looking for Misty Vale."

The young brunette smiled and turned back the way she'd come, leaving him to follow. "I just checked on her. She's fine. Resting. Poor thing, she just overdid it, plain and simple. Working too hard, not getting enough rest. And a woman can't keep that up, not in her condition."

Cullen barely listened to the nurse's one-sided conversation. He barely cared what was wrong with Misty; he just wanted to see her, to know she was all right.

The nurse paused at a closed door, the narrow vertical window above the knob too small to see much inside.

"Don't you worry," the nurse said, patting his arm. "She and the baby are both fine."

Leaving him alone outside Misty's room, she turned and padded back down the hallway.

Baby?

His mind raced, his mouth growing dry.

Baby?

His breathing grew ragged and his palms, he noticed, had begun to sweat.

What baby?

He felt as though his brain was about to explode, his fear for Misty's health mixing now with the news that there was a baby.

Misty's baby.

His baby?

He shook his head, knowing nothing would make sense until he saw Misty with his own two eyes.

Twisting the knob, he pushed the door open and stepped quietly into the darkened room. A low watt fluorescent light was on over an empty bed, the privacy screen pulled to keep it from bothering the sleeping patient.

Cullen tiptoed across the squeaky clean floor until he could see Misty, lying pale against the stark white sheets, her brown hair with its blond highlights the only splash of color in the room. An I.V. tube was taped to the back of her hand and monitors flashed and beeped, tracking her condition.

But what caught his attention, what sent a cold chill snaking down his spine, was the slight bulge of her abdomen beneath the plain cotton sheet.

She and the baby are both fine.

She and the baby...

My God, Misty really was pregnant.

He swallowed hard, not knowing quite what to think as he moved closer to her bedside.

A part of him wanted to be angry with her. Angry that she'd been avoiding him for the past three months. Of course, now he knew why.

Angry that she hadn't told him when she'd discovered the pregnancy, whether it was his child or not. But it was hard to hang on to his anger when she looked so small and vulnerable.

Lifting a chair from the corner, he carried it closer and sat at her side, wrapping his fingers around her still hand. His gaze floated over her face, eyes closed, lips parted gently in sleep. Down to her breasts, which seemed a bit fuller than he remembered. Then on to her belly, where their child rested.

Was there ever really any doubt that it was his baby? No.

As easy as it might be for many men to jump to the conclusion that their pregnant lovers had been sleeping with someone else, Cullen didn't consider it a real possibility.

Throughout their affair, they'd agreed to keep things open. He had certainly dated his fair share of other women, and he knew Misty had gone out a few times, too.

But he didn't think she'd slept with other men in the time they'd been together. It wasn't arrogance on his part, merely his belief that he'd gotten to know Misty pretty darn well in the past four years.

If she'd been sleeping with someone else, she'd have either mentioned it or found it hard to look him in the eye on his frequent visits. After all, she spoke quite openly of the times she'd been asked out by the occasional man and had agreed to go to dinner with him.

Cullen, on the other hand, didn't share the details of his frequent exploits with her. For one thing, they didn't lead to sex as often as he let people believe.

His family was wealthy, its members well-known and easily recognized in the Manhattan area. And he was the playboy of the family, the one who always had a beautiful young woman on his arm.

He'd escorted models, actresses, centerfolds, lawyers, ad executives, boutique owners… You name it, he'd dated it. Just as was expected. And for the better part of his twenty-seven years, he thoroughly enjoyed that lifestyle.

But there hadn't been as many women lately as one might expect. More and more, he found himself distracted by thoughts of Misty. By the desire to be with her and no one else.

He would almost rather go without a woman on his arm—or in his bed—and wait to see her again than be surrounded by attractive, willing females twenty-four hours a day.

Keeping one hand curled tightly around hers, he slid his other along the sheet that covered her to rest on the mound of her tummy.

He felt her stir and tilted his head to meet her eyes. They were a darker green than usual, clouded with distress.

"Cullen," she whispered, her voice scratchy from disuse. "What are you doing here?"

"I heard you weren't feeling well. Thought I'd drop by with some chicken soup."

For a moment, the corners of her mouth tipped up in a grin, but the aura of concern never left her face.

"How are you feeling?" he asked, hoping to distract her.

She blinked, her glance sliding away for a brief slip of time and then back. "I've been better."

"Misty…" He waited until he had her full attention, then flexed his fingers over her stomach so she would have no doubt what he was talking about. "Why didn't you tell me?"

Her eyes filled with tears, and her lower lip trembled. Cullen fought the urge to jump to his feet and gather her into his arms. He wanted nothing more than to comfort her, tell her everything would be all right, but he needed to hear her answer first. Needed to know why she'd kept such a huge secret from him for so long.

"I'm sorry," she said. Her voice trembled and she sniffed once before continuing. "I didn't know how to tell you, and the last thing I wanted was for you to feel obligated."

"Obligated?" he repeated, struggling to keep any sign of irritation from slipping into his tone. "It is my child, isn't it?"

Misty's chest rose as she took a deep breath, her chin lifting a notch. "Yes."

He'd thought her response would bring a sense of relief, but instead he felt nothing. Because he'd *known*. He hadn't needed to ask.

With a sharp nod, he sat up a bit straighter in his chair. There was a lot more he needed to know, but she didn't look in any shape for an inquisition right now.

"It's all right," he told her, squeezing her fingers and brushing his other hand over her brow and through her hair. "We'll talk later. For now, you should rest."

She looked unconvinced, but didn't argue. And soon enough, her eyelids began to droop.

He stayed with her until she fell asleep, thanking God that she and the baby were okay, and trying to formulate a plan for what needed to happen next.

Consulting with the doctor was at the top of his list. He wanted to know exactly what had happened to send her to the hospital in the first place, along with any treatment or special instructions she might need to follow.

Next was to get her home. She would be more comfortable there, as would he.

And then, after those two things were taken care of, he could move on to the really difficult part of his plan.

Convincing Misty to marry him.

Three

Misty entered her apartment two days later, keenly aware of Cullen's arm at her waist. He'd been with her practically every second since he'd first arrived at the hospital—solicitous and concerned.

His dark blue suit was wrinkled after two full days of wear. He kept extra clothes at her place, but he apparently hadn't left her side long enough to drop by and change, though it wouldn't have taken more than half an hour. He'd eaten meals in the room with her, and any time she'd opened her eyes during the night, it was to find him slouched down in an uncomfortable visitor's chair, still keeping watch over her, even in sleep.

It hurt her to realize he was being so sweet and

selfless after she'd spent the last three months avoiding and lying to him.

The guilt hit her like a punch to the gut, causing her to miss a step and stumble slightly. Cullen was there in an instant, catching her up and holding her steady with his strong hands cupping her elbows.

"Easy," he warned, his voice soft and caring as he guided her the rest of the way to the living room sofa.

After easing her down onto the overstuffed cushions, he stepped back and laid the plastic shopping bag that held her personal items on the coffee table.

She'd found out from one of the nurses that he'd paid her to run out on her lunch hour and buy some new clothes for Misty to wear when she was released so she wouldn't have to leave in the tights and leotard she'd been wearing when she was admitted.

"The doctor said you need to rest," Cullen told her, shrugging out of his suit jacket and tossing it over the back of a nearby armchair. "That means you lie down here or in bed. Whatever you need, you let me know. Understood?"

She bit back a smile. This must be what he was like at the *Snap* offices—the confident, commanding executive others saw in the boardroom and at his family's company, Elliott Publication Holdings.

"Yes, sir," she responded with a two-fingered salute.

His brows drew together in a scowl, which only amused her more, but he'd been so good to her, she didn't want him to think she didn't appreciate everything he was doing for her.

Kicking off the sandals that were a touch too large for her, she drew her legs up and stretched out along the full length of the sofa.

Cullen was there, almost before she could blink, fluffing a throw pillow and situating it beneath her head. "Good?" he asked.

When she nodded, he stepped away again.

"What else do you need? Are you hungry? Would you like some toast and tea? Maybe a glass of milk?"

He rocked back on his heels, hands stuffed into the pockets of his rumpled slacks. His hair was mussed, separated in several different places as though he'd been running agitated fingers through the dark locks on a regular basis, and his jaw was shadowed with two days' growth of beard.

She'd really had him worried, and knew she owed him more of an explanation than their brief conversation her first night in the hospital had allowed. Which he'd been polite enough not to bring up again.

Shaking her head, she said, "I'm fine. You look like you could stand to shower and change clothes, though. Why don't you go get cleaned up? I'll stay right here until you're finished. I promise."

His face remained impassive, unconvinced. She smiled, relieved when his shoulders seemed to relax and his eyes softened.

He pulled his hands out of his pockets and scratched absently at his chest. "You sure?"

"I'm sure," she said, offering an encouraging nod.

"All right." He stuck around for another few

seconds, then turned resolutely on his heel and skirted around the living room furniture on his way to the bedroom and master bath.

For the next twenty minutes, Misty lay perfectly still, not tired, but confused knowing that she couldn't break her promise to remain where she was until he got back. Her head ached, and she didn't think it was from the exhaustion that had landed her in the hospital to begin with.

No, she was preoccupied and stressed because she had no idea how things between Cullen and her would play out.

She hadn't wanted him to know about the baby because she suspected he would have had one of two reactions. Either he would be appalled and go running in the opposite direction as fast as modern technology could carry him, or his huge responsibility streak would kick in and he'd insist on taking care of her and their child, at least financially.

She had no doubt he could afford to give this baby the best of everything. The best clothes, the best education, the best toys. Misty could never compete on the modest amount she made with the dance studio...that is, if Cullen allowed her to keep it.

And even though it frightened her to think such a thing, the fact remained that he had the wealth and power to take this child from her, if he so desired.

What if he decided he didn't want to be with *her* anymore, but did want the baby?

What if he decided he wanted the baby to be raised

in New York, with all the respectability and privilege he and his family could provide?

What if he didn't have a problem with the mother of his child being an ex-showgirl, but when he told his family about her and the child they'd conceived illegitimately, they threw a fit and insisted he bring the baby home—without her?

The possibilities rolled through her brain like a dust storm, each one worse than the last.

Cullen was a good man, one of the best she'd ever met. He didn't treat her like an ex-showgirl, which some men equated with an ex-stripper or ex-prostitute.

But their relationship had never exactly been normal. She was a kept woman, plain and simple. And that was okay with her; she'd always been all right with it.

Because she was also self-assured and self-reliant, she'd made a conscious decision to begin an affair with Cullen. To become his mistress.

Getting pregnant changed everything. The un-written rules they'd established along the way no longer applied.

And while her heart told her Cullen was a decent, caring guy, her brain continued to warn that he was an Elliott. A big, rich, powerful Elliott…and as far as his family would be concerned, she was a big, fat nobody.

She was the daughter of a showgirl who'd grown up to be a showgirl herself. Which was exactly what she'd always wanted. From the time she was a little girl, growing up backstage at some of the most glamorous casinos on the Vegas Strip, all she'd ever wanted was to grow up and follow in her mother's sequined, stiletto shoes.

What she *hadn't* wanted was to end up married and divorced several times like her mother, who was currently on husband number four. Happily, having the time of her life, but Misty had still hoped to avoid that particular habit.

She also hadn't intended to be a single mother, but it looked like that was the future she'd mapped out for herself by hooking up with a man to become his mistress and managing to get herself pregnant in the process.

She groaned aloud at the entire mess.

"What's wrong?"

Cullen's deep worried voice from behind her made her jump and twist around on the couch.

"You scared me," she said, her hand over her heart, which was pounding against her rib cage.

"Are you okay?" he demanded, stalking forward.

"I'm fine."

"You moaned."

"Technically," she told him, "I groaned."

Shifting around until she was lying flat on her back, she cast her gaze downward and ran a hand over the swell of her belly, where their child rested. She'd felt it move already, fluttering around inside her womb, reminding her that it was a living being, soon to be kicking and crying and needing her to take the very best care of him or her.

"I was just thinking about what a mess I've made of things. That's groan-worthy, wouldn't you say?"

He came around, hair still dripping, and took a seat in the chair directly across from her. She didn't have to move a muscle in order to meet him eye-to-eye.

He was barefoot, wearing a pair of worn, comfortable jeans and a maroon polo shirt. It was one of his favorite outfits, and he wore it often when he stayed with her for more than a few hours.

It was one of her favorites, too. He looked approachable and normal, and whenever she saw it, she knew she'd have a bit more time with him.

"Don't be so hard on yourself. You weren't exactly alone in the process."

She lowered her gaze, not sure what to say to that.

"We should probably talk about it, don't you think?"

Taking a deep breath, she nodded. "I know you must have a lot of questions."

"I do." Leaning forward, he braced his forearms on his thighs and clasped his hands together. "How far along are you?"

"Sixteen weeks."

His eyes narrowed as his mind worked through the math. "That's four months. Right around the last time we were together."

She swallowed hard, inclining her head for fear anything she tried to say would come out as a strangled squeak.

"When did you find out?"

"About a month later."

A beat passed while he considered that, a slight tick pulling taut the skin of his newly shaved jaw.

"I guess that explains why you stopped taking my calls and never answered any of the messages I left."

"I'm sorry." Drawing herself into a sitting position, she stuffed the pillow against the arm of the sofa and leaned back. "I know that was terrible of me, but I was just so…confused. At first I didn't even believe it. We've always been so careful except for that one time we forgot to use a condom at first. But no matter how many of those home pregnancy tests I took, they all came out the same. Even after I saw the doctor, I think I was still in denial. And I knew that if we spoke, you'd notice something was going on just from the tone of my voice."

She sighed, linking her own fingers in her lap to keep from fidgeting. "I didn't want to lie and say nothing was wrong, so I took the coward's way out and said nothing."

"You were avoiding me?"

"Yes," she admitted, the word coming out breathy with guilt.

"Don't you think I had a right to know?"

The question vibrated with barely concealed anger, snaking around her spine and making her shiver.

"Of course you did. You had every right. My only excuse for not telling you as soon as I found out was that I was afraid. And, if you can believe it, I was trying to protect you."

"Protect me?" he scoffed, jumping to his feet and

beginning to pace. Those long tanned fingers drove through his hair before coming down to settle on his denim-clad hips.

"Yes," she said, with more passion than she had realized she felt on the issue. "Cullen, you're twenty-seven years old. You're an Elliott, the director of sales for one of your family's most successful magazines. You're too young to be tied down by a washed-up dancer with a bum knee and a child you never signed on for. Your family wouldn't thank you for the bad press such a relationship would bring if the media ever found out."

He'd stopped pacing and was now glaring at her hard enough to bore holes through her forehead.

"Do you think I give a *damn* about a few newspaper headlines?"

"Maybe not now," she cautioned, "but how will you feel later, when your family starts to blame you for the damage you've done to their sterling reputation by getting involved with someone like me?"

Cullen narrowed his eyes and consciously tried to unclench his teeth before they were gritted to nubs. He couldn't decide which was closer to the boiling point—his annoyance or his blood pressure.

He hated to hear her talk about herself that way, making an issue of the fact that she was older than he was and assuming his family would disapprove of her simply because she used to be a showgirl on the Las Vegas Strip.

Although, on that last point, she was probably

right. His grandfather, especially, would be livid if he came home with an ex-showgirl mistress and an illegitimate child.

But then again, when was Patrick Elliott ever content with his family's behavior? Nothing any of them did seemed to garner the old man's approval. Cullen, for one, was tired of trying.

And he knew the rest of the family probably felt the same. They didn't so much respect the elder Elliott as they gave him a wide berth and avoided his condemnation as much as possible.

"Someone like you, huh?" His teeth were still clenched so tightly they ached, and if Misty was paying attention, she'd realize just how close he was to the end of his rope.

But she didn't appear to notice. She simply looked up at him with those bright green, almond-shaped eyes that drew him like a moth to a flame.

"We both know I've always been just an amusing pastime for you," she replied quietly. "Our relationship was never meant to become permanent, and I won't change the rules on you now."

One...two...

His nostrils flared as he inhaled sharply.

Three...four...

In. Out.

Five...six...

Inhale. Exhale.

Seven...eight...

If he kept breathing, kept counting, maybe the

curtain of red that fluttered at the edges of his vision would dissipate and he would no longer feel such a strong urge to put his fist through the nearest wall.

Nine...ten...

"Number one," he forced himself to say in a calm, even voice, "you were not just an amusing pastime. I admit things started out hot and heavy between us, and we got involved mostly because the sex was great. But I can get sex at home; I don't need to fly nearly three thousand miles every couple of months for a good lay."

She cringed at his crude language, but didn't interrupt. Good thing, because even the pain of his nails digging into the palms of his fisted hands didn't lessen the fury roiling in his gut.

"Number two, regardless of what our relationship may or may not have been up to now, the rules *have* changed. You're pregnant with my baby, and whether you like it or not, that changes everything.

"Number three, I love my family. I would never do anything to deliberately hurt or embarrass them, but they don't dictate the direction of my life. I make my own decisions. Is that clear?"

Her tongue darted out to wet her dusky pink lips, and he had to remind himself to hold on to his anger instead of stalking over to the sofa and kissing her silly the way his wayward libido wanted him to.

"Is that clear?" he asked again, with just enough sting to hold her attention and draw his own focus back to the matter at hand.

She nodded. It wasn't the most self-assured gesture he'd ever seen her make, but it was enough.

"Good." He loosened the fists at his sides, flexing his fingers to return feeling to the tingling digits. "Because I've made a decision. Not for my family and not out of some misplaced sense of responsibility. For me."

He waited a beat and then told her flat out, "We're getting married."

The color washed from her face until she was paler than she'd been when he'd first walked into her hospital room.

She gasped, her hand at her throat. "Cullen—"

"No," he said, cutting her off. Moving to the chair he'd occupied earlier, he perched on its edge and leaned toward her. "Don't argue, just listen. I want this baby, Misty. It's my child, as much a part of me as it is a part of you. I've already missed the first four months of your pregnancy—I don't want to miss any more. I want to be there every step of the way. I want to rub your feet when your ankles swell, bring you pickles and ice cream at three in the morning and hold your hand during the delivery. More importantly, I want to see the baby every day, not just on weekends or whenever I can manage to fly out here. And the best way to do that is for us to get married."

"Cullen—"

"Marry me, Misty."

Her eyes never left his, and he could have sworn he saw the glitter of tears along her lower lashes. His heart stuttered in his chest, and his mouth went dry as he awaited her answer.

Who could have known doing the right thing, laying claim to his child, would be so damned nerve-racking?

He watched her lips part, begin to move, but nothing could have prepared him for her answer when it finally came.

"I'm sorry, Cullen, I can't."

Four

Misty's heart broke a little more with each word she uttered, her stomach churning as she saw the impact they had on the man sitting across from her. His lips flattened and his expression turned stony.

She was hurting him, when that was the last thing she ever wanted to do. Didn't he understand? Didn't he realize that marrying her would ruin him?

She would step in front of a bus before she'd ever knowingly do anything to cause Cullen pain or humiliation. And whether he realized it or not, marrying her was a one-way ticket to both.

Besides, no matter what Cullen said, she didn't believe his deep sense of duty played no part in his offer. She knew perfectly well that Bryan, his brother, was the result of an unplanned pregnancy. His father had gotten his mother pregnant at age eighteen, and Cullen's grandfather had forced them to marry. But after twelve years of marriage and two children, they'd divorced.

Misty didn't want that for herself or for her child. And she didn't want Cullen sacrificing his happiness and future because of the guilt and responsibility that had been drilled into him from childhood.

She implored him with her eyes to recognize where she was coming from. "Please don't be angry, Cullen. It's a very sweet offer, and I know you're doing what you think is best, but I won't marry you just because the condom broke or we got a little careless."

Resting a splayed hand on her belly, she told him, "I want this baby, too. I'll be a good mother, and you don't ever have to worry that I'll deny you custody or any of your rights as a father. I would never do that."

He studied her for long minutes like a bug under a microscope. Her pulse quickened and she found herself squirming nervously at his close scrutiny. She couldn't even begin to guess what he was thinking or what his response might be.

"Have you given any thought to the doctor's instructions?" he asked finally, obviously struggling to control his emotions. "If you're not careful, you'll wind up back in the hospital—or worse, lose this baby."

At the very thought, a cold chill whipped through her. She wrapped both arms around the innocent life resting safely in her womb and hunched over slightly, her protective instincts already kicking in.

"I won't lose this baby," she said, and it was both a promise and a prayer.

"You will if you keep pushing yourself. The doctor said you collapsed from exhaustion and dehydration. The student from your class who called to tell me you were being rushed to the emergency room said you've doubled up on some of your classes and had extra ads put in the local papers to drum up more business."

"I may have overdone it a bit," she admitted, "but I won't let it happen again."

The blue of his eyes flashed briefly like sapphires under glass. "Why were you doing it at all?"

There it was, the sixty-four thousand dollar question. She took a deep breath, then slowly exhaled.

"You know as well as I do that the studio is struggling. With a baby on the way, I thought it would be prudent to get as much money as possible coming in before I have to stop teaching altogether. Lord knows I can barely support myself right now, let alone a child. I don't even have enough to hire someone to come in and cover for me during the last few months of my pregnancy, until I can get back to teaching the classes myself."

"You think I wouldn't support my own child?" he growled, his brows snapping together in fury. "I've been supporting you well enough for the past three years. Did you expect me to suddenly cut you off because I found out you were pregnant?"

She sighed. As hard as she'd tried to avoid it, she'd managed to bring his anger at her back full throttle.

Sliding off the sofa, she crawled on her knees across the soft beige carpet to his side. She wrapped her arm around one of his legs, her fingers resting on his strong upper thigh.

"Of course not," she replied quietly. "I didn't mean it like that. But, Cullen, I can't keep letting you pay my bills forever. I appreciate everything you've done for me. God knows what would have happened to me after my knee injury if it hadn't been for you. But I told you from the very beginning that I would pay back every penny of the start-up costs you put into buying this building and renovating it so I could live and hold classes here. Not to mention the money you put into my checking account every month, since the studio is still operating in the red."

She frowned at that. If anything, the monthly stipend bothered her more than his setting her up to teach dance classes. It reminded her too vividly of her own inability to fully support herself, of her dependency on a man to put a roof over her head and food on the table, and of the true nature of her relationship with Cullen.

She was his mistress, and for all intents and purposes, he was her benefactor. It was a hard truth to swallow.

"I've told you before you don't have to repay me. It wasn't a loan, it was a gift."

"Hell of a gift," she muttered, only half under her

breath. She knew for a fact he'd put more than a hundred thousand dollars into helping her get the studio up and running, and that didn't include the generous chunk of money sitting in her bank account, earning interest even as they spoke.

"The point is," he said, stressing the words just enough to let her know he was changing the direction of the conversation, "you *aren't* going to be able to teach classes for much longer. You probably shouldn't be teaching at all, considering where it landed you the last time. And then what?"

She opened her mouth to speak, but he held up a hand to stop her and continued.

"I'm sorry, Misty, but I don't want to be a long-distance father. I don't want to be a long-distance father-to-be."

Her heart began to pound, her stomach rolling and pitching like an amusement park ride. "What do you want, then?"

He took a deep breath, his chest puffing out as air filled his lungs, and covered the hand she had on his leg with his own. His long fingers engulfed her much smaller ones, the heat of his palm soaking into her bloodstream warming every inch of her body.

"Come back to New York with me."

"What?" She sat back, startled. It was the last thing she'd expected to hear.

"Come to New York with me. You can't cancel classes and keep the studio open, but you can't continue teaching, either. And I know you, Misty.

Without something to do, you'll be bored out of your mind in a week."

He squeezed her hand, the simple action conveying the importance of his plea.

"So come to New York with me. It will be good for the baby. You need to rest, and my town house is quiet and comfortable. Plus, I'll be there to wait on you hand and foot."

For the first time, she felt a stirring of amusement. "Hand and foot, huh?"

A suggestive sparkle lit his eyes. He slid his fingers beneath her hand and turned it palm up before lifting it to his mouth.

"Hand," he whispered, pressing a kiss to the very center, "and foot."

He molded his lips to the tip of one finger, sucking it gently into his mouth. A tidal wave of desire washed over her, sending her insides quivering. If she hadn't already been sitting, heels propped against her bottom, she thought for sure she would have slid to the floor in a puddle of raw nerve endings.

"Misty?" he asked softly. "Are you listening?"

It took a moment for his words to sink in, and another moment to find her voice. Even then, all she could manage was a weak, "Mmm-hmm."

"Another reason I'd like you to fly back with me is to meet my parents. Now that they're going to be grandparents, I'd like you to get to know each other."

The haze of longing clouding her vision slowly

began to clear. His parents? He wanted her to meet his parents?

Dear God, she could just picture the introductions. *Mom, Dad, this is Misty, my pregnant ex-showgirl mistress.* Their eyes would bug out and their mouths would drop open...but only long enough for them to collect their wits and start in with the hostile glares at her and the lectures to Cullen about mixing his Elliott blue blood with that of a dancer of questionable breeding and obviously low morals.

She'd rather walk naked down the crowded Vegas Strip.

"Come on, Misty," he cajoled. "You owe me."

Her eyes widened. "*That's* what you expect in trade for everything you've done for me?" she asked, incredulous.

"I meant, you owe me a few considerations for keeping this baby a secret from me for the past four months."

Well, he had her there. But still...*meeting his parents?* Wasn't that a bit above and beyond?

"Besides," he went on, "it doesn't have to be forever. Consider it a short vacation. You can come back here any time you want."

Still holding her hands, he got to his feet, pulling her up beside him. He drew her close and she went willingly, because it was where she felt safest, most comfortable.

Being in his arms was like sinking into a warm, scented bubble bath after a long night of dancing under blazing hot stage lights in four-inch heels and a headdress that weighed as much as a small car. Only better.

"And you never know," he murmured next to her ear while he caressed the swell of her waist. "Maybe seeing where I live and meeting my family will change your mind about accepting my proposal."

Leaning back, she met his hopeful, expectant gaze and made her decision. For better or for worse, she did owe him something for keeping the pregnancy a secret for so long, and for all he'd done for her over the years—not the least of which was making her feel protected and special.

"I'll go with you to New York," she told him, and was rewarded with a wide smile that revealed a row of straight white teeth, as well as his pure, unadulterated happiness.

"But I won't marry you," she cautioned before he could get carried away. She waved a pointed finger under his nose for emphasis. "That's not part of the bargain."

His grin didn't waver as he lowered his head and covered her mouth with his own. "We'll see."

Once Misty had agreed to accompany Cullen back to Manhattan, he wasted no time putting the wheels in motion.

He called the pilot of his family's private jet to let him know they would be wanting to leave first thing in the morning, made arrangements for someone to take over the classes at her studio, then carried Misty to the bedroom and deposited her on the mattress near the headboard, pillows propped behind her back.

No matter how much she protested that she was well enough to pack her own bag, he wouldn't hear of it. She had to sit there, watching and talking him in the right direction as he pulled her suitcase out of the closet and proceeded to fill it.

She didn't know whether to laugh or cringe at the way he stuffed her things together without folding, without giving a thought to the fact that the heels of her shoes might snag the delicate fabric of her skirts and blouses. When she pointed it out, he made a valiant effort to fix the problem, but eventually gave up, telling her that he would replace anything that got damaged in transit.

And even though they'd been sleeping together for four years, sharing the intimacies of a married couple, she was amazed to find that she still blushed to see him sorting through her lingerie drawers. He seemed to take great pleasure in picking which items she would take with her to New York, waggling his eyebrows and leering until she doubled over in laughter.

When he was finished, he zipped the suitcase closed and set it aside, then helped her change for bed. Climbing in beside her, he stroked her hair and held her until they both drifted to sleep.

The next morning, they drove to the airstrip in his rental car, and five hours later landed on the East Coast.

The trip passed with surprising ease, a thousand

times more comfortable and quiet than a commercial flight would have been. Cullen even made sure there was food on board so she would have a meal before they landed.

But everything about the posh plane and Cullen's solicitousness only served to remind her of how very out of place she would be in his world. She didn't need to worry about how long she could stand to stay with him at his Upper West Side town house. After a week, he and his family would likely be begging her to leave and forget she'd ever heard the Elliott name.

She'd slept on the plane, so by the time they arrived at his place, she was wide awake and practically shaking with nerves. Why she was so anxious about simply seeing where he lived, she wasn't sure.

A part of her expected to find a brood of Elliotts on the other side of the door, their eyes filled with condemnation, ready to attack. Another part of her thought it was probably the simple act of moving in with him—even for the short term—that had her palms shaking and her knees quaking.

He wanted her to meet his parents. He wanted to be an active participant in the remainder of her pregnancy and in their child's life. That all felt entirely too…domestic to her. Too much as though once she dipped her toes into the pool of his personal life, she would never be able to get out.

It might be a step up for her, but not for Cullen, and she had no intention of dragging him down. If he married her, he would become a laughingstock within his circle of friends, not to mention lose the respect of his peers at EPH and in the business world.

No, she would never put him in such a position. She cared too much about him.

He helped her out of the luxurious black Town Car he'd arranged to have pick them up at the airport, then scooped her into his arms and carried her up the front steps of his well-maintained brownstone.

Setting her on her feet, he dug his keys out of his pocket, then took her hand and led her inside, leaving the door open for the driver to follow with their bags. When that was done, he tipped the man and locked the door again after seeing him out.

He turned back, his mouth curled in a soft smile, his fingers buried in the front pockets of the same jeans he'd worn at her apartment.

"I like your house," she told him, glancing around a second time at her surroundings.

It was obvious someone of considerable wealth lived here, but the place wasn't quite as opulent as she'd expected. Instead, what she could see looked useful and lived-in.

The floors were hardwood, polished to a glossy sheen. Large rooms sat off to either side of the doorway and small foyer.

One was a living room area, complete with a large-screen plasma television, black leather sofa and chairs and a stereo on the shelves along the far wall.

The other room seemed to be Cullen's home

office. A desk stood at the far end of the room, complete with a computer, phone and lamp. The wall shelving on this side of the house was filled with books of all shapes and sizes, and there was even a window seat facing the street where a person could curl up to read on a rainy afternoon.

"Thanks," Cullen said, coming up behind her and curling his hands over her bare shoulders. "I want you to consider this your house, too. Make yourself at home. Snoop around, if you want, so you know where everything is. And if there's anything you need, don't be afraid to ask."

She nodded slightly, but knew she would only ever feel like a guest here.

"Are you tired?" he asked, rubbing the nape of her neck with the pads of his long, strong fingers.

"Not really," she answered, but she couldn't help moaning at the bone-melting sensations he was creating with his talented hands. Her head fell forward and her eyes slid shut.

"In that case, why don't we get you unpacked and settled in?"

His arms dropped back to his sides and he took a step away. She straightened, biting back a moan at the loss of his mesmerizing attentions.

"Then maybe we can crawl into bed," he added.

"I told you, I'm not very tired. I slept on the plane."

One black brow winged upward and a devilish glint lit his blue eyes. "Who said anything about sleeping?"

Five

Cullen sat at the foot of his bed, listening to the sounds of Misty moving around in the bathroom. Every few seconds, he caught a glimpse of her as she set something on the sink or rearranged his toiletries to make room for her own bottles and jars.

It had taken him half the night to convince her to unpack fully and make herself at home, rather than leaving her clothes in her suitcase or in only one drawer, and her makeup and beauty items in their case on the nightstand.

Now she was putting things where they would be if she lived here, but she was doing it reluctantly.

He drew a deep breath and rubbed the lines

forming across his brow. This was going to be more complicated than he'd thought.

Misty and the baby belonged with him. He wanted them in his house, in his life…but he wanted them to *want* to be there.

From the expression on Misty's face every time he made a remark about incorporating her into his home or family, he wasn't sure that would ever happen.

The noises from the master bath died down and he lifted his head to find Misty standing in the doorway. She looked nothing like the woman he'd first seen on that Las Vegas casino stage four years ago.

Then, she'd worn a skimpy, sequined costume that showed off all of her hot feminine assets to perfection and caught his attention faster than a flare gun being fired next to his ear.

Now, she looked like a PTA mother or Manhattan socialite—the sexy kind that got every man's temperature rising and every woman sharpening her claws. And he should know; he'd known his fair share of both.

If she thought she wouldn't fit in with his family, with his lifestyle, or just here in New York, she was wrong. Misty could fit in anywhere in the world, primarily because she was the type of woman who forced the world to conform to her instead of the other way around. Vibrant, beautiful, self-assured. Except for this moment, when she looked nervous and unsure.

Pushing off the bed, he rose to his feet and took two steps in her direction. "Everything okay?"

She nodded, but her teeth worrying her lower lip belied the motion.

"I think so. I'm not sure you'll like where I put everything. I had a lot of stuff and had to move some of your things around."

"I'm sure it's fine."

She cast a glance over her shoulder and Cullen rolled his eyes, deciding he had to do something or she'd fret herself sick the rest of the night.

"Come here, Misty," he said softly.

Her gaze turned back, landing on him. Without question, she drifted toward him, her pink low heeled slides nearly disappearing in the tall thick nap of his bedroom carpet.

As soon as she was close enough, he reached out and engulfed her in both arms, pulling her snug against his chest. "Don't be nervous," he whispered into her hair. "You belong here. With me."

She didn't respond, but he felt the shudder roll through her body. He pressed a kiss to her temple, then her cheek, then her lips, a burst of pleasure filling his chest as she opened her mouth beneath his.

His fingers wound through her hair, holding her in place as their tongues parlayed. Every dormant hormone flared to life and started coursing through his bloodstream like a forest fire.

It had been four months. Four long, dry months when he'd dreamed of Misty, fantasized about taking her to bed, but had been unable to do so because she'd been avoiding his phone calls, hiding her pregnancy from him.

He waited for anger or annoyance or a need for revenge to rear its ugly head, but he felt nothing along those lines. Only lust and a protective instinct so sharp it nearly crippled him.

His hand slid down the line of her body, coming to rest on the mound of her belly. On his child.

He lifted his head, breathing heavily. "I want to make love to you, but I don't want to hurt you."

"You won't," she said, her voice thin and feathery.

With his left hand cupping her stomach, he brought his right hand around to cradle her face. "But I've never made love to you before while you were pregnant, and you just got out of the hospital."

She mimicked his posture, putting one hand at his waist and placing the other along his jaw. "I was in the hospital because I wasn't careful enough with my health, not because there was something wrong with the baby. They kept me there until they were sure I was okay, and you've taken excellent care of me ever since. You won't even let me walk around on my own, if you're there to carry me," she added with a teasing grin. "I'm fine. And I want you to make love to me."

His gut clenched until he thought he might double over with the impact her words had on him. She had humbled him, while at the same time making him feel like the most powerful man in the world. She treated him like a hero…her hero, and damned if he didn't want to be one for her.

He released her long enough to walk around the bed and fold back the covers, dimming the lights while he was there. When he returned to her side, he tipped her head back and kissed her, letting her know how much he wanted her, how he felt about her.

At the same time, they began to slowly undress. His hands slipped beneath the hem of her sweater, luxuriating in the silken smoothness of her waist as he pushed the top upward. Her fingers fiddled with the buttons at the front of his shirt, loosening them one by one.

Raising her arms, she allowed him to strip the top up and over her head. As soon as she was free of the garment, she returned the favor by running her hands over his bare chest and pushing his shirt off his shoulders. Her touch raised trails of blazing heat beneath his skin, causing his breath to catch.

She pressed her lips to the hollow at the base of his throat and Cullen had to clench his fists to keep from throwing her down on the bed and taking her like some hardened criminal newly released from prison.

He focused his attention instead on the front closure of her robin's-egg blue slacks, shucking them down her legs and letting her use his shoulders for balance while she stepped out of them, leaving her shoes on the carpet, as well.

Straightening once again, he took in her tall lush form. She was only a few inches shorter than his own six foot one, and she'd always been curvy enough to make a grown man weep.

But now, four months into her pregnancy, she looked positively mouthwatering. One part Madonna, one part sex kitten. Cullen wondered what he'd done in his life to deserve such a gift.

Beneath the lacy cups of her demure white bra, her breasts were larger than before, but it was her belly that drew his gaze. His child rested inside that hard, half-a-basketball-size mound.

Dropping to his knees, he settled his hands on either side of her waist, then leaned forward to press his lips to her taut skin. He had the sudden, inane urge to talk to the little life on the other side. To say hello and tell his child he couldn't wait to meet him or her. To promise his unconditional love and protection.

Instead, he tilted his face up, meeting her emerald eyes. "What does it feel like?" he asked in a low tone. "To be pregnant?"

For a minute, he thought she might laugh at such a ridiculous question. He should have known better. Misty would never mock another person's sincere, heartfelt emotions.

The tips of her fingers feathered his hair as she looked down at him, a small smile playing on her lips. "What part?" she wanted to know. "The morning sickness? The tender, enlarged breasts? Or the bizarre midnight cravings?"

"Everything. I want to know everything."

Still on his knees, he turned her until her back was to the bed, then shifted her around to sit on the end of the mattress. It wasn't easy to stay where he was, but he needed to hear this, needed to know what he'd missed.

"The morning sickness wasn't fun. I suffered with that from the moment I woke up in the morning until mid-afternoon every day for the first three months."

She made a face and the corners of his lips tugged upward.

"My breasts are getting bigger," she told him with a pointed look at her chest, "but I imagine you'll enjoy that. And they are tender, but not unbearably so. Just be careful."

He nodded. She didn't need to worry about that. She already felt like a porcelain doll in his big hands. He had no intention of doing anything that would hurt or even discomfort her.

"The cravings have been interesting. I've been told they'll get worse the farther along I am, but I've already found myself starving for strange things like asparagus and maraschino cherries." She lowered her gaze, her cheeks turning an attractive shade of pink. "And there was one time that I raided an all-night convenience store for powdered donuts. I bought every box they had of both the regular size and the minis, then went home and ate them all with about six glasses of milk while I watched re-runs of *I Love Lucy*."

He chuckled, imagining the sight of her curled up on the couch amidst an avalanche of white powder, and wished he could have been with her. Wished he could have been the one to run out at 3:00 a.m. to find whatever odd food item she was hungry for at that particular moment.

"What about the baby? How does it feel to have a brand-new life growing inside you?"

She licked her lips, her breasts rising as she drew a deep breath. "Do you really want to know?" she asked.

More than anything. "Of course."

"Terrifying."

His brows knitted in a frown. That wasn't at all the sort of answer he'd expected.

"Every day," she continued, "I wake up to find something else changed about my body. My breasts will be larger, my stomach will be rounder, my hands or ankles will be swollen. And then there's the thought of how little the baby is."

She splayed her hands over her middle, covering his own hand that still rested there.

"I know it's growing more every day, but it's still just a tiny, completely helpless being, relying on me to take care of it for nine whole months. I worry about everything I put in my mouth. About how much sleep I get, the shoes I wear, if I'm sitting too close to the television…"

Her expression turned earnest and she clutched at his wrists. "I mean, I've been so careful, honestly I have, but look what happened—I still ended up in the hospital. Can you imagine what might have happened if I hadn't been paying attention to every meal and every step I take?"

Tears filled her eyes as her voice drifted off, and he

reached up to dab the moisture from her lashes. "You're doing a great job," he reassured her. "You were just working too hard, and even that was for the baby."

Her lips continued to tremble, so he covered them with his own, hoping to kiss away any lingering doubts she might have about her abilities as a mother. He kept them light and comforting, sipping at the sweet nectar of her mouth rather than devouring her the way his libido urged.

When he pulled back, the uncertainty had fled her face, replaced by a simmering passion that mirrored his own.

"Have you felt the baby move yet?" he asked, not surprised when his voice came out rough and ragged.

She nodded, and the gesture sent a jolt of arousal straight to his groin.

"Will you let me know the next time it happens? I'd really like to be there, feel it for myself."

"Of course," she all but whispered.

It was enough. Now that he'd gotten the answers to his questions, they could move on to more pleasurable pursuits.

Shooting her a wicked grin, he rose to his feet, hooked her under the arms and lifted her farther back on the bed. He stretched out above her, admiring the view and thinking of all the things he wanted to do with her. They might not get through the entire list tonight, but they had time.

With luck, they would have a lot of time together.

He ran his fingers through her hair, spread in a

brown and blond halo around her head. "Have I told you lately how beautiful you are?"

Her lips turned up at the corners. "Not that I recall."

"How remiss of me," he murmured, kissing the slope of her shoulder.

He slipped his index finger under the strap of her bra and slowly drew it down her arm. Then he repeated the process on the other side.

"You are, you know. Beautiful."

She arched her back a little as he reached beneath her and released the set of hooks at her spine. The filigreed cups came loose from her voluptuous flesh and he removed the garment altogether, tossing it over the edge of the bed.

"I thought so the very first time I saw you. You were on stage with all those other dancers. Attractive women, every last one, but still you stood out."

She inhaled sharply as his fingers and then his tongue found a nipple and began to play.

"I saw you, too," she rasped. "Every once in a while, through a break in the lights, I would look out and there you were."

Her nails raked his biceps, her breaths coming in pants as he took turns licking and teasing the tender peaks of her breasts. He remembered what she'd said about their sensitivity and was careful to use just the right amount of pressure.

He slid his hands down, over her distended belly to her hips, catching the lace of her panties with his thumbs. She moved for him, helping him to get them down her legs and over her dainty feet with their rose-tipped toes.

"It's your turn to undress," she told him, when he returned to nibbling her lips. Her bare knee rubbed against his jeans.

"Mmm. Let me just take care of that. You will be here when I get back, won't you?" He shot her an errant grin, knowing full well he had her right where he wanted her.

"I'll try not to run off," she returned with a grin of her own.

While he moved off the bed, kicking away his shoes and socks and shrugging out of his pants, Misty wormed her way higher on the mattress. She fluffed the pillows at her back, reclining like an Egyptian princess awaiting the dutiful attentions of her myriad servants. If he'd had a bunch of grapes, he would have been more than happy to feed them to her one by one as he worshipped her ripe, luscious body.

But he didn't have any grapes, so he would have to simply worship.

Naked now, he crawled toward her, like a great cat stalking its prey. He didn't need a mirror to tell him his eyes burned with longing. He could feel it pulsating through every cell of his being, heating his blood, raising his temperature, sending pulses of desire to his already throbbing erection.

Kneeling in front of her, he pulled her up by her wrists. He stared at her for several long seconds, taking in her heart-shaped face, the glow of her em-

erald-green eyes and her velvet smooth lips, swollen
from his kisses.

Wrapping one hand around her neck, beneath the
curtain of her hair, he kissed her again. Devoured her
mouth, suckled her tongue. He could kiss her forever,
he thought, and never grow tired of her feel, her taste,
her scent.

His lips still locked with hers, he shifted his
weight until he was lying flat on the mattress, Misty
hovering above him. Her stomach nestled against
his, her breasts brushing his chest. She straddled his
hips, coming close enough for her feminine heat to
seep into his skin.

"It's been too long," he said, drawing her closer,
urging her to take him inside before he exploded.

"I know."

Reaching between their bodies, she caressed him,
making the breath hiss through his teeth and his hips
hitch off the bed, straining for more of her magical
touch. And then she slid down, taking him to the hilt.
She fit him like a glove and felt like heaven, surrounding him with her warm wetness.

Four months since he'd last tasted her sweet
mouth, cupped her full, bountiful breasts, had her
tight sheath clasped around him.

How had he ever survived that long without her?

How had he ever thought another woman could
take her place, or adequately fulfill his needs in
between trips to Las Vegas?

And it wasn't just the sex. His head arched into

the pillows and his mouth opened on a gasp as she rose up, then dropped back down, sending ripples of ecstasy coursing through his nervous system.

When he could breathe again—albeit raggedly—he realized his last thought before she'd sent his brain spinning was still true. The sex was great—fabulous, amazing, earth-shattering—no doubt about it. But there was more to this attraction than that.

He'd asked her to marry him back at her apartment because he thought it was the right thing to do for her and for the baby. But now…now he actually wanted it for himself, too.

Being saddled with Misty for the rest of his life wasn't the worst thing he could imagine. And having her in his bed each night would be the icing on the cake.

Bracing her hands on his chest, she increased her pace, driving all rational thought from his mind. He squeezed her hips, helping her to rise and fall, rise and fall. Faster, stronger. Her inner muscles clenched around him and he gritted his teeth to keep from flying apart too soon.

"Cullen," she moaned, tossing her head back so that her hair fell in glossy multicolored waves over her naked shoulders and biting her bottom lip so hard, it turned white.

"Misty," he returned with equal emotion.

She cried out again, a high-pitched sound that reverberated into his skin, his bones, his very soul. She shuddered above him, her nails curling like claws into his pectoral muscles as she came, and he followed her. Followed her into bliss...into their future.

When she started to collapse, he caught her and rolled them to their sides to accommodate her rounded belly.

"Well," she said, tiny beads of perspiration dotting her blushing cheeks and brow, "that was certainly an impressive way to welcome me to your home."

He chuckled, hugging her tighter and tucking strands of damp hair behind her ear with its sparkling blue-and-green stones dangling from the lobe.

"That wasn't welcome-to-my-home sex," he told her. "That was this-is-just-one-of-the-many-perks-you-can-expect-by-marrying-me sex."

He felt her stiffen in his arms even before he met her shimmering gaze, but didn't give her time to reply. "Marry me, Misty. Say yes."

Six

The lovely warmth of afterglow coursing through Misty's veins cooled at his words.

If only he knew how much she wanted to say yes.

Like most little girls, she'd spent much of her childhood and adolescence imagining her own personal happily ever after. Meeting her Prince Charming, having him sweep her up onto his white steed and carrying her off to a castle far, far away where they would live and love forever, just like a fairy tale.

But the older she'd gotten, the more she'd come to realize how much of a fantasy those daydreams had been. Men were only human, it seemed. There were very few princes in her kingdom, and many of them had more in common with the ogres who lived under the castle's drawbridge.

Cullen was definitely one of the better ones, more princely than most, but it didn't take Merlin to figure out how mismatched they were. She just wasn't the right princess for him.

Her lungs emptied on a resigned sigh as she traced patterns on his bare chest, avoiding his intense gaze. "Cullen, I told you before, I can't marry you."

Instead of arguing with her, as she'd expected, he merely shrugged one broad bronzed shoulder and said, "You can't blame a guy for trying."

She could, but she wouldn't. The fact was, even though she couldn't accept, she found his offer— *offers*—extremely flattering. And it only made her respect him more for wanting to give his child a real family and his very influential last name.

"Just…don't ask me again, okay?" she asked softly. It was too painful to be reminded of what she couldn't have, and she knew it was only going to get harder to turn him down.

"Sorry," he replied glibly, turning his body until he hovered above her and braced his weight on his strong muscled arms. "I can't make any promises."

And then he was kissing her, making her forget all her reasons for saying no.

The next morning Misty's pulse was racing and she was sweating as though she'd been sitting in a sauna for the past two hours. Her stomach lurched, and if she didn't know better, she would say she was suffering from morning sickness all over again.

This was terrible. Horrible. Pure torture. How could Cullen ask her to marry him one minute, then turn around and treat her this shabbily the next?

Meeting his parents. My God, what was he thinking?

When he popped his head in the bedroom door, she had the sudden urge to lob something at his head. Unfortunately, the only objects within reach were a drawer full of lacy undergarments. And he would probably like it if she tossed one of those at his face.

"You about ready?" he asked.

She glanced down at herself, standing in the middle of his bedroom wearing nothing but a pink bra and panties.

"Do I *look* ready?" she snapped, then felt immediately contrite. It wasn't his fault she was a nervous wreck. Although it *was* his fault she had to meet his parents.

The pregnant mistress being brought home to meet Mom and Dad. It was enough to cause heart palpitations.

Tears filled her eyes, but she turned away quickly before he noticed. She wanted to believe she was simply overly emotional because of the pregnancy, but knew it was more than that.

She was thoroughly terrified about what the next few hours would bring. Fires, floods, pestilence… The list went on and on in her head.

"Hey."

His soft low voice reached her from behind her left ear, and his hands sliding over her shoulders and down the length of her arms. Goosebumps broke out along the bare flesh.

"What's wrong?"

She gave a short bark of laugher. What *wasn't* wrong?

"I don't want to do this," she told him truthfully. "Your parents are going to hate me. They'll blame me for corrupting you, and accuse me of trying to trap you by getting pregnant, and I don't know what to wear to my own persecution." Her tirade ended on a high note, panic seeping into the words.

Cullen chuckled, rubbing her upper arms comfortingly. "Sweetheart, you're worrying for nothing. My folks are dying to meet you, and they are *not* going to treat you badly. I wouldn't allow it, even if they tried."

His reassurances were helping. Not putting an end to her fears altogether, but lightening the pressure around her lungs and diaphragm.

"Now, far be it from me to tell a woman what to wear, but as much as I'm personally enjoying your outfit, you might want to put on a few more clothes before Mom and Dad get here."

She gave a small squeak when she realized she was still in her underwear, jerking away from him and racing to the closet.

Of course, not a single thing she'd brought with

her seemed appropriate for meeting her lover's parents. At the moment, she doubted a nun's habit would have looked demure enough.

"I can't believe I let you pack for me," she ranted, her stress level rising once again. "All you brought is sexy lingerie. I can't meet your mother and father in sexy lingerie. What were you thinking?"

"I was thinking you look hot no matter what you're wearing."

He crossed the room, moving in front of her to sort through the closet's offerings. "Here, this isn't sexy lingerie."

She studied the skirt and top he was holding. It wasn't exactly demure, but it wasn't awful. A seashell pink skirt with a flounce at the bottom that would almost reach her knees, and a floral blouse with a plunging V-neckline and loose ruffled material at the shoulders in place of sleeves.

The front was a little low, but maybe she could pull it closed with a safety pin. And the pink, wine and brown floral pattern would go a long way toward camouflaging her expanding middle.

"All right," she said, taking a deep breath as she reached for the hanger.

"It even matches your bra and panties," Cullen announced proudly. "See, I'm not so bad at packing for you, after all."

Making a noncommittal sound at the back of her throat, she struggled into the skirt, fitting it around the bulk of her belly and straightening the seams.

Then she pulled the top over her head and hurried to the bathroom to check her reflection in the mirror.

She didn't look like a Mensa member, but she didn't look like the stereotypical ex-showgirl either. It would do.

Thankfully, she'd talked Cullen through the packing of her shoes and accessories, so she had chocolate-brown mules for her feet and gold hoops for her ears.

The doorbell rang just as she was arranging the earrings next to the diamond studs she rarely removed from her second holes. She jumped at the noise and began to panic all over again.

"That will be them," Cullen said, stepping into the bathroom with her.

He smiled encouragingly and pressed his lips to her cheek. "You look great. Take a deep breath and relax, then come down when you're ready, okay?"

She swallowed hard, taking that deep breath he had suggested. The chime sounded again as his foot-steps moved out of the room and down the stairs.

Her stomach rolled as if she were riding the Tilt-A-Whirl at the state fair, but she forced her fingers to put the finishing touches on her loose hair and stroke on one last coat of lipstick.

She could do this, she told herself. All she had to do was put one foot in front of the other and make her way downstairs…straight into the lion's den.

Despite his claims that Misty had nothing to worry about, Cullen had to admit he, too, was nervous about this meeting.

Soon after discovering that Misty was pregnant, he'd phoned both of his parents from the hospital to let them know they were going to be grandparents. Since Daniel and Amanda Elliott had divorced long ago, it had taken two separate calls and two separate confessions about his four-year-long affair with Misty.

His father had gotten himself into a similar situation at the age of eighteen and had been forced to marry his mother by his old-fashioned, overbearing father—Cullen's grandfather, Patrick Elliott. So in many ways, Cullen had expected a lecture.

He should have been more careful; he never should have gotten involved with a showgirl to begin with; she was likely nothing more than a manipulative gold-digger…. But since the horse was out of the barn, so to speak, it was time for Cullen to step up and do the responsible thing.

He'd expected to hear all of that and more from his father. Instead, Daniel had been sympathetic and understanding of the situation his son found himself in. He'd offered only one piece of advice: Do what you feel is right.

His father hadn't spoken the words, but his meaning was clear: He didn't want Cullen making the same mistakes he had, letting himself be forced or guilted into marriage simply because a child was involved.

Cullen got the feeling that if he married Misty, his father would be accepting of his decision. And if he decided to be a long-distance father, that would be okay, too.

The call to his mother had been very different in tone, but essentially the same. Amanda Elliott may have been a high-priced Manhattan attorney, but her voice had grown thick and waterlogged the minute she heard she was going to be a grandmother. She'd begged him to bring Misty to New York as soon as she was feeling well enough. Or, if that wasn't convenient, Amanda herself would fly to Las Vegas so they could meet.

The topic of marriage had never come up. Either because his mother expected him to do the right thing, or because it simply didn't matter to her. Only the impending grandchild mattered.

Then last night, after he and Misty had arrived at his town house, he'd phoned them each again while Misty was unpacking her things and invited them over to meet their future daughter-in-law. He hadn't said anything about his proposal or the fact that Misty had turned him down—twice.

After taking the steps two at a time, he crossed the small foyer to the front door and yanked it open before the bell could peal again. The sound was beginning to grate on his nerves, and he could only imagine the effect it was having on Misty.

His mother and father stood on the other side of the ornately carved door. It wasn't very often that he saw them together, and he was struck once again by what a handsome couple they made.

He'd come to terms with their divorce years ago, but the little boy in him still wished they could have made things work. That he and Bryan hadn't had to go through the emotional upheaval of their split.

He didn't want that for his child. If Misty ever agreed to marry him, he would move heaven and earth to make sure they stayed together.

"Hey, Mom. Dad." He stepped back and waved them inside.

"Oh, Cullen," his mother cried, throwing her arms around his neck and hugging him tight. "I'm so happy for you."

When she let go, he noticed the hint of moisture in her brown eyes. "I know all of this came as a surprise, but you're going to make a wonderful father."

"Thanks, Mom."

Covering her heart with her hand, she went on as though he hadn't even spoken. "And *I'll* finally get to be a grandmother."

Cullen turned to face his father. "Dad."

Daniel Elliott put his hand out to shake, then pulled Cullen close and patted his back in a supportive, fatherly gesture.

For a minute, Cullen thought he might tear up himself, but cleared his throat and was relieved when the sensation passed.

"So where is this young woman we're supposed to meet? The one who's carrying our grandchild." There was no censure in his tone, only curiosity.

"She's upstairs. She had a bit of trouble deciding what to wear."

"I know the feeling," his mother replied with a smile.

"Look," he told them, stepping closer and lowering his voice. "Misty is really nervous about meeting the two of you, so try not to make her any more uncomfortable than she already is. No nosy questions or inappropriate comments about her former choice of profession, okay?"

A flash of hurt crossed his mother's face, and he felt immediately contrite.

"We wouldn't dream of it, dear."

He released a pent-up breath, rubbing his damp palms on the legs of his chinos. "I know. I just...I don't want her getting stressed out and landing in the hospital again."

His dad clapped him on the back and shot him a teasing grin. "Stop worrying, son. Your mother and I will be on our best behavior."

While they waited for Misty to make an appearance, Amanda said, "Did you hear about your cousin Scarlet and John Harlan?"

Cullen's brows knit. "No, what about them?"

"They're engaged to be married," Daniel supplied.

"Isn't that wonderful?" Amanda asked.

"Yeah." That certainly explained their odd behavior at Une Nuit the last time he'd seen them, Cullen thought. "I'll have to be sure to give them both a call to congratulate them." Not to mention give his friend a rough time for keeping him in the dark.

Before Cullen could say more, he heard a sound at the top of the stairs and spun around to see Misty standing on the second-story landing. She looked beautiful and his heart swelled with pride.

This was the woman he planned to marry. The mother of his child. The only woman he'd ever intentionally introduced to his parents.

And even though he was slightly anxious about how this morning's gathering would go, he wasn't uneasy about Misty or embarrassed by her in any way.

He hoped his family wouldn't be, either.

"Misty, sweetheart. Come on down here and meet my parents."

Her heart was racing, her palms sweating and for a second, dizziness washed over her so that she had to clutch the mahogany railing even tighter in her already white fingers.

It didn't help that Cullen had called her sweetheart. She couldn't remember him uttering the endearment in the four years they'd been sleeping together, and now he was using it in front of his mother and father.

As she moved slowly down the steps, she took in the couple standing beside Cullen.

Only about an inch shorter than his son, Daniel Elliott was dressed in a dapper dark blue suit, the jacket left unbuttoned for a more casual look. His jet black hair and blue eyes were so much like Cullen's, it was obvious they were related, though it was hard to believe Daniel was old enough to be Cullen's father. She knew he had to be in his late forties, but he could easily have passed for five or ten years younger.

Amanda Elliott had dark brown hair that fell to her chin, and equally brown eyes. She was a few inches shorter than both her ex-husband and son, with a curvaceous figure tucked into her stylish red skirt and matching jacket.

At the moment, all three Elliotts were standing at the base of the stairs, watching her descent with what appeared to be a mixture of eagerness and trepidation.

She didn't blame them. If it weren't for Cullen flashing her that encouraging smile, she'd have run back upstairs and locked herself in the bathroom long before now.

As soon as she came within reach, Cullen took her hand and pulled her close to his side. She went willingly, needing both his physical and emotional support. He kept his fingers wrapped around hers and slipped his other arm around her waist, so that his palm rested on the curve of her pregnant belly.

"Mom, Dad," he said proudly, "this is Misty Vale."

A beat of complete, taut silence passed, and then his mother threw up her arms and gave Misty an enthusiastic hug. "Welcome to the family," she singsonged. "And, oh, look at you!"

Leaning back, she curved both hands over Misty's protruding stomach, circling the firm, round mass. Misty stiffened, surprised by the woman's forwardness. But then she relaxed, reminding herself that this was Cullen's mother…her child's grandmother.

"Misty." Cullen's father reached around his ex-wife's exuberant form to shake her hand. "Like Amanda said, welcome to the family."

Her chest swelled at their kindness, and for a minute, she felt like an Elliott. Like Cullen's true fiancée rather than his pregnant mistress.

She cleared her throat, praying her vocal chords would work. "Thank you, but I'm not really family. I'm just—"

Daniel cut her off before she had a chance to grope for the appropriate description. "You're carrying my son's child, the next generation of Elliotts. That makes you family."

Tears burned her eyes and her lungs refused to take in air. She turned her gaze to Cullen, squeezing his hand in a death grip, desperate to be rescued before she collapsed into a grateful, sobbing mess in front of his parents.

"Why don't we go into the kitchen," he said, flexing his fingers around hers reassuringly. "Misty and I haven't had breakfast yet. You're welcome to join us, or I can get you a cup of coffee while we talk."

Seven

While they chatted, Cullen made omelets. Misty told him she wasn't hungry—in truth, she still felt too nervous to eat—but he insisted. She was eating for two now, he took great joy in pointing out, and then he proceeded to fill her beaten egg mixture with every possible fresh vegetable.

She had to admit, it was delicious. The first few bites had been forced to keep from hurting his feelings, but now she realized just how famished she'd actually been, and ate with relish.

Having already eaten before their arrival, Daniel and Amanda passed on the offer of breakfast, settling for cups of coffee instead.

Misty knew they were divorced, and from what

Cullen had told her about the split, she understood things hadn't always been amicable. But no one would know it by the way they were acting this morning.

Daniel had pulled out Amanda's stool for her before taking a seat at the counter beside her. And when Cullen had handed them mugs of steaming black coffee, Daniel had automatically flavored his ex-wife's with cream and sugar.

And Amanda had let him. She'd acted as though such behavior was completely normal.

Hmm. Misty wouldn't say anything to Cullen in case she was wrong, but it looked to her like a few sparks might be flaring to life again between them.

"It's not that I'm not delighted for you," Cullen's father said in a reserved tone, "but you know how your grandfather is. He's sure to have something to say about this, and it probably won't be nice."

Misty chewed carefully, watching the three Elliotts exchange knowing glances.

"Well, you know how I feel about that," Amanda replied, fingers wrapped tightly around her ceramic cup. "I'd tell the old coot to go to hell. How you live your life is nobody's business but your own. My own life certainly would have turned out a lot differently if Patrick Elliott hadn't been such an overbearing tyrant."

Though the words were caustic, Amanda's voice held no hostility. She seemed to be merely stating facts and telling her son not to let his grandfather's opinion influence his actions in any way.

Misty didn't know what to think. She'd been expecting Cullen's parents to treat her with derision, but they hadn't. And now they were telling her that his grandfather likely would. It was enough to send Cullen's light-as-air omelet sinking like a stone in her stomach.

"I can't help what Granddad thinks," Cullen told his parents, his mouth turned down in a hint of a frown. "If I get the chance, I'll drive out to the Tides and talk with him. Maybe he'll handle the situation better if he hears it directly from me."

Daniel nodded solemnly. Amanda sipped at her coffee and refrained from comment.

Setting her fork down, Misty pushed her plate away and folded her hands in her lap, appetite suddenly gone. The entire scene made her uncomfortable. They were discussing her as if she wasn't even in the room.

She understood that her unexpected pregnancy impacted the entire Elliott family, but didn't want to be a bone of contention between anyone. Especially if it meant that Cullen's relationship with his father or grandfather would be negatively affected…or Daniel's relationship with *his* father.

"You don't have to do that," she told Cullen. "I don't want to cause trouble with anyone in your family. I can just as easily go back to Henderson and—"

"No." His response was sharp and fast. "You're staying here. And you're not causing trouble…you're having my baby. Granddad can accept that or not. The choice is his, but it doesn't affect us."

"Cullen…" she tried again.

"Misty…" he said with a smile, then swooped in for a quick, hard kiss. "No. Let it go."

She wasn't sure how to respond to that, at least not without starting a heated argument in front of his parents.

Daniel checked his watch, then cleared his throat to break the uncomfortable silence as he pushed back his stool. "I'd better get going. *Snap* won't run itself, you know. Although I'll understand if you don't come in for a couple of days," he added with a pointed glance at his son.

"Oh, my goodness, look at the time." Amanda jumped up, too, tugging at the hem of her tailored jacket. "Daniel isn't the only one who needs to get a move on. I've got to meet a client. Misty, it was lovely to meet you. I'm looking forward to spending even more time with you while you're in town."

She rounded the counter to give her son a peck on the cheek, then wrapped Misty in a smothering hug. "You two have fun today, and take care of my grandbaby."

Misty jumped as Amanda's manicured hand once again rubbed her belly, but managed a nod. In fact, Amanda's unconditional acceptance of her choked her up.

Amanda left the kitchen with Daniel on her heels.

"I'll walk you out," Cullen said. He ran a hand absently across Misty's arm before following his parents. "You stay here and finish your omelet."

Misty could see the three of them clearly from

her perch in the kitchen, and noticed that when Amanda stopped to retrieve her purse, Daniel laid a hand on her shoulder. There was definitely something going on between them, she decided. And in a way, it gave her hope.

Knowing that Daniel and Amanda could be forced to marry because of an unexpected pregnancy and still care for each other all these years later made her think she and Cullen might have a chance, too.

If she agreed to marry him, would they be doomed for failure...or might they eventually grow to love each other?

Cullen stood inside the open door, waving goodbye to his mother. His father stood on the front stoop a moment longer, and as soon as Amanda was out of sight, turned back to face him.

"If you do speak with your grandfather, let me know what he says. I agree that you shouldn't let his rigid and sometimes outdated views control your life, but he could make things difficult for both you and Misty. I just wanted to warn you of that."

The shadows in his dad's eyes told him better than words how much Daniel regretted parts of his own past. Cullen didn't want to make the same mistakes, but so far, it seemed he was following pretty darn closely in his father's footsteps.

"Thanks, Dad. I know Granddad won't be too happy when he hears I got a former showgirl pregnant, but hopefully in time he'll come around."

"Yeah, hopefully. In time," Daniel agreed with a twist to his lips. "Look, son, it's none of my business, but have you considered doing the right thing by her? Marrying her, I mean."

"I asked," Cullen admitted. "She turned me down."

His father's eyes widened, but to his credit, he kept his mouth shut.

"Don't worry," Cullen added, "I'm working on it. And I fully intend to change her mind before long."

After a moment, Daniel nodded. "I'm sure you will."

Seconds ticked by while Daniel remained just outside the front door, not meeting Cullen's gaze, but not walking away, either. Clearing his throat, he said, "There's something else I've been meaning to tell you. My marriage to Sharon is finally over."

Cullen watched the tension flash across his father's face, disappearing with his announcement. His divorce from his second wife had been long and drawn-out, with Sharon doing her best to take Daniel for everything he was worth.

Laying a hand on his father's arm, he gave a quick, supportive squeeze. "I'm glad, Dad."

Daniel nodded and they said their goodbyes before Cullen headed back to the kitchen. Misty hadn't eaten any more of her omelet, he noted, but she'd finished off the glass of milk he'd poured for her.

Good. He knew she was taking prenatal vitamins, but he intended to make sure she ate well while she was here, too.

"So…what did you think of my mom and dad?" he asked, helping her hop down from the stool. He held her a few seconds longer than was necessary, enjoying the feel of her bare arms under his hands and her belly bumping into his.

"They were very nice. Wonderful, really." She chewed thoughtfully on her lower lip. "I didn't expect them to be so accepting of me or our situation."

"I told you they would be. My mother is through the roof at the prospect of being a grandmother." He shot her a wide grin. "In case you couldn't tell."

She chuckled and threw her arms around his neck. "I noticed. I've never had someone spend so much time feeling my belly."

"Oh, yeah?" He slipped his hand between them and did just that.

"Well, except for you, of course. I don't think you stopped touching my stomach all night, even in your sleep."

"Get used to it," he told her. "I have a lot of lost moments to make up for, and I plan to spend as much time as possible caressing your adorable pregnant body."

His palm slid around her waist, to the small of her back, then the curve of her buttocks. A moan rumbled in her throat as her head fell back and he covered the pulse there with his lips.

"So what do you say?" he murmured against her warm skin. "Ready to marry me yet?"

He felt her muscles tighten for a second, then relax.

"Not yet," she answered just before turning her face to his for a slow, lazy kiss.

Maybe she was coming around, he thought as her fingers danced down his arms and her tongue began to do wild, sexy things inside his mouth.

Because *not yet* didn't necessarily mean *no*.

They made love right there in the kitchen, with Cullen being as careful with her as he would be with a delicate piece of china.

Then, after rearranging their clothes, Cullen offered to show her the city. He'd taken the day off, anyway, and she'd never been to New York before.

He wouldn't let her overexert herself, so they took a cab to Central Park, where they spent hours of a sunny May afternoon strolling hand-in-hand, admiring the trees and fountains and children playing.

He showed her the Statue of Liberty, the Empire State Building, Radio City Music Hall and gave her a leisurely tour of the Elliott Publication Holdings building on Park Avenue, between Fiftieth and Fifty-first Streets.

The lobby alone took up two stories, with tall windows, granite floors and so many live trees and plants that it looked like a conservatory.

Cullen stopped at one of the large granite security stations to check her in and get her a guest pass. It probably wasn't necessary, he told her, but this way she wouldn't cause questions or concern if they happened to split up.

At the bank of elevators, he scanned his own identification card and they headed upstairs.

Mailing and shipping for the entire building took up the third floor, the cafeteria the fourth, and the gym was on the fifth. She knew for a fact Cullen spent a good amount of time using the weights and machines there; she felt the proof of that beneath her fingertips every time they made love.

They skipped levels six through eighteen and twenty through twenty-four, which held various meeting rooms, boardrooms and magazine offices, heading straight for *Snap* on nineteen.

As the elevator whisked them silently upward, he explained which magazines were housed on which floors and what the publications entailed in a way he hadn't before. She was familiar with EPH, of course—soon after they'd begun their affair, she'd made a point of studying as much as she could about the Elliott empire without letting him know—but he seemed more in his element now, more willing to take the time to share details.

The fifteenth floor, he told her, was dedicated to *HomeStyle* magazine, known for its focus on fashion for the home; seventeen housed *Charisma*—fashion for the body; and *Snap* was sandwiched between their showbiz publication, *The Buzz,* on eighteen and *Pulse* for the news on twenty.

It was enough to make her head spin, but she listened intently and nodded in all the right places because Cullen's job and his family's business really did fascinate her.

The elevator doors swished open and Cullen led her off the car. With her hand in his, she stopped in her tracks and stared.

"Oh, Cullen, it's beautiful."

He threw her a pleased smile. "We like it."

The entire floor was decorated in black and white and screamed Old Hollywood. Small framed photographs of Marilyn Monroe and James Cagney adorned the walls, along with much larger prints of some of *Snap*'s most famous covers.

It made her think of old black-and-white gangster films and starlets with breathless voices and hourglass figures today's women could only dream of—which she supposed was the point.

Over the years, he'd described parts of his work environment, but she'd never imagined this. And now that she'd seen it, she knew she would never be able to picture him anywhere else. It suited him.

He introduced her to *Snap*'s petite brunette receptionist before she buzzed them through the glass doors that divided the reception area from the rest of the floor. Voices, ringing phones and the sounds of a bustling business filled the air as they moved between cubicles toward his office.

Misty was impressed by how many of EPH's employees—Cullen's coworkers—greeted him with a smile and wave, and seemed more than willing to accept her as one of Cullen's close personal friends.

She wasn't sure if they saw her as simply that—
a friend—or assumed more was going on between
them. They didn't ask and Cullen didn't tell. But
either way, they were warm and pleasant, and made
her feel more than welcome.

When they reached his office, he opened the door
stamped *Cullen Elliott, Director of Sales* and ushered
her inside.

"Very nice," she told him, noticing that the room's
vintage décor matched the rest of the floor's.

"Thanks." He let go of her hand and rounded his
desk. "Let me just check a couple of things, then we
can get going."

"Take your time."

She wandered around the room, studying some of
the framed magazine covers on the wall, his business
degree and personal pictures.

Near his desk, she chanced a glance over his
shoulder as he sifted through phone messages and
memos. It took her a moment to realize he'd stopped
moving and was now looking directly at her.

"Sorry." Her cheeks heated and she took a step
back, ready to return to her perusal of his photo gallery.

"Don't be silly." He grabbed her hand and pulled
her onto his lap. "I was just thinking how beautiful
you are, and how I wish I never had to come into
work again so I could stay home twenty-four hours
and worship you like the goddess you are."

"Cullen…" Her laugh sounded brittle as she
slapped at his chest.

"What's the matter?" he asked with a chuckle of his own. "You don't think I could do it?"

"Oh, I have no doubt you could do it, but—"

"Kiss me."

"What?"

"Kiss me. Give me something to fantasize about when I'm locked in this dark, dreary office, working my fingers to the bone."

She hardly thought of his office as *dreary,* even with a copious amount of black mixed with the white. But she leaned in and kissed him all the same, enjoying the warmth of his lips, his hands at her back.

"Knock, knock."

Misty jumped at the unexpected female voice, quickly breaking away from Cullen's embrace and getting to her feet. She turned her attention to the tall, attractive blonde standing just inside the room, her hand still on the doorknob.

"Hey, Bridge," Cullen said, though he sounded less than pleased by the interruption.

"Sorry, didn't mean to intrude, but I heard you two were in the building and just had to come up and meet Misty for myself."

She moved forward, holding her hand out for Misty's. Misty took it and let the woman shake her arm exuberantly.

"Misty, this is my cousin Bridget. She's the photo editor for *Charisma* down on seventeen. Bridget, this is Misty Vale."

"It's nice to meet you," Misty said reflexively.

"It's *really* nice to meet you," Bridget returned, then backed up a few steps and plopped down in one of the guest chairs positioned in front of Cullen's desk.

She was wearing a tight black skirt and black heels. Her blue blouse was sheer, with draping medieval sleeves and a low neckline that did a great job of showcasing her cleavage. The girl had fashion sense, that was for sure, and Misty found herself liking Cullen's cousin immediately. She was even thinking of asking where she'd gotten her top.

"I have to tell you, Misty, you're the hottest topic to hit the Elliott grapevine in ages. Granddad's furious. 'No grandson of mine is going to marry a stripper,'" she mimicked in a low, crusty tone.

Bridget made a face, rolling her eyes. "Please. If you ask me, the Elliotts could use some fresh blood in the old family tree. And it doesn't get any fresher than a Las Vegas showgirl," she added with a grin.

Misty felt the blood drain from her face and held a hand out toward the desk in case she started to sway.

"Bridge…" Cullen muttered in warning, apparently noticing her distress.

"Uncle Daniel and Aunt Amanda are over the moon, though. They're so excited about Cullen getting married and giving them a grandchild, they're just about floating. I wouldn't be surprised if Aunt Amanda is already planning the wedding."

"Bridge…"

"And you absolutely *must* tell me how the two of you met and got together. I have yet to hear the real story. All I've gotten are snippets, and I think most of them are merely conjecture. I'd much rather get it from the horses' mouths, if you—"

"*Bridget!*"

Bridget blinked her blue eyes, her mouth left open. "Yes?"

"Shut. Up."

Eight

Bridget blinked again, the shock on her face showing she was completely unaware of why Cullen was yelling at her. He took a deep breath and unclenched his teeth, trying to shake off the annoyance his cousin's little diatribe had created.

"I didn't mean to snap," he told her calmly, "but I think you're making Misty uneasy."

Bridget glanced at Misty, her eyes going wide in comprehension. She leapt out of her chair and raced to give her an apologetic hug. "Oh, my gosh, I'm so sorry, I had no idea."

When she returned to her seat, she dragged Misty along, urging her into the chair beside her. "I didn't mean to offend you or make you uncomfortable. I'm just so excited about having you in the family, my mouth got away from me."

"As usual," Cullen mumbled, then shot his cousin a wink and a grin when she scowled at him.

"It's all right," Misty said, smoothing a hand over her stomach, then clutching the arms of her chair until her fingers whitened.

"No, it's not. I shouldn't have come on so strong. You've only been in town for one day. You probably haven't even unpacked, and here I am putting you on the spot about the rest of your life."

She shook her head, sending her shoulder-length hair into motion before reaching over to clasp one of Misty's hands. "Forgive me. I'd like for us to be friends, and I don't want you to think that I'm going to be the nosy or presumptuous kind."

Cullen watched the two women exchange a look. As soon as Misty began to smile, Bridget did, too. His heart, which had stopped beating for the barest space of a second, picked up again and he released a silent sigh of relief.

He hoped Misty and his cousin could be friends. The more Elliotts who welcomed Misty with open arms and treated her like family right off the bat, the better his chances of convincing her to marry him…convincing her to stay.

"So what do you say I give you a call one of these days and we can go out to lunch, maybe do a little shopping?"

Misty's lips tipped up in pleasure. "I'd like that."

"Great. I'd better get back to work," Bridget said, patting Misty's knee and rising to her feet. "And leave you two to get back to whatever you were doing."

She flashed Cullen a teasing grin, wiggling her fingers as she waved goodbye. Cullen couldn't help but grin himself as the door closed behind her.

"In case you missed it," he deadpanned, "that was my cousin, Bridget."

Misty gave a breathless laugh. "So I gathered. She's very…"

"Yeah, she is. But she's a terrific girl. If she calls to ask you out to lunch or shopping, you should take her up on it. I really think you two will hit it off."

Pushing back his rolling leather chair, he stood and moved in front of Misty and took her hands. She offered them willingly, and he pulled her up until her long, lithe body rested all along the length of his own. He leaned back against the edge of the desk, taking her with him.

"Now, where were we?" he asked, looking deeply into her emerald-green eyes.

"You were checking your messages," she answered almost too innocently.

The corners of his mouth stretched in a grin. "That's not how I remember it. As I recall, you were sitting on my lap and I was wondering if I could talk you into a little interoffice hanky-panky."

"Why, Mr. Elliott," she said, feigning offense, "that could be construed as sexual harassment."

"Only if you work for me, which you don't.

And only if you aren't interested, which I'm pretty sure you are."

She made a purring sound of agreement, her fingers toying with the hair at the nape of his neck. That action alone sent shivers of desire sliding in a domino effect down the line of his vertebrae.

He was just leaning in to kiss her, hoping for a lot more, when the phone rang.

"Son of a…" He scowled at the offending object, silently wishing it to Hades.

"Aren't you going to answer it?"

Careful not to dump her on the floor, Cullen got up and set Misty on her feet. "Hell, no. Let it go to voice mail. I'll deal with it tomorrow."

Taking her hand, he straightened a couple of things on his desk, then led her to the door. "Let's get out of here before something—or some*one*—else interrupts us."

On the way to his town house on the Upper West Side, Cullen told the cab driver to take the long way, cruising down Broadway so Misty could *ooh* and *ahh* over the brightly lit marquees.

She'd never seen a Broadway play before, and he promised to escort her to any shows she wanted, any time she wanted. Of course, there were entirely too many to choose from, and in order to attend more than one or two, she would have to stay in Manhattan with him…and she wasn't at all sure that was how things would work out.

They arrived home late in the afternoon, and though she had expected him to pick up where they had left off in his office, when they reached the bedroom, he instead insisted she lie down to rest. She was having too much fun and didn't want to sleep, but he promised to take her out to dinner if she did—to his brother's restaurant, Une Nuit, no less.

It was an offer she couldn't refuse, and as soon as her head hit the pillow, she realized she must have been exhausted after all, because she drifted immediately off to sleep.

When she opened her eyes several hours later, Cullen was seated on the edge of the bed, smiling down at her. She startled at first, then pulled herself up to sit with her back against the headboard.

"How long have you been watching me sleep?"

"Just a few minutes."

She ran her fingers through her hair, sure it was a mess, then brushed at her mouth and the corners of her eyes. "Did I drool?" she wanted to know.

He chuckled. "No. You're beautiful—and very ladylike—when you sleep."

"Thank goodness. Is it time to go to dinner?"

"We can go any time you're ready. Bryan has the family booth reserved for us, so there's no hurry."

He'd exchanged his casual clothes for a more formal pair of tailored black slacks and jacket with a white dress shirt underneath. Thankfully, she'd brought a black knit dress along that would be appropriate for dinner at his brother's upscale restaurant.

"Let me change," she said, throwing back the covers and sliding off the king-size mattress.

She thought he'd leave the room while she got ready, but he stayed where he was, watching her every move. If she hadn't spent the past four years walking nearly or fully naked around him, she might have been embarrassed.

As it was, she barely would have noticed his presence if she hadn't felt the heat of his gaze searing her skin while she stripped out of her skirt and top and slipped into black stockings and the versatile little black dress. Thankfully, the material stretched to cover the bump of her belly without needing alterations or camouflage to look decent.

Ten minutes later, she was ready to go. Cullen held her hand as they left the house and slowly walked the two short blocks to Une Nuit.

The restaurant was brimming with people when they arrived. Customers, dressed to the nines, smiled and laughed over their meals while the waitstaff bustled between tables taking orders and serving food.

Misty was immediately impressed by the ambience and popularity of Bryan's establishment. Black suede banquettes and armchairs surrounded copper-topped tables, with low red lighting illuminating the entire space. She was used to bright and glitzy, but Une Nuit was the epitome of trendy but romantic.

As soon as the maitre d' saw them, he smiled and led them through the main dining room to a private booth reserved for members of the Elliott family whenever they chose to drop by. Cullen gestured for her to take a place behind the table, then slid in next to her, thighs brushing.

She was almost too distracted by her surroundings to think about eating, but Cullen leaned close to tell her about the different appetizers and entrées; which ones he'd tried, which were his favorites, which were restaurant specialties. Everything sounded wonderful to her.

After they placed their orders, Cullen moved in tighter, putting his arm around her shoulders.

"What do you think?" he asked, tipping his head toward the center of the dining area.

"If the food is half as wonderful as the atmosphere, I'll think your brother is a genius. This place is amazing."

"Hey, you finally landed a smart one, little brother."

Misty jumped at the intrusion, but Cullen merely grinned up at the man hovering behind them over the back of the booth.

So this was Bryan she thought, as he swung around and took a seat across from them. He was tall, with the same black hair and blue eyes as his younger brother and father had. The family resemblance was so strong, even if a person hadn't known they were Elliotts, they would immediately realize the three men were related.

"Misty," Cullen said, waving an arm in his brother's direction, "meet my brother, Bryan. He's the owner of this fine establishment and an all-around pain in the ass."

"Funny," Bryan remarked, "when we were kids, that's what I used to say about you."

They were like two puppies wrestling over the same chew toy, and she couldn't help but smile.

Bryan held his hand out over the table's centerpiece, a shallow bowl of water with three floating lighted ivory candles in the shape of some stunning exotic flower.

Misty returned his quick shake.

"It's nice to meet you, Misty. Is my brother treating you okay?"

"I'm treating her just fine," Cullen answered for her. "Unlike some men, I know how to treat a lady."

"Don't let him fool you," Bryan said, flashing her an amused wink. "Everything he knows, he learned from his big brother."

Cullen scoffed, and Misty could only grin.

"So how are you two doing?" Bryan asked, turning serious, his gaze focusing mainly on Misty. "Has the family given you a warm and friendly welcome?"

She toyed with the rim of her drink glass, feeling suddenly nervous, just like she did every time the topic of Cullen's family—or being welcomed into it—came up.

"Oh, yes, they've all been very nice."

"Even Granddad?" This time, his clear blue eyes went straight to his brother.

"He'll come around," Cullen responded simply.

Bryan's attention skidded away from them to a spot far beyond their booth. "Sorry I can't stick around, but I'm being beckoned. A restaurateur's job is never done. Misty, it was great to meet you. I'm looking forward to having you as my sister-in-law."

He flashed her a smile and offered his hand again. "Enjoy your meals. Order whatever you like, it's on the house."

"That isn't necessary," Cullen told him.

"Of course, it is. Consider it my gift to you to celebrate your engagement."

He waved his arm one last time before disappearing into the heart of Une Nuit.

"Our engagement?" Misty repeated, brows arching with interest as she sipped her nonalcoholic cocktail.

Cullen cleared his throat. "I may have mentioned something along those lines when I told him we'd be dropping by."

"But we're not engaged," she pointed out.

"We would be if you'd say yes to one of my proposals."

She fought the grin that threatened to break out across her face. He sounded petulant, as though she was keeping him from something he really, really wanted. It was flattering and warmed her deep down in places only Cullen seemed capable of touching.

Still, she didn't want to joke about marriage to him or lead him to believe she would eventually accept—no matter how much she might want to.

"I'm sorry, Cullen," was all she could think to say.

For a moment, his stern expression remained, and

then his eyes lightened from a dark, stormy blue to the color of the sky in summer.

"Don't apologize," he told her. "I fully intend to wear you down. Besides, I didn't bring you here to propose to you again, or to make you feel guilty for saying no. I brought you here for dinner, and to impress you with another branch of my family tree so you would have an inkling of what awaited you if you ever did say yes. Are you adequately impressed?"

The tilt of his lips was too adorable to resist. She leaned over and pressed a kiss to his cheek.

"I'm very impressed," she said softly. "Thank you."

Their meals came then and they spent the next hour eating, talking and flirting. Cullen fed her bits of his entrée from his own fork, and she returned the favor, until things turned so hot, she was afraid they'd set the room on fire.

The sight of his lips moving as he chewed set her skin to tingling. The feel of his thigh pressed to hers heated her blood to a near boil. And from the look in Cullen's eyes, he was as aroused as she was.

"Let's get out of here," he said, snagging her hand and sliding out of the booth as soon as they'd finished the last of their desserts of crème brûlée flavored with mango and passion fruit juices.

"What about the check?"

"I hadn't planned on it, but I think I'll take Bryan up on his offer."

He stopped in the middle of the restaurant, nearly causing her to bump into his back. Spinning on his heel to face her, he drew her close and kissed her like a man stranded in the desert without food or water who had suddenly stumbled upon a bubbling oasis.

She responded, heedless of the fact that they were standing in the middle of his brother's very popular and very crowded restaurant. When he finally pulled away, diners were staring at them, but Misty couldn't find it in her to care.

"I'll pay him back later," he rasped in her ear. "For now, I just want to get you home so I can strip you down and make love to you for the rest of the night."

That sounded good to her. Heart pounding in her ears, legs the consistency of grape jelly, she nodded and uttered the only word her passion laden brain would allow. "Okay."

Nine

As much as he did not want to, Cullen returned to work the next day. Luckily, his eyes popped open a little before 6:00 a.m., before the alarm could wake Misty. Lifting her arm from his chest, he climbed carefully out of bed and began getting dressed.

Somewhere deep in his gut, he liked the idea of having her curled up under the covers every morning while he got ready to leave for the office. He liked watching her while she slept, knowing that if he climbed back in beside her, she would welcome him with open arms and use her hands and mouth to convince him to call in sick.

Stifling a groan, he tightened the knot of his tie, gave his libido the "down boy" command and forced himself to walk out of the room with only one last wishful glance at her lush sleeping form.

The morning moved at a snail's pace and he could barely concentrate on the tasks in front of him until he glanced at his watch and realized Misty would likely be out of bed by now.

He picked up the phone and punched in his own number. It rang several times before voice mail kicked in.

Dammit. Knowing Misty, she probably didn't want to answer his home phone because she knew—or rather, assumed—no one would be calling there for her.

He hung up and immediately redialed. He'd keep trying, he thought, but if she still didn't answer, a quick trip home wasn't out of the question.

"Hello?"

Her voice was tentative, nervous.

"Good morning, sexy."

"Good morning," she said, her tone still low, but sounding much more confident. "I didn't know if I should answer your phone or not, but when it kept ringing, I thought it might be important."

"For the record, you *can* answer my phone. Don't forget, Bridget might call to invite you out. If it's anyone else, you can take a message." A beat passed while he let that sink in, then he added, "And it is important. I miss you."

Silence greeted him for the space of several seconds before she murmured, "I miss you, too. This place is awfully big and quiet without you."

Damn. He thought of her in his big empty town house and went hard. He thought of her in his big empty town house, missing him, wishing he were with her, and that hardness turned to a throbbing painful ache.

"I'm coming home," he grated out through a throat gone closed with desire.

She laughed, the light tinkling sound carrying over the phone line. "No, you aren't. You have work to do."

"It can wait." He didn't think making love to her could.

"Don't be silly. You've taken enough time off to cater to me, and I'll still be here when you get home."

Cullen didn't know which warmed him more—hearing her call his place "home" or hearing her say she'd be there when he got back. A part of him knew she could pick up and fly back to Nevada at any moment. He could walk in the door one day and find her gone.

"In the meantime, I thought I'd wander around, snooping in all your cupboards and drawers," she went on. "Are you hiding any naughty secrets you don't want me to find?"

His lips curled up in a grin. "Sweetheart, for you, I'm an open book."

"Mmm," she purred in response. "Interesting concept."

"Well, if you're not going to let me come home and rock your world, then I suppose I should get back to work."

"All right. I'll see you tonight, then."

"I'll call if I'm going to be late."

"Okay."

"Hey, Misty," he said before she could hang up.

"Yes?"

"Will you marry me?"

He could almost see her eyes widen in sudden panic, the pulse in her neck pick up speed.

"Not today," she finally answered. "But thank you for asking."

Despite being rejected for what must have been the fifth or sixth time, he found himself smiling. "I guess I'll just have to ask again tomorrow."

The next day, and every day after, Cullen called home several times, just to hear Misty's voice. And while he had her on the line, he always made sure to ask her the same question. "Will you marry me?"

Each time, her answer remained unchanged, but he didn't stop trying. If anything, her refusal made him more determined. Like a medieval warrior, he would continue to storm her castle walls until they crumbled and she gave in to the inevitable.

A week or so later, Cullen made his way to the EPH gym where he was meeting his brother for a midday exercise session. He tried to work out for an hour every day, and whenever Bryan could make it, he joined in.

After changing into shorts and a sweatshirt with

the neck and arms cut out, Cullen headed for the free weights. Bryan joined him and they both began to do arm curls.

"So how are things going between you and Misty?" his brother wanted to know.

"Great," Cullen answered honestly.

Things between them were fabulous. The sex was earth-shattering, as always, and he found her near-constant company more intriguing than he could have imagined.

He was never bored with her, and that was more than he could say about any other woman he'd ever dated. If only she would accept one of his countless marriage proposals, life would be perfect.

"Has she taken you up on your offer to marry her yet?"

Cullen ignored the slight smirk on his brother's face. "No. I'm still working on it, though. She'll come around eventually."

"Are you sure you want her to?"

At Bryan's softly spoken question, Cullen's movements slowed. "What's that supposed to mean?"

"Hey…" Bryan held up his free hand, continuing reps with the other. "I'm not trying to piss you off. I'm just asking if getting married is what you really want, or if you're only asking because you got her pregnant."

If a comment like that had come out of anyone else's mouth, he'd have already driven his fist into the offender's teeth. But his brother was his best friend and confidant, and Cullen knew he meant well.

"I'm not sure," Cullen said, for the first time putting voice to his true feelings. "I want to marry her. I just don't know if it's out of a sense of duty or because I truly care for her."

"Don't you think that's something you should figure out before you walk down the aisle?"

"If only it were that easy," he said, once again finding the rhythm of his pumping arm.

Bryan switched the weight he was using to his other hand, then took a seat on the empty bench next to Cullen's. "Look, you're not the only one who had responsibility with a capital *R* drilled into him all his life. Dad and Granddad both made sure we knew what they considered the measure of a man."

Cullen huffed out a breath. "And we saw where that got Dad, didn't we? Forced to marry when he was eighteen because he and Mom got themselves into a sticky situation."

"Isn't that the same situation you're in now?"

"Yeah," he reluctantly replied. "Which is why I'm not sure whether I'm pressing Misty to marry me because I want to be with her, or because I'm predisposed to follow in Dad's footsteps."

After lowering the heavy metal dumbbell back to its place on the weight rack, Cullen sat back, wiping sweat from his brow. "I don't want my child to grow up without a father, Bryan. I don't want to be a part-time dad, either, and I don't want Misty to be a single mother. Her life has been difficult enough without the opportunities we've had. She works hard to support herself and doesn't need to spend the rest of it scraping by."

"You'd never let that happen. Even if you decided not to be involved in the child's upbringing, you'd make sure they both had whatever they needed financially."

A ripple of acknowledgment skated through his belly at the truth of his brother's words. He could never stand idly by, knowing that his son or daughter was in need of something the Elliott wealth could provide.

But then, he wasn't sure he could just stand by and watch. He wanted to be there, elbow deep in dirty diapers and feeding schedules. He wanted to see his child's first smile and first steps and first time climbing on the bus to school.

"You can be a good father without marrying the child's mother, though," his brother volunteered when the silence stretched too long between them. "You can support them both, and either convince Misty to move to New York or fly out to Nevada as often as necessary to be with them and see your kid grow up."

Cullen studied his older brother from beneath lowered lashes. "What would you do if you were in my shoes?"

Bryan considered that for a second, then replaced the weight he'd been using in the only empty space left on the rack. "I guess that would depend on whether or not I was in love with the baby's mother. If not, I'd do everything I could to let my child know I loved him and was there for him. But if I was..."

He paused for emphasis and looked Cullen straight in the eye. "I'd move heaven and earth to make sure we were together."

Cullen spent the rest of the day haunted by Bryan's heartfelt statement. He had to admit, his older brother might just be wiser than he'd ever given him credit for.

The question was, was he in love with Misty or did he simply want to be a good father to their child?

When he arrived home that evening, he was no closer to finding an answer than he had been earlier, he only knew that his instincts were telling him to marry Misty, make the most of what they had together and see where the future took them. But if things didn't work out, it would be the child who suffered.

Misty greeted him at the door, looking as delectable as ever. She'd found his laundry room and mentioned that she might do a load of laundry if she started to run out of clothes. But she'd also discovered that a pair of denim shorts and one of his T-shirts made a good enough outfit to wear around the house.

He wholeheartedly agreed. Pregnancy only enhanced her already abundant curves. The jean shorts hugged her bottom and thighs, and she'd knotted the hem of his gray T-shirt to the side, offsetting the rise of her breasts and the small swell of her belly.

She looked hot…and he'd seen her both naked and in those skimpy sequined concoctions she used to wear on stage.

"How was your day?" she asked, bouncing up to take his jacket as he shrugged out of it.

"Good." He bent to place a chaste kiss on her lips. This was definitely something he could get used to—coming home at the end of a long day to her smiling face and sweet, welcoming mouth. "How about you?"

"Fine. I decided to take your advice and explore the city a little bit."

"Did you call the car service I told you about?"

"Yes." Tiny wrinkles appeared in the center of her forehead as she frowned. "I didn't want to. I thought I would call a taxi instead, but then I realized I don't have any money with me."

"The family has an account with the car service, that's why I mentioned it."

"I know, which is why I ended up going with them, after all."

His arm snaked out to catch her around the waist and draw her close.

"Then why are you still frowning?" he asked, kissing away the signs of her distress.

"Because I don't like being dependent on you for every penny I spend. I know it was your money paying for everything back in Henderson, but at least that felt different because I was teaching classes and bringing in *some* income."

"You're going to be my wife," he told her. "What's mine is yours."

If anything, that caused the lines in her brow to deepen. "I'm not going to be your wife, and I should be able to support myself and my child."

"Our child," he corrected firmly. Then his tone lightened. "Look, while you're in New York, you're my guest. I don't want you to worry about that sort of thing. If I didn't have to go into work, I'd spend every day with you, anyway. So let me leave some money for you tomorrow, along with a couple of credit cards and phone numbers, and if you need anything else, you can call me."

She gave him a look that clearly said he had missed the point.

"Humor me, would you, please?" he asked, giving her shoulders a squeeze. "We can discuss the division of assets after we're married."

Thankfully, she let the subject drop. With any other woman, he might have been suspicious, but with Misty, he knew that was just her way. If something was worth arguing about, she'd fight to the bitter end, but as far as she was concerned, some things weren't worth the effort.

"All right. Dinner's getting cold, anyway." Taking his hand, she led him through the house to the kitchen.

"You cooked?" he asked, genuinely surprised.

"Of course. Why else do you think I needed to go out today?"

When they reached the kitchen, pots were steaming on the stovetop and she released his hands to deal with them.

"Have a seat," she said, indicating the places she'd already set at the island.

He did have a dining room, which he was sure

she'd discovered during all of her alleged snooping, but the kitchen was cozier and less formal for just the two of them.

"No offense," she said, "but you were down to cocktail olives and crackers."

He winced. "Yeah, sorry. I try to keep the basics stocked, but I've been kind of distracted lately. My grandmother keeps telling me I should ask my house-keeper to shop for me, too, but I can't see the point, since I eat out more often than not or pick something up on the way home from work."

"Well, don't get too excited. This is nothing elaborate."

"It smells delicious."

He admired the smooth flow of her movements as she stirred and tasted. She strained a pan of pasta, then scooped generous portions onto two plates, covering them with red sauce. Returning to the island, she set a serving at each of their places before climbing onto her stool.

She looked so eager for his opinion of her culinary skills that he spread the linen napkin over his lap and immediately dug in. She'd added shrimp and chunks of portabello mushroom to the sauce, and flavors exploded along his taste buds.

"Mmm," he uttered in appreciation. "Very good."

She beamed at his compliment, then speared a forkful of pasta for herself. They ate in silence for several minutes before Cullen caught her eyeing him warily.

"What?" he asked, glancing down at his shirt front. "Did I drip?"

"No," she said on a half laugh. "I was just thinking... If we did get married, would you expect me to be a housewife and stay-at-home mother? Cleaning the house, having dinner on the table every evening when you got home from work?"

Though the question was posed innocently enough, he sensed the seriousness behind the words. This was also the first time she'd spoken about *if* they married, rather than remaining adamant that it would never happen.

He set his fork on the side of his plate and swallowed, considering his answer carefully.

"I wouldn't expect anything," he told her honestly. "I would want you to do whatever made you happy. If you wanted to stay home to raise our children, that would be fine with me. And if you enjoyed cleaning or cooking, that would be fine, too. But I have a housekeeper, and we could also hire a cook, if you wanted, so it wouldn't have to be an issue."

"What if I wanted to work outside of the house?"

"I'd be okay with that, too. Misty," he said, stretching his arm across the corner of the island to squeeze her hand, "whatever you want to do with your life, I'll be agreeable. Within reason, of course," he added, flashing her a grin. "I don't know how thrilled I'd be with the idea of you jumping out of airplanes or running into burning buildings. But if you wanted a position at EPH, I'd do whatever I could to

get you a job there. If you wanted to teach dance at
Juilliard, I'd support you on that, too."

"Juilliard," she scoffed, rolling her eyes. "Right.
Like they would want a former Las Vegas showgirl
on their faculty."

"You're a great dancer, Misty. You worked as a
showgirl, but we both know you're talented at other
forms of dance, too. You could wipe the floor with
those Juilliard stiffs, if you wanted to."

When she beamed at him, it made all the moments
of doubt and disappointment at her rejections fade
away. He understood now—at least in part—why
she continued to turn him down.

She felt out of her element. The thought of
marrying him scared her because she considered
herself not good enough for an Elliott, far from socialite material.

He hated that she thought so little of herself. If she
only knew how much the Elliott family needed her—
how much *he* needed her—to add a spark to their
lives and loosen up some of the rigidity Patrick Elliott
had drilled into all of them from infancy.

His mind flashed back to his brother's remarks
that afternoon at the EPH gym. Bryan was right. He
needed to decide if his proposals to Misty were based
on emotion or an ingrained sense of responsibility.

He was beginning to believe it was the former.
Love might be too strong a word. After all, he'd never
been in love and wasn't quite sure how a sensation
like that would feel. But he cared for her deeply. So

much so that he wanted to marry her, raise their child together, spend the rest of his life with her.

He *wanted* those things, he realized. He wasn't selflessly offering to take them upon his shoulders because it was the decent and respectable thing to do.

They finished the rest of their meals in a comfortable silence, but when Misty rose to carry the dishes to the dishwasher, Cullen wiped his mouth with his napkin, knowing he needed to ask one more time.

"Hey, Misty?"

She acknowledged him without turning around, her light brown hair with those streaks of blond falling over her shoulder and back as she bent to fill the bottom rack.

His throat closed for a minute, the words sticking as his chest tightened and a wave of unexpected emotion washed over him. He'd asked her to marry him a dozen times before, but for some reason, he suspected this time was different. This time, her refusal just might crush him.

He swallowed hard, his fingers turning white as they clutched the edge of the island. "Will you marry me?"

She stopped what she was doing and turned to meet his gaze. Sadness and regret flashed through her eyes for a split second, and he knew what was coming.

"I'm sorry, Cullen, the answer is still no."

Ten

Two days later, Misty was wandering around Cullen's town house, trying to find something interesting to occupy her time. She'd already straightened the kitchen and bedroom, flipped through channels on the television in the living room and read the first few chapters of a popular fiction paperback she'd found in the den.

It wasn't even noon and she was bored already. Cullen had assured her she wouldn't be expected to be a housewife or stay-at-home mom. She could go out if she wanted, find a job or other activity to keep occupied.

If she married him. Which she wouldn't. Couldn't, no matter how much her heart might protest the decision of her better judgment.

She would still see him. He would come to Nevada to visit his child, and she was sure he'd ask her to fly east with the baby a few times a year. They could spend time together then.

Things might not be the same between them—their sexual relationship would likely transform itself into something more platonic—but at least he would still be in her life. She wouldn't lose him completely just because she refused to love, honor and cherish him.

She didn't need vows for that. She already felt all of those things and more for him. But she wouldn't intrude upon his life, forcing him to make room for her and a child when she was sure that had been as far from his plans as flying to the moon.

It hadn't exactly been in her plans, either, but she could incorporate the role of single mother into her everyday life much more easily than he could incorporate a pregnant ex-showgirl into his.

With a sigh, she plopped down on the sofa in front of the TV, contemplating another run through the channels to see if anything interesting had come on in the past ten minutes. She could go out—it was a balmy May afternoon—but had already done about as much exploring as she cared to do on her own. Or maybe…maybe she should think about going back to Las Vegas.

Back to her dance studio and normal routine. She might not be able to teach classes quite the way she had in the past, but there were adjustments that could be made to allow her studio to remain open. A couple of the students had been taking classes from her long enough to pick up the slack and demonstrate moves she was no longer capable of.

And there was no sense dragging out the inevitable. She would have to return home eventually. Maybe sooner would be better than later, especially considering the tension that had developed between Cullen and her ever since that night in the kitchen when he'd asked her one more time to marry him.

One last time, it seemed, since he hadn't broached the subject again.

Where he used to propose several times a day, it had now been several days since the topic of marriage had even been discussed. They still made love, still slept in each other's arms and he still called from work to check on her. But what he didn't do was ask her to marry him morning, noon and night.

She missed it, she thought with a pang low in her belly. As many times as she'd turned him down, it was horrible of her to be sorry he'd stopped, but she was. She missed the tiny thrill of anticipation that used to sing through her veins every time the phone rang or he walked through the door.

She'd said no because it was the right thing to do, but it had been flattering to hear him pose the question over and over, as though he really meant it.

When the doorbell chimed, her heart lurched and she jumped to her feet, thinking it might be Cullen. A second later, her senses returned and she realized he would simply use his key, not ring the bell.

Still, a visitor would be a nice distraction. She almost didn't care if it was a door-to-door salesperson wanting to demonstrate the amazing power of a new vacuum cleaner, or a neighbor looking for her toy poodle.

What she didn't expect to find when she pulled open the door was Cullen's cousin Bridget. Misty hadn't seen the woman since their amusing and slightly embarrassing encounter in his office a couple of weeks ago, but that didn't keep her from stepping into the foyer and greeting Misty with a wide, bright smile.

"Hi, there," Bridget said enthusiastically, tossing her lime green handbag over one shoulder. "I hope I'm not intruding."

Misty shook her head. She hadn't even gotten the chance to say hello, but was beginning to realize this was probably typical of encounters with Bridget. The young woman was energetic almost to a fault, and brought a smile to Misty's lips without even trying.

She was wearing an orange sleeveless top with a small tie holding together the two sides of the deep V-neck. Her skirt had an angled hem and a swirl design that incorporated the same colors of her blouse, purse and brown shoes. Her dark blond shoulder-length hair was pulled back on either side with rhinestone clips that sparkled in the sunlight shining through the front windows.

"I'm so glad." A determined light played across her blue eyes. "Now tell me you don't have plans for the day."

Misty shook her head again. "No. Why?"

Bridget released what must have been a pent-up breath. "Great, because I came to take you to lunch."

"Excuse me?" Misty blinked, feeling somewhat disconcerted.

"Lunch. You know, the meal between breakfast and dinner. The activity in which women get together for a little gossip and girl talk."

She flashed a grin and moved forward to squeeze Misty's arm. "Come on. I know Cullen is at work and you must be going stir-crazy cooped up here by yourself. We'll go out, grab a bite and I'll fill you in on all the best need-to-know about the Elliott clan. You can ask me how to get on Granddad's good side—if he even *has* a good side—" she added with a roll of her eyes, "and what Cullen was like as a kid."

That last was icing on the cake. Misty had been almost desperate to find something to do, and since she liked Bridget immensely, going out to lunch with her sounded like fun. But now that she'd mentioned it, Misty did want to know more about Cullen's childhood and the man who would be her child's great-grandfather.

"Let me just grab my purse," she said, turning to head upstairs. "I should probably phone Cullen, too, to let him know I won't be home for a while."

"He already knows," Bridget called after her.

Misty paused halfway up the steps.

"I told him what I was up to before I left EPH. He said we should enjoy ourselves and bring him some leftovers." Bridget crossed her arms over her chest. "As if. Let him find his own food. If we talk as long as I think we will, we may still be out at dinnertime."

Misty chuckled before running the rest of the way to the bedroom to retrieve her small clutch purse. When they stepped outside, she noticed Bridget had a Town Car from the same service Cullen had recommended waiting at the curb.

"I'm not allowed to let you overdo it," Bridget said as they slipped into the air conditioned backseat.

"I feel fine," Misty felt the need to put in.

"I'm sure you do, but Cullen told us about your hospital stay—scared ten years off of him, I'd venture to say—and he just doesn't want you getting sick or risking the baby. You're lucky he doesn't have you on bed rest, whether the doctor suggested it or not," she said with a wink. "The Elliotts are like that—stubborn, determined know-it-alls."

"You included?" Misty asked with a small smile.

"Of course." Bridget didn't seem the least offended or put off by the description. "As much as I hate it sometimes—especially Granddad—I'm lucky I was born into this family. Anyone else's and they'd have probably tied me up in a burlap sack and tossed me into the East River years ago. As it is, they consider me hell on wheels. Most of the time, I think they all stand back and hope that if I do anything really stupid, I won't take them down with me."

"It must be nice to belong to such a large, close-knit family."

"It is," Bridget replied without hesitation. "It can be a pain in the butt, too, but any time I'm in trouble or need something, I know I can turn to them."

A beat passed before Bridget said, "You can, too, you know. Once you and Cullen get married, you'll be as much an Elliott as the rest of us and can come to me or the others whenever you need anything."

Misty started to protest that she and Cullen weren't going to marry, then thought better of it. He had probably already told his family they were, and no amount of argument from her would convince them differently.

Besides, she really didn't want to bring Cullen's cousin into the debate. It would become clear enough to everyone that a wedding wasn't going to take place when no plans were made and she flew back to Las Vegas.

She also took exception to the idea that she would fold naturally into their family and automatically become *one of them* just because she married Cullen. Bridget herself had said that their grandfather, Patrick Elliott, had been overheard claiming, *no grandson of mine is going to marry a stripper!*

She wasn't a stripper and never had been, but doubted the eldest Elliott would appreciate the distinction.

A lot of people felt the same way, so she could hardly blame him for the misconception. It bothered her more that he had apparently made up his mind about her and her relationship with Cullen before even meeting her. But then, she couldn't blame him for that, either. In his shoes, she probably would have had a similar reaction.

From the outside, she was sure she looked like a gold digger, out for the Elliott money. An ex-showgirl, searching for a way out of Las Vegas and into one of the wealthiest and most successful families in the northeast.

First, they would say, she lured Cullen in with hot sex and a convenient affair. Then she managed to get herself pregnant and trap him into a loveless marriage.

If only people—Cullen's family included—knew the truth. How much she really did care for him, and that this pregnancy had been as much of a shock to her as it had to anyone else.

Her hand moved to cover the slight bulge in her lap as the Town Car moved through the stop-and-go Manhattan traffic.

That was another reason she couldn't marry Cullen—because no matter what they did or said, no one would ever believe she hadn't gotten pregnant on purpose to tie him to her and gain ready access to his money.

She might be a kept woman, but she wasn't a gold digger and didn't think she could live with the knowledge that everyone in the world thought she was.

Hours later, Misty and Bridget sat at a white latticework table on the patio of a local delicatessen. A slight breeze ruffled the umbrella over their heads as they made slow work of their sandwiches and fruit salad.

They probably would have been at the restaurant much earlier, except that Bridget had insisted they stop along the way. After hearing about what Misty had done so far on her first visit to New York, she had declared Misty's outings boring and pedestrian and decided to give her a taste of what the Elliott women considered a fun day of shopping.

She had taken Misty to several jewelry stores and boutiques, encouraging her to buy something at each. She kept telling her *he wouldn't mind,* and a part of Misty knew it was true. But she felt extremely uncomfortable at the notion of making or asking Cullen to pay for anything more than necessities for her.

Providing for their child was one thing, but she refused to accept baubles and superfluous gifts that would make her feel like more than just a mistress. They would make her feel like a whore. No better than the type of woman everyone already assumed her to be.

She didn't say as much to Bridget, even though she suspected the woman would have understood if she'd explained. Instead, Bridget had shrugged one slim shoulder each time Misty declined to make a purchase and went ahead to buy a hat and pair of calf-high boots for herself.

On and off while they strolled through the shops and rode through town in the luxury sedan, Bridget filled her in on all kinds of family gossip and the goings-on at EPH.

Some of it made her laugh, such as the story Bridget told of one of *The Buzz* employees attending a meeting with the word *Urgent* stamped across the back of his rumpled shirt, giving everyone a pretty clear idea of what he'd been up to in the copy room with one of the magazine's young receptionists.

Other parts made her wonder, like the apparent competition Patrick Elliott had set up between his children by issuing the challenge that whichever one of them made the biggest success of his or her magazine by the end of the year would be given the position of CEO of EPH when Patrick retired.

Misty couldn't imagine pitting siblings against one another in any manner, let alone over something as inconsequential as a family business. She realized how large an empire EPH was, but it was still just a company, just a job, not nearly as important as family and children, love and respect.

Hearing such a thing about the man who would be her own child's great-grandfather made her feel slightly ill. She wasn't particularly looking forward to meeting Patrick, but she swore that no matter what, she would protect their child from him and his gruff demeanor, his disdain—or outright hatred, as the case may be—and his manipulative personality.

"He's a controlling old bastard, is what he is," Bridget told her, munching on her sandwich as she continued on the topic of her grandfather. "His interference in my life and the rest of the family's lives drives me insane. Somebody needs to either shake some sense into him or tell him to leave us the hell alone."

Misty sipped at the glass of cranberry juice she'd ordered with her meal, nodding in agreement. She certainly didn't have anything to offer other than her own personal concerns about how Patrick would affect her and her baby's life, and Bridget seemed content to have a captive audience while she talked.

"He made Uncle Daniel marry Aunt Amanda when she got pregnant right out of high school. And I guess we should all be grateful or we wouldn't have Cullen to love." She shot Misty a knowing, lopsided grin. "But they still should have been allowed to make up their own minds about how to handle the situation. They might have ended up together anyway, and then wouldn't have gotten divorced. Even if they wouldn't have, I'd bet you anything Daniel still would have been a great father and done right by both Amanda and Bryan."

She washed down the sandwich with a gulp of soda. "And forcing Finola to give up her baby when she got pregnant at fifteen was just *wrong*. I mean, I don't think poor Aunt Finny has ever gotten over it. She's let her job as editor in chief of *Charisma* completely take over her life. She won't even date."

Leaning back in her chair, Bridget added, "I don't want the magazine to take over my whole life, that's for sure."

A second later, she leaned forward again and whispered conspiratorially, "If I tell you something, will you promise not to breathe a word of it to anyone? Not even Cullen?"

Misty sat in stunned silence for a moment. She felt both honored that Cullen's cousin wanted to confide in her and unworthy at the same time. But she nodded, anyway, stretching over her plate to hear what Bridget had to say, because she was loathe to put an end to the camaraderie she'd found with this young woman.

"Cross your heart?" Bridget demanded.

"Cross my heart..." she promised, forming the invisible symbol on the front of her shirt.

"I love running the photo department at *Charisma*, don't get me wrong. And I've never told this to anyone before, but... I've been working on a tell-all book about the Elliott family. Granddad would *die* if he knew. As it is, he'll probably kill me when he finds out. But it has to be done. Somebody has to let the world know what kind of man Patrick Elliott really is and what he's done to get where he is."

Almost before Misty had a chance to digest all that, Bridget's expression went from harshly determined to soft and unsure.

She huffed out a breath and shoved a wedge of cantaloupe in her mouth. "Do you think I'm crazy? Do you think I'm risking not only my grandfather's wrath, but my entire family's rejection?"

"I don't know," Misty answered honestly. She didn't know any of them, save Cullen, well enough to predict how they would react to Bridget's clandestine actions or to a tome that would reveal to the world the inner workings and private scandals of the Elliott family dynasty.

"I think…" She took a deep breath and then dove in with her honest opinion. "I think you need to do what feels right to you. It sounds like you're very passionate about this project, and I can only think that's a good thing. You shouldn't spend your life working at a job you don't love or doing something that makes you feel unfulfilled."

She took another sip of juice before bravely forging on. "Just because you write this book doesn't mean you have to seek publication for it. You could do it for your own satisfaction and no one else would ever need to know."

At that, Bridget's face fell. It was obvious her aspirations for this tell-all were much larger than simply a secret hobby.

"But if you do publish it… I'm not an Elliott, so maybe I shouldn't even be saying this, but maybe airing out some of the family linens is exactly what your grandfather needs to realize he's been too controlling of his children and grandchildren."

"Really?" Bridget reached across the glass-topped table and squeezed Misty's hand. "Oh, Misty, thank you. That makes me feel so much better. At least you understand. Someone has to be brave enough to tell the truth about the Elliott family—not just the truth as Patrick Elliott has concocted it."

The rest of their lunch passed without any more

heavy disclosures, but Misty still felt herself with-drawing emotionally. She liked Bridget very much, but knew that forging too much of a friendship with her would be unfair when she probably wouldn't be in town much longer and might never return to New York after that.

When they pulled up in front of Cullen's town house, Bridget immediately leaned across the seat to embrace Misty before she could step out of the car. Misty hugged her back, her eyes stinging with tears as she realized she'd finally met someone with whom she could truly become friends.

And that she might never see the young woman again.

Eleven

"How was your lunch with Bridget?"

Misty was sitting at the kitchen island, staring at, but not really solving, the crossword puzzle from yesterday's paper.

She raised her head at Cullen's question, realizing she hadn't heard him come in. Hadn't heard the front door open…his footsteps across the hardwood floor…his keys hitting the hall credenza. He'd shrugged out of his suit jacket and set down his briefcase, but she hadn't heard or witnessed those actions, either.

And it was no great mystery why. Spending the afternoon with Bridget had filled her mind with a million different thoughts, all of them centering on

Cullen and whether or not she should risk staying with him in New York any longer.

Scratching her head in a distracted gesture, she pasted a smile on her face that she didn't quite feel and twisted around on her stool.

"Good. I like your cousin," she answered. "How about you? How was your day?"

"Good."

He continued forward until he stood directly in front of her, hedging her in, his breath dancing over her cheeks, her lashes, her lips. Lifting his hands, he set his palms against the edge of the island on either side of her and leaned in.

"I missed you, though. I was thinking," he murmured, his mouth grazing her temple, them moving down along the line of her jaw, "maybe tomorrow you could come into work with me. That way, whenever I start daydreaming about you, you'll be right there instead of so far away."

The corners of her lips turned up in amusement at his exaggeration of the distance between his office and his house.

"Wouldn't that be distracting for you?" she asked, driving her fingers through his hair and letting her head fall back as he kissed a molten path down the column of her neck.

"Not half as distracting as it's been wanting you and not having you in easy reach."

Her heart gave a little flip at his words, and her toes curled inside her shoes.

She wanted to ask if he'd found her equally distracting for the past four years, while they'd been carrying on their affair, living at opposite ends of the country. But she was too afraid of what his response might be. Too afraid he hadn't thought of her much at all, while she'd thought of him each and every day.

His nose nuzzled the scoop neck of her shirt just above her breasts, his tongue darting out to wet her rapidly heating skin. Her eyes slid closed and a low purr sounded at the back of her throat.

"Let's go upstairs," Cullen growled.

"Aren't you hungry? Don't you want dinner first?"

He straightened and her eyes popped open. Before she could guess his intent, he scooped her up in his arms and turned for the foyer.

"The only thing I'm hungry for right now is you. Food can wait."

He took the stairs quickly but carefully, moving toward the bedroom like a man on a mission. When he reached the foot of the bed, he laid her gently atop the mattress and followed her down.

The look in his eyes was intense, possessive... adoring, and it caused her stomach to clench with regret. She would miss him so much when she left.

And she would leave. She had to. But it would be one of the hardest things she'd ever had to do. Because she loved him.

Deep down in her soul, she knew she always had. All the denials and claims that she was in the affair because he was a good man and treated her better than any of the guys from her past were just so much smoke.

She loved him in a way she hadn't known possible, and for the first time thanked God she was carrying his child. It might be selfish of her to think it, but at least by having his baby, she would always have a piece of him, always have a connection to him that no one and nothing could break.

If she could, she would marry him, spend the rest of her life with him. But that would require her to have been working as something other than a showgirl when they met, and for their relationship to have begun as something other than an illicit, red-hot affair.

His being an Elliott didn't help, either. Maybe if he weren't, then some of the hurdles between them wouldn't have looked quite so insurmountable.

Moisture prickled behind her eyes and she bit the inside of her lip, blinking rapidly to keep her emotions in check. If Cullen noticed she was close to tears, he would want to know what was wrong, and wouldn't let up until she told him.

But how could she tell him that she was leaving him because she loved him? Tell him and make him understand that it was for the best—for everyone.

She knew Cullen would try to talk her out of it. When that didn't work, he would try to argue her into changing her mind. And if she was still determined to go, he would likely tie her to the bed until she came to her senses.

A smile tugged at the corners of her mouth. His

stubborn streak and single-mindedness were two of the things she loved most about him. They made her feel cared for and protected.

But this time, she couldn't let his Elliott arrogance stop her from doing what she knew was right.

Brushing his thumbs over the twin arches of her brows, he stared down at her, his body pressed along hers from shoulder to ankle.

"You look so serious," he said softly. "What are you thinking?"

The words *I love you* were on the tip of her tongue, but she couldn't let them escape.

For one thing, love hadn't been part of the agreement when they'd first started sleeping together; it wouldn't be fair for her to bring such a sentiment into the deal now.

For another, she couldn't bear to tell Cullen she loved him and not hear the words in return. Or worse, to see his face turn stony and tense as he tried to figure out a way to extricate himself from a mistress who had suddenly become too clingy and emotionally involved.

Pregnancy or no pregnancy, shared child or no shared child, she had to remember that they were still only a mister and mistress.

She shook her head, raising her arms to run her fingers through his silky hair.

"Nothing important," she answered in response to his question, pushing all other thoughts and feelings to the back of her mind. "I was just thinking about how nice it is to be someone's substitution for food and drink."

"Not someone's," he growled. "Mine."

His teeth closed on the muscle in her throat, over the jugular vein, in predatory possessiveness. Her pulse sped up, pumping blood even harder past the area where his hot, wet tongue now swirled against her skin. She writhed beneath him, wanting closer, wanting more.

He released her throat and moved to her mouth, kissing her with a heat and passion that sucked the air from her lungs and left her breathless.

While his tongue parried with her own, his hands caressed her arms, her waist, her breasts.

Little by little she felt her clothes loosen and begin to fall away. Rolling and shifting, she let him strip the black slacks and hot pink top from her body, leaving her in only panties and bra.

Returning the favor, she slipped the end of his tie through its knot and pulled the entire length away from his collar. Next, she slowly ran her fingers down the front of his shirt, releasing each of the small buttons until the material gaped open, leaving his broad, smooth chest bare to her touch.

He inhaled sharply, his abdomen going rigid as her nails trailed along his sides and into the waistband of his dress pants. She flipped the catch open with her thumb and forefinger, easing the zipper down as she continued to drink from his lips, nipping, licking, sucking.

When she delved into his briefs to gently cup his straining erection, Cullen pulled away and jumped to his feet to shed his shoes and trousers so quickly, she chuckled. He came back to her blessedly naked and wasted no time freeing her from the constriction of her matching bra and panties.

Their mouths met. Breaths mingled and limbs tangled as they twisted and rolled around on top of the bedclothes. He kissed the side of her neck, drew the lobe of her ear into his mouth, then his lips moved lower, across her chest, until they reached the peak of one breast.

He circled the budded nipple before pulling it into his mouth, at the same time using the pad of his thumb to tease and torment the tip of her other breast.

She arched her back, pressing into the sensations he stirred to life, straining for relief as the pressure built and pulsed through her, gathering force at her very core.

Misty pulled her legs up, wrapping them around his waist, and he slid into her easily in one fluid stroke. Her muscles clutched at him automatically, making her gasp as pleasure washed over her like an ocean wave.

Her fingers played along his back, his shoulders, the planes of his chest. His jaw tightened, the cords of his neck standing out in stark relief as his hips flexed, pounding into her again and again.

The world ceased to exist, narrowing to a pinpoint of space and time where only the two of them existed, in this room, at this moment. All other thoughts and concerns disappeared. The air filled with the sounds of heavy breathing and moans of intense pleasure.

Cullen's hands stroked down her sides, one coming to flex and rest on her hip while the other delved into the folds of her slick, swollen sex. His thumb sought and found the bud of her desire, and pressed, shooting lightning bolts of pure ecstasy through every pore and cell of her body.

Her back arched, her heels dug in, and her nails curled into his shoulders as she came with a long keening cry. Leaning in even closer, Cullen continued to thrust, continued to rub and tease her so that the spasms rocking her body went on and on. And then he stiffened, pouring into her with a heartfelt groan.

When her heart had stopped pounding in her chest like a marching band on parade, Misty opened her eyes to find Cullen staring down at her with those stark blue eyes. He held himself above her, away from the mound of her belly, his arms straining with the effort.

And then he grinned, leaning forward to press a firm, satisfied kiss to her mouth before rolling to his side. "I don't know about you, but I'll take that kind of meal over boring old meatloaf any day."

Even as her eyes drifted closed, her lips curved in agreement. "Mmm."

Pulling the sheets and comforter loose from beneath them, he covered them both to their chests and snuggled up to her.

They were on their sides, with him pressed behind her, spoon fashion. His arm was curled around her waist, his lips brushing her neck and shoulder.

Dragging in a deep breath, she tried not to let it stutter back out as she exhaled. She didn't want him to know she was crying. If he realized, he would want to know why and would pressure her with questions she didn't have answers to.

His fingers played absently along the taut, bare flesh of her protruding stomach, which only made her heart lurch and her throat clog with emotion.

He was such a good man, and there was nothing she wanted more than to lie here with him every night for the rest of their lives. To know that she belonged to him...with him...that a future together shone brightly before them.

But she didn't, and she knew what she had to do. No matter how much it might hurt.

Twelve

When Cullen arrived home from work the next day, he found himself whistling as he took the front steps two at a time.

That's what a good woman could do for you, he decided. Make you feel like skipping even after a long, hard day. Make you eager to get home and do more than pop a single serving frozen meal into the microwave or crash in front of the TV for a few hours before crawling upstairs to bed.

It bothered him that she wouldn't marry him, there was no doubting that. In fact, if he were honest, he'd have to admit it was more along the lines of crushed.

He'd never asked anyone to marry him before. Never cared enough about any woman to ask.

But he cared about Misty. And he cared about their unborn child.

He wanted her to be his wife, dammit. But he'd asked...at least a hundred times. And she'd turned him down...at least a hundred times.

He didn't know what more he could do to convince her, short of tossing her over his shoulder and carrying her off somewhere to perform Chinese water torture until she gave in.

Which left him with only one final option: take what he could get. She wouldn't agree to marry him, but she seemed happy enough to live with him here in New York.

So that was what they'd do. It might not be ideal, and his family might not offer their one hundred percent approval, but it could work.

They could live together and raise the baby together. Just one big, happy family, even without the sanctity of marriage.

His gut clenched at the idea; his fingers tightened on the front door handle.

He'd always been the playboy of the family, with pretty women hanging on his arm and his every word. His bed had only been empty when he wanted it to be.

So why did it suddenly feel imperative that he tie the knot, not just shack up with Misty?

Because they were having a child together?

Because she was the one woman for whom he was willing to give up all other women?

He honestly didn't know. He'd asked himself the

same questions numerous times but still didn't have the answers.

But vows or no vows, they could still make it work. They *would* make it work. He would see to it.

Pushing the door open, he stepped inside the town house, cocked his head and listened for signs of Misty. He often found her in the kitchen, throwing together something for dinner. Or in the sitting room, reading a book.

He set down his briefcase and shrugged out of his suit jacket, then made his way down the hall. He didn't smell anything coming from the kitchen, but that didn't mean she wasn't in there.

When he reached the back of the house, however, the room was empty. No pots or pans heating on the stove, no place settings laid out on the kitchen island.

He checked the living room next, and then the den. His brows knit as the first niggling sense of concern started to tickle at the base of his spine.

It probably shouldn't worry him that Misty wasn't downstairs when he arrived, but it did. Only because she always had been before. And because she was pregnant and had had complications before.

These days, he seemed to carry a pocket of constant fear and concern with him everywhere he went. Concern for Misty's health and safety. Fear that something could happen to send her to the hospital again and that she might lose the baby.

He tamped down those worries on a daily basis, not wanting her to know that impending fatherhood had turned him into a writhing mass of raw nerve endings and quivering gelatinous goo.

She was fine, he told himself, but hurried up the stairs to the second floor, just in case.

"Misty?" He called her name, expecting an immediate response. Instead, his query was met with silence.

Perhaps she was in the shower. Or taking a nap. He understood that pregnant women got tired easily and needed extra rest.

When he got to the bedroom, he found the door ajar and quickly stretched out an arm to push it open the rest of the way.

Instead of finding Misty in bed, he saw her standing beside the king-size mattress, folding clothes and packing them neatly inside her open suitcase.

Cullen stood in the doorway, frozen in place by the sight before him. The blood in his veins turned thick and sluggish. His brain strained to function, but failed.

"Hey," he forced past his tongue, which felt twice as large as normal inside his mouth.

Her movements halted and she slowly turned her head, meeting his gaze. The sadness in her eyes slammed into his solar plexus like a fist. But what drove the air from his lungs and made the room spin around him was the determination written plainly on her face.

"What are you doing?" he asked, afraid he already knew the answer.

She turned back to her task, finished folding a pair of black slacks and tucked them into the luggage. "I'm packing."

"I can see that. Where are we going?" he asked, striving for levity, praying his suspicions weren't valid.

"*We're* not going anywhere," she said. "*I'm* going home."

Oh, God. "This is your home."

"No, Cullen," she said softly. "This is *your* home. My home is in Nevada."

That was enough to get his blood pumping again, followed by a quick surge of panicked annoyance. He strode across the room, reaching her in three long strides, and grabbed her arm before she could pick up the next item of clothing.

"Your home is with me," he told her firmly. "Where we live is irrelevant."

"Cullen…"

She pulled her arm away, and he let her go. Her lashes fanned across her cheeks as her gaze floated to the floor, then back up again.

"I'm sorry, but this isn't going to work. I appreciate everything you've done and everything you've tried to do these past weeks."

Her fingers rubbed absently along the edge of the suitcase while she struggled to keep her eyes locked with his.

"And you know I won't try to keep you from the baby—that isn't even an issue. But I can't stay here any longer, pretending to be something I'm not…pretending *we're* something we're not."

"No one asked you to be anything but who you are."

She shook her head, sending her brown and blond

hair swinging around her shoulders. "You want me to be your wife, when I am definitely not Elliott material. Your grandfather wants me to be a socialite instead of a dancer, when I'm well past the age of being molded into someone I'm not."

A fine sheen of perspiration broke out along his skin, slid down his back and turned his palms damp with apprehension. He could feel her slipping away from him, and was damned if he knew how to stop it.

"To hell with what Granddad wants," he growled brutally. "To hell with what I want, for that matter. What do *you* want?"

Her breasts rose as she drew a deep breath, then gave a heartfelt sigh. "I want to go back to the way things were. I'm not sorry about the baby," she said, laying a protective hand on her belly, "but you have to admit it's complicated our lives. I won't complicate your life any longer, though. That's why I'm leaving."

Complicate his life? Didn't she know she made his life *better?* That she was like a rainbow after a summer storm…a roaring fire on a cold winter day…his soft place to fall when everything else around him was a whirlwind of stress and confusion?

She'd been the one constant in his life, from almost the moment they had met. Always welcoming him with open arms, ready and willing to listen and accept him as he was.

How could she not know that?

How could she not know he loved her?

The truth slammed into him, stealing his breath and nearly sending him staggering backward.

He loved her. It was so simple. So obvious, he couldn't believe he hadn't realized it sooner.

He didn't just find her attractive, wasn't only interested in her body. And he didn't want to be with her simply because she was pregnant with his child.

He wanted that child, but he wanted her, too. Wanted her as his wife, his lover, his partner from now until the day they died.

It was no wonder he hadn't been able to give her up over the years. Regardless of the other women who'd passed through his life or the number of times he'd told himself he should break things off with Misty, he never could, and now he knew why.

He had been in love with her all along. Deep down, in a place even he hadn't known existed.

"Misty."

His voice broke on her name, but he wasn't embarrassed. He was shocked, amazed…ecstatic. He wanted to grab her up and squeeze her tight, swing her around and shout at the top of his lungs about his newfound revelation.

"Why now?" he asked instead. "I thought you were happy here, that *we* were happy here, and you were enjoying getting to know my family. What happened to change your mind?"

Her gaze skittered away from his own and she turned back to her packing. This time he let her go, more eager to hear her answer than hold her undivided attention.

"Nothing happened," she said. "I just realized that I've been here longer than I planned and need to get back to the studio and my classes."

He didn't believe her, but wasn't going to press the point. It didn't really matter, anyway.

"What if I told you I love you?" he blurted out almost desperately.

Her movements halted, a pair of panties hung limply from her fingers. As though in slow motion, her body twisted around until she was facing him once again. Her eyes were wide, the muscles in her throat convulsing as she swallowed hard.

"What did you say?"

He stepped forward. His face split, he was sure, with a goofy grin. His hands closed on her upper arms, his thumbs stroked her in a reassuring caress.

"I love you, Misty. I think I always have." He lifted a hand to stroke her cheek and comb his fingers through her hair. "You were never just a mistress to me. From the moment I met you, I knew you were more than that. I may not have been willing to admit it at the time…"

He gave a harsh laugh. "Hell, I may not have been willing to admit it now, except that I'm scared to death about losing you."

His fingers flexed on her bare skin. "I don't want you to go," he told her simply. "But if you feel you have to…if Nevada is where you really want to be, then I'll go with you."

"Cullen—"

"I'll leave EPH if I have to. Or find a way to work for the family long-distance. I don't care, as long as we're together."

She shook her head, blinking rapidly as her gorgeous green eyes glittered with unshed tears.

"I can't, Cullen," she said, her voice clouded with emotion. Twin drops of moisture formed on her lashes before spilling over to streak down her cheeks. "I love you, too, but I don't want to be the reason you eventually come to hate me."

His heart kicked into a gallop. He was so delighted by her admission of being in love with him, too, that at first he didn't catch the rest of her pronouncement.

When he did, his smile slipped and he started to get that sick, slick feeling in his gut again.

"What are you talking about?" he asked, thoroughly perplexed. He couldn't imagine anything she might do or say to ever cause him to hate her.

"I'm not the right woman for you. You need a wife you can be proud of, one your family will approve of. Not a mistress you felt obligated to marry just because she got pregnant."

She sniffed, valiantly wiping the tears from her face only to have more fall in their place. "I know you feel responsible for me and the baby, and that you want to do the right thing by us because it's what your father and grandfather have raised you to do. But I won't be another duty you feel compelled to fulfill, and neither will this child."

Cullen could only stare at her, stunned by her words. He did think of her and the baby as his responsibility, but because he *loved* them, not because he felt trapped or obligated. Where would she have gotten the idea that—?

His crossed brows began to lift, the corners of his mouth moving from their downward tilt into a lopsided grin.

"Bridget," he breathed, not sure whether he should be furious or amused.

Shaking his head, he said, "Bridget filled your head with stories about how my father and then my brother and I were raised, didn't she? Told you all about Granddad and how overbearing he can be, always drilling into us that an Elliott takes responsibility for his actions. Am I right?"

She started to nod, but he didn't need even that much confirmation.

"I love my cousin, but the next time I see her, I swear I'm going to wring her neck," he muttered.

"Listen to me, Misty."

He ran his hands up her arms, over her shoulders, until they came to rest on the slope of her long, slim neck. His fingers dug gently into the base of her skull, his thumbs framing her jawline.

"I love you. I love our baby. You are not an obligation to me, a duty. You are a gift. A blessing I didn't even know I needed until you came into my life. And I'll thank God every day for the rest of my life that you did. I never want to spend another moment apart from you."

Closing his eyes, he lowered his head until their foreheads touched, then he opened his eyes again and stared directly into those deep emerald pools he hoped he would be lucky enough to gaze into for the rest of his life.

"Marry me, Misty. We'll live anywhere you want, do anything you want. Just marry me. *Please.*"

Misty inhaled a deep, ragged breath, her heart beating so hard behind her rib cage, she knew he must be able to feel it against his own chest. Tears continued to roll down her cheeks, but they'd transformed into tears of happiness rather than tears of sadness and regret.

There wasn't a doubt in her mind that Cullen meant what he said. He *didn't* think of her as a responsibility to be handled with a stiff upper lip.

And most importantly, he *loved* her. As much as she loved him.

Clearing her throat, she opened her mouth, hoping her voice would work—now, when she needed it more than ever.

"I remember the first night I met you, when you came backstage after the show," she said softly, touching his handsome, familiar face, so dear to her, with the tips of her fingers. "I knew from that very moment that my life would never be the same."

Pressing her mouth to his, she let her eyes slide closed for a brief moment before opening them and whispering against his lips, "Yes. I'll marry you."

He pulled back, only slightly, and she watched the

smile form on his face, growing wider until pleasure filled his gaze from the inside out.

"Finally," he breathed, then wrapped his arms around her and hugged her tight.

"You've made me a very happy man," he said just above her ear. "I promise you won't be sorry."

She laid her cheek on his shoulder, her nails curling into the material of his tailored brown suit jacket. "You're sure it doesn't bother you I'm five years older than you are, or that everyone will know you married an ex-showgirl?"

"Are you kidding me?" he returned.

He shot her a wide, wicked grin and added a wink that made her toes curl inside her pretty pastel slides.

"Older women make better lovers. That's what the song says, right? I happen to know whoever wrote it is one hundred percent on the money. And as for you being a former showgirl...if anyone gets on my case, I'll simply explain that you can cross your ankles behind her head. They'll not only understand, they'll beg me to introduce them to some of your dancer friends."

They both knew the situation was more serious than that, but she buried her face in his chest and laughed, anyway. His sense of humor was another one of the traits she loved best about him, so as long as he could hold on to it through thick and thin, she really believed they would be all right.

"And your grandfather...?" she ventured.

"Granddad will learn to accept you. And if he doesn't, then he'll learn to keep his mouth shut or he won't be allowed to see his first great-grandchild."

"Oh, no, Cullen—"

He covered her mouth with two fingers. "Don't worry," he said. "We'll work it out. Whatever it is, we'll work through it *together*. Together, okay?"

"Together," she whispered, and they sealed the deal with a kiss.

Thirteen

Two weeks later

Cullen stood outside the Tides, the Elliott family's palatial estate in the Hamptons, tugging at the bow tie of his black tuxedo. The darn thing was all but cutting off his circulation.

And his brother was late, dammit.

Everyone else was inside, flowers were arranged, his family and the minister were present, guests were seated. Only Bryan—his best man—had yet to show up.

Even to the casual observer, Cullen would probably look nervous. And considering that it was his wedding day, he figured he had every right.

But he wasn't. His tie was too tight and he was starting to get annoyed with his brother's continued absence, but he was far from anxious.

He'd been wanting to marry Misty for too long— longer than he'd even realized until recently—to think about backing out now. If he had his way, he and Misty would be standing at the altar already, saying their vows. Then he would be that much closer to whisking her away on their honeymoon.

He'd wanted to take her somewhere such as Paris or Greece, but since she was already five months into her pregnancy and had suffered complications early on, it was recommended that she not fly very far.

Actually, the doctor had said it would probably be okay, but Cullen had nixed the idea. He might not be a nervous groom, but he was an exceptionally nervous and overprotective father-to-be.

They'd already flown back to Vegas once so that she could gather more of her belongings and deal with a few aspects of the dance school, but he didn't want to risk letting her board another plane until after the baby was born.

So instead, they were spending a long, uninterrupted week at the Carlyle, right in Manhattan. She'd never been there and had always wanted to see the inside of the luxury hotel.

And see the inside of it, she would. Once he got her to their suite, he didn't plan to let her leave—not even for a meal—for at least forty-eight hours.

And God help any member of his family who dared to disturb them. He had already threatened them with dire consequences if they so much as tried.

Blowing out a huff of breath, he checked his watch and went back to pacing along the edge of the circular drive that fronted the foyer entrance of the Tides.

Where the hell was Bryan?

His brother should have been there an hour ago. He had the rings for the ceremony, and they were supposed to take their places at the front of the church well before Misty walked down the aisle.

He was about to go back inside to try reaching Bryan on the phone when he heard tires squeal and an engine rev. Next thing he knew, Bryan's silver Jaguar Xje careened up the drive and skidded to a stop sideways behind another car parked several feet away.

Cullen rolled his eyes at his brother's dramatic entrance and started forward with purpose.

"It's about time," he said as Bryan opened the driver's side door and climbed out.

He was dressed in worn, comfortable looking jeans and a plain blue button-down shirt. He also had a split lip, and when he moved to slam the car door closed, Cullen noticed he was walking with an obvious limp.

"What happened to you?" Cullen asked, halting in his tracks.

Bryan shook his head. "Fender bender," he said casually. "I knew I was running late, and wasn't paying close enough attention on my race to get here.

Of course, having to stop and exchange insurance information didn't exactly help matters."

Cullen glanced from where Bryan was poking gently at his split lip to the bumper of his car. Not a scratch anywhere that Cullen could see, front, back or side. And the cut on his face was already scabbed over.

Cullen's brows drew together and he'd opened his mouth to question his brother further when Bryan slapped him on the back.

"Come on, little brother. It's time for me to get changed into my monkey suit, and for you to tie the knot."

Cullen's gut dipped in anticipation as they headed back to the house. The Tides was a sprawling, two-story stone structure bought by Patrick Elliott forty years before. Located on five acres on a bluff above the Atlantic Ocean, the entire house had been lovingly decorated and filled with family photographs and memorabilia by Cullen's grandmother, Maeve.

Throwing together and carrying out a ceremony of this size with only two weeks' notice had been no simple feat, but there had never been a question that it might be held anywhere other than the family estate. His mother had taken her role as wedding planner seriously, clearing every detail with him or Misty, but not letting her soon-to-be daughter-in-law raise a finger.

Cullen couldn't remember the last time he'd seen his mother so excited or determined. She was obviously thrilled at the idea of seeing her younger son married and expecting a child in only four more months.

And Patrick had, surprisingly, been more than willing to allow the event to be held on his property. At the very least, he hadn't put up a fuss.

Ever since he and Misty had announced their engagement, Cullen had expected a call or visit from his grandfather. A lecture about the evils of mixing his fine Elliott blood with that of a lowly showgirl. A demand that he call things off and send Misty and the baby off to be hidden away from the rest of the world, someplace where they wouldn't bring embarrassment to the family.

He'd been braced for it, ready to defend his future wife to his last breath, if necessary. But Patrick hadn't called, and he hadn't stopped by Cullen's office at EPH to confront him.

Cullen hoped his grandfather's silence meant he had accepted Misty's addition to the Elliott family, but a part of him was still waiting for the inevitable.

He and Bryan made their way across the marble foyer to the library and master suite behind it. The groomsmen were using it as their changing area, while Misty and her bridesmaids occupied one of the upstairs bedrooms. Amanda had insisted on the wide separation to avoid any chance of the groom accidentally seeing the bride in her gown before the ceremony.

The old wives' tale about bad luck befalling them if such a thing happened didn't worry Cullen. He didn't believe anything could ruin their day, or the many glorious years they had ahead of them.

The wedding itself was being held outside, on the pristine back lawn. A dark pink satin aisle had been laid on the grass, with chairs set up on either side, draped in a lighter pink fabric. A trellis stood at the end with red roses climbing over the white latticework.

"Hurry up," he told his brother, shoving a garment bag with the last remaining tux at his chest. "You've held me up long enough, and I don't want Misty thinking I got cold feet."

"Are you kidding me?" Bryan retorted. "You chased her so hard, I'm surprised you didn't just elope on your last trip to Vegas."

"It crossed my mind, believe me," Cullen muttered. It would have saved everyone a hell of a lot of trouble, and if they'd done that, Misty would have his ring on her finger and be Mrs. Cullen Elliott right now.

They would be at home, snuggled in bed or holding hands over their breakfast plates, discussing names for their future little bundle of joy. And he wouldn't be chomping at the bit to get out there and say *I do* already.

Bryan unbuttoned his shirt and kicked off his boots. "You'd have to be barefoot in Antarctica to get cold feet, and Misty knows it. You two are so damn happy together, everyone around you needs a shot of insulin to keep from going into sugar shock. It's sickening."

A small smile stole across his face. "Yeah," he agreed softly. "I know."

Cullen slapped the black tuxedo pants into his brother's hands as soon as Bryan kicked out of his jeans. "Now shut up and get dressed."

Misty stared at her reflection in the full-length mirror and felt her heart stop.

She couldn't believe this was her wedding day. That in less than half an hour, she would be walking through this massive house that intimidated her right down to her fishnet stockings, and across the expertly manicured lawn toward Cullen.

Her future husband. The man of her dreams.

In all the years she'd been with him, been secretly in love with him, she had never truly believed they could ever be together. But now she knew they would never be apart.

Despite their differences—age, upbringing, social status—she knew that he loved her. And there was no doubt that she loved him.

He'd been willing to give up his family for her—or his grandfather, at least—and his life in New York so they could be together. Compared to that, giving up her dance studio in Henderson and moving to Manhattan to try her hand at being an Elliott wife seemed a small price to pay.

And she knew she could be happy here. His entire family might not be thrilled that they were getting married, but most of them accepted her and had already made it clear they supported Cullen's decision.

She had no intention of being a housewife or

stay-at-home mother, though. She was content to stick close to the Upper West Side town house until the baby was born—and maybe for a time after. But she and Cullen had also discussed the possibility of her getting a job as a dance instructor somewhere, or perhaps opening another studio of her own in the city.

She wasn't sure yet what she wanted to do. She only knew that she didn't want her options limited just because she'd agreed to marry into the Elliott clan.

"You look beautiful." Breaking into Misty's thoughts, Bridget came up behind her and slipped into the mirror's limited view.

Her heart began to race again and she swallowed past the lump in her throat. "Are there people out there?" she asked timidly.

"Of course," Bridget offered with a laugh. "You're about to marry into the esteemed Elliott family. No one who's anyone would dare miss it. Relatives from both families are here, along with any member of the media who could beg, borrow or steal an invitation. Your mother hasn't stopped crying since she got here, by the way. Come Monday morning, your face and Cullen's will be plastered on the cover of every newspaper and magazine in America."

"Oh, God." Misty fought the urge to bend over and stick her head between her knees—mostly because, these days, bending wasn't as easy as it used to be.

"Relax." Bridget patted her back and fussed with the folds of Misty's white gown.

Misty had at first resisted the idea of wearing white on her wedding day. It seemed somewhat improper and not the tiniest bit ridiculous, considering she was five months pregnant and looked as if she'd swallowed a volleyball. But Cullen's mother had insisted, and Misty had finally agreed once she'd tried on the dress for the first time.

The entire gown was made of the same silky satin, but the smooth, unadorned bodice ended just below her breasts in the empire fashion and an overlay of gossamer with tiny seed pearls fell to her ankles, almost entirely masking the bulge of her belly.

"You look amazing," Bridget continued in an attempt to allay her fears. "All you need to remember is that this day is for you and Cullen, no one else. When you walk out there, pretend you're the only two people in the world. Keep your eyes on him and ignore everything else."

When she put it that way, Misty didn't think she'd have any trouble getting through the ceremony, no matter how many guests were watching or how many flashbulbs were going off in her face. To her, having eyes only for Cullen was as natural as breathing or waking up in his arms.

She gave herself a final once-over in the long oval looking glass, nodded and turned to face the woman who was quickly becoming her new best friend.

Bridget was wearing one of the strapless lilac bridesmaids' gowns Amanda had chosen, her blond hair swept up and decorated with sprigs of spring flowers.

"Thank you. And thank you for all of your help this morning. I couldn't have done it without you."

Bridget had picked her up at Cullen's town house bright and early, whisking her away to the Tides for what would turn out to be several hours of bridal preparations. She'd done Misty's nails, hair and makeup, then even helped her get dressed when it became obvious Misty couldn't see her feet, let alone slip into delicate stockings or a handmade, nearly priceless gown.

The other woman grinned. "That's what maids of honor are for."

They were gathering Misty's bouquet and getting ready to head downstairs when a light knock sounded on the bedroom door. Bridget hurried over, prepared to bar the groom's entrance on the off chance Cullen had decided to risk his mother's wrath and try to get a peek at the bride before the ceremony.

"Granddad," she said flatly, stepping back to let the older man inside.

Patrick Elliott was tall, with short gray hair, and though Misty knew him to be in his late seventies, he looked about ten years younger. His eyes were a twinkling blue, making it clear who had passed that color on to most of the other Elliotts.

She'd only met him once before, at a small Elliott family gathering where Cullen had stayed by her side and remained staunchly protective of her. And though Parick had been cool toward her that day, he hadn't seemed outwardly hostile.

Today he was dressed in a crisp gray suit and looked only slightly nervous about entering a room that was so clearly the domain of wedding-minded women.

"I'd like a private word with the bride-to-be, if that's all right," he said.

His voice was deep, but not as gruff or demanding as one might expect from others' description of him.

Bridget crossed her arms over her chest belligerently. "I don't think—"

But Misty interrupted. "Of course."

Every anxiety that Bridget's encouraging words had managed to calm flared to life again in screaming apprehension, but she would never refuse to speak to Cullen's grandfather. Not even if she expected that she was about to get the dressing-down of a lifetime.

The man had made it clear—albeit through second parties—that he disapproved of her. Of her upbringing, her choice of career, her involvement with Cullen. But he was still going to be her relative by marriage, and he would be her child's great-grandfather by blood. The least she could do was let him speak his piece.

But no matter what he said to her, or how upsetting the encounter might turn out to be, she was still going to walk downstairs and outside and exchange vows with the man she loved.

"Are you sure?" Bridget asked, doubt, concern and more than a little loathing of her grandfather written clearly on her face.

Misty forced the corners of her mouth to curve

upward in a show of confidence she didn't entirely feel. "I'm sure."

With a reluctant nod, Bridget opened the door again. "I'll be right out here if you need me."

She cast her grandfather one last distrustful glance, then disappeared into the hallway.

Patrick watched her go, then turned back to Misty. "Thank you."

She inclined her head, her mouth too dry with uneasiness to speak.

He looked around the room, taking in all the signs of wedding day preparations. Discarded clothes and shoes, flower arrangements, trays of makeup, nail polish and perfume. Then his eyes moved back to Misty, sliding down her shapely frame, only to settle on the swollen bump at her middle.

"I've seen a change in my grandson since the two of you started seeing each other." He stuffed his hands in his pants pockets and rocked back on his heels, clearing his throat before saying more. "I started to notice it a few years ago, when he first took up with you, I believe, but it's become more obvious since you came to New York and moved in with him."

Misty's pulse was pounding so hard it echoed in her ears. She opened her mouth, closed it in hopes of creating enough saliva to form words, then opened it again.

"I'm sorry," she told him. "I know you don't approve of Cullen's involvement with me, but—"

The elderly man shook his head, his brows

coming together sharply and his mouth turning down in a frown. "That's not what I mean. What I'm trying to tell you is that Cullen seems happier these days, more at ease. He obviously loves you very much, and is excited about this baby."

He nodded in the general direction of her stomach and made an all-encompassing up and down gesture with one hand.

"You've been good for him. Even a hardheaded old man like myself can see that."

He cleared his throat again, and this time Misty realized he was nervous. Patrick Elliott, patriarch of one of the wealthiest, most influential families in New York, was uncomfortable around her.

Her, a former Las Vegas showgirl from a humble background who'd become his grandson's mistress, for heaven's sake. She found it almost beyond belief.

"I'm glad you're joining the family," he added in a harsh tone. "I have a feeling you'll do us all some good."

Stunned, Misty could only stare, wide-eyed for a moment. And then she forced herself to offer a feeble, "Thank you."

"Yes, well…" Patrick's gaze darted around the room as he began backing toward the door. "That's all I wanted to say, really. You look lovely, by the way, and I'm sure Cullen is eager to get this show on the road, so I'll leave you to…whatever it is you were doing."

He waved in her direction one last time before escaping the same way Bridget had, leaving Misty standing in stunned silence. Two seconds later, Bridget returned, casting a wary glance at her grandfather's retreating back through the crack in the door before closing it behind her.

"What did *he* want?" she asked cynically.

Misty tried to shake off the shock of Patrick's strained declaration, but seemed incapable of movement.

Cullen's grandfather hadn't apologized for the comments he'd made soon after her arrival in New York—the ones about no Elliott marrying a stripper. But he had approached her today, privately, when he didn't have to. He had welcomed her—in his own way—to the family.

"He better not have said anything to upset you," Bridget growled protectively. "If he did, I swear—"

"No." Misty shook her head, blinking several times in an attempt to clear the fog of astonishment from her brain. "You'll never believe it, but—"

Off to the side, a cell phone chirped.

"Oh, damn, that's mine."

Bridget bustled off toward the bed, digging her purse out from under the mountain of clothing that had been tossed there while the bridal party changed into their gowns.

She found her phone and flipped it open, lifting it to her ear. "Hello?"

Misty watched as Bridget riffled through her bag for a pad and pen, taking notes while she listened to whoever was on the other end of the line.

"All right. Yes. Thank you."

She closed the phone, returned it to her purse and spun back to Misty, fiddling with a few loose strands of Misty's hair, tucking them under the rhinestone headpiece where they belonged.

"You'll never believe this," she said almost breathlessly. "I just got some information about what could be a very big break on the story I'm working on for my book. It means I'll have to leave right after the reception, though."

Misty frowned in concern. "Where are you going?"

"I don't want to say just yet, but I promise to call as soon as I get there to let you know I'm all right."

She took a step back and smiled encouragingly. "Now, tell me what Granddad said so I know whether I need to sic Cullen on him or not."

Misty took a deep breath and shared what she still wasn't entirely sure had happened. "He told me I was good for Cullen and said he was glad to have me in the family."

"*What?* Are you serious?" Bridget's blue eyes were round with surprise. And then they narrowed with suspicion. "That doesn't sound like my grandfather. Are you sure you heard him correctly?"

Misty chuckled. "Yes, I'm sure. Although I admit I was as shocked as you are."

For a second, Bridget continued to scowl. Then her expression brightened and she shrugged one slim bare shoulder. "Maybe he's finally coming to his senses. Whatever the reason for his change of heart,

I'm happy for you. The rest of us always knew you'd be a wonderful addition to the family. Cullen loves you, and that's all that matters."

At the mention of Cullen's name and the reminder of how much he loved her, Misty's mouth curved up in a grin. "I know."

"Should we go downstairs and tell them we're ready to get this party started?"

Her fingers flexing around the base of her rose and lily bridal bouquet with strips of pink ribbon hanging nearly to the floor, she nodded. "Yes, let's."

With her hand in Bridget's and butterflies dive-bombing low in her belly, Misty left the room, walked down the hall and stairs to the lower level of the sprawling mansion, and toward the back of the house where her other bridesmaids were waiting to precede her down the makeshift aisle.

Bridget left her at the back of the gathering, rushing around to match up each bridesmaid, including herself, with the appropriate groomsman.

Cullen's father, Daniel, would be escorting Misty down the aisle, and as he approached, she saw a glint of emotion dampening his eyes. Close to tears already, she quickly looked away, linking her arm with his and busying herself with the folds of her gown and ribbons of her bouquet.

Once everyone was lined up and ready to go, Amanda gave the signal for the orchestra to begin playing "The Wedding March." As the first strains began, Misty's heart lurched in her chest, and she had to tell herself over and over again to take deep breaths and relax.

She may not have wanted to step outside and have hundreds of guests gawk at her, but she most certainly wanted to get to the end of this day and finally be Mrs. Cullen Elliott.

The minute she saw him, standing in front of the flower-strewn trellis at the other end of the pink pathway, her nerves left her. A sense of calm swept over her entire body and a gentle smile curved her lips.

Cullen smiled back, and from that moment on, they had eyes only for each other.

When they reached the minister, Daniel kissed her cheek, then turned her over to Cullen. Their fingers twined and he gave her hand a gentle squeeze. She squeezed back, never taking her gaze from the man she was about to marry.

The minister spoke of love and commitment, and before she knew it, it was time for them to exchange their vows. In turn, they each promised to love, honor and cherish, which Misty knew would never be a problem for either of them. And then the minister told Cullen he could kiss the bride.

"My pleasure."

Cupping her face in both hands, he leaned forward until their breaths mingled. "I love you," he whispered, for her ears only.

She blinked rapidly, feeling her heart swell near to bursting inside her chest. "I love you, too."

And then he was kissing her, a soft, chaste

meeting of their mouths that still managed to convey all the passion and devotion their future together would hold.

Epilogue

"That was some pretty incredible newlywed sex," Cullen said, combing the hair away from his damp brow before pressing a line of kisses down Misty's throat, chest, the underside of her breast.

They were in their suite at the Carlyle, blessedly alone. The wedding reception had dragged on forever—at least it had seemed that way to Cullen—until at last he'd been able to whisk Misty away.

A limo had brought them back into the city, and he'd had the honor of carrying her—in all her bridal finery—into the hotel lobby, up in the elevator and across the threshold to the honeymoon suite.

She'd protested that she was too heavy, too largely pregnant, but to him she was light as a feather.

Even if she hadn't been, the adrenaline pumping through his veins would have allowed him to carry her the entire length of Manhattan.

Not one to overlook even the smallest detail, his mother had made sure that the room was filled with fresh flowers, gourmet chocolates and two bottles of chilled champagne—one regular and one nonalcoholic.

It was lovely, and everything a newly married couple could hope for, but Cullen had barely given it a second glance.

Instead, he'd carried his new bride straight to the king-size bed and slowly peeled the pristine white gown from her luscious body, languorously making love to her for the first time as her husband. The experience had been so moving, so elemental, he'd wanted to cry.

The second time, he had realized that Misty really and truly belonged to him. Forever.

He was one hell of a lucky man.

"If I'd known," he added, "I'd have wrangled you down the aisle years ago."

She laughed, the sound skating down his spine like chips of ice while she rubbed the back of his calf with the arch of her foot.

"I still can't believe you wore fishnet stockings under your gown."

When he'd run his hand under her dress, only to find the sexy, revealing things covering her shapely thighs, it had been quite a surprise. But in a good way. A very good way.

"I thought they were appropriate," Misty said. "As a reminder that even though you made me an Elliott today, I'll still always be a showgirl at heart."

"Amen to that," he muttered with feeling.

And then his hands began to wander again. His palms circled and stroked the taut mound at her middle, followed by his lips. "Have I ever told you how sexy I find your pregnant belly?"

"I don't think so," she said with a chuckle, feathering her fingers through his hair.

"I love touching it, feeling the baby move inside and knowing I played a part in putting it there."

"You certainly did."

"And now we have the birth to look forward to. Diaper changes and midnight feedings. Maybe even siblings."

Keeping his hand on her stomach, he kissed a trail back up to her mouth. "Have you thought of any names yet?"

"No," she answered, looking drowsy and sated, lying naked on the silky sheets. "Have you?"

"A few. And I'm sure my family will have some suggestions of their own."

He was watching her sparkling emerald eyes, so he saw the slight shuttering of her gaze at the mention of his family.

"What's the matter?" he asked.

She shook her head, her teeth toying distractedly with her bottom lip.

A stab of concern hit him low in the gut. "Tell me," he said, stilling his caress of her body.

"It's nothing bad, I just didn't have a chance to tell you before the wedding."

Releasing a breath, she turned her head on the pillow, looking him straight in the eyes. Her arm moved until she found his hand and linked their fingers together.

"Your grandfather came upstairs to see me before the ceremony."

Cullen reared back, shocked to the soles of his feet. "What? What did he say to you? Did he upset you? Threaten you? Did he offer you a bribe not to marry me?"

"No. No, no," she quickly assured him, stroking her free hand over his bare shoulder in a soothing gesture. "That's the thing. He was nice to me, and sort of…welcomed me to the family. I think."

For a few seconds, all he could do was stare down at her as though he'd been smacked between the eyes with a brick.

"Well, I'll be damned," he finally found voice enough to mutter. "I have to admit, I never expected Granddad to come around. I'm glad, though."

He pushed the hair back from her brow and lightly kissed the corner of her mouth. "Now do you believe me when I say you'll make a fine Elliott?"

"I don't know. But it certainly is a relief to know your grandfather doesn't hate me anymore…and won't end up hating you in the process."

"Wouldn't matter if he did," he replied confidently. "You're mine, and I won't let anyone tell me we can't be together."

She brought her hand from the back of his head to hold out in front of them—her left hand, with its obscenely large diamond ring and bright gold wedding band flashing in the light of the bedside lamp. And then she touched that same hand to the side of his face.

"Here's to four years as your mistress," she murmured, "and the rest of my life as your wife."

"I'll drink to that," he said before covering her mouth with his own. "Later."

* * * * *

HEIRESS BEWARE

BY
CHARLENE SANDS

Charlene Sands resides in Southern California with her husband, high school sweetheart and best friend, Don. Proudly, they boast that their children, Jason and Nikki, have earned their college degrees. The "empty nesters" now have two cats that have taken over the house. Charlene's love of the American West, both present and past, stems from storytelling days with her imaginative father sparking a passion for a good story and her desire to write. When not writing, she enjoys sunny California days, Pacific beaches and sitting down with a good book.

Charlene invites you to visit her website at www.charlenesands.com to enter her contest, stop by for a chat, read her blog and see what's new!

Special thanks to Jefferson County Deputy Sheriff
Jackie Tallman for her help and guidance in
getting the facts straight.

My heartfelt gratitude goes to one time Navarro County
Deputy Sheriff Betty Swink and Hollis Swink for
their help and constant loving support.

A big thank-you to senior editor Melissa Jeglinski for
creating such a great cast of characters for
THE ELLIOTTS continuity series.

One

"Don't you dare die on me," Bridget Elliott pleaded for all she was worth. But the darn rental car died despite her plea. The motor shut down and no amount of key turns and pumps to the gas pedal would do any good.

She peered out the windshield to view nothing but vast dry Colorado land, an abundance of road ahead and a bright dawning sun that promised a sweltering day to come. A born and bred New Yorker, she was accustomed to scorching June days, but she'd never been to Colorado, and from the look of the place, she hoped she'd never have reason to come here again.

But her mission was just, and the hot tip she'd received last night during her cousin Cullen's wedding reception had put her on a late-night plane. She'd flown all night,

making plans and hoping to add one last chapter to
the book that would expose secrets and lies her grandfather had imposed on their family for two generations.
Patrick Elliott, the family patriarch, owner and CEO of
Elliott Publication Holdings, one of the largest magazine
empires in the world, would finally be exposed for the
man behind the image. There'd be no more positive spin
on the Elliott clan. Bridget planned to clear the air,
uncover family secrets and expose scandals with truths
that could knock her grandfather off his feet.

He deserved it. The last stunt he'd pulled, earlier in
the year, had stunned and angered the whole family.
He'd announced his impending retirement, but instead
of picking his successor, he thought to make a bitter
game of it, pitting his four children against one another
for the job.

It had been the last straw for Bridget.

So for the past six months, she'd been searching for
Aunt Finola's child. The baby, conceived when her aunt
was a teenager, had been given up for adoption—an
adoption forced upon her by her own father, Patrick
Elliott. Bridget suspected her dear aunt had never gotten
over the loss, choosing instead to devote her life to
Charisma magazine to fill the void. Being the photo
editor at *Charisma,* Bridget often witnessed the sense
of loss in her aunt's eyes, even now, more than twenty
years later.

And Bridget had finally made a breakthrough with,
hopefully, a reliable tip from someone who claimed to
know the identity of the child. She had to get to Win-

chester. She had to locate Aunt Fin's daughter. Finding her aunt's child would secure the ending chapter in her book. The world would finally see the kind of man her grandfather really was.

It was close to 6:00 a.m., yet not a soul appeared on the road. Of course, if she'd broken down on Highway 25, she would have been rescued by now, but the directions given by her tipster had taken her off the well-traveled road to this two-lane highway.

Bridget sighed, slumping in her seat. She didn't have time to waste. Then she remembered her cell phone. At least she could call for help, maybe get a replacement car out here quickly. She reached into her purse, coming up with the phone. But her hopes dimmed immediately. Dead battery. Heck, Bridget was forever forgetting to plug the darn thing in to recharge. That made two dead batteries in the span of a few minutes. At least, she *thought* her car's battery had died. But maybe not. Maybe it was just a fluke.

She tried the key in the ignition one more time. "Come on, please," she pleaded to the car gods. "Start, damn it."

Like an unruly child, the Honda Accord refused to comply. Nothing. Not even a little grunt of a sound. "The rental company is going to hear about this," she muttered, slinging her purse over her shoulder and exiting the car.

She slammed the door shut and began walking. Vaguely, she remembered seeing a sign a while back that Winchester County was ten miles ahead. If her calculations were correct, she'd have about a five-mile trek to reach her destination.

"I can do this," she said, her three-inch-heel boots grinding on the asphalt. Always fashion conscious, a true-blue testament for *Charisma*, Bridget now wondered why she hadn't thought to pack her walking shoes.

Where were her Nikes when she needed them?

Sheriff Macon Riggs bounded out of his patrol car and strode with purpose toward the woman lying on the side of the road, her body motionless and damn close to the edge of the cliff. She would never have survived the steep drop had she fallen. The woman faced sideways, with her legs twisting awkwardly, but it was the blood at the back of her head that worried him the most. No doubt she'd hit that sharp wedge of granite beside her, the one smeared with blood.

As he came closer, he noted a face devoid of expression, but beautiful all the same. Dark blond hair framed her face, and her lips, still pink with life, were slightly parted.

He took her hand and gave a squeeze. "Miss, can you hear me?"

Mac hadn't really expected a response, but the woman's eyes snapped open immediately. She stared up at him, blinking several times, and he gazed into amazing lavender-blue eyes. The combination of blond hair, fair skin and that particular shade of blue made the woman memorable by anyone's standards.

He leaned in closer and reassured her. "I'm Sheriff Riggs. You're going to be all right. Seems you had an accident."

"I did?" She spoke softly, with furrowed brows and a puzzled expression that suggested she was dazed from the head injury.

"Looks that way. You hit your head on a rock."

Again, she appeared confused.

"Hang on and don't move. You're close to the edge of the cliff. I'll be right back."

Within a few seconds, Mac returned to her side with the first-aid kit he kept in his patrol car. "I'm not going to move you until you give the okay. Do you feel pain anywhere?"

The woman shook her head slightly. "Not really, except my darn skull's pounding like a son of a—gun."

Mac held back a grin, admiring her attempt at restraint. "I bet. You think you can sit up?"

"I think so."

He knelt down, wrapped his arms around her shoulders and helped her to a sitting position. The material of her raspberry-pink sweater bunched up in back under his fingertips, but it was the V-neck in front that drew his attention. After one swift glance, he kept his eyes averted from soft skin and mind-blowing cleavage, focusing instead on helping the injured woman. "That's good. I can look at the back of your head now."

"Does it look bad?"

Mac did a cursory examination. The blood had clotted to her hair and there was no further oozing. No telling how long she'd been unconscious, though. It was a good thing Mac thought to patrol this road from time to time. Or she might just have rolled the wrong way, right smack into Deerlick Canyon.

"Actually, you're pretty lucky. It doesn't look too bad." Mac sat behind her, positioning himself to attend to her injury. He dabbed at the gash with moistened gauze, parting her hair to see the extent of the wound. "Does this hurt?"

"No. Keep going."

"What's your name?" he asked, to distract her from discomfort she refused to admit. He'd seen her flinch the moment he touched the gauze to her head.

"My…name?"

"Yeah, and while you're at it, want to tell me what you were doing up here? What happened? Did you fall?"

The woman tensed, her body becoming as rigid as a plank of wood.

When she still hesitated, Mac softened his tone. "Okay, first let's start with your name."

"My name is…" she began then started again. "My name is…"

She scooted away from him enough to turn around. She stared into his eyes, blinking, with a panicked look on her face. "I don't know," she said, her voice elevating. She paused again, her eyes darting in all directions, seemingly searching her memory. "I don't know who I am! I can't remember anything!"

Tears pooled in her eyes and she blinked hard, trying to keep them at bay. With desperation in her voice, she repeated frantically, "I don't know. I don't know."

Mac stood, then reached down to take both of her hands and slowly help her up. With her erratic behavior, he wanted her away from the edge of the cliff.

"It's going to be okay. We'll have the doctor check you out."

"Oh, dear God. I can't remember anything. I don't know who I am, what I'm doing here." Pleadingly, she tugged on his sleeve. "Where am I?"

"You're in Winchester County."

She stared at him blankly.

"Colorado."

She shook her head hard, her eyes wide, and Mac saw the determination on her face as she tried urgently to remember something. "Do I live here?"

"Don't know. Seems you were on foot. But we'll search for a car later. There's no sign of your belongings, either. No purse or backpack or anything. If you had anything with you, I'd guess it went over the edge when you fell down. That's *if* you fell. But I can tell you one thing for sure, with those boots you're wearing, I doubt you were hiking."

She glanced down at smooth black leather boots, then noted the rest of her apparel. Designer jeans, lightweight cashmere sweater, a black suede belt that slanted over the material and across her hips, but oddly, no jewelry other than a watch with one bright diamond on the face. She took all of this in with no recognition. It was as if she were staring down at a stranger's clothes. "I can't remember. Dear God. Not one darn thing!"

"C'mon, let's get you to Dr. Quarles." Mac took her hand, but her legs buckled when she took her first step. "Whoa," he said, catching her.

He turned her toward him, her body pressed against

his. She clung to him, wrapping her arms around his neck, leaning in for support. He held her for a minute as she rested her head on his chest. She seemed to need this moment to regain her composure, or maybe to simply lean on him for moral support. He understood her alarm. Waking up in a strange environment, with no sense of who she was or what she was doing up here, had to be frightening.

As Mac patiently held her, his own sense of composure came into play. A professional lawman, he denied the pulsing thump in his throat and the slight acceleration of his heartbeats. Yet, she was soft and beautiful and felt damn good in his arms. It had been quite a while for Mac. He'd almost forgotten what it was like to hold a woman. But her next words brought him back to task.

"My head's spinning."

Mac didn't hesitate. He lifted her up in his arms and walked slowly to the patrol car. Before setting her inside, he took a few seconds to make a mental scan of the area. No car, no sign of her belongings anywhere. Later he'd come back with a few deputies to scour the vicinity. Right now he had to get this young woman to the doctor.

And then he'd try to learn her identity and unravel the mystery of her appearance here.

She didn't know who she was. She didn't remember one thing about herself. Her mind spun and she focused her eyes solely on the man holding her in his arms. Sheriff Riggs. He held her gently, but with strength, and she felt protected and safe. She depended on the comfort he lent as she gazed into his dark eyes. He had nice eyes, she thought, and probably a good smile when he let his guard down. But she got the feeling Sheriff Riggs didn't do that all too often.

She'd been lucky he found her when he did. She'd been lucky she hadn't rolled off that ridge into the canyon. But that was where her luck ended. She searched her mind over and over during these past few minutes, hoping that something would register. Anything.

Nothing did.

The sheriff placed her in his patrol car, leaning in awkwardly, brushing her body with his. As he released her, his arm grazed just under her breasts and she silently gasped at the accidental contact.

"You okay?" he asked, his face inches from hers.

He paused a moment and stared at her, their eyes locking. She nodded, breathing in his aftershave, a subtle manly, musky scent that defined the sheriff. She got the feeling he'd protect her with his last breath if need be. Instinct told her he took his job and his life seriously.

He got into the driver's seat and started the engine. "Let me know if anything looks familiar," he said, slanting her a glance as they drove off.

Again, she nodded. She peered out the window, watching as the high ground they'd traveled became level. They'd entered a valley where cattle and horse ranches lined the highway. Mountain ridges off in the distance provided a majestic backdrop to the rest of the scenery. Again she searched her mind endlessly for any hint or clue as to her identity. Did she live here? Was this her home? Or was she on a mission of some sort? Or a vacation? Was she meeting with someone?

When nothing came to mind, she closed her eyes, willing the dizziness away. She prayed the doctor would have good news for her.

"Stay put," Sheriff Riggs said once he pulled into a driveway and parked the car in front of a small medical building. "I'll come around and get you."

"I think I can walk." She opened the car door and let herself out. Warm air hit her and she took a steadying breath, leaning on the car for support.

Sheriff Riggs was beside her instantly, looking at her with concern. "Not dizzy anymore?"

"I didn't say that," she said, feeling the effects again of standing upright. "But it's getting better."

Without hesitation, he wrapped his arm around her waist and helped her into the doctor's office.

Thirty minutes later, after Dr. Quarles had given her a full examination, he called for the sheriff. "Mac, it seems this young lady has a form of amnesia. With retrograde amnesia, the patient can't recall anything that happened before the accident or incident. A blow to the head could have caused it, but this kind of amnesia can also be brought upon by stress. The good news is that she has no permanent damage. Physically, she's fine. Oh, she'll have a headache for a day or two. Wouldn't be a bad idea to have a few tests done at the hospital to be sure, though. The injuries are minor, but I'd feel better if she—"

"When will I get my memory back?" she asked pointedly, interrupting the doctor.

Dr. Quarles shook his head, peering down at her through his glasses with kind brown eyes. "I can't answer that. Could be hours, days or weeks. Sometimes a patient goes for months without regaining his memory. Usually, with this kind of amnesia, you'll start recovering older memories first, but I have to warn you, you may never remember ones that might have caused the amnesia in the first place. The mind tends to block those out."

"Then I may never remember why this happened to me?"

"That's right. There's a chance of that," the doctor answered. "And let me know right away if those headaches don't subside. You should feel much better by tomorrow."

"But…but," she began as her situation became clear in her mind, "you're saying I'm not going to regain my memory soon?"

"Soon?"

"Today. Doctor, I need to know who I am. Today!"

"I'm afraid that might not happen. There's no way of knowing."

"Surely there's something you can do." Alarmed, she began to tremble, her body shaking uncontrollably. "No," she said, rubbing her forehead. "No, this isn't happening. Where will I go? What will I do?" She refused to cry, but couldn't control her shuddering. Panicked, she shook even more. She didn't know a soul in Winchester County. Or anywhere else, for that matter. She didn't know if she had family here. She didn't know anything about herself. She searched her mind again, trying hard to recall one memory, just one. But nothing came to mind. She didn't even know her own name! This all seemed like one horrible dream.

Dr. Quarles glanced at the sheriff before settling his gaze on her. He spoke softly, in a reassuring way that gave her reason to believe that the good doctor had met his true calling in life. "My wife and I have a spare room in our house. Used to be our daughter Katy's room, but now she's grown and married. You're welcome to stay with us until we can sort this all out."

She was at a loss. She didn't know what to say to such a generous offer. Words weren't enough to express the gratitude she felt. Her throat thick with emotion, she managed to murmur, "Thank you, thank you."

"Well then, it's settled. Let me just call my wife and let her know we're having a houseguest."

Her gaze shifted to the dark, unreadable eyes of Sheriff Riggs. For some odd reason, she needed his approval. In just a short time, she'd come to rely on the man who had most likely saved her life this morning.

The sheriff stared at her for a long moment, as if making up his mind about something. His lips quirked for an instant, not quite in a smile, but something just short of one.

"Wait up, John," Sheriff Riggs said in a commanding tone, stopping the doctor before he exited the room. "I have another idea." Then he turned his attention to her, with a dark piercing gaze. "She should stay with me."

Two

Maybe it was because he felt responsible for her safety, or maybe it was the way she looked up at him with those amazing blue eyes, but Mac couldn't abandon his "Jane Doe." Not even to John and Doris Quarles, one of the nicest couples in Winchester County.

Something inside him just couldn't do it, and the invitation fell from his lips without hesitation.

Jane stepped off the examining table to look him squarely in the eye. Her brows furrowed and she spoke in a tone that seemed…hopeful. "You want me to stay with you?"

He nodded, but added clarification. Hell, he wasn't propositioning her. If he'd met her under different circumstances, without a doubt he'd be interested. And not too many women interested him lately. But Mac was wiser and much more cynical when it came to the opposite sex now. He'd had a bad track record, a failed marriage among other things, to prove it. But something about Jane Doe struck a nerve. He'd lend her his help, food and shelter, and that would be it.

"It's strictly business. I live behind the jail and it will make my investigation into your past easier if you're close at hand. Dr. Quarles lives—" he glanced at John, hoping to get this right "—at least fifteen miles out of town. Correct?"

Dr. Quarles nodded. "That's right. Doris and I have a nice place, but I'm afraid it's outside the city limits."

Mac explained, "I live with my sister, Lizzie. You and I won't be alone, trust me. Lizzie's a schoolteacher. She's around teenagers all day long. She'll love the adult company."

"Doctor, that does make more sense," Jane explained to John Quarles. "I need to work with the sheriff to find out my identity. Thank you for the offer. Both of you have been so kind and generous to me." Jane Doe smiled, and dimples peeked out from the corners of her mouth. Mac took credit for that smile and immediately halted that train of thought. No sense getting caught up in blue eyes and a curvy body. He had a job to do. And he'd bet the woman would get her memory back real soon. Either that or someone would come looking for her.

"Are you through with your exam?" Mac asked the doctor.

"Yes, I've given her a prescription for pain, but I

want to know if there's more dizziness, fainting or anything unusual."

"You got it," Mac said. Then he faced his new house-guest. "Are you ready, Jane?"

"Jane?" She wrinkled her nose.

"Jane Doe," he said softly. Hell, he had to call her something. "Unless you prefer another name?"

"My real name would work wonders," she said a little sadly, with a slant of her head.

"I'm gonna work on that straightaway."

Again she looked at him with hopeful eyes, then shrugged a shoulder. "Jane's as good a name as any, I suppose."

"Okay, Jane. Let's get you home." And for the first time in his life, Mac was taking a woman home to meet his doting younger sister.

You'd have thought he'd been the one who'd hit his head on a rock.

"Don't let me keep you from your work, Sheriff," Jane said, sitting across from him in his cozy kitchen. He'd driven her to his house, after showing her the Winchester County Sheriff's Station, which was just yards away, up on the main street of town. His house sat on a quaint residential street just behind the jail.

While the sheriff's station could be considered contemporary, with angles and large floor-to-ceiling windows, the sheriff's home was anything but. She liked the charming three-bedroom house the minute she'd stepped inside. There was a lived-in warmth about the place.

"Call me Mac," he offered with the slightest hint of a smile. "And this *is* work. I hope you're up to a few questions. I'm going to take a drive out later today with my deputies to scour the area where you fell." Mac slid her a cup of coffee and a turkey sandwich he'd whipped up at the counter.

"Oh, thank you."

"It's my job," he said automatically.

She chuckled. The man was all business. "No, I meant for the meal."

He glanced at her for a moment, staring into her eyes. "It's hardly a meal. Lizzie's better at cooking than I am. She'll be home after three."

"I hope she doesn't mind having me here."

Without pause, he stated, "She won't. If anything, she'll talk your ear off. My sister loves a good conversation, especially if she's the one doing all the talking."

"Oh, I get it," Jane said, teasing the all-too-serious sheriff. "That's why you wanted me here. Takes a load off, does it?"

Instead of a sharp denial, he played along, much to her surprise. "You got it. You're nothing if not perceptive."

Jane drew air into her lungs. With her situation so desperate, she couldn't put much energy into being witty. "Thanks for the sandwich." She took a bite, then sipped her coffee. "What did you want to ask me?"

Mac scratched his head, then leaned forward. He paused a moment, his gaze traveling the length of her. When his eyes stopped on her chest for the briefest of seconds, Jane's breath caught. Electricity sparked in the air, filling the small kitchen. He liked what he saw, and though he had tried, he couldn't conceal that initial jolt. After all Jane had been through today, that brief instant in time brought her a definite dose of satisfaction.

Silly, of course, but true. Jane didn't know much about herself, but she understood something about the opposite sex. And Sheriff Macon Riggs, physically fit and mentally sound, was one heck of an appealing man.

"I need to know if you came up here on your own. Or if someone meant to do you harm. Sorry, but I have to ask."

The thought of someone out to harm her hadn't crossed her mind, yet she didn't feel alarmed. In truth, she felt blank, like an unused sheet of paper. Jane searched her memory, hoping for a flicker of recognition. "I don't know. I can't remember. Do you think it's possible that someone deliberately left me up on that cliff?"

"I don't know. Maybe. A jealous boyfriend? It's been known to happen, but the reality is that you've got no identification on you. I didn't see a car abandoned on the road, but we'll check that out. And you had nothing in your possession."

"I know," she said, tamping down her frustration. She knew the sheriff was only trying to get at the facts. "It's strange, but I have no answers for you. The only thing I remember is waking up on that road, with sunlight warming my body, looking into your eyes. I remember thinking you had nice eyes," she said, revealing aloud what she meant to keep to herself.

The sheriff stared at her, again with an unreadable expression. Jane shrugged off her embarrassment at that last statement, reminding herself to keep her most private thoughts to herself. She realized, though, that she might not know enough about herself to keep quiet. Each new revelation, even one as small as Mac's attractive dark eyes, meant something to her. She had so little to go on and knew so little about herself that she felt as if each new observation could be a clue to her identity.

She wondered, this time definitely keeping her thoughts to herself, if her attraction to Mac Riggs was a natural reaction borne out of his rescuing her, or if she might have automatically categorized him as "her type." She wondered if she liked the tall, dark and deadly serious kind of man, ones with strong features and sexy eyes.

"Anything else?" she asked, grabbing for the plates.

Mac immediately reached out, brushing his hand over hers, taking the plates from her. The contact startled her and she froze, her heart leaping in her chest. His touch sent shivers down her spine in a decidedly good yet unwelcome way. Jane had enough to worry about without lusting after the man who had been kind enough to take her in, offering her shelter and protection.

"I don't expect you to wait on me," he said firmly.

The breath whooshed out of her. "And I expect to pull my weight around here. Now, if you don't have any more questions, I'll clean up the kitchen. Don't you have an investigation to carry out?"

Mac blinked and his lips thinned, but Jane was certain he held back a grin. "Yes, ma'am. I'll get right on it." He snapped to, standing tall and puffing out his chest. Once again taking control. "Lizzie'll be home shortly. You need anything before then, call the jail." He scribbled a number on a notepad on the counter. Then he clapped his tan hat on his head, scowled once as she began clearing the rest of the table, and nodded in farewell.

He strode to his patrol car, which was parked on the driveway. As she watched from the doorway, she decided he was just as appealing from the back side, wearing a pair of tan pants hugging a tight butt and a chocolate-brown uniform shirt stretching across very broad shoulders. He slid into his car and started the engine, taking one last glance at her before pulling away.

Funny, with Mac around she'd felt safe and protected. But as soon as he left, her bravado failed her. She was alone. Not just in a strange house, but alone in her head. She had no memory, nothing to call upon, nothing to seek solace in, and that more than anything else frightened her.

Jane wandered from room to room, getting acquainted with a home she did not know, ready to meet a woman, who, regardless of all of Mac's assurances, might not appreciate an intruder.

Jane crossed her arms and hugged herself, warding off another case of trembles. She didn't know if she had the fortitude to survive without her memory. Right now nothing seemed real. She walked into the room Mac had designated as hers for the time being, and lay down on the bed. The full-size mattress accommodated her comfortably and she noted the cheerful surroundings. She guessed Lizzie was the decorator in the family, the whole house having female touches like lacy curtains and wall sconces with scented candles, so unlike the no-nonsense Sheriff Riggs.

Jane curled up on a soft chenille quilt and closed her eyes, as fatigue from a harrowing day caught up to her. She only hoped that when she woke up, somehow her memory would return.

And this nightmare of a day would be over.

Jane woke to the sound of humming, some catchy tune she didn't quite recognize. She opened her eyes to unfamiliar surroundings, blinking as she darted her gaze around the room. Everything seemed…off. For a second nothing registered. Then, in an instant, it all rushed back to her and she remembered her sudden appearance here in Winchester County. She remembered Sheriff Riggs taking her in. She'd fallen asleep in the guest room in his home.

Jane sat upright in bed, hoping that she'd remember something more than the past few hours of her life. When nothing jumped out at her, she rose quickly and peeked her head out the bedroom door in search of whoever was humming.

"Oh, hi! I didn't mean to wake you," announced a slender woman with short auburn hair and Mac's espresso-brown eyes. She approached, walking down the hallway wearing a big smile. "It's the song. I just can't seem to get it out of my head. I didn't realize I'd been humming and disturbing your peace all at the same time. Some songs just do that to you, you know."

"I didn't recognize it," Jane said, searching her mind for any clue. "Should I?"

"Not if you don't listen to country music. It's Tim McGraw's latest."

"Oh," Jane said with a shrug, learning something new about herself. "I guess I don't like country music."

The woman smiled once again and put out her hand. "Hi, I'm Lizzie, Mac's sister. Don't worry, a few days around here and you'll hear every doggone country tune known to man."

Jane took her hand and, instead of a shake, Lizzie placed her other hand atop hers and squeezed gently. "Mac told me all about your situation. Sorry to hear about your amnesia. That must be strange, not knowing who you are." She cast her a warm, soothing smile. "You're welcome here for as long as it takes to regain your memory. Don't tell him I said so, but Mac's the best there is. If there's a way to discover who you are, he'll find it."

Jane nodded. She had already pegged him as a dedicated lawman. "He's calling me Jane Doe."

Lizzie frowned. "Now, isn't that original. That man has no imagination."

"It's fine, really. Call me…Jane."

"Okay, Jane. Nice to meet you. And welcome. *Mi casa es su casa.*"

"I can't tell you how much I appreciate your hospitality. Your brother has been so kind. And now you. Thank you from the bottom of my heart."

Lizzie waved off her thanks with a quick gesture.

"I'm glad to have the company. Mac told you I teach at the high school. Little devils, all of them. But I love them, just the same."

Jane laughed. Lizzie had a way about her that put a smile on your face. "It's easy to see you love your job."

She nodded. "I do. But I'm ready for a break. School's out soon and I have the whole summer off."

Jane wondered about her own job status. Did she have a career? Would someone be missing her soon? Or had she traveled here on some kind of vacation? It seemed that all of her conversations reverted right back to square one. Who was she? And why was she in Winchester County?

"Tell me," she asked Lizzie curiously, "that song you can't get out of your head. What's it about?"

"'Live Like You Were Dying'? It's about living life to the fullest. About getting the most out of life while you're still here on earth." She lifted her shoulder in a little shrug. "At least, that's my interpretation."

"And do you?" Jane asked, nearly certain at how Lizzie would respond. "Live life to the fullest?"

Lizzie's smile faded some and she gave serious thought to her answer. "No, I wish I could be more adventurous, but I've never been a risk-taker."

Surprising. Jane didn't quite know what to say, but Lizzie bounced right back, grinning. "Besides, who would watch out for Mac? He needs me. He doesn't have anyone special in his life. And he hasn't for quite awhile. Divorced, years ago."

Jane didn't know Mac Riggs very well, but she'd

gotten the distinct impression that the big strong sheriff didn't need anyone watching out for him. He appeared quite capable in all regards, a man who didn't want or need complications in his life. He seemed to like his life just the way it was. Jane guessed that Mac kept his sister close so that he could watch out for *her,* regardless of what Lizzie might think. And she also guessed that Lizzie had sacrificed something in her life for her brother's sake.

Though it wasn't any of her business, Jane felt obligated to comment. "He's lucky to have you, Lizzie. In fact, you're lucky to have each other. I only wish I knew if I had any siblings."

Lizzie reached out to take her hand, her brown eyes warm and reassuring. "You'll get your memory back soon. It might even happen tomorrow. But in the meantime, know that you've got a friend here in Winchester."

Jane didn't know anything about herself, but she believed that she would have liked having Lizzie Riggs as her friend. "Thank you."

"Here I am, going on and on, and I haven't even asked if you'd like to get cleaned up. Would you like a hot shower or a bubble bath? I bet you'd love to get out of those clothes."

Lizzie's perception and her generous attitude made Jane feel at home. For that, she would be eternally grateful. "I would. I don't know why, but I feel like I've been in these clothes for twenty-four hours." She glanced at Lizzie, her mind whirling. "Maybe I have."

Lizzie nodded. "Maybe. All the more reason to get you out of them and into something else."

Jane had nothing else to wear, and just as she was about to relay those sentiments, Lizzie spoke up. "Let me take care of that. I've got it all under control. Just relax and enjoy. I'll show you to the bathroom. Lavender bubbles await."

Jane suddenly couldn't wait to get out of her clothes and cleaned up. And she'd learned one new thing about herself.

She preferred a steamy hot bubble bath to a shower any day of the week.

Mac entered the kitchen through the back door, unfastening his gun belt and yanking off his hat. He hooked both on a wooden rack that had seen better days. Lizzie had been pestering him about updating the kitchen, but Mac liked things as they were. Change made him uneasy, and he'd grown accustomed to the chipped tiles and outdated curtains. "Hey, Liz," he called out.

"Not Lizzie," a voice corrected, and he spun around to come face-to-face with Jane. "Just me."

He took a step back, seeing her in his kitchen, her face clean, her blond hair wet and combed back, falling to her shoulders. Those lavender eyes seemed larger now and more expressive as she examined him for a moment, before she turned toward the oven.

"Lizzie's taking a Pilates class right now. She trusted me with heating up your dinner. I hope that's okay."

Mac grunted. "Fine."

"She said not to wait dinner on her. She had some errands to do after that. Looks like you're stuck with me."

Being "stuck" watching a beautiful woman make him dinner wasn't half-bad, Mac thought. He stood there staring, watching Jane busy herself around his kitchen, wearing what he recognized as Lizzie's clothes. Levi's hugged her bottom like a baby to her mama, and the Winchester Wildcats T-shirt she wore never fit his sister that way. Lizzie was nothing if not loyal to the high school football team, but hell, Mac hadn't seen anyone fill out a T-shirt so well.

Detective skills aside, any red-blooded male would notice that Jane wasn't wearing anything under that shirt. Brown-and-white material stretched across her chest, exposing twin tips jutting outward, and each time she moved, everything jiggled.

Hell.

He wouldn't even think about what she might not be wearing under those Levi's. "More like you're stuck with me. Need some help?" he asked.

Jane stopped with oven mitts in hand, ready to put the roast in the oven. "I've got it covered. But thanks. Dinner should be ready in an hour."

He headed for the refrigerator, stifling the heat crawling up his neck, remembering why he'd come home early in the first place. He had news for Jane. "Want a beer?" he asked, yanking out a Bud.

Jane closed the oven door and stood to face him. "I don't know. Do I like beer?"

Mac grabbed a second bottle. "Only one way to find out."

He handed her a beer and gestured for her to sit at the table. Both took seats facing each other. "How're you doing? Feeling okay?" Even though she looked great, he had to ask. He felt an obligation to see to her care. And Mac never took his responsibilities lightly.

"I took a little rest earlier, and it really did me a world of good. I'm feeling much better."

"No headaches?"

Her damp hair framed her face when she shook her head. "Nope. No headaches."

Relieved, he nodded, realizing that Miss Jane Doe had been on his mind most of the day. He'd been concerned about the fall she'd taken this morning, and how she would fare the rest of the day. "I took a few deputies and went out to the site where I found you."

Jane played with her bottle, twisting it back and forth in her hands. Her eyes were wide, and Mac noted the anticipation on her face. "And?"

"Well, we can't be sure, but there's evidence that a car had pulled off the road about a mile and half back from where I found you. We found fresh tire tracks in the dirt. If it was your car, chances are it's been stolen. Then again, it could be completely unrelated."

"That's it?"

Mac shook his head. "I'm sorry it isn't better news."

Jane took a swig of her beer and Mac waited for her reaction. She kept on drinking until she'd emptied half the bottle.

"Guess you're a beer drinker, after all."

She shrugged, her eyes downcast. "So I like beer and hot bubble baths."

Mac didn't need a reminder of how Jane looked, cleaned up. He'd already had enough to deal with, watching her busy herself around the kitchen, but the thought of her naked and soaking in a steamy tub of bubbles sent his mind spinning. He took a swig of his own beer, and then a longer drink. Hell, he couldn't recall a time when a woman made him feel so unsettled. He'd taken a few jabs of ribbing at the station when he'd quit to come home early today. That teasing was bound to escalate once his deputies got a good look at her.

She peered up at him with those large questioning eyes. "What now?"

Mac returned his mind to her situation. He scratched his head, laying out his next plan of action. "Routine stuff. We'll check the local area reports of missing persons. We'll run your fingerprints tomorrow and see if we get a hit."

"Fingerprints? Do you think I could be a *felon?*" She whispered the last word, as if appalled by the notion. She had trouble meeting his gaze as she tried to mask her distress.

Mac shook his head. Instincts told him Jane Doe wasn't a criminal. He wanted to reach out to her, to reassure her and lend her comfort. But the lawman in him couldn't do it. He knew he stood behind a firm, defined line. He couldn't breach that line. Sometimes, even the most innocent-appearing people held the worst kinds of secrets. Mac had been a lawman fifteen of his thirty-five years, and he'd seen enough to harden him. "Not necessarily. Criminals aren't the only ones who get fingerprinted. We go through Automated Fingerprint Identification System, an automated way to identify persons in the military and law enforcement, too. If you've ever applied for a liquor license or been caught with a concealed weapon, your fingerprints should be on record. The system is designed for identification purposes."

"But mostly it's used to identify criminals, right?"

"Yes, that's true. Do you have a prob—"

Jane shook her head quickly. "No, no. I'm willing to do whatever it takes. I don't have a problem with that."

"Okay, that's our next step. Might take a while, so don't set yourself up for disappointment, okay?"

She nodded, and cast him a brief smile. "Okay."

Mac stood and walked toward the hall, ready to change into his street clothes. He grabbed his gun belt on the way out. Habit had him keeping the gun in his room at night, rather than out in the open where a perpetrator might find it. "Oh, one more thing," he said, turning again. Jane stood to face him, lifting her blond brows.

"Do you, um, have any unusual or identifying marks on your body?" He swept his gaze over her, unable to limit his focus to her face. Suddenly the three feet that separated them no longer seemed enough. It was one thing interviewing a victim at the jail and another thing entirely speaking of such a subject in the privacy of his own home. Or maybe it was just asking those personal questions of Jane that swamped his body with heat. "Tattoos, body piercings, anything like that?"

She shook her head. "Nothing like that. But I, uh…I do have a birthmark." She blushed, her face coloring quickly.

Encouraged, Mac asked, "Where?"

She bit her lip and turned sideways, pointing to an area just above her derriere. Lizzie's low-rise Levi's covered the spot in question. "I don't quite know how to describe it. It's kinda hard for me to see."

Mac swallowed, cursing himself for asking the question in the first place. Always the dutiful lawman… He stood there, staring at Jane's perfect butt.

"Is it important?" she asked, "because you could— I mean, I would let…"

Mac stared into clear blue, earnest eyes. He stepped back, shaking his head. "I've tangled with some pretty tough characters, Jane, but sorry. I'm just not that brave." Or stupid, he wanted to add.

He exited the room quickly, his body tight and hot, but even worse, his ears burning with Jane's quiet chuckling.

Three

"I gathered my things, if you want to take a look at them," Jane said, holding the pile of newly laundered clothes. She stood by the screen door, waiting for Mac's response.

He sat comfortably in a white wooden lawn chair, looking out at the backyard garden, which was full of trimmed shrubs and colorful spring flowers that Lizzie prided herself on. She'd given Jane a quick tour of the grounds when they'd met earlier today.

Lizzie had been kind enough to wash and dry all of her clothes, except, of course, the cashmere sweater. It was ruined anyway, ripped a bit and stained with red dirt from when she'd fallen.

After dinner, Mac had asked to see Jane's belongings, meager as they were.

"Bring them outside," he said now. "It's a nice night. I made coffee."

The screen door slammed shut behind her as she exited the house. Two mugs of coffee sat on a white wicker table beside Mac. She took the other seat, somewhat touched that he had included her in his little respite.

"I can vouch for my coffee. I make a mean cup."

"That's good, I think," she murmured, setting her clothes on her lap.

Mac cleaned up nicely, she thought. She'd been taken aback earlier this evening when he'd entered the kitchen for dinner dressed in casual street clothes—faded jeans and a black polo shirt. Tanned and well muscled, he seemed less formidable out of his uniform, but just as appealing.

She wondered what it would take to bring down his guard. She had yet to see him smile.

"I have to thank you again for all you're doing for me."

"It's my—"

"And don't say it's your job, Sheriff Riggs," she interrupted, wagging a finger at him. "You went beyond the call of duty by taking me in. You have a lovely home and your sister is as friendly as can be. Both of you have made me so welcome. Under the circumstances, I feel pretty lucky. One day I hope to find a way to make it up to you."

Mac glanced at her, his dark brows arching. His lips quirked and he shook his head. "Don't offer to show me your birthmark again and we'll call it even."

Completely stunned, Jane gasped, barely managing to utter the words, "My birthmark? I thought it would… help," she said, her voice rising once again as she nearly bounded from her chair. The only thing stopping her were the clothes on her lap, which she tried darn hard not to drop. "I would never have made that offer if I wasn't desperate to find out who I am, you idiot." She barely contained her temper, but she did take a swat at his arm. His well-honed instincts must have kicked in, because he jerked away quickly.

Mac laughed then, a full-out, deep laugh, and the change in his face was astounding—so much so that for a moment Jane forgot all about her anger. She stared at him, her heart doing major flips. Oh God, she thought wryly, he's gorgeous. Amazing.

"Don't get me wrong, Jane. It's the best offer I've had in five years."

Jane sank back down in her seat, staring at him and shaking her head. "Only five?" she said with sarcasm. Despite her cutting remark, she was still awed by the transformation on the lawman's face. And the fact that he had stayed single all this time.

Mac took hold of the clothes she'd brought outside, removing them from her lap. "Beer, bubble baths and bad temper. At least we're learning something about you, Jane."

She countered quickly, "And to think I was beginning to believe the good sheriff wasn't human."

Where had that come from? Jane chided herself on her cynical tongue. The words just poured out of her. And she learned that when backed in a corner, she came out fighting.

Mac's smile faded and he pierced her with dark probing

eyes. He spoke in a low, sexy tone, more like a whisper meant for her ears alone. "Believe me, I'm human. That birthmark of yours will be in my dreams tonight."

He kept his eyes focused on hers, but the heat of his stare and the implication of his words poured through her like molten lava.

"Oh," she said quietly, fully aware of the sparks igniting between them. But it seemed they both came to their senses at the same time. They leaned back in their chairs, and Mac began examining her clothes.

The moment had come and gone, and Jane was grateful. She didn't need any complications right now. Admitting that Mac Riggs was an interesting and appealing man was one thing, but allowing anything to develop between them was something else again. How could she? She didn't know who she was or where she belonged.

"Lizzie said your clothes were high-end." Mac became all business again, studying the designer label on her jeans.

"I suppose."

He ran his hands up and down the material, then looked inside the waistband.

"Size five."

Jane rolled her eyes. Didn't the man know not to announce to the world a woman's dress size? After her last few sardonic remarks to him, she decided not to comment.

"Why do women spend a fortune on Gucci and Guess and Ralph Lauren, when Levi's works just fine?" He glanced at her jeans and nodded.

"Maybe because women want to look better than 'just fine.'"

Mac grunted.

Then he lifted her watch and brought it close to his face, examining the diamond. "Pretty good size diamond in there." He flipped it over. "No inscription."

He set the pants and the watch on the table and moved on to examine her sweater. "Why would you be wearing a sweater, cashmere no less, in the middle of June?"

She shrugged, her frustration mounting. Nothing in her possession seemed to lead to any clues as to her identity. "I don't know, but I got the feeling that I'd been in my clothes a long time."

"Meaning?"

"That maybe I slept in them. Or traveled in them a long while. I'm not sure."

Mac drew oxygen into his lungs. "Maybe. That could mean you came a long way. If you traveled during the night, you'd most likely need warmer clothes. That would explain the sweater. And the fact that you don't know much about Colorado in June. Hell, it gets sweltering hot here during the day this time of year."

"That's not much to go on, is it?"

Mac sipped his coffee, staring out into his backyard, contemplating. "It's something, at least."

Then he glanced her way. "For what it's worth, I don't think you're from this area at all."

"Why?"

"Just a hunch." Then he lifted her wide, black suede belt and studied it. "This isn't a western belt. Won't fit through any loops. In fact, it looks pretty darn expensive."

Jane didn't have any answers. She couldn't respond.

She felt at such a loss, as if trying to put together a puzzle where none of the pieces seemed to fit.

She took her first sip of Mac's mean cup of coffee. "Not bad, Sheriff Riggs."

"Is there a compliment somewhere in there?"

"I won't lie. This is good coffee."

He nodded, sipping from his own cup. "Thanks."

He set the belt down beside the rest of her things and stood up. Jane hadn't the nerve to let him see her underwear. She'd kept them hidden in her room. She couldn't stand to let Mac know that she'd worn a teeny, minuscule scrap of material that one might mistake as underpants.

That was just too much information for the sheriff to have.

"I'll take you by the station in the morning and we'll get started on your case."

Jane rose, picking up her things and hugging them to her chest. They were all she had in the world right now. She felt the evening coming to an end, and she needed the comfort. "Okay."

"Well, good night." Mac tipped his head in a brief nod of farewell.

But Jane couldn't let him go. Not before she apologized. She'd been out of line, and he deserved more for all he'd done for her. "Wait. I, uh, can't say good night without apologizing for how I behaved earlier."

Mac smiled then, with a quick flash of white teeth and full lips. "Don't apologize, Jane. I haven't had a good laugh in way too long."

"Really?" she asked, puzzled. "What was so funny?"

"You," he said. "No one's dared call me an *idiot* since I was nine years old. Back then, I bloodied the kid's nose and got sent to the principal's office."

"Oh," she said, realizing her sharp tongue had indeed insulted the sheriff. "Now I really feel bad."

Mac grabbed her hand and squeezed, ready to say something. But just then they heard a car pull up. "That'll be Lizzie," he said, dropping her hand and stepping back. And within a minute, Lizzie had their full attention.

"I guessed at the size," Mac's sister said, displaying half a dozen items of lingerie that she'd purchased for Jane. She'd also bought a hairbrush, comb and toothbrush, as well as a small travel kit filled with lotion and shampoo, lip gloss and other makeup essentials. "You needed some things of your own, especially something to wear to bed tonight."

Jane cleared her throat, glancing at the personal items Lizzie had laid out on the kitchen table as Mac lodged himself against the counter, watching. So many emotions whirled around inside her that she had trouble naming them all—gratitude, for one, but embarrassment as well, along with an uncanny sense of helplessness. "I don't know what to say. I can't possibly pay for these right now."

"It's okay, Jane. Call it a loan. Besides," Lizzie said, looking over Jane's head to wink at her brother, "I put them all on Mac's credit card."

Jane whipped her head around to find him shrugging.

Lizzie took her hand and squeezed gently. "It's okay. Mac's got more money than Donald Trump. The only difference is that my brother doesn't flaunt what he has. He can afford it."

Jane eyed the pretty pink nightie, a matching light-weight robe and four pair of underpants, each a different style, from full cotton panties to a lacy red thong, with the others in between.

"I didn't know your preference," Lizzie explained.

"Oh, Lizzie. This is so thoughtful and generous. They're all perfect. Thank you," she said, then turned again to catch Mac's stare. "And I'll find a way to pay you back."

He shook his head. "Don't worry about that right now."

"As soon as I can, I'm taking you shopping," Lizzie said. "You'll need more than my hand-me-downs to wear."

"I don't mind," Jane said, feeling overwhelmed. She didn't have any means to pay either of them back for their kindness and generosity. Lizzie's clothes fit her well enough, even though they were a tad on the tight side. "Besides, I'm hoping to get my memory back before there's a need to go on a shopping spree."

Lizzie smiled warmly. "I hope so, too, Jane. But just in case, we'll make a day of it, sometime soon. Right now, I'm knee-deep in finals. School will out by the end of the week, and after that I'll have some free time."

Jane hoped with her whole heart it wouldn't come to that. She hoped to regain her memory very soon. But Lizzie seemed intent on planning a shopping day, and the last thing Jane wanted to do was discourage her enthusiasm. "Okay, then, I'll look forward to it."

Mac's sister beamed. "Good."

"Thank you, Lizzie. I think I'll take my things and head off to bed. I have to be up at the crack of dawn. Mac is taking me to the station tomorrow to get finger-printed." She turned to him. "Shall I set my alarm?"

He came forward, his gaze focused on the red thong panty atop her stack of new lingerie. "I'll give a knock at your door when it's time. No need to get up too early." His gaze finally rose to meet hers, and the unmistakable gleam in his dark eyes was enough to send Jane off to bed with a bad case of tingles.

"Rise and shine, Miss Doe," Mac said from outside Jane's door. His knocking had woken her from a sound sleep. She opened her eyes slowly and lay there, allow-ing the events of the last twenty-four hours to sink in. She knew she'd slept in a strange bed, but oddly enough, she'd fallen asleep almost immediately. And she'd dreamed.

She'd hoped to dream about something from her past, something that would give her a clue as to her identity, but that hadn't been the case at all.

She stared up at the ceiling, hugging her pillow. "I dreamed of Sheriff Mac Riggs," she whispered incred-ulously. And she recalled her dream vividly, almost a complete replay of how Mac had found her lying in the dirt up on that canyon road. She'd dreamed of him holding her in his arms, bringing her to safety, but that was where the dream got fuzzy.

She'd woken up awash with warmth.

"Jane, did you hear me?"

"Oh, yes," she said, recognizing that familiar deep voice from her dream last night. "I'm awake. I'll be dressed in a few minutes."

"Take your time. Coffee's brewing in the kitchen," he called through her door. "Help yourself to breakfast. Lizzie had to rush off to school early. I'll be in the garage."

"Okay," she said, then added quietly, "Thanks."

Lizzie had left a few tank tops and several blouses on her dresser. Jane decided the black blouse with lacy trim would look a little more appropriate for the sheriff's station than the hot-pink or lime-green tank tops. She slipped out of her nightgown and into the borrowed clothes. Jane opted for her own boots this time, feeling more comfortable in them than the tennis shoes Lizzie had provided.

Jane took a look at herself in the mirror, hoping that something more than lavender-blue eyes and blond hair would register, but nothing came to mind. She recognized the face staring back at her, but that was all. No past, no history. It was as if her life had begun the minute Mac had found her up on that road. She promised herself to keep positive and remain patient. She trusted Mac Riggs, and placed her faith in him. And she prayed that something would turn up today.

She took a minute to brush her hair, apply lip gloss and brush a few swipes of mascara on her eyelashes. She made up the bed and tidied the room, then headed to the kitchen. She could really use a big cup of Mac's mean coffee.

Jane stopped short when she entered the kitchen. The table was set for one, complete with napkin and place mat, even a thin-stemmed red rose in a tall glass vase. Eggs, bacon, oatmeal and biscuits were laid out in bowls, buffet style. Jane shook her head. She couldn't possibly eat all this food.

The rich scent of coffee filled the room and she poured herself a cup, then sat down, once again over-whelmed. She filled half a bowl with oatmeal and ate it quickly, then covered the rest of the food with foil and placed it in the refrigerator.

She took a second to savor the sweet scent of the rose, a thoughtful gesture on Mac's part, then poured a second mug of coffee, and with two mugs in hand, strode pur-posefully out the back door to the garage.

Coffee spilled from the mugs when she stopped suddenly, realizing her mistake. "Oh, uh, sorry. I didn't mean to interrupt."

She glanced at the coffee stains on the garage floor, cursing her own stupidity for seeking Mac out.

"Hey, Jane," he said. "Morning. And you're not in-terrupting. I'm almost through."

Jane shot him a half smile, trying not to stare, but it wasn't easy, seeing him in a pair of gray sweatpants and nothing else, lifting weights. Beads of perspiration coated his bare chest and his skin gleamed in the morn-ing light filtering into the garage. His arms bunched and muscles popped as he finished his repetitions with arm weights.

Pulse racing, Jane set the mugs down on a worktable,

fearing she'd drop them otherwise. Pumped up and hard, Mac was the most physically fit man she'd ever seen.

So *that* was what lay beneath his tan-and-brown sheriff's uniform.

Jane's mouth went dry. She sipped her coffee, acting nonchalant and trying to keep her focus. She'd come out here for a reason. Ogling the sheriff hadn't been her intent, yet she couldn't deny the attraction. She felt drawn to Mac Riggs and that wasn't a good thing.

Mac finished his workout and sat down on a bench, wiping sweat from his brow. Jane watched him swipe at his torso with a small white towel. "I want to thank you for breakfast," she stated quickly. "I ate oatmeal. I guess I'm not much of a breakfast eater."

He swept a long, leisurely look over her body. Heat crawled up her neck and suddenly she felt self-conscious in Lizzie's tight clothes.

"Guess not. I should have known."

"Now we do know."

"Right," he said, his gaze lifting from her chest to her eyes.

"I guess you don't need coffee," she said lamely, showing him the mug.

He brought a big bottle of water to his lips and took a swig. "No, but thanks for the thought."

"Speaking of thoughtful," she said, "I really liked the red rose. Is it from your garden?"

He sipped water again, and Jane watched his throat work, taking it in. "Lizzie's doing. I cook. She sets the table. She loves her flowers."

"Oh," Jane said, kicking herself for the assumption. Of course Mac wasn't the sentimental or romantic type. Why would he have put that rose on the table for her? She was his houseguest, not his lover. "I'll have to thank her. So is this your hobby?"

Mac glanced around the garage at his workout stations. Jane figured he had half a regular gym in here, from free weights to Nautilus machines, mats and benches.

"It's my job," he said, and when he met Jane's eyes, she chuckled.

He cracked a smile and she realized that they had their own private joke. "Okay, I have to keep fit for work. It's just easier doing it at home, on my own schedule. And I guess I do enjoy it. I run through a thirty minute workout most mornings before work, and when I'm off duty, I go an hour or two."

Jane swept another gaze around the garage. "For a home gym, it's quite impressive." And so was he.

Mac nodded. "Thanks. You know, not that you need it, but you're welcome to use my equipment anytime you want. It's always good to stay in shape."

"You are," she blurted, and then caught herself. She added quickly, "Very nice to offer. Maybe I will sometime."

Use your equipment. Oh boy, Jane, she thought. Get out of here before you make a complete fool of yourself.

"What time will you be ready?" she asked.

"Give me ten minutes to take a quick shower, then we'll be out of here."

"Okay, fine. I'll meet you inside."

And she made herself a mental note not to go traipsing after Mac Riggs when he worked out in the garage. It was far too dangerous.

Four

Half a dozen deputies huddled around Jane, waiting on introductions. "Back off," Mac said. "Give the lady some breathing room."

The deputies didn't budge, except to bump each other as they offered handshakes and made small talk with her. Deputy Sheriff Marion Sheaver, his favorite colleague, if the crustiest deputy on the force, pulled him aside. She was six months from retirement and always had an opinion.

"She's beautiful," she said, "and quite a big deal around here. It's been a slow week and a mysterious woman with no memory can liven things up. Let the boys talk to her. I bet she could use some new friends."

"Friends?" Mac glared at his deputies, trying to shake

off the protective feelings he had for Jane. She was his responsibility, nothing more. But sensations whirled through him as he watched his men gawk at her as if she were some prize to be won at the county fair. "I doubt *friendship* is on their minds."

"And what about you, Mac? What's on your mind?"

"She's just a case, Marion."

"You took her in," she said, raising her graying brows. "She's living with you."

"Me and Lizzie. And don't forget, when I found her she had no memory, no money, no identification. She's not the type of woman to go into a shelter, for Pete's sake. She was pretty freaked out about her situation."

Marion scratched her head and eyed him. Mac always hated that particular look on her face. It usually meant a lecture was coming. Or an opinion he didn't want to hear. "She's beautiful."

Mac folded his arms, ready for battle. "You said that already."

"You like her."

"I don't know her. Hell, *she* doesn't know her. Jane's got amnesia, remember. She's just learning about herself."

"Mac, it's about time you got involved with a woman again. If not your Jane Doe, then someone else." Marion shook her finger at him. "You're too good a man to live alone."

He rolled his eyes. "Not this again."

"You had a bad experience, but that was years ago."

"Deputy Sheaver, don't go there."

"Don't pull rank on me, Mac. You know I'm gunning for you."

"Yeah, it's your mission in life to see me tied down before you retire."

"And let Lizzie have a life of her own."

Mac's eyes went wide. "I'm not stopping her from anything. She's a grown woman. She can do anything she wants."

Marion shook her head and closed her eyes briefly. "If you believe that, then you're missing all the clues. And for a man in your profession, that's a real crime."

Mac stalked off, heading for Jane, parting his men and taking her arm. "Ready?" he asked her, making eye contact with each one of his deputies. Funny thing, but the only men seeking out her "friendship" were his unattached bachelor deputies. "Let's get those fingerprints now."

He glanced at his staff. "Don't you have work to do?"

Jane smiled at the officers. "Nice meeting you all."

Mac grunted as the men slowly made their back to their desks.

"Is everyone in Winchester County so nice?" Jane asked, and Mac realized that she had no clue as to how attractive she was. He found that quality endearing. He wondered if she came by that trait naturally, or was it due to her recent memory loss? Who was the real Jane Doe? And why was it so hard containing his attraction to her?

"Nosy is what I'd call them. Good men, each one, but your appearance here in Winchester has caused quite a stir."

"Really? Why?"

Mac shrugged, then placing his hand on the small of her back, led her down the hallway to be fingerprinted. Maybe they'd get lucky and get a hit before the end of the day. Then this unsettled feeling he'd been experiencing would disappear—when Jane left town.

"It's a small community. We get petty thefts and local disputes, but we've never had an amnesia victim show up on our doorstep. You're quite a mystery."

"I wish I wasn't."

"Maybe we'll have some luck through AFIS. Let's hope for good news."

"But what if that doesn't work? What if my fingerprints aren't in there?"

Mac halted, hearing the slight desperation in her voice. "Don't worry, Jane. There's more to do. We have a protocol. The next step would be to go to the local media. That's why I asked about identifying marks on your, uh, body." Mac immediately recalled their conversation about Jane's birthmark. He hadn't dreamed of it or her, like he'd said last night, but the woman had never been far from his mind since he'd met her, birthmark and all.

Jane's blond brows rose to attention and she had this uncanny way of raising one brow higher than the other that drove him wild. "You mean for me to go on television?"

"Not exactly. We'd release a picture of you for the newspapers and television stations, along with what we know about you. We'd do spots on local radio stations as well, with your description and details about how you were found. We'd publicize anything that would help someone identify you."

"Oh, when would we do that?"

"We can do so as soon as I can make the arrangements."

"What do you think I should do?" she asked, looking up at him with those big blue eyes. It was clear that she trusted him, and he didn't want to abuse that trust.

Mac placed his hand on her back again and they began walking slowly. "I say go for it. The more we do, the faster we can get results. I only hesitated about the media because being exposed like that tends to make some people uncomfortable. We can wait on it and hope you remember something, or we can move straight ahead."

Jane listened intently, then nodded. "Let's move ahead. And I hate to be a pessimist, but what if nothing works?"

Mac held her stare, reassuring her. "There's more to do if we come up empty with all of this."

"Like what?"

"DNA samples, hypnotist… But let's not jump the gun. I'll explain all this to you later." He stopped again once they reached the window whose sign read Fingerprints. "Here we are. Margie will take you through the process. I'll be in my office. Check with me when you're through."

Jane nodded and Mac left her, heading back to his office. Jane was one concern, but now Marion had planted a bug in his head about Lizzie.

And it was all Mac could think about the rest of the day.

"You're home earlier than I expected," Lizzie said, as she set down a mass of papers on the entry table and walked over to the living room sofa. Jane had spent the bulk of the afternoon reading. She'd found a Dean

Koontz novel on the fireplace mantel and figured it would be a good way to pass the time.

"Hi, Lizzie. I could say the same about you. Finals all through for the day?" She set the book down, happy to have Lizzie's company for the moment.

"Yep, and I thought I'd bring the essays home, rather than read them in the classroom. This way I can get comfy and put my feet up. Makes for a more generous grade for my students." She grinned.

"I bet you're pretty generous to them, anyway. What subjects do you teach?"

Lizzie sat down next to her on the sofa and sighed. "What subjects don't I teach? I've been around a while and I've taught everything from home economics and art to journalism and English. Right now I'm teaching tenth grade English and history."

"Wow, that's pretty impressive. Do you have a favorite subject?"

"Mmm, I love American history. But it's a challenge getting my students excited about our heritage."

Jane couldn't remember her school days, so she had little to add. She didn't know her favorite subject or whether she had appreciated American history while she was in school.

"How was your day?" Lizzie asked, making herself comfortable on the sofa. She kicked off her sandals and lifted her legs, tucking her feet under her. Her earnest approach and guileless nature was what Jane liked best about Lizzie Riggs. She felt immediate warmth and a budding friendship with her.

"My day went well. Your brother's doing all he can for me. I spent the morning getting fingerprinted, and then Mac had me go through some missing persons reports. I guess time will tell. But I did meet some of the nicest deputies today. Everyone seemed so friendly. One of the men asked about you. A Lyle Brody?"

Lizzie's brown eyes rounded in surprise and her voice went raspy. "*Lyle* asked for me?"

It seemed that Lizzie's whole demeanor changed then. Her face lit up like a Christmas tree and she sat up, leaning in, on full alert. Her body language couldn't be mistaken. Lizzie had the hots for Lyle Brody.

"He sure did. He said to say hello and that you should stop by the jail again real soon."

Lizzie's face took on a dreamy quality. "He didn't."

Jane grinned. "He did. He also said that I was lucky to be staying with you, because you're the best cook in Winchester County. Did you cook for him?"

Lizzie beamed, though she tried darn hard to hide the fact. "Well, yes. But not really. I mean to say, Mac started this thing at the jail. The last Friday of every month they have Potluck Pantry. He's got so many darn bachelors on the force that he decided once a month his deputies should get a decent meal. So some of us pitch in and cook them up enough food for lunch and dinner."

"That's nice. And Lyle likes your cooking in particular?"

Lizzie shrugged modestly. "I suppose."

Jane figured Lizzie to be in her late twenties. She was cute and friendly and had a great personality. There had to be a reason why she wasn't married, or at least dating. And Jane had a feeling that the reason had to do with Mac. Lizzie had made a comment once before about her loyalty to her brother.

"So, if he likes your cooking so much, why not cook him up a meal…in private?" Jane pressed.

Lizzie nodded. "I've thought about it, hundreds of times, but…"

"But?"

"It's complicated."

"So, un-complicate it."

"If only Mac would settle down again," she said quietly, and Jane guessed that she hadn't meant her comment to be heard.

"Mac is a big boy, Lizzie," Jane said sweetly. She didn't want to overstep her bounds, but she also wanted to help her new friend.

"I know. But he's taken care of me for fifteen years. I can't abandon him now. I can't…leave my brother alone."

"Have you spoken to him about this?"

Lizzie shook her head. "No. Mac's protective. You know, the big brother syndrome. He doesn't think anyone's good enough for me. He's kind of in the stone age about things like that."

"Maybe it's time you shook him into the twenty-first century."

Lizzie took a good long minute to think about it, then smiled, her face beaming again. She gave Jane the oddest look and patted her knee. "Maybe I should. Thanks, Jane. I think you've hit upon something here."

She grabbed her essay papers and sighed with content-ment. "I'll be hibernating in my room for two hours, then I'm off. I have a dinner meeting tonight. I'll be home kind of late. You don't mind cooking a meal for Mac, do you?"

"No," Jane said, watching her leave the room with a bounce in her step. "Of course not."

The strangest sensation swept over Jane. She shud-dered involuntarily. Relying on her powers of deduction as well as a gut feeling, she surmised that something sig-nificant had just happened, something to do with her and Lizzie's hunky brother.

Mac entered the kitchen and cursed under his breath. "Where the hell is Lizzie?"

"What?" Jane turned around from her task at the kitchen counter, looking puzzled. "Did you say some-thing?"

"It's nothing," he answered, hanging up his hat and gun belt on the hook by the door. He already knew the answer. Lizzie's car wasn't in the driveway and she wouldn't be home for dinner tonight. Again. This made three consecutive nights that she had been long gone when he arrived home from work.

Mac knew exactly what his little sister was up to. Lizzie and Marion had been prodding him for years to get involved with a woman again. Lizzie's absence again tonight, the fact that she'd chosen the most reveal-ing clothes to give Jane to wear, the fact that Jane looked like a damn cover model in those clothes, all had Mac's nerves on edge.

Yeah, he knew what Lizzie was up to—and it was working.

Damn. Spending a good part of his days with Jane and the better part of the evenings hadn't helped his resolve to keep his distance. He was drawn to her like a moth to a flame.

Tomorrow her picture would be splashed all over the television screens and newspapers. Her description would air on the local radio stations as well. Soon Jane Doe would be a household name in Winchester County.

But right now she stood in his kitchen, looking too much like she belonged there, cooking up his dinner.

Mac took a big breath to steady his nerves. Jane caught his deep sigh, and so he said quickly, "Something smells good."

She smiled and even the specks of flour dusting her face couldn't mar her beauty. Her clothes fit her like a glove. Lizzie's Levi's hugged her hips, and Jane wore a white, sleeveless button-down blouse two sizes too small for her, each button seeming to strain to keep the material from separating. Mac had had trouble keeping his eyes averted today at the jail, and he couldn't miss his deputies' conspicuous interest, either. Jane turned heads wherever she went. He had to do something about her attire. She was pretty enough to draw attention without those revealing clothes, but with them, Mac hated to admit, the woman turned him on.

He forced his body not to react while at work. But seeing her in his kitchen, and being alone with her, well, hell. He was human. And hard as a rock.

"It's nothing special, just baked chicken and potatoes. I tried making biscuits, too. I'm sure you'd prefer Lizzie's cooking over mine."

Mac ran his hand through his short-cropped hair. "Same restaurant, different chef. Good cooking is good cooking, Jane. I'll be back in a few minutes to help set the table."

With that, Mac headed for an ice-cold shower.

Thirty minutes later, he entered the kitchen again after the icy assault and the stern, wordless lecture he'd given himself. He felt relieved and much more in control.

He could manage living with the lovely blonde without getting personally involved. He knew something of self-discipline.

Until he took one look at Jane's face.

She turned to him from the stove, her face flushed, her eyes moist and her body trembling.

The smoke alarm began to chirp wildly.

He glanced down at the pan of chicken, the charred and blackened pieces almost unrecognizable now, surrounded by twice crisped potatoes and toasted biscuits that would chew like leather. The house smelled like a Wildcats football rally bonfire—after the fact—and was just as smoky.

Mac grimaced at the scene, feeling things he had no right feeling. Caring too much. He'd never been one to lose his heart to a woman. Not even his one-time wife.

"Jane, what the hell?"

Upon hearing her name, she burst into tears. Her body shuddered uncontrollably and she broke down, crying quietly. Her silent sobs wrenched his heart.

He reached for the kitchen window, sliding it open quickly, and smoke found its way out. He turned to her. "It's just dinner," he said roughly. "We'll get pizza."

"I…told you, Lizzie's a better cook. I…don't…know what I'm doing here," she managed to blubber, waving her arms in the air.

"Okay, so maybe Lizzie's a better cook. Maybe cooking isn't your thing."

"It's not just dinner…you, you…"

"Idiot?"

"I didn't call you an idiot. I learned my lesson the first time."

"But you were thinking it."

Jane sopped up her tears then glared with those lavender-blue eyes that went dollar size on him.

"What?" he growled. What the hell had he done wrong?

She tossed the kitchen towel at him.

Surprised at her gumption, he caught the towel before it slammed into his face. "Damn it, Jane. I can't figure you out."

"That makes two of us!" Her breaths shaky, she continued, "I can't figure me out, either! I don't know a thing about myself. I can't cook worth a darn, that's a given. But what else do I know? Nothing. Not one darn thing."

Mac played with the kitchen towel, which sported blue ducks and yellow daisies. Jane had a temper. She had spirit and pride and intelligence. He already knew she was a knockout in the looks department. His mind in turmoil, he couldn't tell if he was more pissed off or more aroused.

Neither emotion would do.

"Is all this about one burned dinner?" he asked, trying to make some sense of her outburst. He couldn't claim to know what she was going through right now, but he'd done and would do everything in his power to help her regain her memory.

She pursed her lips and shook her head.

"No? Then what?"

Jane lowered her head, her eyes downcast, as if staring at the ruined meal, but Mac knew she didn't really see any of it. "Deputy Brody called while you were in the shower. He said…he said that, uh, my fingerprints didn't come up with a match. I was supposed to relay the message."

Damn, Lyle should have run that by me privately.

When she glanced at him this time with a face devoid of hope, a body slumped in defeat, Mac couldn't hold back another second. He took the steps necessary to reach her. He swept her into his arms, pulling her close, resting her head against his chest and tucking her hair under his chin.

"It's okay, Jane," he whispered, brushing his lips to her forehead. "Don't give up hope."

She clung to him, and he realized that maybe this had been what she needed all along—someone to hold her. To tell her everything was going to be all right.

He glanced down to where her breasts crushed against him. The top button of her blouse popped open, exposing creamy skin, right down to the white lace bra she wore.

He slid his eyes shut, but her image, and the sweet

fragrant scent of her hair, sent him over the edge. He was rock solid against her and didn't give a damn.

"Mac," she whispered softly.

When he looked down he met her gaze, and Mac realized it wasn't just comfort Jane wanted. He tipped her head and bent his, watching acceptance and desire sweep across Jane's lovely face. He brought his lips down on hers, claiming her mouth in a kiss that began slowly, softly, a test to where they would go from there. A little throaty sound slipped from Jane's lips and Mac drew her closer, cupping her face in his hands, then sliding them farther back, to flow through her blond waves.

She pressed in, wrapping her arms around his neck, her fingers digging into his hair. Her mouth was soft and warm and giving, and Mac deepened the kiss, exploring her lips thoroughly until she sighed with pleasure.

He hadn't been with a woman in quite a while. Fact was, he'd dated some, slept with others, but he couldn't recall a time when a woman had crept into his bones like this. He couldn't remember ever needing this way.

He parted Jane's lips and kissed her openmouthed, losing some of his usual self-control as their tongues danced together, a gentle ballet that soon became a wild tango. Lips and tongues and bodies touched and meshed and blended. They created heat together, a blaze that brought sweat to their brows. Hearts pounded. Bodies cried out for more.

A thought struck Mac. He pulled back, breaking off the kiss, and looked deeply into Jane's eyes. "You could be married."

She shook her head, lifting her left hand and wiggling her ringless ring finger. "I don't think so."

"You could be engaged. Maybe there's a man out there waiting to marry you."

Again, Jane shook her head. "There's no one. Don't ask me how I know, I just do."

Mac wasn't so sure. Jane Doe didn't appear to be a woman who'd be alone in the world. She'd shown him passion and vulnerability, as well as strength and intelligence. She was beautiful and sexy and feisty as hell. How could a woman like that be unattached?

She still had her arms around his neck. Mac relished their contact one minute more, taking her in another deep, long, deliberate kiss, before he reached down to the slope of her breasts.

She waited, her expectant gaze fastened to his. Mac touched the top button that had popped open. She took in a deep breath, straining the material even more. He hesitated, realizing the implications of his next move. He wanted nothing more than to slip his hands inside her blouse and stroke her flesh. To feel the soft, ripe swells.

Slowly, with deft fingers, he refastened the button and backed away. He blinked from the impact of leaving her, giving up the best gift he might ever receive. Clearing his throat, he lifted his gaze to look into her baffled blue eyes. "Tomorrow, we go shopping. You need clothes of your own."

Five

"Well, here we are," Mac said as he pulled into the Winchester Mall parking lot. "It's not fancy, but I think you'll find something you might like here."

Jane glanced at him, sitting in his black Trailblazer, looking as if he wished he were anywhere but here. He wore blue jeans that fit him too well and a white tank with four large brown initials, WCSD. Winchester County Sheriff's Department.

She decided Mac Riggs was one with his job. Whether off duty or on, his job, his commitment to the county, defined him. She respected him for his dedication and knew she was nothing more to him than an obligation.

But she hadn't felt like an obligation when he'd kissed her last night. She been swamped with emotions, wondering about herself, struggling with the meal. And when Deputy Brody had called with the disappointing news, Jane had gone into meltdown.

She hadn't expected to fall into Mac's arms that way, or to kiss him for all she was worth. She hadn't expected to feel more alive in that moment than she had for the last four days, ever since she'd woken up with no memory.

The kiss had been wonderful, but it had caused them awkward moments the rest of the evening. They'd shared a pizza, perhaps to prove to each other that they could handle what had happened, or rather *not* happened, between them. But their stolen looks, averted glances and stilted conversations had sent Jane to bed early.

For both of their sakes.

Yet she couldn't deny she'd wanted to curl up next to Mac on her bed. She wanted his arms around her, comforting her and making her feel alive and vital once again.

"This is going beyond the call, Mac. I bet this is the last place you want to be on your day off."

Mac glanced at her lime-green tank top, his eyes holding begrudged appreciation. "It's necessary."

"But Lizzie said if you'd only waited until the weekend, she would be happy to take me."

Mac bounded out of his car, slamming the door. He came around to her side quickly and opened hers. "Necessary for my general health, Jane."

His brows rose and he shot her a direct look. She glanced down, seeing herself as he might see her. True, she'd felt packed into her clothes like a sardine, but she hadn't realized how that might make her appear to Mac.

Up until last night she hadn't thought he'd even given her a second look.

"You've got a body on you," Mac said, walking toward the mall entrance. "And I'd rather not be reminded of it every time I look at you."

Jane stepped down from the Trailblazer, slamming the door also, nearly having to break into a run to catch up with him. He'd infuriated her with that last comment. As if Jane had had a choice in the matter! She'd been left with only the clothes on her back. She couldn't help it that Lizzie's wardrobe didn't quite fit right. Jane would have seemed ungrateful to complain.

"That shouldn't bother you, Sheriff. You've got enough willpower for both of us."

Mac slanted her a look. "Don't be too sure of it."

"Is that all it takes to get you interested?"

He stopped in his tracks and stared at her. "What?"

Flushed now and nearly out of breath, Jane said softly, "I think you heard me."

"I *can't* be interested, Jane. Don't you get that? You're living under my roof, under my protection. Whether you think so or not, you may have ties to other people. People who love and care for you."

"Yes, I get that. I *got* that last night. You made yourself pretty clear."

Mac shook his head, his expression grim. Jane frustrated him, and she was beginning to understand why. He protected his heart well. So well that he wouldn't even open up enough to take a chance. His dedication to his profession wouldn't allow him to compromise his position. She *got* all of that.

But she also *got* that he had everything to lose. What if she had a past, a family who was looking for her? What if she had a man searching for her? Jane could only see the small details of her life now, living here in Winchester, but Mac could see the whole picture.

She couldn't blame him for backing off. She took hold of his hand and gave a gentle squeeze. "Listen, I'm sorry. I owe you so much for everything you've done."

"You don't owe me, Jane."

"I do. And today, well, you're doing such a nice thing by taking me shopping. Let's not argue. Let's get this over with. I promise I'll be fast. I won't prolong the torture."

Mac grinned then, a quick lifting of the corners of his mouth. His teeth flashed, white and straight and her heart did that thing again. Mac had a killer smile.

"You're really something, Jane Doe."

She cocked her head to one side. "Do you really have Trump money?"

He laughed. "Nobody has Trump money."

"Don't worry, I'll go easy on your wallet."

He placed his hand on her back and led her inside the Winchester Mall. "I'll bet you a week's worth of laundry duty you'll empty me out within an hour."

"Deal."

"Hey, you're that woman with no memory, right? I saw your picture on the news early this morning," the young salesgirl announced, scrutinizing Jane's face. "You were found up by Deerlick Canyon. What's it like, not remembering who you are?"

Jane's expression faltered for a moment. "Well, I, uh, it's not something I would wish on anybody."

Mac stepped up to the sales counter, presenting his credit card. "All through here?" he asked.

The salesgirl, who was named Luanne, according to the pink tag pinned to her chest, took the credit card. "I heard you were injured, but no one really knows how." She glanced at Mac's card, then nodded. "Oh, you're the one who found her. The news said to contact the sheriff's department if anyone recognizes you."

"Yes, that's right," Jane said, her body language telling Mac that she wanted out of this conversation.

"Well, I don't." Again, Luanne studied Jane's face. "Nope. I don't recognize you. Can't say that you've ever been in our store before."

"Thank you. We'll keep that in mind. Could you hurry up with that," Mac said, pointing to the card and the clothes Jane had set on the counter. "We've got a lot to do this morning."

"Oh, sure." Luanne popped her bubble gum a few times as she rang up the sale, and had Mac sign for the purchases. "I bet someone recognizes you, though. I saw your picture on the front lawn as I was pulling out of my garage."

"On your front lawn?" Jane asked.

"Front page of the *Winchester Chronicle*. Boy, I can't imagine. Must be kinda strange."

Jane sent her a weak smile. "It's very strange."

Luanne slipped the clothes into a shiny black bag and handed Mac his credit card and Jane the sack. "Here you go."

"Thanks." Mac grabbed the card and Jane's hand. They strode out the door quickly. "I guess it's going to be like that from now on."

"Like I'm in a fishbowl and everybody's suddenly got the urge to stare at the weird fish?"

Mac squeezed her hand once before letting go. "Not weird, Jane. Intriguing. You're a mystery here, that's all. We'll run the news spots a few days and if no one steps up with information, we'll take another route. You won't enjoy your celebrity too long."

"Celebrity? More like freak show."

Mac shook his head. There was nothing freaky about Jane. Although she found herself in a precarious situation, she'd held up remarkably well, despite the meltdown she'd had last night. She was a strong woman, Mac surmised, and someone who certainly knew how to put herself together. He wasn't an expert, but he'd waited and watched as she tried on clothes, picking out colors that emphasized her pretty complexion and showed off her flawless figure.

She had class, he'd give her that, and a good sense of style. Even though the highly anticipated and newly built Winchester Mall couldn't compare with big city shopping centers, so far Jane had managed to pick out the right clothes to suit her personality.

Unfortunately for Mac, she looked just as sexy in

them. It didn't matter that the clothes were her correct size and there wasn't a designer label to be had; Jane still looked like a million bucks.

"Where to now?" she asked.

Mac glanced down at her black leather boots. "C'mon. We've got to get you some decent shoes. Summer's just around the corner."

"I'm not ungrateful, but Lizzie's shoes hurt my feet. They are just a little small for me."

They strode toward a store called the Shoe Salon, a small intimate shop that carried nothing but finely detailed women's shoes, the displays themselves nearly a work of art. Mac figured Jane wasn't the department store type. And he also figured she'd be glad to get into something less confining. "I bet those boots can't be any more comfortable than Lizzie's shoes," Mac said.

"Actually, my boots are the most comfortable shoes I own. They're from a little town in Italy. The shoemaker only makes two pairs a month. He makes a mold of your feet and customizes accordingly."

Mac halted abruptly. "What?"

Jane continued walking. "I said, the shoemaker makes only two—"

She stopped and turned to him, her eyes rounding in complete surprise. She stared at Mac for a moment as realization dawned. "Oh my God." She dropped her shiny black bag right where she stood. "Mac, I remembered something," she whispered. Then she repeated, louder this time, her face breaking out in a big smile, "I remembered something."

She rushed into his arms, surprising him once again. "Oh, Mac."

Her joy was contagious. He held her a moment, squeezing his eyes shut and relishing the brief contact.

She pulled away quickly and grinned. "This is good."

"Very good. What else do you remember? The shoe-maker's name? The town in Italy? When did you get the boots? Were they a gift?"

Jane smiled again, shaking her head. "I don't know any of that. I can't recall anything else, but this is a good sign, isn't it? Should we call Dr. Quarles and let him know? Maybe there's something I can do to help my memory along now."

"Not a bad idea. We'll give him a call later."

"Oh, Mac." Jane fell into his arms again. She pressed her head to his chest and he took her in, holding her tight. They stood between Trixie's Toys and Fashion Fare in the middle of the mall, like two teenagers crazy about each other. "Thank you."

She looked up and kissed his cheek.

"What's that for?" he asked, guarding his heart from the unwelcome sense of loss he experienced in that one moment, when he thought Jane might have regained her full memory.

"For being here. For helping me. For giving me your support."

"It's my—"

A flicker of disappointment crossed Jane's face.

"Pleasure. It's my pleasure, Jane."

She smiled again, big and wide, and Mac nudged his

misgivings away. True, she was his case and it was his job to help her, but he finally admitted to himself that he'd do everything in his power to help Jane, whether or not it was his job.

The thought unsettled him. Shook him to the core.

The woman had gotten under his skin.

Tonight, tomorrow or the next day, she might regain her full memory. Then she'd be gone.

"I feel so safe when you hold me, Mac. Like everything's going to be all right."

Mac felt just the opposite. When he held Jane, he felt like nothing in his life would ever be the same.

She pulled away, grabbed his hand and tugged. "Come on, you have summer shoes to buy me."

Jane spread out her new clothes on the bed, arranging the blouses and slacks, the jeans and shorts, making outfits, mixing and matching. She'd been happy with her purchases, realizing that with one week's worth of clothes, she could actually put together nearly a month's wardrobe. All in all, she'd done a decent job. And she hadn't cleaned Mac out, either. She'd been prudent, checking price tags, making sure that she could justify the cost of each piece.

"Wow!" Lizzie knocked on the open door, then came bounding into the room, her soft brown gaze lit with pleasure as she scanned Jane's clothes. "Would you look at all this! These are great, Jane. I love the raspberry outfit. It'll look great with your hair and eyes."

Jane couldn't help smiling. "It was fun, and so sweet of Mac. You both have been so kind."

Lizzie flipped over a price tag, then gave Jane a look of admiration. "Great deal. Did this blouse come in other colors?"

"About five others."

Lizzie smiled. "Mac loved it, you know."

Puzzled, Jane frowned. "The blouse?"

"No, silly. Taking you shopping."

She blinked and her voice rose slightly. "He told you that?"

Lizzie shook her head and wispy auburn bangs fell into her eyes. "Big brother would never admit to actually enjoying a shopping trip. But," she said, looking deeply into Jane's eyes, "he didn't complain. Not once. I think my brother likes you."

Jane's face warmed considerably and she knew a flush of rosy color reached her cheeks. She felt obliged to comment. "He's a nice man," she murmured, though she could describe Mac in much more accurate ways. Strong and steady. Protective yet guarded. Dependable. Commanding. And, oh yeah, sexy as sin. He had a way of looking at her lately that made goose bumps erupt on her arms, and when he held her close, simmering heat spread throughout Jane's entire body.

"That's it? You think he's *nice?*" Lizzie stacked some of Jane's clothes on top of each other and made room for herself on the bed. She sat down, crossed her legs and leaned back, bracing her palms behind her.

"Yes, I do." Jane lifted a white, sleeveless summer dress and put it on a hanger. It was a last-minute purchase, an item Mac had encouraged her to buy. She'd need at least one dress, she figured, so she hadn't argued about it. She hung up the dress in the closet, then turned. "What are you getting at?"

Lizzie shot her a mischievous smile. "Mac needs a woman in his life."

"Oh, Lizzie. And you think it's going to be me?"

"You like him, Jane. I can see how you look at him."

"Of course I like him. He saved my life, took me in." With a sweep of her hands, she gestured to the clothes on the bed. "He put clothes on my back. I'm grateful to you and Mac, but there's no future for us, I'm afraid. I don't know who I am. Mac is right to guard himself from the likes of me."

"So you don't think he's a great guy?"

"Lizzie, Mac is a great guy and he certainly doesn't need you matchmaking for him," she said softly. "So why are you? And what about your own love life?"

She let out a deep, gloomy sigh. "What love life?"

Jane sat down next to her. "What about Deputy Brody?"

Lizzie shrugged, but her eyes lit just at the mention of his name.

"Tell me," Jane said gently. "I'd love to help."

"It's just that… I think he's afraid of what Mac might say."

"Lizzie, you're a grown woman and you have a right to make your own choices in life. Besides, Lyle Brody is a decent man, from what I've seen of him. Why would Mac object?"

Again, Lizzie shrugged. "It's complicated." She searched Jane's face for a moment, as if deciding whether to confide in her. "I want to see Mac happy, for one. He deserves it. He's been alone too long and, well, I'd feel like I'd be abandoning him. Sure, he's overbearing at times and we butt heads on occasion, but I know in my heart that he'd give his life for me. He's a great brother."

Jane understood Lizzie's loyalty, to a point. And while she thought it wonderful that Lizzie and Mac shared such a special bond, she wondered about her own life. Did she have a brother somewhere searching for her? Was there anyone out there willing to lay down his life for her? It was moments like this when Jane felt so alone, so lost. The hollowness inside ate at her at times, until she had to mentally obliterate those feelings of despair before they took her down.

Jane had hope now. She'd remembered something today. It had to be just a matter of time before her memory returned. She clung desperately to that hope. She'd tried to speak with Dr. Quarles this afternoon, but he wasn't in his office. Tomorrow she'd make an appointment to see him.

"Mac wants you happy, Lizzie. I'd bet my last dollar on it." Then she grinned. "If I had one, that is."

Lizzie smiled too, only briefly. "But there's more, Jane. And I'm not sure Mac would appreciate me talking about this."

"I understand," she said, though she was dying to know what else Lizzie had to say.

"Of course, if you forced it out of me, then I couldn't be blamed."

Jane grinned again, realizing why Lizzie was a favorite among her students at Winchester High. She was so childlike in her own way, but still a woman with needs and desires that shouldn't be ignored. Lizzie deserved to have a life of her own. She deserved a man to love, a home and a family. Jane had a hard time believing that Mac would deny her those pleasures.

"I'm officially forcing it out of you. I'll take all blame. I'm not giving you a choice." She winked and nodded.

"Okay," Lizzie said, picking up the shoe box holding Jane's new, strappy tan sandals. She lifted the lid off, then replaced it. "Ask me about Lyle."

"Why doesn't Mac want you to see Lyle Brody?"

"Well, because you're forcing me, I'll tell you. Mac was married to Lyle's sister, Brenda Lee."

The air rushed out of Jane's lungs. She felt empty, deflated, and she couldn't quite understand why. She'd known that Mac had been married once, but speaking about it, giving the woman a name, made it all seem so real. Jane had no right to feel even the slightest bit of jealousy, but she did, and the fingers of that emotion inched up her spine in a slow crawl. "Oh my."

Lizzie breathed deeply and nodded. "You see now. The breakup wasn't pretty, and of course, Lyle's just as protective of his sister as Mac is of me. They respect each other professionally, but Lyle is Mac's ex-brother-in-law. Makes it kind of tricky, doesn't it?"

"And you're in love with Lyle, aren't you?"

"I think I could be, Jane. But we haven't been able to explore the possibilities."

Sensations washed over Jane as she thought about

Mac and his marriage to Lyle's sister. She had a burning desire to learn about his failed marriage and couldn't resist prying, just a little. "So what happened with Brenda Lee?"

"Oh, she and Mac never really were suited for each other. Once they married, Brenda Lee thought she could change him. She wanted to leave Winchester in the dust and she thought she could convince Mac to take her away from here. Mac struggled with it for a long time, but he couldn't change who he was. She never got that Mac was a small-town sheriff, and he'd always be one. Mac likes his life, this town, his job. He never expected that she'd demand such drastic changes. Mac couldn't stop being Mac, not even to save his marriage."

"Wow."

"Yeah, but Brenda Lee got what she wanted. She lives in New York now, remarried, with two children."

"So, you'd feel disloyal to Mac on both fronts, if you got involved with Lyle."

"Yes, that's so true. When you entered the picture and I saw how Mac reacted to you, I can't tell you the sense of relief I felt. Mac hasn't been interested—I mean seriously interested—in a woman in a long time."

"He keeps telling me that he's not, Lizzie. I hate to break the bad news to you, but Mac sees me as his responsibility, nothing more."

"Right, and the sun doesn't set in the west every afternoon."

Flustered, Jane didn't know what to say.

"My brother doesn't invite women into our home,

whether or not she has amnesia. He doesn't take her shopping and then buy her gifts if he's not interested." Lizzie reached into the pocket of her blouse and pulled out a gold box. "He wanted me to give this to you."

Jane accepted the gilded box Lizzie shoved her way, staring at her with total surprise.

"Well, open it. I'm dying to see what it is."

Slowly, with deft fingers, Jane pried open the box. "Oh," she said softly, as tears pooled in her eyes. She pulled out a set of matching, stamped silver earrings, necklace and bracelet—large round hoops connected by smaller links. "I took one long look at these in the window while we were shopping. I didn't think Mac noticed. I didn't want him to notice, Lizzie. I couldn't possibly expect him to buy me jewelry."

"But he did."

"Yes, he did," Jane said quietly, hugging the box to her chest and hard-pressed to name all of the warm emotions whirling by. "Why didn't he give them to me himself?"

Lizzie's smile widened. "Probably because he couldn't take seeing that look in your eyes. You've nearly got me teared up, too."

"I don't know what to say."

"Just do me a favor? When you thank him, don't make a huge deal about it. Mac's not into big thank-yous. It's enough that he sees you wearing them."

"I'm not sure I should even accept them, Lizzie."

"They didn't break his bank account, Jane. And you'd hurt his feelings, big time, if you sent them back."

Jane fingered the necklace, playing with the hoops

and admiring the fine details. Of all the expensive jewelry she'd seen today, stealing glances in shop windows, this simple silver set had impressed her most. And Mac had picked up on that.

Small wonder. He had great investigative skills and good instincts.

"On second thought, I couldn't possibly send them back. Help me put them on?" She handed the necklace to Lizzie.

"Sure, but on one condition. When I get back from my trip, you'll help me tackle a whole new wardrobe. I need to go on a shopping spree of my own."

"I'd love to, Lizzie. Sounds like fun. But where are you going?"

"North Carolina. My best friend, Caitlin, is delivering her baby earlier than expected. And her husband, Joe, is on a mission overseas. The marines won't send him home anytime soon. I'm going to be her birth partner and the baby's godmother."

"That's wonderful. How long will you be gone?"

Lizzie bounded up from the bed to fasten the necklace around Jane's neck. "I'm leaving on Sunday and I'll be gone less than a week. But long enough for you and Mac to figure out where you stand."

Jane stood there, wearing the jewelry Mac had given her, shaking her head at Lizzie. "Mac's going to think you're matchmaking."

"It's not my fault that Caitlin had some complications. They're taking the baby early, by caesarean section. I can't let my friend down. A promise is a promise, and I'm thrilled to be a part of the birth." She smiled, showing a beautiful set of white teeth, so much like her brother's. "But I have to admit," she added, cocking her head, "the timing couldn't be more perfect."

Six

Jane stood at the back door, debating about going into Mac's garage this morning. She'd heard him exit the kitchen, and berated herself for not rising earlier to catch him during breakfast. He hadn't come home for dinner last night after their shopping trip, Lizzie explaining that he'd been called into the sheriff's station for an emergency. And Jane had yet to thank him for his generous gift.

She wore the jewelry today, the silver pieces setting off her new sleeveless lilac blouse and lightweight black slacks very nicely. It completed the outfit, making her feel more put together than she had all week. The weather had warmed up considerably, the Colorado summer taking hold, and Jane's new clothes lent her the cool comfort she needed. She'd even put her hair up in a ponytail, and wondered if that was something she'd been inclined to do. Was she the tomboyish, ponytail type of woman? She didn't know, but right now having her hair up brought a cooling breeze to her neck and throat. Something she figured she'd need, if Mac were working out in his gym as she suspected.

She heaved a heavy sigh and strode toward the garage. She knew one thing about herself—her thank-yous couldn't wait. But just as a precaution, instead of entering the garage, she decided to steal a quick peek through the window. She saw no sign of Mac in there and didn't know if she was relieved or disappointed. Just as she began to turn away, his voice boomed in her ear.

"Looking for me?"

She whirled around and found him leaning against the fence post, sipping from his water bottle. His bronzed chest glistened under the Colorado sun, and once again he wore nothing but his sweatpants and a white towel draped around his neck.

"Oh, Mac. Yes, I was. I…didn't want to interrupt your workout."

"I'm through," he said, taking a last sip from his bottle. He set it on the post and approached her.

It was all Jane could do to keep from backing away. Mac stared at her in a way that made her heart race, her nerves jangle and her lips pucker, among other parts of her anatomy. She saw his gaze flicker to her throat, taking in the necklace, then the bracelet and finally catching the gleam of the hoop earrings she wore.

"You look pretty," he said as he came to stand before her.

She blushed, swallowing hard. Her hand instinctively reached for the necklace. It was the first time Mac had paid her a direct, unabashed compliment. "Oh, um, that's why I came out here. To thank you. I love the jewelry, but then you must have known that."

He nodded, and Jane didn't gush with thanks, keeping in mind what Lizzie had told her. "It was a nice surprise."

"Jane," Mac began, staring into her eyes. Her pulse escalated until she thought she'd faint. She waited for him to continue, but when he only stared, she realized it was the first time she'd seen him at a loss for words. She didn't know what to make of it.

"Did you want something?"

He lifted one corner of his mouth, not in a smile as she knew it, but more a sardonic expression. "Not a good question to ask of a man who wants…"

"Wants? What do you want, Mac?"

As if catching himself for mistakenly revealing a real, undisguised emotion, Mac started to retreat. Jane grabbed both ends of the towel hugging his neck and tugged, refusing to let him go.

She stood toe to toe with him, looking up into his handsome face.

His eyes darkened to nearly black. Then his gaze focused on her mouth.

Swamped with heat, pulsating with desire, Jane parted her lips.

Mac groaned, closing his eyes briefly.

"What do you want?" she asked again, this time as softly as a summer wind.

"Not here," he said enigmatically, puzzling Jane even more. Then he took her hand, tugged her along with him into the garage and pressed her up against the wall. Bracing his hands on either side of her, trapping her, he lowered his mouth on hers for a deep, long, openmouthed kiss.

Jane moaned, sighing with pleasure. She hadn't expected this—not anything like this—but she wasn't complaining. Though it was totally insane, she couldn't deny Mac this kiss, or anything else he might want.

She stroked his smooth, slick skin, running her hands up and down his chest, curling her fingers into the mass of curling hairs. He was firm and well muscled, and Jane couldn't get enough of Sheriff Mac Riggs. Her hands slid over him again and again, until he, too, couldn't get enough. He pressed his body closer, his tight, hard erection rubbing her belly. Jane thought she'd die from the sensations.

"Oh, Mac," she breathed, willing him to take everything he wanted. And somehow, a moment later, Jane's blouse was undone, and Mac was there, sliding his hands inside, caressing her sensitive flesh.

He flicked his thumbs over her nipples, back and forth, heightening her pleasure until she wanted to scream out. Mac kissed her again and again, trailing his lips down her throat, licking her skin until the anticipation grew too much. Jane arched for him, offering herself, and he bent his head to take her inside his mouth, hot and moist and slick.

"You're so damn perfect," he whispered in a husky voice, lifting up to kiss her again. "I want all of you, honey."

Jane searched his gaze, finding desire there, a stark, dark desperation in his eyes. She felt the same, and nodded as much. She wanted Mac to make love to her, to find a place inside her and stay until both of them were sated and spent and exhausted. She wanted that connection. To feel. To belong. She wanted all that. And only with Mac.

He moved her along with him, without breaking the connection until he lowered her down onto his workout bench. Within a second his body covered hers, and she noted how careful he was, how much he held back so as not to crush her.

He moved slowly, taking his time now, kissing her, stroking her, his body rubbing hers in all the right places. She ached for him. Everything inside her cried out for completion with this man.

And when he finally reached for the zipper of her slacks, Jane sucked in her breath, making it easier for him.

Bells rang.

At first Jane thought it was a school bell. Or the clanging of a fire truck.

Mac stopped midway with her zipper.

He listened.

Then he sat up, and she felt the immediate loss.

"What is it?" she asked.

"My cell phone, Jane. Something's up. Either at the station or with Lizzie."

Yet he allowed the ringing to continue. He glanced down at her, and she felt suddenly exposed and vulnerable. But his eyes held hers, telling her in unspoken words that it was okay. And with that one look he vanquished any embarrassment she might have had.

He reached for her hand, lifted her to an upright position on the workout bench and sighed. "Jane, it's a good thing the phone rang."

She didn't agree.

"I didn't even think about a condom."

Jane buttoned her blouse, and he watched until she was fully dressed again. She sensed his retreat, the backlash of his actions to follow.

"This is crazy," he said, standing now, admonishing himself. Mac wasn't a man to lose control, and Jane figured he'd be blaming himself for this. "I wasn't thinking, period. How are you going to forgive me?"

She stood then, mustering her courage and tamping down her anger. "Shut up, Mac."

He snapped his head up. "What?"

"Don't you dare apologize to me. I'm a big girl, fully capable of making decisions for myself." Jane turned away so he wouldn't see her distress. "Don't you have to see about that phone call?"

"Jane?"

"Just go, Mac," she said forcefully. Then more softly, she repeated, "Just go."

"Are you all right?"

Jane wanted to scream "No!" She wasn't all right. Nothing had been right since she lost her memory. But for a few brief moments this morning, she'd thought that maybe everything would be all right. With Mac. And her.

"I'm fine."

Mac lifted the cell phone from the worktable and glanced at the number. "It's the station."

"So, call them back."

He glanced over at her, standing there by his workout bench, the place where both of their lives might have changed this morning. "I'm—"

"Don't say it, Mac. I'm warning you."

He actually smiled, as if her tone amused him, then turned to make his phone call.

Jane bounded out of the garage, filled with enough emotions to sink a cruise liner. She needed out of here, fast.

And that was exactly what she decided to do.

Leave.

Mac stepped out of the shower, dried off quickly and dressed. He had to get to the station as soon as possible, and he had to speak with Jane. The news he'd gotten involved her, but Mac wasn't too thrilled to have to spend any more time with her this morning. Hell, what had he been thinking earlier, in the garage? He'd almost made love to her like some smitten, hormone-crazed teen without the sense God had given him.

It wasn't like Mac to lose control like that. He'd prided himself on his rationality and good judgment. He'd been alone a long time, he told himself. And he was sexually attracted to Jane.

What living, breathing man wouldn't be?

But he'd thought he could manage having her live under his roof. After all, they had Lizzie as a chaperone. The thought that he *needed* a chaperone around Jane made him nuts. Where had all his willpower gone?

He'd like to turn his baby sister over his knee just thinking about her obvious ploy to shove Jane at him every chance she could. Lizzie had *never* been out of the house this much. She'd never had "meetings" or "appointments" in the evenings that kept her out late.

As soon as Jane had arrived on the scene, his sister had made herself scarce.

Mac made a mental note to read her the riot act the next time they were alone. Lizzie didn't know she was playing with fire. Mac had already been burned once, and though he'd gotten over the searing pain a long time ago, he wasn't stupid enough to jump into the flames again. And Lizzie's latest news, about leaving on Sunday to spend nearly a week with Caitlin, wasn't what he wanted to hear.

"Babies come when they want," Lizzie had said, "and I can't help it if this one is coming early. Caitlin had some complications and she needs a C-section. You know, darn well I promised I'd be there, Mac."

Yeah, Mac had known, but he hadn't planned on being left entirely alone with Jane for all that time. Still, he couldn't really fault Lizzie on that one, but he didn't have to like it.

He'd made himself a personal vow to keep a safe distance from Jane, but that wasn't easy when he spent time with her during the day for duty's sake, and nights with her at home. Hell, there was no use starting up something with a woman who was here only temporarily. He berated himself again for not exercising more caution when it came to Jane.

But when he'd seen her today, looking bright and pretty in her new clothes, wearing the jewelry he thought she'd deserved, something inside him had snapped. A possessive, almost carnal urge had taken hold. The jewelry had glistened on her skin, catching the light and beaming at him, and Mac had found himself at a loss. He'd only wanted one thing.

Jane.

"And look where that got you, buddy," he said ruefully.

He managed to stop himself in time, but if his phone hadn't chimed, ringing loud enough to wake the dead, would he have had the good sense to call a halt to making love to her?

"You only managed to confuse her even more," he said quietly as he stepped out of his bedroom. He knew that the last thing Jane needed in her life was more chaos and uncertainty. And he also knew he'd blown it with her in a major way. He didn't think he would ever forget that look of hurt and disappointment on her face when he'd come to his senses. Hell, he'd been damn disappointed, too. But he'd never be able to convince Jane of that. She wasn't too happy with him right now, but he had to face her, to tell her the news he'd received this morning.

"Jane," he called out, walking through all the rooms in his house. An eerie silence followed.

He heaved a sigh and went searching. Five minutes

later, after checking and rechecking the house and grounds, Mac got in his patrol car and slammed the door. His heart beat like crazy as he wondered where she was. The lawman in him hated the fact that because of the way he'd found her—alone, abandoned on that ridge—he hadn't really ruled out foul play. Had someone come searching for her? Had someone meant her harm?

It wasn't like Jane to leave the house so abruptly. Mac hated the route his mind had taken. He pressed the gas pedal and took off slowly, scouring the streets of Winchester in hopes of finding a gorgeous blonde with a hot temper.

When he finally found her, he had to tamp down his own raging temper, allowing himself one brief moment of relief. He spotted her on the main street of town, speaking to—no, actually laughing with—Lyle Brody. If he recalled correctly, this was his deputy's day off, and the fact that he wore jeans and a blue plaid shirt verified Mac's assumption. They stood in front of Tyler's Market, Lyle shifting a bag of groceries in his arms.

Mac parked the car ten yards down the street and waited. When neither looked his way, he counted to ten, a precaution he'd learned to take whenever he felt the urge to do something impulsive, then got out of his car.

He leaned against the passenger side door and waited, arms folded.

Whether Jane didn't see him or just refused to acknowledge him, he couldn't be sure. After another round of counting to ten, he approached, keeping his stride and his demeanor casual.

"Morning." He spoke to Lyle.

Both seemed truly surprised to see him standing there, which only added to his irritation. What had been so dang interesting that the two had blotted out the rest of the world?

"Hey, Sheriff," Lyle said, straightening up and wiping the grin from his face. "Look who I bumped into. Jane and I were—"

"I'm here on official business. I need to speak with Jane," Mac interrupted. It grated on his nerves, seeing the two of them so chummy.

"Sure thing. I'd better get these groceries put up." Lyle cast Jane a quick smile. "Nice seeing you again."

"Same here, Lyle. Remember what I said."

Lyle nodded, darting a glance at Mac, and once again Mac wondered what the hell was up. "Will do. See you around."

Jane folded her arms across her middle and stood ramrod still. "Well, that was rude."

"What's rude, Jane, is leaving the house without telling me where you were going."

"I went for a walk, Mac. That's all. No great mystery here. Sometimes I need to get out and clear my head."

Mac figured it was more than that. Both had been left anxious and unnerved by what had happened in the garage this morning. And in Mac's case, filled with sexual energy that he had a damn hard time shutting down. "Next time, leave a note. I'm still responsible for you."

Jane shook her head. "Listen—"

"I have news about your case," he said, avoiding

what was certain to be an argument coming. "Take a drive with me."

"News? About me?" Jane's expression changed, her blond brows lifting and her blue eyes gleaming with hope. At the very least he had managed to get her out of her sour mood. He only hoped that once he took her to the scene, she would remember something. Part of him wanted Jane to regain her memory and leave Winchester for good, while the other part struggled with the idea of her leaving.

When he'd found her gone this morning, he'd worried about her for professional reasons, but he'd also worried about her for personal ones. And those sentiments could get a man like him in big trouble.

"C'mon." Mac began walking toward his patrol car. "They're waiting. I'll fill you in on the drive out of town."

"So this is it," Mac said, parking the car on the bank of Cascade Lake. "Looks like our timing is perfect."

Jane glanced around, her nerves frazzled from all that had happened this morning. Now maybe she had a chance, a clue as to her identity, and though Mac had warned her on the way up here not to get too hopeful, she couldn't quite help it. "It's beautiful," she said, staring out onto the lake. Deep blue waters glistened under the Colorado sun, tall trees in springtime hues lined the far shore and the last vestiges of winter snow tipped glorious Pike's Peak in the background.

"There's a lot of history here," Mac said. "This was one of the first places to be settled in the West."

But the grind of heavy machinery marred the moment, and both she and Mac turned their heads toward the sound.

"Looks like a red Mustang."

A team of local lawman stood on the sidelines as the car was dragged out of the lake.

They exited the patrol car, Mac coming around to stand beside her. "All you have to do is take a look. See if it sparks your memory in any way. It's a long shot at best, Jane. But, since we believe you were driving a car that we have yet to find, this could make sense. We've found two other cars this way, stripped of any identity, no registration, no license plates, but we've managed to find one of the owners."

"Were the cars stolen?"

"Yeah, we think it's nothing more than joyriders, since they don't strip the cars for parts. We have an idea about who's doing it, but what we don't have is proof."

"So, you think that someone might have stolen the car I'd been driving?"

Mac shrugged. "It's a possibility. Let's get closer to take a better look."

Jane reached the vehicle, with Mac standing right beside her. She stared at the Mustang, which was drenched, and coated with debris from being at the bottom of the lake. She looked long and hard, then shook her head. "Nothing comes to mind, Mac. I don't think I've ever seen this car before."

Mac pressed the small of her back and urged her forward. "Take a look inside."

She did. She glanced inside to see a soaked, yet barren interior, devoid of any signs that might give her a clue. She shook her head again.

"We still have the trunk. One of the cars we found like this had nothing inside to help us out, but the other did. We found a few items along with a grocery receipt lying on the floor of the trunk. From that, we were able to locate the owner. They'll tow the car in and check the trunk at the station."

"When were the other cars found?" she asked.

"This month. The investigators believe that there's a gang of teenagers out for some fun. Troublemakers mostly, and not the kind of kids you'd want to have around. We'll find them. It's only a matter of time."

Jane faced the car once more, studying it with intensity. Again, she shook her head slowly, not seeing or feeling what she'd hoped. "I don't think this is my car, Mac."

"Probably not, but we'll find out for sure once the trunk is opened. If it is yours, there might be luggage or other identifying items in there. We can rule out the other car we found, since it showed up well before you landed in Winchester."

"What now?"

"Give me a minute. I have to speak with Sergeant Meeker with the Pueblo PD."

"Okay."

Jane watched Mac head toward the hub of lawmen huddled together at the rear of the Mustang. She stared out onto the lake, breathing in fresh, crisp air, enjoying the scenery once again and allowing the calm serenity to dip inside and soothe her nerves. She couldn't recall ever having seen such a lovely spot, not that she would, of course. But Cascade Lake was something special. The surrounding wildflowers in lavender, blue, pink and yellow made a colorful array against the water. She walked a little along the bank, away from the crime scene. She thought she'd like to come here again one day, when there wasn't so much tumult in her life. She'd like to simply sit by the water's edge and drink in the view.

"Jane?"

She turned to find Mac behind her, watching her with those dark, knowing eyes.

"Want to take a walk?"

She nodded.

They began to stroll along the shore, both deep in thought. Finally, when a large grouping of rocks prevented them from going any farther, they stopped. "Let's sit for a while," Mac said.

They found a long flat boulder and sat down next to each other. "I've got good memories of this place," he said quietly as he gazed across the expanse of the lake. "Used to come down here and skip rocks when I was a kid. Had my first kiss here, too, when I was twelve."

Jane laughed. "Twelve?" Mac lifted his lips, the brilliance of his seldom-seen smile tugging at Jane. "Seems you were an early learner."

"Bungled my way through, and both of us nearly landed facedown in the lake. Man, I was so nervous."

"But determined."

Mac nodded. "Always."

"And was she your girl from then on out?"

"You kidding? She dumped me the next day," Mac said, chuckling. "Can't say as I blame her."

Jane imagined Mac as a young, eager boy, long and lanky and probably awkward as heck trying to impress a young girl. He certainly had improved his skills since then. Jane had been swept away this morning by Mac's "skill" and found him passionate, caring and thoughtful. She'd been overwhelmed by desire, and she doubted she'd ever met a man in her life that could measure up to him.

Even though she didn't know about her life, she felt sure in her heart that no man could possibly make her feel the way Mac did.

Mac's smile faded then and he turned to meet her eyes. "About this morning, Jane—"

She put up a hand. "Don't."

"I'm not apologizing," he said quickly. "But I am taking responsibility. I should have known better. It was more than an innocent kiss and we both know where we were heading."

Jane nodded, unwilling to sugarcoat what had happened this morning. Mac was right—if that phone call hadn't broken the spell, they would have made love, right there on the workout bench and who knows where else. It was that intense. That powerful.

"But it can't happen, Jane. You don't know your circumstances, and until you do…"

"What, Mac? There are never any guarantees in life."

"I know that," he said with a long, laborious sigh.

"But I got involved with a woman once who didn't know herself. She thought she could be content with life as it was, but once we married, nothing was enough for her. *I* wasn't enough for her. We'd be foolish to think that your life, your *real* life, won't take precedence over anything you might find here with me."

"No, I can't guarantee that. I know what you're saying is true, Mac. But I have little to go on here. I only know what I feel."

Mac smiled broadly and her heart flipped over itself again. "I know what I feel, too."

"And what's that?" Jane asked, her heart pounding hard.

He hesitated a few seconds, then said, with clear honest eyes, "I want you."

Warmth spread throughout her body, and Jane realized she had to be content with that knowledge. She wouldn't press Mac. He was trying darn hard to be reasonable, rational and responsible.

The rat.

"I know about your wife, Mac. Lizzie sort of filled me in."

He scowled.

"Don't be angry with her. She only wants your happiness."

"She's a pill."

Jane laughed, and the sound echoed against the wall of trees surrounding the lake. "She's a sweetheart."

Mac granted her half a smile. "That, too." Then he took a long, drawn-out breath. "Listen, you know Lizzie is leaving on Sunday. It's not what I had planned when I invited you to stay with us. We're going to be alone, and if you don't want to—"

"Do you want me to leave?" Jane asked, point-blank. Heart racing, she had to know the answer. She didn't want to overstay her welcome, and if Mac thought her leaving would make his life easier, then she'd go. Earlier this morning she'd called Dr. Quarles to make an appointment, and once again, he had been gracious to offer her an open-ended invitation to his hospitality.

"No," Mac stated immediately. "I was only asking for your sake. Not mine."

"If it makes you feel any better, I won't be home all that much. Lizzie helped me get a job at Touched with Love. I'll be volunteering at the bookstore every day." She beamed him a smile. Once she'd finalized the arrangements today, the thought really took hold. She couldn't wait to get started and to do something productive with her life. "Rory assured me that my working there wouldn't interfere with our investigation. Anytime you need me I can be available. And in between times I'll be helping him out over there."

"Lizzie arranged that for you?"

She nodded. "Yes, she's very friendly with Rory Holcomb. Seems his grandchildren have been in her classes, all six of them. And it's close enough for me to walk to work and back."

Mac's expression faltered. "It's not that close to home, Jane. I'd rather you didn't work at night."

"Oh, so you want me home nights. Alone. With you?"

Mac pursed his lips, then shook his head in resignation. "All right. You've made your point. But I'll be picking you up from the shop when you do work nights. And that's *not* negotiable."

"It's a deal. I can't wait to get started," Jane said with a happy sigh. "It's the one positive thing I have to look forward to."

"Is that where you went this morning?"

"Yes, I'd heard his used book store was charming. I wanted to meet Rory in person and see his place."

"And you failed to tell me. Made me worry like crazy."

Jane turned her head to look him in the eyes. "You worried?"

Mac scratched his head and rose abruptly, refusing to answer. "I've got to get back to work."

Jane walked back to the car with him, struggling with her thoughts. She'd thought she'd angered Mac by taking off without his permission. She thought it more an ego thing on his part. She hadn't thought about him worrying about her. Worrying meant caring. And caring led to other things.

After this morning she knew Mac wanted her. But that had been sexual. He'd been attracted to her physically. But Jane hadn't thought past that. She hadn't thought he actually cared for her. Not in the personal, intimate way a man cares for a woman.

She was his responsibility. Hadn't he told her that a dozen times? He felt duty-bound to help her.

Jane picked up her pace and reached the patrol car before Mac. She got in, slamming the door and staring straight ahead. She couldn't possibly afford to think that Mac actually cared for her. It would be dangerous to believe so. Yet her heart burned with the thought.

Putting distance between them would be the wisest route to take. Jane had the means now, by working long hours at the bookstore. She planned on staying far out of Mac's reach.

His heart wasn't the only one that could get broken.

And in her vulnerable state, Jane knew she would shatter to pieces if that happened.

Seven

The next morning Jane stepped into Touched with Love and a great sense of belonging swept over her. She breathed in the musky scent of yellowed pages turned by loving hands, of aged bindings holding leaves together by vintage strength, and of softly worn leather sofas placed in a semicircle in one corner of the bookstore. The "reading cove," as Rory had affectionately called it, was a place for old and young alike to gather. In the afternoons, children clustered on the sofas and listened as Rory read them their favorite tales. The evenings were shared by the Women of Winchester, a historical reading group, as well as the Book Banterers, an eclectic group who delved into elements of the paranormal.

All in all, Jane felt welcome here. She fit in somehow,

and a sweet, sweeping sensation of rightness filled her. Not even the softly played country tunes wafting in the air could stifle these newfound impressions of belonging. She'd come to know the likes of Toby and Martina, Kenny and Shania, George and Tim. Living in the Riggs household, she hadn't had a choice. Good thing the rock and twang had seeped into her soul. She'd caught herself toe tapping to the tunes often enough.

She had to admit she enjoyed listening to KWIN, and all the antics of the radio station's disc jockeys. Though originally she'd been stunned, she had eventually gotten accustomed to hearing her description play on air, as well. "The young blond woman with blue eyes, an amnesia victim found on the outskirts of town. If anyone has information regarding Winchester's own Jane Doe, please contact the Winchester County Sheriff's Department."

"Morning," Rory said, looking up from a stack of paperbacks ready to be shelved. "You're here bright and early."

"Hello, Rory. I couldn't wait to get started."

"We're not officially open for half an hour. I was just about to have a cup of coffee and a doughnut. Marietta bakes them up fresh every morning. She brings me a batch for my customers. It'd be nice to have someone to share them with. Come, let's sit awhile. I don't expect a crowd until later in the day."

"I'd love to."

After two cups of coffee and a sugar doughnut, Jane set about her work. She organized a stack of mysteries, alphabetizing them, but not without reading their back cover blurbs and perusing their first pages. The feel of the books, the print on the page all seemed so familiar to her, yet she had no real recollection, no hint as to why. All she knew was that she liked being here, and it felt darn good finally being able to do something productive.

The day flew by. She worked alongside Rory, and when he had to leave the shop for an hour, he entrusted it to her care. He brought them both back lunch, and in between helping customers, they stuffed down their sandwiches.

Rory turned over the children's reading hour to her, introducing Jane to the children as his new "reading buddy." Rory had paired up the children, teaming them so that when they had an opportunity to read, they could work out the tougher words together. Sometimes Jane would read a story, and sometimes the children would read one to her.

"Aren't you getting hungry?"

"A little," Jane answered automatically. Her head down, she was focused intently on a compelling thriller she hadn't been able to shelve just yet. When she glanced up, she found Mac leaning beside her in the mystery section, watching her with interest.

"Oh, hi," she said lamely, amazed at how his presence always seemed to fluster her lately, and now his scent, that fresh lime aftershave, mixed with his own essence, remained with her even after he'd stalked off somewhere. "What are you doing here?"

"It's almost eight. Rory left hours ago. His oldest grandchild, Jimmy, is working the cash register now, readying to close up."

"Oh," Jane said, remembering that she'd bade Rory farewell earlier. He'd told her to go on home, and Jane had planned to, but she'd gotten involved in the thriller. "I lost track of time."

Mac took the book out of her hand, closing it and eyeing the title. "Good?"

"I couldn't put it down."

"I'm starving," he said. "Let's go eat."

Surprised, Jane followed him to the cash register. "You haven't eaten yet?"

"Nope." He shook his head, and Jane was too dumbfounded to realize that Mac had paid for the book she'd been reading. When he handed it to her with a quick lift of his lips, she blinked.

"Why not?"

He shrugged as he headed for the front door. "I had a late call tonight. You weren't home when I finally got there, so I drove over to pick you up."

Jane finally glanced down at the book in her hands. She reminded herself not to read too much into simple gestures of kindness, but those gestures, coming from the stanch and stubborn sheriff, sent her mind spinning.

Dusk had settled on the horizon and she realized that Mac felt duty bound to pick her up this evening. She abhorred being a complication in his life, and at the same time felt as though it was more than that. Her heart warmed considerably at the notion. She'd tried to stay away today, losing herself in the bookstore and her volunteer work. She'd had a nice day, actually, but nothing compared to being with Mac.

He stood tall, wearing his tan uniform proudly, watching her, and Jane nibbled on her lower lip, staring at her reflection in his silver badge. "I'll make dinner when we get...*home*." Using the word in that context set her mind spinning again. She was beginning to feel that 2785 Crescent Drive was her home. And she had handsome Mac Riggs waiting on dinner for her.

"No need. We're going out. Best place in town."

Jane glanced down at her clothes. She'd known she would work in the bookstore today, shelving, opening cartons and getting down on the floor with little ones to help them pick out books, so she'd worn her old jeans and a nothing-special blouse. "Should I go home to change?"

Mac grinned and placed a hand on her waist, urging her to his car. "Not a chance, Jane. You're dressed exactly right."

"I still say you're chicken, Jane."

She sat at the back end of Mac's Trailblazer in Colorado Chuck's parking lot, dangling her feet and eating an Aspen burger with pickles and tomato out of a cardboard box. Mac opted for a Pike's Peak, a mountainous burger filled with chili and cheese and onions and heaven knows what else, definitely the more dangerous choice. Jane's stomach rumbled at the sight of the monstrous meal.

"Not chicken, just smart." She pointed at his burger. "I hope you have a jar of antacids at home."

"I have a stomach of steel." He took a giant bite of his burger.

Jane couldn't disagree. She'd seen his bare chest, the rippling muscles and hard-packed abs. The image stayed in her head until she shook it free. "You'll need it. If the burger doesn't kill you, the fries surely will."

"Ah, but what a way to go." He popped a fry into his mouth.

Jane smiled, nibbling on her meal while she watched Mac indulge in his. "You sure know how to treat a lady," she teased.

"You ain't seen nothing yet," he bantered back, and it was clear he took no offense in her statement. "You haven't experienced Winchester until you've had one of Colorado Chuck's Pike's Peaks." He shook his head. "Too bad, Jane. You don't know what you're missing."

"Maybe next time. I mean...if I come back here... sometime...ever again."

With his burger halfway to his mouth, Mac stopped to look at her squarely. Their eyes met for a long moment and he let out a long sigh. The fact that Jane would leave Winchester someday, maybe sooner than later, lay like a deep sea of doubt between them.

Jane swallowed the lump in her throat and took a small bite of her burger.

"Do you know how many little towns and villages there are in Italy?" Mac said, finishing his meal and crumpling his napkin. "Hundreds."

"Wow," Jane said, glad Mac changed the subject. She didn't want to think about leaving Winchester, or Mac, anytime soon. But she couldn't wait to regain her memory and find out about herself. She felt stuck between a rock and a hard place, the catch-22 of her situation not lost on her. "I guess I might have known that at one time. So, no luck finding our friendly little Italian shoemaker?"

Mac answered with a shake of his head. "We're not giving up. Would help if we had the cobbler's name, though. Anything else come to mind?"

Jane finished her burger, leaving the fries untouched and finally washing it all down with a strawberry shake. "No, sorry. I've thought about those boots over and over. You've got me dreaming of stiletto heels and black leather, but nothing comes to mind."

Mac nearly choked on his chocolate shake. He sputtered, spraying chocolate onto the asphalt parking lot. "Man, Jane. I think I'll be the one dreaming of stiletto heels and black leather tonight."

Jane punched him playfully on the arm, but the heat of his gaze froze her in action. He wasn't kidding. Desire burned in his dark eyes and her body heated quickly.

One passionate look from the sheriff was all it took to turn Jane's subdued demeanor into a sizzling wreck of nerves.

The remembered feel of his lips on hers, his hands caressing her body, his long lean form atop her on that workout bench yesterday, filled her mind and put an ache in her heart. She grabbed both cardboard boxes, jumped down from the back of the SUV and walked over to the trash, dumping everything inside.

When she turned back around, she found Mac

speaking with a woman, a young, pretty brunette with a curvy body and a proprietary hand on his arm. The woman hadn't wasted any time in approaching Mac as soon as the coast was clear.

Jane hesitated a few seconds, then, with decided assertion, walked right back over to them. "Hi, I'm Jane." She put out her hand.

The taller woman shook it, a quizzical look on her face. "Lola. I'm a…friend of Mac's."

Jane nodded and smiled. "That makes two of us."

Mac sat silently by, watching the exchange, offering nothing.

"Mac and I go back a long way," Lola said, smiling at him. "Don't we, Sheriff?"

He shrugged, sipping his shake. "Guess we do. We were both born and bred in Winchester."

"School chums, then?" Jane asked, though she really didn't enjoy being a part of this conversation. Her heart raced, but a deep sense of dread overshadowed any other sensation she felt at the moment. While half of her cried out with jealous regret, the other half felt heavy, like a lead weight around Mac's neck, pulling him down. Since being found up at Deerlick Canyon, Jane had tied up all Mac's time, taking him away from any personal life he might want to have. She'd been his responsibility, and hadn't thought about how her being here had affected his life.

The woman chuckled. "Schoolmates and then some, right, Mac?" She tilted her head so that her long, shiny brown locks rested on his shoulder.

"Ancient history, Lola." Mac stepped back and raised the hatch of his car.

"Well, I didn't mean to interrupt," the woman said, staring at him with bright, interested eyes. Jane knew that look, the way one female knows when another is flirting, even if the man is too dim to figure it out.

"Good seeing you again, Mac. Don't be a stranger."

Mac nodded and headed for the driver's door. "Take care, Lola."

Jane took her seat quietly and closed her eyes, stunned by her own rude behavior. "I'm really putting a damper on your social life."

Mac gunned his car out of Colorado Chuck's parking lot. Both were silent on the short drive home until he parked the car in his driveway.

Jane made a move to exit the car.

"Jane, listen."

She turned to him, her eyes bright with unshed tears. She couldn't name all the emotions churning around inside her gut, but she did know one thing. She didn't want Lola, or any other woman, hovering around Mac. And that made no sense at all. Jane had no right to him. He was free to see any woman he wanted, except her. He'd made that clear, yet when he'd showed up at the bookstore tonight, Jane's rational mind had shut down and she'd lost herself in foolhardy notions.

"Mac, don't try to convince me that my being here hasn't changed your life."

"Damn it, Jane. You're not stopping me from anything."

"You're just being sweet," she said softly.

Mac stormed out of the car, slamming the door. "I'm not *sweet*," he said, grinding out the words.

Jane stepped out of the car as well and together they walked up the steps to the front door. "Okay, so you're not that sweet. I never really thought so. Feel better now?" she said, smiling.

Mac paused, pursing his lips and blinking. "You never really thought so?"

She shook her head, so hard her hair whipped against her cheeks.

Mac ran a hand down his face in what she feared was utter frustration, but when she could finally see his mouth, the corners had lifted up and he laughed. "What am I going to do with you?"

She joined in the laughter, happy to have gotten him out of his bad mood. Then on impulse, she planted a quick kiss on his cheek. "Talk to me?"

Mac's eyebrows rose. "About?"

"About Lola, and how I'm not interfering in your life."

She sauntered past him when he unlocked the door, and stood waiting for his answer, arms folded.

Mac stared at her a moment, then his gaze dropped down to her chest, where she'd crossed her arms. Jane didn't flinch, though the heat of his perusal was enough to knock her off her feet.

Mac broke eye contact and moved to the window, his arms braced on the windowsill as he focused his gaze into the darkness of the night. "Lola and I are friends, Jane. Nothing more. We dated a while, after my divorce, but that's the end of it. We both moved on."

"She's not married."

Mac turned to her. "No. She'd drive any man insane, and you didn't hear that from me."

Jane chuckled, garnering satisfaction that Mac hadn't found the brunette irresistible. "Why?"

"Never mind. I've said enough."

"And what about other women, Mac? You're not dating anyone. You don't have a girlfriend. I find that hard to believe, since you're so…"

"So hard to deal with?" he finished for her. "Or maybe, stubborn? Too dedicated to my work? Name any of the above."

Jane softened her expression and took a seat on the sofa, looking up at him. "I was going to say so easy on the eye."

Mac sat down on the opposite end of the couch. He looked at her with a gleam in his eyes. "Now you're being sweet. But the truth is, sure, there are women who occasionally look me up. Sometimes I date, but it'll never amount to anything. I'm not looking for anything permanent. I've done the marriage thing. It isn't for me."

What a waste, Jane thought. Mac had too many great qualities to give up on sharing a life with someone.

"Too bad," she said aloud.

"I'm happy with my existence, Jane. Why do all the women in my life feel the need to push me into something I don't want? And," he said, leaning forward, pointing his index finger her way, "that goes for you, too. You're so sure you're wrecking my social life, but the truth is I don't have one. So no more talk about that. Don't worry, Jane."

"So, you really didn't want to spend time with Lola tonight?"

"I'm here with you, aren't I?"

Jane nearly snorted. "I guess I have my answer. Tell me, just where, exactly, did you go to charm school?"

"What?"

She cast him a slow smile and stood. "It's nothing, Mac. I think it's time for bed."

She walked over to him to say good-night, endeared to him more than she should be. Mac had been earnest with her. He'd shared part of his life. He'd tried to explain himself to her, the best he knew how. And now he stood before her, blocking her way to the hall leading to her room.

"Don't worry about anything but regaining your memory," he said, touching the tip of her nose.

The touch carried her over the edge. This time she kissed him fully on the mouth, surprising them both. Mac groaned, but he didn't back off. Instead, he wrapped both arms around her and held her loosely, allowing her to lead the way.

Jane knew she was in deep trouble the minute their lips met again. She'd longed for this, for his lips to warm hers and for the heat of their bodies to carry them away. "Definitely not sweet, Mac. But so much more." She parted her lips and their tongues met, the mating a sacred kind of homecoming.

Mac tightened his hold on her, drawing her up against

him so that she felt his heart beating, each pulse in sync with her own. "Sometimes you amaze me, Jane," he whispered into her mouth.

"I amaze myself, too," she whispered back.

Just as their lips met again, Lizzie barged into the room, stopping short the minute she spotted them. "Oh, sorry!"

Jane immediately backed away from Mac and stared at his sister, the red heat of embarrassment climbing up her throat.

Lizzie, on the other hand, was beamimg. "On second thought, I'm not sorry. It's about time!"

"Lizzie." Mac offered up a stern warning. "You and I need to have a little talk."

"Can't, big brother. I'm all packed. I'm leaving first thing in the morning for Raleigh."

"Okay, then, we'll talk on the way to the airport. What time?"

Lizzie smiled at Jane, her eyes bright with appreciation. "Oh, I already have a ride to the airport. Jane made the arrangements for me."

Mac looked at Jane with a quizzical expression. "You made arrangements for her? How?"

She smiled tentatively at Lizzie, ignoring his intense stare.

"Jane?" Mac moved to face her. "What did you do?"

"Nothing much, really," she said, trying to shrug it off.

Impatient with her evasion, he turned to his sister. "So, who's taking you to the airport?"

Chin up, Lizzie tossed out the one name that could make Mac crazy. "Deputy Lyle Brody."

* * *

Two nights later, Jane shelved the last of the children's books, tidied up the reading cove and met Jimmy at the cash register.

"All done," he said, his blond hair flipping onto his forehead when he glanced up. Jane liked Jimmy a lot and she was sure with his clean-shaven, earnest good looks, he would melt more than one young girl's heart. Yet he was always polite, a hard worker, and she knew that his grandfather adored him.

"So am I."

Both headed for the front door, Jane watching Jimmy lock it up good and tight before turning to her. "Are you sure you don't need a ride home?"

"I'm sure. Sheriff Riggs will be here shortly," Jane said, glancing up and down the darkened street, looking for Mac's black Trailblazer. Sometimes he picked her up in his patrol car, so she kept an eye out for that, too. She found it odd that he wasn't parked outside waiting for her. Mac never arrived late to pick her up. "You go on home, Jimmy. I'll be fine."

Jimmy frowned, shaking his head, but with a little more urging, Jane finally convinced him to leave. She stood outside Touched with Love, waiting. When Mac didn't appear for five full minutes, she began walking. She didn't mind. She had a lot to go over in her head, and the hot summer day had finally cooled to a warm breezy evening.

Mac had been furious with her the other night, and she'd walked in the chilling shadow of his cold shoulder for the past two days. He hadn't been happy with her interference in Lizzie's life. He'd been blunt, almost cruel. She'd never forget the look of contempt on his face once Lizzie had left the room that night.

"It's none of your concern, Jane," he'd said sternly. "You don't know all of it," he'd added. "You have no right butting into my business."

That last statement stung, and she'd tried defending herself valiantly, but Mac wouldn't hear anything she had to say. He'd simply shut down, refusing to discuss Lyle or Lizzie or why he felt so strongly about Lizzie getting involved with his deputy.

Jane had no choice but to back off, but the damage had been done. Mac barely tolerated her now, keeping a safe distance away even though she'd catch him at times peering at her from across the room. Still, the budding friendship they'd slowly developed had vanished.

Mac had never once made her feel like an intruder, but she had to believe that now he wanted her gone. Perhaps she should consider Dr. Quarles's invitation. Maybe it was time to leave Mac's home. There was no telling how long it would take to regain her memory.

She hadn't had any new revelations lately. She hadn't recalled anything else other than that she owned custom-made leather boots crafted in some small village in Italy. Nothing much had happened with the media blitz the sheriff's department had put out, either. Oh, there'd been one guy claiming her as his fiancée, but it turned out the man had been investigated as a single white male who had failed relationships with three online dating services. Jane couldn't help feeling sorry for him, but at the same time she'd been greatly relieved to find that she wasn't in any way tied to him.

There was only one man Jane wanted in her life and he was late picking her up. And just as she turned the corner on Elkwood Street, she heard the familiar rumble of a motor from behind.

Mac pulled up close to her, slowing the patrol car. He rolled down the window and Jane's ready smile disappeared. "Get in, Jane" was all he said, a deep frown marring his handsome face.

She raced around to the passenger side and slipped in. Realizing that something was wrong, she turned to him immediately. His face was bloodied and bruised, and he held one hand to his chest. Jane quaked with fear. "Mac, you're hurt."

The car moved forward and Mac nodded ever so slowly, the action causing him to wince even more. "Bad asses thought they could wreck Sully's place. Had to go in there and straighten them out."

Her mind jumbled, all she could think about was the extent of Mac's injuries. He still held that hand to his chest and hadn't let go. Blood oozed down his face where he'd been cut. "Where are you hurt?"

"Probably bruised a few ribs. Got a few cuts and scrapes. That's all."

"All?" Jane couldn't stand to see him in any pain. "You need to go to the hospital, Mac."

"No way, Jane. I'm fine."

"You don't look fine," she said, her voice rising. "You look like you've been run over by a truck."

"Gee, thanks. Appreciate the thought."

"I'm not kidding, Mac. Just how many were there, and what kind of place is Sully's, anyway?"

"About half a dozen. Bar and grill," he answered, his tone clipped. Jane feared he had broken, not bruised, ribs.

"Six of them and how many of you?"

"Two of us, until we got backup."

Jane's heart pounded. Up until tonight she hadn't thought much about Mac's profession, the dangers and pitfalls. Winchester was a small, quiet town. But seeing him in pain, barely able to drive, she felt the reality of Mac's job hit her with stark and unnerving force. Just like any other professional lawman, Mac put his life on the line each and every day. Jane couldn't shake that notion loose. It stayed with her, swamping her with fear. Then she noticed that his shirtsleeve was rolled up. "Looks like your arm is bandaged. What happened?" she asked.

"It's just a cut."

"A cut? Are you saying someone attacked you with a knife?"

He nodded. "Assault with a deadly weapon. It's been taken care of. The paramedic team patched me up."

Jane's gut tightened. Dear God. Mac could have been killed tonight. And that thought nearly destroyed her. Her feelings for Mac Riggs ran deeper than she'd believed. "Why didn't they take you to the hospital?"

Mac lifted one shoulder in a small shrug as he pulled into his driveway. And then it dawned on her. The paramedics would have taken Mac to the hospital if he had allowed them to. Instead, he'd shown up on Elkwood Street in his patrol car to pick her up. "I'm fine, Jane." He killed the engine and got out of the car.

Jane raced around the vehicle to meet him at the driver's side door. He stepped away from the SUV, hunching over a bit as he did so.

"Lean on me," she said firmly, bracing his body with hers.

He pursed his lips, deciding, then finally nodded once Jane had given him her most obstinate look. He wrapped his good arm around her shoulders and she braced his weight the best she could.

Together, they made their way slowly to the front door. Mac handed her the key and she opened the lock, then slanted her body sideways so they both would fit through the opening. Once inside, Jane led Mac to his bedroom.

She helped him sit down on his bed, and he took a minute, breathing deeply.

"Is your head spinning?" she asked.

He let out a wry chuckle. "You might say that. Of all the ways I've dreamed of getting you into my bedroom, this wasn't one of them."

Jane smiled, reveling in his earnest admission. "Lie down, Sheriff."

Mac obeyed, closing his eyes as he lowered his head and stretched out his long legs on the bed. Jane fussed with his pillow, propping it behind him.

She gave the pillow one last blow, then stood over Mac, gazing down at him. "You know, this isn't exactly how I'd hoped to get into your bedroom, either."

He opened one eye and peered at her, but she held her stance, refusing to let any embarrassment come through. The truth was the truth. "Now, stay put. Your forehead is bleeding again. I'll be right back."

She walked out of the room to the sound of Mac's groan. This time she knew it wasn't pain causing it, but her remark. At least Mac knew where she stood. There would be no second-guessing and no mistake. Jane wanted him, but tonight she'd realized something even more powerful. When she'd seen him bruised, battered and in so much pain, she knew she couldn't deny her feelings any longer. She knew that to lose him would be to lose herself all over again. She'd fallen for him.

Jane Doe was crazy in love with Sheriff Mac Riggs.

She took a minute to let her feelings sink in and accept what had been inevitable. She'd seen it coming, yet hadn't the power to deny or refuse the love that had begun building from the first moment she'd looked up into Mac's piercing dark eyes on that canyon road.

With a heavy sigh, Jane grabbed the first-aid kit out of the bathroom and gathered up the other supplies she needed, then headed back to Mac's room. She found him lying on the bed right where she'd left him, with eyes wide open, watching her.

She scooted next to him and dabbed at his head wound, the antiseptic oozing onto the cut above his eye. "Sorry, this must sting."

He grunted a denial.

"I think your ribs might be broken."

"Nah. I've broken ribs before when I played quarter-

back for the Wildcats. I know the difference. They're
bruised, that's all."

Jane knew she had to get Mac more comfortable on
his bed. "Can you get out of your clothes, or do you
want me to do it?"

Mac cocked her a lopsided smile. "You do it."

Jane snorted. "This isn't funny, Mac. You scared me
half out of my mind. It wasn't so thrilling seeing you
bloody and bruised, slumped over the steering wheel. I
just about had a heart attack."

"Sorry, Jane." He reached for her hand and she
allowed him to hold it. He stroked his thumb gently
across her palm, sending goose bumps all over her body.
"Fact is, Winchester is a quiet town. We don't get a lot
of excitement around here." He winced, his eyes shutting briefly, and she sensed the pain he was trying hard
to conceal. "But June has been an unusual month. First
with a beautiful amnesia victim landing on my doorstep
and then tangling with a bunch of out-of-towners
looking for trouble."

"Don't forget the joyriders abandoning cars in the lake."

"That, too. But for the most part, my job's pretty
mundane. It's been a curious time in Winchester lately.
Now, didn't I hear something about you undressing me?"

Jane twisted her mouth. "Taking unfair advantage,
Sheriff?"

"Just need a little TLC, Jane." Then he lowered his
voice, brought his lips to her outstretched palm and
kissed her there. "From you."

Jane's heart stopped with that kiss, the moisture from

his lips seeping into her skin. Reluctantly, she pulled her hand free to reach for the buttons on his uniform shirt. Carefully, she unfastened each one, then gently slid the shirt off his shoulders. She held back her own wince when she saw up close the bruises on his chest and the bandage on his arm.

Jane dipped a washcloth into a bowl of water and cooled down his heated skin, her fingers sliding leisurely over his chest. On impulse, she bent down to plant a tiny kiss on one of the larger bruises. Mac lifted his good arm and stroked her head, weaving his fingers through her hair. Then he guided her head up and leaned forward, showing Jane what he wanted. Their lips met briefly, a sweet, healing kiss that made her heart flip and Mac smile. "You give great TLC."

Jane withdrew, stood up and headed for the end of the bed. She took a daunted look at his boots, then, with a steadying breath, pulled and twisted and finally yanked, until one boot came off, sock and all. "Not such good TLC here," she offered.

"I'm not complaining."

The other boot came off easier, and Jane felt a surge of satisfaction. She walked over to Mac, lying there bare-chested, looking vulnerable and sexy all at the same time.

"Can you manage your pants?" she asked, holding her breath.

Mac tried leaning forward, then bit back a howl of pain. He rested his head on his pillow. "Don't think so."

"Okay," Jane said, reaching for his belt. She unhooked it, then slid her hands down to his zipper, the evidence of his bulging manhood hard to miss. "Mac, I thought you were injured."

He didn't bother holding back a devilish smile. "Nothing hurts below the waist."

Jane stared down at him.

"Touch me there, and I can't be responsible for my actions."

Jane swallowed. "Is that an invitation or a warning?"

"Both," Mac said, the teasing glint in his eyes gone now. The heat of his gaze penetrated her, warming her all over. "It's crazy, you know. Denying what we both want."

Apparently, Mac had sifted though his own denials, to come up with the truth, too. "I know," she whispered, though she knew that she wouldn't deny Mac anything, not ever again.

Jane reached for his zipper.

Eight

Mac had been furious with her when she'd butted into Lizzie's business. He hadn't wanted anyone, especially Jane, to interfere in his relationship with Lizzie. Jane had just come to Winchester and she didn't know his history. She didn't know the heartache Mac had endured trying to salvage an unsalvageable marriage. She didn't know how Lyle Brody had interfered on his sister's behalf, causing even more strife between them.

But the minute he'd walked out of Sully's tonight, bloodied and bruised, the knife swipe having just missed his chest, cutting instead into the beefy part of his arm, all Mac could think about was Jane.

Getting to her.

Seeing her.

Wanting her.

He'd wasted too much time with her, too much of his life. That close call had him forgiving Jane everything. He'd forgotten all about his anger, and thought only about being with her.

And as she slowly slid his zipper down, the proof of his feelings were reflected in a powerful erection that only Jane could satisfy.

He watched her work his pants off without too much difficulty. She looked at him tentatively as she held his trousers to her chest protectively. "Wish I could undress *you*," he admitted softly.

Jane smiled, her lips parting in a subtle move. She dropped his pants, letting them fall at her feet. Without a second thought, she removed her tank top, the material catching on her breasts before being flipped over her head.

Mac sucked in oxygen. "Wow," he muttered, watching her necklace catch the moonlight where it nestled in the hollow between her breasts. She wore the jewelry he'd given her every day, and he'd felt a stirring of pride and possession.

She stood beside him now and leaned over. "You could unhook me."

Mac reached up behind her to unfasten her bra. He tugged slightly and the white cotton undergarment fell through his fingers. Her breasts toppled out, full and lush, and he groaned. "You're killing me, Jane."

"That's not what I had in mind to do to you, Mac." She bent down for a kiss, but he grabbed her around the waist, pulled her onto the bed and settled her on his thighs. She straddled him, her legs on either side of him. But he needed to feel her, skin to skin, so he guided her body down until her breasts rested on his chest.

His lips met hers urgently, sealing their fate with a long, hot, wet kiss that went on and on. He drove his tongue into her mouth, searching for and finding its mate. They sparred and teased and played feverishly, Mac stroking his hands through her soft blond hair, his fingers tugging and releasing the strands.

The feel of her breasts pressing into his chest, the soft subtle sounds she made, the unabashed passion she gave him were almost too much. Mac didn't think his erection could become any more potent.

Finally, she pulled away slightly, her breathing as labored as his. "I'm crushing your chest. It must hurt," she said.

Mac shook his head. "Only when you leave me."

Jane bit her lip, unsure.

"I mean it, sweetheart. You're not hurting me."

Jane settled back down, and Mac realized that nothing had felt better, or more right, in his whole life.

He kissed her deeply again, then lifted her easily at the waist, guiding her higher so that he could moisten the very tip of her nipple with his tongue.

"Oh, Mac," she moaned as he cupped her breast and continued to slide his tongue up and around and over the rosy tip until it peaked and pebbled.

Her next long, pleasured moan nearly brought him to the edge. "I need to be inside you, Jane," he managed to gasp, his voice hoarse with need.

He reached down to her jeans and fumbled with her zipper. Jane helped him, and he almost lost it again when she shimmied out of her pants. She helped get his boxers off, then did a little wiggle to get out of her own panties.

"Reach over to my nightstand, sweetheart. We need protection."

Mac prayed he still had a condom or two in there. It'd been a while.

When Jane carefully slid across him, coming up with one, Mac silently sighed with relief and quickly managed to secure the condom in place.

He held her waist and guided her body, positioning her over him and lowering her. He slipped his full erection inside her, joining them together with one slow, deliberate thrust.

As she took him in, she closed her eyes, parted her moist lips and tossed her head back as if savoring the moment. Mac had never seen anything quite so beautiful in his whole life. Deep, heady sensations washed over him as he watched this sexy, mysterious woman slowly move on him, her body's natural instincts taking hold as she raised and lowered with each of his thrusts.

In sync, in rhythm, they moved together, Jane huffing out little throaty breaths and Mac moving more forcefully now as their momentum escalated, higher and higher.

He reached up to caress her breasts, rubbing his thumbs over her peaked tips until she ground out his name. The intense look on her face brought him a new brand of pleasure as he watched her ride the waves of their passion. Up and down, faster, harder. Mac took hold of Jane's hands, interlacing their fingers, connecting them in every way possible.

He felt her shudder. Her muttered moans and pleas as she breathed out his name gave him the ultimate satisfaction. "Oh, Mac."

He plunged deeper, thrusting one final time as she came down hard, and then, in tandem, they both shuddered violently with completion.

Mac lay breathless, Jane atop him.

They stared into each other's eyes.

Moments ticked by and yet neither spoke.

Jane appeared a little stunned.

Mac felt the same way.

Finally, he lifted his lips in a crooked, cocky smile.

Jane smiled back.

Then he kissed her deeply. "That was worth the wait."

Jane slid her body sideways to curl up beside him, her arms wrapped around his neck. "Mmm. I don't think I've ever…um."

Mac lifted his head to stare down at her. "Ever?"

She cast him a shy smile. "Not that. I mean, I don't think it's ever been so good."

He inhaled deeply. "You don't know that, for sure."

"Oh, I think I do, Mac."

He trusted her on that one. Of course, it did his ego good to do so, and he believed a woman would simply *know* those things. But there was so much to Jane that neither of them knew about. There was so much he wanted to know and so much he feared knowing.

He reminded himself that her memory could return

at any moment, but it was too late for guarding against his heart. He couldn't think rationally when it came to Jane. Not anymore. Not after tonight.

For once in his life, Mac took a chance that fate might work in his favor. He couldn't think past that. He didn't want to. This time around, he would take a gamble.

Jane was worth the risk.

Bacon sizzled in the pan, eggs boiled and Jane stared out the kitchen window, still in awe, her body humming from making love to Mac last night. He'd been breathing strongly and steadily when she'd left him minutes ago to allow him the rest he needed. He'd been injured last night, and Jane couldn't contain the fear she'd felt seeing him bruised like that. She couldn't contain her relief, knowing that his injuries weren't life threatening. But mostly Jane couldn't contain the love swelling up inside her. Deep, fresh emotions sang in her veins, and her heart was awash with guarded joy. She wanted to feel every sensation, let it seep in and take hold, but a part of her held back. A part of her worried about Mac's reaction.

He had been reserved—resigned, really, to not getting emotionally involved with her. He'd been the responsible one, the one who faced facts. Jane didn't know her past, but that didn't mean she didn't have one.

She prayed that Mac wouldn't wake up this morning and tell her that they'd made a mistake last night. She couldn't bear the blow to her heart if that happened.

Just as that thought settled in her gut, Mac stepped up behind her, wrapping his arms around her waist and dragging her body up against his. She leaned back against him, resting her head just under his throat.

"Morning," he said, nibbling her earlobe, his lips warm and inviting.

"Oh, Mac," she said quietly, relishing the feel of his arms around her once again. "It is a good morning, isn't it?"

"The best," he said softly, running his hands up and down her rib cage in a soft, sensual caress.

The frying pan crackled as the scent of bacon permeated the air, reminding her of the breakfast she'd wanted to present to Mac this morning.

She turned around in his arms to look at his face. Dark patches of bluish-purple appeared harsher in the daylight, more pronounced, but his eyes held hers with warmth and feeling. She reached up to gently outline a bruise just above his temple. "How are you this morning?"

"Pretty darn good, sweetheart."

"Really? I thought after you got hurt last night you'd wake up sore. How's your chest? Can I do anything to—"

He bent his head and kissed her soundly, pretty much cutting off her words. She had trouble formulating any coherent thoughts as well, falling into the kiss with total abandon. Mac was a take-charge kind of guy, and Jane decided she liked that about him, especially now as his mouth claimed hers and his hands took charge, roaming over her backside, stirring up wildly wicked thoughts.

"That'll do just fine," he said, ending the kiss and

taking a step back. He sighed and scrubbed his jaw. "I missed you in bed this morning."

"I wanted to make you breakfast. You need your nourishment, Mac. Especially after last night."

He cocked her a lopsided smile. "Seems to me I held up pretty well. You're the one who didn't want a second—"

"Mac!" Jane's jaw dropped. She couldn't believe he would be so open and earnest about their lovemaking. Jane hadn't wanted to exhaust him after he'd been involved in an altercation that left his ribs bruised and his body battered. It had been hard refusing him, and Lord knew she wanted him again, but she'd been worried about his physical condition. "I was speaking about the fact that you'd been in a fight last night."

Mac laughed and spun around to turn the knob on the stove. "Appreciate the thought, but I'll have to take a rain check on breakfast. I'm late getting to the station. I need to make out my report."

Jane hid her disappointment. She'd hoped it wouldn't be business as usual today. "Okay."

"Are you…okay?" he asked. "About what happened last night?"

She wouldn't pretend; she knew he was referring to the night they'd spent in bed together. "It was wonderful, Mac."

"Yeah," he said, and then he sighed again. "Are you going to the bookstore today?"

She nodded. "I had planned on it."

"Could you take the afternoon off?"

"Sure. Do you need me to do something? Is it regarding my case?"

He shook his head. "No, nothing like that. I'm going in to fill out my report, then I'm taking some time off. There's something…someplace I want to show you. Will you come with me?"

Does the sun shine? Is Paris a city? "I'd love to."

"Great, I'll pick you up at the bookstore later on. Oh, and wear comfortable clothes, nothing fancy, and don't wear those boots. They'd get ruined where we're going."

"Is this all yours?" Jane asked, her gaze roaming across the land surrounding a beautiful adobe ranch house. Mac had driven twenty miles out of town, to the verdant side of a mesa. Pike's Peak could be seen in the distance, and he had pointed out the amazing Kissing Camels rock formation.

"About twenty acres of it is mine," he said, and she couldn't miss the obvious pride in his voice. "This place was a wreck when I bought it. The house was in shambles and the property was in foreclosure."

"How long have you had it?" she asked, still pretty much stunned at this new facet of Mac's life. He was a private man, with private thoughts, and the fact that he wanted to share this with her was nothing short of spectacular.

"About eight years. I've been working on the house in my spare time."

Eight years? About the length of time Mac had been

divorced. Jane wondered if he'd needed a place, something to rebuild, something to make his own, after his marriage failed. Perhaps working on the house, fixing it up had been a sort of therapy for him.

"It's lovely."

He chuckled and guided her forward. "Wait until you see it up close before you say that."

Mac showed her in, and the massive ranch house instantly became a cozy refuge once she stepped foot inside. "I've got more work to do, but—"

"No buts, Mac," Jane said, taking a leisurely walk around, making note of a stone fireplace, wood beam ceilings, an inviting sitting area, wide bay windows that brought the outside prairie land inside. "This is unbelievable."

She turned to face him. He let out a deep breath and smiled. "I'm glad you like it."

"What's not to like?"

"Some people would think it too…rustic, too remote. It's just a rural home."

"It's more than that. I love it. When do you have time to come up here?"

"Weekends when I'm not working. Vacations. It's not so far that I can't stop by in the evenings, either. Sometimes Duke and Daisy Mae get lonely."

Jane raised her brows in question.

"My horses. Well, Duke is mine. I bought Daisy Mae for Lizzie. She comes up and rides with me once in awhile. I hired the neighbor's daughter, Angie, to feed and ride them when I can't get up here. She's real good with the horses. I was hoping you'd like to ride today. Do you know how?"

Jane thought for a moment, unsure. "I don't think so. But I'm willing to learn."

Mac smiled.

Overwhelmed with emotion, she walked over to him. "I'm glad you brought me here. It's a lovely home and I want the whole nickel tour." Then she put her arms around his neck, tugging him down to her level. When he expected her kiss, Jane surprised him instead by whispering quietly near his mouth, "A tour that ends in your bedroom, Mac. Do you think the horses will mind waiting?"

Mac pulled her closer, her body meshing fully against his hard, tight length. He took her lips in a long, sweeping kiss that left her completely breathless. "We'll give them extra carrots."

This time Mac did undress her, and he took his own sweet time. He peeled one article off after another, with calculated moves that swamped her body with slow, simmering heat. He touched her, caressed her and kissed her with such unhurried deliberation that she wanted to scream out.

"Be patient with me," he said, standing by his massive cedar-and-oak four-poster bed. "I want to know all of you."

Jane stood before him, watching afternoon light cast him in sun and shadows, defining his strong jawline and dark intense eyes. And when she was fully unclothed, she reached for him, to begin unbuttoning his shirt.

"No, not yet," he said, taking her shoulders and spinning her around. He brought her up against him, her derriere to his groin, her back to his chest. With a hand, he pushed her hair to one side and nibbled on her neck, planting light kisses there while the other hand held her hip, keeping her body firmly in place.

"Relax, Jane," he whispered in a husky tone.

Heart racing, Jane knew that was impossible to do. Her soft skin pressed against his rough jeans and she felt the heat of his hard, tight shaft. She took a deep breath and his heady musky scent enveloped her. "Mac," she muttered, but no other words formed. None were necessary.

His hands came up to stroke her breasts, the twin round globes aching for his touch. He stroked her gently, almost reverently, and whispered on a breath, "You're perfect, sweetheart."

Jane's legs nearly buckled, her body weakening at his touch. She rested against him, arching up, and Mac groaned, tightening his hold on her, rubbing her skin more fervently now.

He roamed over her body, splaying his hands, sizing her up, his fingers exploring every inch of her. With one palm on her belly, he let the other slide lower, and Jane felt a burning warmth between her thighs. Raw heat coursed through her, and when Mac finally found her core, cupping her, she moaned with relief, letting out a little gasp.

Mac kissed her neck again, moistening her skin with his tongue, while he continued to stroke her. Her body instinctively moved, and they swayed together as he continued his ministrations. His fingers parted her skin, and he found her center. Electric sparks flew, her body picking up the rhythm of his strokes. Her release building, Jane gave in, letting herself go. She moved without thought, without shame. Mac urged her from behind with sweet, sexy words that she felt more than heard.

Her climax exploded, shattering her and making every sensation become more vivid, more intense. Her pleasure heightened, but the love she felt for Mac wedged its way even deeper into her heart.

She collapsed against him, letting him hold her as she slowly recovered.

Outside, she heard the trees rustling and birds chirping, but inside, she heard only the beating of her heart.

Mac waited patiently, holding her without saying a word, as if he knew she needed this time. And when she was ready, she turned to face him.

His eyes sharpened on her, the brown nearly black and his expression unguarded, open. "I need you inside me now," she said, whispering the same words he had said to her last night.

Mac smiled as he dug into his pocket, then removed a handful of condoms. He tossed them onto the night-stand. Jane took one glance and grinned.

She lay down on the bed and waited. Mac undressed in front of her, his body gleaming and more than ready. He came down beside her.

"I want to know all of you," she said boldly, reaching for him.

Mac groaned as she took him in her hand. "I've always liked a woman with a thirst for knowledge."

"Really?" Jane's own voice was husky now. Unmercifully, she stroked the silky length of him. "Then relax and enjoy the ride, Mac. 'Cause there's a lot I want to learn."

Nine

Jane stroked Daisy Mae's mane, the coarse hair sliding beneath her palms. "Hi there, Daisy Mae. You're a pretty one, aren't you?"

The mare nuzzled her throat in response, seemingly happy to be out of the stable and in the fresh late-afternoon air.

"Careful," Mac said, "she's good-natured, but she doesn't know you yet."

Jane smiled. "I think we're going to be friends."

Mac stared at her for a moment, then nodded. "She's a chestnut quarter horse. Workhorses back in the Old West, but now she's got it soft."

Jane glanced at the ink-black horse that stood alongside Mac, nudging him occasionally for attention. "What about Duke?"

"Duke's a gelding quarter and a great guy." Mac stroked the horse's snout with tender care, much like he'd made love to Jane, just an hour ago. For all his gruff ways, Jane couldn't miss the gentle side to Sheriff Mac Riggs. He was hard as steel when he had to be, but Jane had seen his tender side, and both facets of the man fascinated her.

"Want to give it a try?" Mac said, gesturing toward the two saddles in a paddock to her right.

"Sure. As long as you take it slow."

He nodded and cast her one of his killer smiles. "I can do that."

Heat crawled up her neck. Jane remembered how well Mac could take it slow. So much so that her breath hitched as she recalled how controlled, how incredibly restrained Mac could be, just to ensure her own pleasure. "Okay, then."

Mac saddled both horses, giving her quick directions. "Mount from the left, hold the reins loose, but with enough tension to let Daisy know you're in control." He ran his hand along Jane's upper thigh, the simple touch enough to make her heart race. "Use this part of your body to lean in and let her know which way you want to turn. Horses understand body language. Don't solely rely on the reins."

Jane nodded, peering up into his dark eyes. "Okay, I think I've got it."

Mac helped her mount, handed her the reins and looked up at her. "Don't let Daisy know you're worried.

Ride with confidence. I've got your back, Jane. I won't let anything happen to you."

Jane let out the breath she'd been holding. For all she knew, this was the first time she'd ever been atop a horse. "I trust you, Mac."

His brows rose and something powerful flashed in his eyes. "Okay, here we go."

Mac mounted Duke, and Jane was amazed at how much taller he sat on his horse. She pictured him as a sheriff in the Old West, ready to lead a posse out on the range to capture a villain. Silently she laughed at the thought, but her amusement caught his eye.

"What?"

She shook her head. "Nothing. It's just that you look like you belong here, Mac. This place suits you."

He leaned over and kissed her quickly, the familiar warmth of his lips sending her heart racing again. "Let's go."

Mac led the way, and Daisy seemed to follow Duke without any help from Jane. Before long, Jane forgot that she sat upon a horse, instead enjoying the scenery and Mac's comments about the land and history of the area. They rode the perimeter of his property as the sun began its descent behind the mountain range.

Mac had them back at the house before dusk, Jane insisting on helping him bed down the horses for the night. Daisy Mae didn't seem to mind Jane's unsure hands as she used the leather-handled body brush, making sure she cleaned the brush with the curry comb. She worked as hard as Mac, giving Daisy a good brushing as Mac explained it helped to keep her skin clean and open up her pores. Then, with great care, she sponged Daisy's eyes and nostrils, cleaning them and washing her down.

"I'm impressed," Mac said as they entered the house.

"You are?"

He nodded. "Lizzie hates the clean-up part. Especially using the water brush on Daisy's tail."

Jane laughed. "I can see why. It's dangerous back there."

Mac chuckled, too, swinging his arms around her. He locked his hands behind her back, trapping her against him. "You're grimy, Jane. I think you need a shower."

"You're a mess, too, Mac." She lifted her nose in the air. "And is that horse dung I smell on you?"

"There's only one shower," he said, eyes twinkling.

"That's all we need."

Their clothes were off by the time they reached the bathroom. Mac entered first, adjusting the temperature, getting the water just right. "It's safe to come in."

Jane stepped inside, realizing that Mac's big muscular body took up most of the space. "I'd hardly call this safe." She gulped, staring at him as water rained down on her.

Mac didn't respond. Instead, he took the bar of soap and began lathering her all over. His slick hands soaped her up and down, his palms both smooth and a little rough on her skin. Raw need rippled through her body as Mac touched every part of her, his hands moving on her possessively.

She went through periods of holding her breath, then
letting it out in a pleasured sigh. Mac massaged her
backside thoroughly, the scented soap slipping and
sliding. Then he turned her around and worked her
upper body, his hands skimming her breasts, the quick
brief touches enough to make her cry out. He moved
lower, soaping her belly, and lower yet, his hands
spreading her legs, to clean her inner thighs. Every now
and then he'd kiss her, sometimes on her lips and sometimes on the very part of her he was washing.

Hot water rained down, creating steam enough to
fog the glass panes. Jane was sure that they'd be encased
in their own cloud of passion, regardless. And when
Mac had finished, he handed her the soap, claiming it
was her turn.

Jane took hold of the soap and worked up lather on
Mac's formidable chest, her hands spreading the tiny
bubbles across it until he was richly coated. She slid her
hands up and over, curling her fingers in the chest hairs,
grazing his flat nipples until they peaked.

Neither could ignore Mac's full erection, which stood
like a barricade against Jane's body, but she continued
on, soaping him up, giving as good as she'd gotten. She
lathered his strong thighs and bent to do his calves, elic-
iting a deep groan from Mac when she went higher to
work her hands over that area of his body that had grown
hard and tight.

But she wasn't quite through with Mac yet. She spun
him around and massaged his broad shoulders, working
down his back with the soap. Its citrus scent permeated

the room as she continued on, moving lower, to caress the slope of his buttocks, and causing her a deep intake of breath. But before she could finish, Mac spun around abruptly, shaking his head. "Can't take much more, sweetheart."

Jane braved a glance downward and nodded, the sheer, massive power of him overwhelming. He bent his head, taking urgent claim to her lips, his tongue probing. The hungry kiss led to more caresses, more urgency, until Mac maneuvered Jane against the tiled wall of the shower. Out of the steady stream of spray now, he lifted her up and impaled her with his shaft, entering her in one long, full thrust.

"Oh, Mac," she cried, holding his shoulders and wrapping her legs around him.

"That's it, baby," he rasped, his hands behind her urging her on, and together they rode the wave of their passion.

Eyes closed and heart racing, Jane reeled with the heady sensations of slick bodies, heat and steam. She met each of Mac's thrusts, oblivious to all else, until one niggling, unwelcome thought struck. She stopped and opened her eyes. "Mac, wait."

He halted, his eyes dark with desire, but wide with curiosity. "What's wrong?"

"We have no protection," she said, her breaths labored.

Mac froze for a moment, deep in thought, then he shrugged. "Doesn't matter," he said, and the implication was clear. He wasn't speaking of health issues here, but the thought of conceiving a child. And Mac didn't seem to think it a problem. His quick admission told Jane in so many words that what they had went beyond a summertime fling. Her heart soared with the notion, and she tossed her reservations away. No matter what her other life might have to offer, Mac had to be in her life from now on, she knew.

"It doesn't?" she asked, only for clarification.

Mac shook his head. "Not to me," he said. "I want you to know that. But you're right. You can't afford to get caught up in something that might be bigger than both of us. You have another life somewhere out there, Jane. And it's my job to protect you."

Jane tugged him closer and brought her mouth to his in a long hot kiss. "Thank you, Mac."

He lifted her in his arms and brought her to the bedroom, protecting her from everything but the one thing that he couldn't control—her unquestionable love for him. They joined bodies once again, finishing what they had started, but their hot, urgent mood had suddenly changed to reverent caresses and sweet indulgence.

Mac woke in the early morning with Jane in his arms. He lay curled around her body, the fit and feel of her something he would never forget. Her freshly showered scent filled his nostrils as sunlight poured into his bedroom, casting golden light on her honey-blond hair. He tightened his hold on her, bringing his body even closer. They'd spent the night here, at the ranch, and Mac held close to his heart the memories of sleeping with her last night and waking to the soft sounds of her breathing. Aside from Lizzie, he hadn't brought another female here, to his refuge, his home away from home.

He smiled, thinking of Jane atop the horse, hanging on for dear life, and then later, her attempt to groom Daisy Mae. She'd been happy to learn, eager to participate. Mac hadn't met too many women like Jane Doe, the mystery lady with the unknown past.

He sighed deeply, the sound resonating inside the room. Jane turned in his arms and opened her pretty, lavender-blue eyes. "Hi."

"Morning," he said, kissing the dimples at the corners of her mouth. "It's a workday, sweetheart. I need to get going."

"Mmm."

"I'll see what I can find for breakfast. Must have some cereal and dry milk in the pantry."

"I'm not hungry, Mac."

"No, neither am I." He flopped onto his back, staring up at the ceiling. He let out another long sigh, one he couldn't contain. He had something to tell Jane, something that he should have told her yesterday.

"What's wrong?" she asked, her hand gently caressing his wounded arm. He turned to look into her eyes, finding concern there. "Did we overdo it yesterday? Is it your chest?"

She slipped her hand onto his torso, her fingers splaying across his ribs with tenderness.

He covered her hand with his and laced their fingers. "No. I'm feeling better, just bruised."

"Then what's up?" she asked, again with concern.

"When I went into the station yesterday to file my report, we had some news about your case. Seems the investigation has turned up eight potential shoemakers that design custom boots like yours. It'll take a few days to track down a list of their clients. The boots are high-end, as you know, ranging in price from two to three thousand dollars a pair."

Jane sat up on the bed and leaned forward, clutching the sheet to her bare chest. She looked so beautiful sitting there with hope filling her eyes that Mac couldn't pry his gaze away. Yet he ached for her in ways he never had before in his life. The lawman in him knew it was his duty to find out who she was and to return her to the life she'd once led, the one she'd had before he'd found her up on Deerlick Canyon. But Mac cursed the news, as well. He'd come to dread the day when Jane Doe found out her identity.

"Are you saying I might find out soon who I am? That one of the names on the list might be mine?"

Mac nodded, gauging Jane's reaction. She smiled then and lay her head down on her pillow slowly, her eyes bright with anticipation. "I wonder what my real name is. Where I live. There are so many things I've wondered about."

She reached for his hand and squeezed it. "Just think, Mac. In a few days I'll know who I am."

"Maybe. I don't want to get your hopes up. Not yet. Not until we have something more concrete. That's why I held off telling you. But now...well, I figured that you and I have to face facts."

Jane wrestled the sheets off and sat up on her knees, naked to the world and beautiful to him. "What facts?"

Mac remained silent. He was torn with wanting what was right for Jane and the nagging pain in his gut telling him that she'd be gone before long.

She stared into his eyes and he couldn't hide the indecision he felt, or the pain.

Jane immediately responded. "It won't change anything between us, Mac. It can't."

He tossed back the covers and got out of bed. "*Everything* is going to change, Jane. We can't pretend it won't." He picked up his clothes and began dressing.

"I wasn't pretending…about anything," she said honestly, before getting up and grabbing her own clothes.

Mac waited for her to slip on her pants and blouse. "I wasn't, either. Let's just wait and see what happens." He wrapped his arms around her to reassure her, but he had doubts. He'd been a fool to get involved with Jane in the first place. Hell, he'd tried not to. Tried to ignore every sweet aspect of her personality, the tempting allure of her sexy body and those big lavender eyes. But from day one, he'd been a goner, and now they'd both pay the price. The last thing he wanted to do was hurt her.

Jane rested her head on his chest. He brought her closer, their bodies touching intimately, with a familiarity Mac had known only one other time in his life, with his wife. But nothing compared to how Jane felt in his arms, the rightness of it. Desire surged again, but he held back, needing to hold her more than anything else.

"I never thought that learning my identity might hurt me."

"It won't, Jane. I promise it won't. You'll be glad when you find out about yourself."

She lifted her chin and he felt her eyes on him. "Will I?"

He nodded. "Yeah, you will."

"And what about you?"

"Me?" he asked, looking away, ignoring her penetrating gaze. He didn't want her to see his face when he told the biggest lie of his life. "I'll be glad, too, Jane. It's what we've been working for all this time. Now, we both have work to do today. Are you ready?"

Jane glanced around the ranch house with sadness in her eyes. "Yes, I'm ready. Let's go home."

The words stuck in Mac's head all the back to Winchester. He hadn't planned it, didn't know how or when it had happened, but he'd come to think of Jane as "home."

"What do you mean, you're moving out?" Mac interrogated Lizzie from across the parlor.

"Exactly what I said, Mac. I found a place and I'm moving out. It's time, big brother. Doesn't mean that I don't love you, or I don't appreciate you taking care of me all those years when I was a kid. But I'm not a kid anymore."

Jane watched the scene unfold from the doorway of the parlor, frozen to the spot. She'd known things would change between her and Mac when Lizzie arrived home this morning, but she couldn't have guessed this turn of events. Jane didn't want to interfere, felt it wasn't her place to listen in on this conversation, but Lizzie had asked her to be there, to act as a buffer when she told Mac the news. Jane couldn't refuse Lizzie's request. Both siblings had done so much for her. And she wanted to help Lizzie. She wanted to see her happy.

"Hell, I know you're not a kid. That's not what this is all about."

"It's about me gaining some independence. It's about giving you the space you need, Mac."

He gestured widely, his arms outstretched. "It's a big enough house. I have all the space I need."

"Then maybe I don't have all the space I need," she said quietly, looking at Jane. Jane nodded, giving her encouragement. Mac was formidable, a man you wouldn't want to cross, but Lizzie had rights, too, and Jane wouldn't refuse her support. "I found a place just a few miles from here, Mac. It's great, really. And I have plans for fixing it up."

Mac stared at her, then at Jane. He paced the floor, his face a study in fury. He shook his head over and over, breathing deeply.

Jane hated to see this confrontation. These past few days with Mac had been glorious. After they'd returned home from his ranch house, they'd gotten into a domestic routine like any other happy couple. Mac would go off to work and Jane would spend time volunteering at the bookstore. She'd come home and fix dinner, then they'd spend quiet time sitting together outside, talking about mundane things until they fell into bed. Nothing was mundane about their lovemaking, though. It was hot and passionate one time, then sweet and lazy the next.

The only bleak spot marring their days had been with the news that Jane's identity was still a mystery. The investigators, including Mac himself, had located every woman who'd had boots made by the eight shoe-makers on the list. Every one had checked out. Every single woman had been accounted for. Mac had come home that night with a dozen red roses, gently breaking the news to her. Jane had been sorely disap-pointed, her hopes dashed, but Mac had been so sweet and tender, holding her and making love to her throughout the night, that Jane had woken with a newfound feeling of hope. And it had little to do with learning her identity.

"Damn it!" Mac's curse brought her back. He threw his arms up, his voice filled with disgust. "Maybe Jane can talk some sense into you."

Jane walked over to him, put her hands on his arms and said gently, "Maybe you should *talk* to Lizzie, Mac. All you've been doing since she told you her plans is shout. Sit down and listen to her." Jane turned to Lizzie. "Both of you, listen to each other."

Mac opened his mouth to comment, but a knock at the door stopped him. He walked over and yanked the door open.

Deputy Lyle Brody stood on the threshold.

"Morning, Sheriff."

Mac grunted, his face grim. "Brody. What's up? Hell, it's Sunday. Is there a problem at the station?"

Standing tall, Lyle peered into the house, meeting Lizzie's eyes. He smiled, and Mac turned his head in his sister's direction to find Lizzie smiling back. Jane walked up to stand beside her. "Actually, boss, I came here to see Lizzie."

"This isn't a good—"

Lizzie rushed up and slipped out the door to stand right next to the deputy. "Hi, Lyle."

"Lizzie," Lyle said, "it's good to see you. Do you have time to take a walk with me?"

Lizzie turned her back on Mac and answered, "I'd love to."

Mac turned to Jane, his face wrought with emotion. He slammed the door after the two had taken off down the street. "What the hell's happening around here?"

Jane took his hand and led him over to the couch. "Sit."

He glared at her with defiance, but Jane knew him better than that. She knew his gruff facade was only window dressing, covering up a more vulnerable man underneath. That guarded vulnerability was one of the reasons she loved him so much. She reached up to kiss his lips, and gave a little shove. "Sit down."

The shove wouldn't have budged him if he hadn't wanted to comply. He sat down.

She planted herself atop his lap and wrapped her arms around him. "Things are changing, Mac. And it's okay."

"It's not okay."

"Lizzie doesn't want to hurt you. Don't make it

harder on her than it has to be. She adores you, Mac. But it's time to let her go."

"Don't give me the if-you-love-her-you'll-let-her-go speech, Jane."

Jane's chuckle broke the tension and she grinned. "You know me so well, Mac."

He didn't budge, his expression still grim. "What's she doing with him, anyway?"

"Lyle? She likes him. A lot. And apparently the feeling is mutual. She only wants your blessing. And in this day and age, I'd say that was something special."

Mac sighed heavily, closing his eyes. "He's not right for Lizzie."

"Mac, listen to me. I think I've figured out why you're so opposed to Lizzie seeing Lyle."

Mac tipped his chin up to listen, but with narrowed eyes. Jane knew she had to tread carefully. Mac was a prideful man who didn't like anyone analyzing his motives. "I'm listening."

"All your life you've been in control of things. You took care of Lizzie when she was younger, being both brother and father to her. You worked hard at your job, and built a wonderful career as a sheriff who is highly respected. You're handsome and strong and perfect in almost every way."

"I don't think of myself like that, Jane."

"I do."

His lips broke into a reluctant smile, but a smile nonetheless. "Yeah?"

She nodded. "Yeah."

"Are you trying to get me into bed, honey? Because I'm pretty much a sure thing."

Jane let out an unexpected chuckle. "I'm glad, but let's get back to the real subject here. I think that having Lyle around the station house is one thing, but you don't want to see him anywhere else. You don't want Lizzie to have a relationship with him, because every time you see him, it's a reminder of the one failure in your life, Mac. I'm not saying your divorce was your fault. I don't think it was, but Lyle Brody reminds you of something you couldn't fix. Something that you couldn't control. You don't have anything against Lyle personally. In fact, I think you like him. It's what he represents that bothers you."

Mac sat there quietly, absorbing her little speech, staring off into space.

"Am I close?" she asked.

He lifted her off of him, gently setting her down on the sofa, then stood up to face her. With hands on hips, he stared into her eyes, his expression pensive. "I don't know, Jane. I'll give it some thought."

Jane stood to face him, and her encouraging smile was enough for Mac at the moment. He couldn't remember a time when he'd been happier. She wrapped her arms around his neck, her expression so open and honest. "I meant all those things I said about you, Mac. You're a special man."

Mac had to face facts. He was crazy about Jane. *She* was the special one, the woman who had filled his life and brought him a kind of joy he'd never known before.

It was time he owned up to his emotions. It was time to admit to Jane what was in his heart. "Jane, I'm—"

A hard knocking at the door interrupted Mac's confession. With a deep sigh, he glanced at the front door. "Lizzie must have gotten locked out," he said, shuffling aside his annoyance. His sister had lousy timing, but he wasn't angry with her. Not anymore. Thanks to Jane, he decided to cut his sister some slack. "Maybe it wouldn't be such a bad thing to have her move out," he said, striding to the door. "At least this place would quiet down some."

"I'll be in kitchen making coffee," Jane said, grinning, and Mac figured she wanted to give him a chance to speak with his sister alone.

Mac opened the door. To his surprise, it wasn't Lizzie standing on the doorstep, but an impeccably dressed man with jet-black hair, looking him directly in the eye. "Sheriff Riggs?"

Mac nodded, a sense of dread he couldn't explain invading his chest.

"I'm here for Bridget Elliott."

Ten

Mac swallowed hard. He sized the man up in one quick moment and his instincts told him this was the real deal. The air of confidence about him, the way he looked Mac squarely in the eyes and his well-groomed appearance told the lawman that the mystery surrounding Jane Doe would soon be over.

In a smooth move, the stranger produced a wallet-size picture. His heart in his stomach, Mac took a quick look, seeing Jane smiling at the camera, with this man's arms around her. "You do recognize the woman in the photo? Is this the woman who's been living here?" he asked, and Mac came out of his stupor to realize that he should be the one asking questions.

"Before I answer that, let me ask how you arrived on my doorstep and who are you?"

The man shot him a no-nonsense look. "I've been searching for Bridget for ten days, Sheriff. I have contacts that led my search here."

Mac didn't miss the note of softness in the man's tone when he spoke Bridget's name.

Bridget?

Was Jane's name really Bridget Elliott?

"What kind of contacts? Who are you?"

"My contacts aren't any of your concern. All that matters is finding Bridget."

"I still don't know who you are," Mac said firmly.

"My name is Bryan. I'm Bridget's—"

"Mac, coffee's ready," Jane called out, and Mac gauged the man's reaction at hearing her voice. His eyes widened and he tried to peer into the house. "That's her voice," he said decisively. "May I?" He took a step forward to enter.

Mac wanted to block the doorway. He wanted to send this man packing. He didn't know a thing about him, except he *did* know. The truth. This man had come to take Jane home.

A soul-searing pain settled in Mac's gut. Everything inside him ached with the knowledge that Jane was lost to him now. This man named Bryan had come to claim her. A quick glance at his left hand said he wasn't married to her. But that didn't mean that they weren't deeply involved. Maybe engaged? All of Mac's initial fears and apprehensions had come full circle now. And another emotion he hated to admit tore at him. Jealousy. So deep, so raw, that it shook him to the core.

He forced himself to step away and allow the man entrance. Both men stood just inside the house.

"The coffee's hot, Mac," Jane said, coming out of the kitchen holding a steaming mug. She shot him a look, then her gaze flew to the man who called himself Bryan. "Oh hi, Bryan. What are doing…"

Jane stopped, the mug in her hand, shaking. She blinked, and Mac noted the revelations, her past instantly becoming her present, all reflected in her deep lavender eyes. She took a moment, as if she'd been hit with the fast-forward button to her life. There was no doubt that her memory had returned. He saw it all in her expressive face.

Slowly, she set the mug down, then smiled at Bryan with such warmth that Mac felt as though an elephant had trampled his body. "Bryan!"

She raced into his outstretched arms and he swung her around, lifting her off the ground, joy evident on both of their faces. "Oh my God," she said, "Oh, my God. You're here, you're really here."

Bryan set her down. "I'm here, honey. I've been searching for you. You gave us all a big scare."

"I had amnesia, Bryan. But everything came back to me. Just now. Seeing you. I can't believe it. Everything's back."

"That's great, honey," Bryan said, his gaze roaming over her, as if making sure she was all right. That proprietary look struck Mac like a sharp knife to the gut.

Mac had been the one seeing to Jane's welfare all this time. He'd reserved that right for himself.

"I'm glad I found you," Bryan continued. "What the hell happened to you?"

"I remember now," she began after a brief pause. "I flew to Colorado nearly two weeks ago, after Cullen's wedding. My rental car broke down, so I started walking up the canyon road. I fell and hit my head. That must have been when I lost my memory. Mac found me. He and his sister, Lizzie, took me in." She glanced at Mac, her face beaming. "Oh, sorry. Here I am, going on, and I haven't introduced you. Bryan, this is Sheriff Mac Riggs. Mac, this is my cousin, Bryan Elliott."

"Cousin?" Mac couldn't help blurting out. Stunned, he shook the hand Bryan had offered, still reeling with this new turn of events. Relief swamped him, and Mac took his first calm breath since the man had showed up on his doorstep.

"Yep. Bryan and I are cousins. And I have a whole family back in New York, Mac. A whole big crazy family. I can't wait to tell you all about them."

Mac ran his hand along his jaw, his lips pursed, listening to Jane—to Bridget Elliott—as she filled him in about her life. She'd smile as the memories washed over her, reciting them to him but at the same time seeming to relive them.

Mac cursed his bad luck. Bridget Elliott was a rich New York socialite, whose family had an estate in the Hamptons, no less. Her family owned one of the most prestigious magazine publishing houses in the world. Bridget was the photo editor for *Charisma,* a high-end fashion magazine that catered to the rich and beyond. Hell, he'd been sleeping with a woman who under any other circumstances he wouldn't have given the time of day. Bridget Elliott was way out of his league.

He'd already had one failed relationship with a woman who had higher aspirations than bedding down with a small-town sheriff. Mac couldn't help but place Bridget—he'd have to get used to calling her that—in the same category. Bridget Elliott might look like Jane Doe, might talk like Jane Doe, but Mac wouldn't deceive himself. They were worlds apart.

Bridget Elliott had money to burn.

Her family could probably buy the whole of Winchester without so much as blinking their eyes.

"Bryan owns this very trendy restaurant called Un Nuit. His place is great. I can't wait for you to see it, Mac."

Mac held himself in check. "Bridget," he said awkwardly, using her real name for the first time. "Your cousin Bryan might own a restaurant, but there's more to him than meets the eye."

"What do you mean?"

"Your family is powerful and wealthy, yet they couldn't find you. But Bryan did. And he wouldn't speak of his methods. Take it from a man in law enforcement, your cousin isn't exactly who he seems."

"Oh, don't be silly, Mac. Of course he is. Bryan just likes to be…cryptic at times."

Mac nodded. "That's one way to describe him."

But Bridget was eager to go on. "And guess what, Mac. The boots. I know why you couldn't track them down in Italy. Poor little Carmello DiVincenza, a genius at shoemaking, died two years ago. My boots were the very last ones he'd made. No wonder I cherish them. He lived and worked and died in this little village just south of Florence called Micello. I remember doing a photo shoot there for a story with *Charisma*. He insisted on creating the boots especially for me."

"So you trot around the world, doing whatever you do for this magazine." Mac leaned back on the sofa, glad that they were alone. Lizzie was still out with Lyle, and Bryan had left a few minutes ago, to give Bridget time to collect her thoughts. Of course, he wouldn't say where he was staying. He'd just used the classic Arnold Schwarzenegger line: "I'll be back."

"No, not always. I work in the offices at EPH—that's Elliott Publication Holdings—but on occasion, I go on location for a shoot. I love Europe, and Italy is my favorite country."

"So you're the one with Trump money." Mac couldn't keep the edge out of his voice. Bridget couldn't help who she was, but he didn't have to like it.

She stared at him. "Mac. I know what you're thinking, but I'm not a spoiled little rich girl. In fact, I deplore everything my family stands for. It's the reason I came to Winchester to begin with. My family is full of secrets."

"What family doesn't have its secrets?"

"Oh, but my family is different. We have a whole

volume of secrets. And I plan to expose them all—and expose my grandfather for the man he truly is. There'll be no whitewashing my accounting of his life. I'm writing a revealing book to expose his self-serving manipulations. My book will uncover truths that have been secret for decades."

Mac shook his head, staring at Bridget, seeing her with clear eyes. She wasn't his Jane Doe anymore. She was a cynical woman bent on…what? Revenge? Payback? Or did she feel that her tell-all book would somehow be justified?

"Sounds like you're going to hurt a whole lot of people."

"To clear the air, Mac. Patrick Elliott, my esteemed grandfather, has gotten away with too much to get to the top. He's got the media in his back pocket. All these years he's covered his tracks well. He needs to be stopped. He's only getting what he deserves."

"And you think a book is going to solve all the problems?" Mac rose. He set his hands on his hips, staring down at her. "Innocent people will get hurt."

"But innocent people *have* been hurt, Mac. I came here because I received an anonymous tip that my aunt Finola's child might be living right here in Winchester. A child my grandfather forced her to give up for adoption when she was just fifteen years old. He'd used his power and influence over her and it nearly destroyed her. *Charisma* is all the life she has now. It's not fair, Mac. She shouldn't have to go through life not knowing her daughter. I came here to find her. I know she was adopted by a couple living here in Winchester."

"That's what brought you here?"

She nodded, standing to face him. "It's the sole reason. I came here to find and reunite Aunt Fin with her daughter."

"It's none of your business, Bridget." Mac still couldn't get used to her real name. It sounded false on his lips, as though he wasn't speaking with the same woman who'd had come to mean everything to him. "It's not your battle."

"It is my battle. Fighting my grandfather and uncovering the truth about him is what I set out to do six months ago. The book is the means to the end. It'll put a stop to all the scandals. My family can then put the past behind them. Finding Aunt Fin's child will make her happy and will send a message to Grandfather Patrick that he can no longer mess with our lives. Aunt Fin has suffered for too many years. Her daughter would be twenty-three now."

That rang a bell with Mac. Could it be that it was his friend Travis's daughter whom Bridget was looking for? Jessie was the right age, twenty-three, and she'd been adopted as a baby from a teenaged mother. Travis didn't talk much about Jessie's adoption now, having fallen in love with his daughter from the moment he'd laid eyes on her. No one would guess that Jessie and Travis didn't hold a flesh-and-blood bond.

Mac and Travis went way back, and recently the rancher had been helping Mac fix up his ranch house.

Hell, the last thing his friend needed was to have his life turned upside down by Bridget's interference. It was bad enough that Travis lost his wife a few years back.

"You're messing with people's lives, Bridget." Mac stood firm, speaking adamantly. "Don't do this."

"I have to."

"No, you don't!" He turned his back on her and threw his arms up in disgust. "Of all the rotten luck. I can't believe I fell in love with a rich bitch, willing to destroy so many lives." Then he turned to her, hot anger reaching the boiling point. "You're not the woman I found up on Deerlick Canyon. Not if you do this. That woman isn't vindictive. She's not so cynical that she feels justified in damaging lives. Let it be, *Bridget*."

"I can't, Mac," she said, facing him squarely. "Don't you understand? The book is nearly finished. Finding Aunt Fin's child will be the final chapter."

Mac stared into those vivid, gleaming blue eyes. He realized he'd finally opened his heart to allow love inside, to have it all shatter around him in one quick instant. Bridget Elliott—bitter, cynical and so damn beautiful that she took his breath away—wasn't the woman for him. She'd been born with a silver spoon in her mouth and could be doing something positive with her life; instead she chose to cause misery and heartache to those around her.

Mac wouldn't allow her to cause that misery here, not now, not in his town and not in his house. He wouldn't do that to Travis or to himself. There was only one solution. "When your cousin returns, I think you should leave."

"Mac," she said in a quiet voice, tearing his heart out with her plea.

He held firm, but he had to force the next words. "If you intend to go ahead with your plans, you have no place here."

Slowly she nodded, and Mac cringed inwardly. She wouldn't give up. "I have to finish what I started."

"Then we'll have to say goodbye. Go back to New York, Bridget. It's where you belong."

Lizzie burst through the door, her face awash with joy. "Lyle asked me out on a date! And he offered to help when I move into my apartment. Jane, we have to shop. I need your help in finding the perfect outfit."

Mac took a last look at Jane, or the woman he wished was Jane, then directed his gaze to his sister. "She's not Jane. Her name is Bridget Elliott and she'll be on the next flight to New York."

"I can't thank you enough, Bridget. I couldn't have put together these outfits without your help. But with all that's on your mind, I can't believe you still wanted to help me shop," Lizzie said, plopping her shopping bags on Bridget's bed.

Bridget sat down on the bed and soon Lizzie joined her. "I made you a promise, Lizzie. Besides, you've done so much for me and I wanted to return the favor. It was fun. Took my mind off…things."

"Like the fact that your plane leaves in three hours? I can't help it. I wish you weren't leaving," Lizzie said with great sadness. "My brother needs you."

Bridget leaned back to rest her head against the pillow. She closed her eyes, and visions of Mac rushed forward. His rare smile, the way he would hold her, the tender way he made love to her. "Mac doesn't understand what I'm trying to do."

"No, and he probably won't change his mind, either. He's always been so sure of what's right."

Bridget snapped her eyes open. "So you don't think I'm doing the right thing, either?"

Lizzie took hold of her hand. "It's none of my business, really. It's between you and my brother." She squeezed her hand firmly. "I know Mac's hurting, too. He didn't say much, but it's all on his face, the pain of losing you. You have to promise me one thing, Bridget."

"Anything."

"Don't return a thing he's given you, not the clothes, not the jewelry. And for heaven's sake, don't you dare try to pay him back. I know my brother. That'll just about kill him."

Bridget nodded. "I'm glad you told me. But I want to do something to return your kindness."

"Just be my friend, Bridget. That's all I need. Maybe give me some fashion advice once in a while?"

Bridget chuckled. "Sure."

"I'm going to miss you."

Tears stung Bridget's eyes. She'd come to love both brother and sister in this household. And she knew that her life would never be the same since knowing them. She wrapped her arms around Lizzie and they hugged tightly.

"Me, too. But do yourself a favor, Lizzie. Don't back

down with Mac. Don't change your mind about moving out or your plans with Lyle."

Lizzie sat thoughtfully for a moment. "But my brother—"

"Lizzie," Bridget began firmly, "don't you dare. You've devoted your life to Mac. You've been a good sister, and I think Mac really does want your happiness. I'm hoping I got through to him, at least about that."

Lizzie smiled. "I hope so, too."

Bridget rose and began filling the duffel bag Lizzie had given her. Within a minute, she was all packed and ready.

Mac popped his head in the doorway. "Your cousin's here to pick you up."

"Oh." It all seemed to be happening so fast. Bridget turned to stare into Lizzie's pretty brown eyes. "I have to go."

Lizzie nodded and stood. "I know."

"Bye, my friend." Bridget held back the flood of tears surging forth. Crying wouldn't help the situation. What was done was done, and Bridget knew her time in Winchester was over.

"Goodbye," Lizzie whispered, giving her one last hug. "I'll entertain Bryan while you two say goodbye."

Lizzie left and Bridget stared into Mac's dark eyes. She grabbed the straps of the duffel bag, which was filled with things that would be a constant reminder of Winchester County and Mac Riggs. Things that held special meaning…things she couldn't part with. "I guess it's goodbye, then."

Strong and tall and always in control, Mac nodded,

keeping silent. Bridget walked over to him. "I can't leave without thanking you for everything, Mac," she said softly, drinking in the sight of him. She hoped she'd never forget those intense dark eyes, the way the tic worked in his jaw when he thought about something too long, or the way his eyes softened on her when they made love. "You're an excellent lawman and a wonderful man."

With that, Bridget reached up to kiss his cheek, giving him a soft, subtle peck that belied her true feelings. But Mac didn't want her to kiss him. He didn't want her in his life or in his house. She'd been effectively tossed out. Not even his admission of love earlier helped this moment, since his next words, "rich bitch," had cut deep into her heart. He didn't want to love her. And that hurt the most, because Bridget loved him with everything she had inside. She loved him no matter what. But their differences had torn them apart.

"I'm going to miss Winchester," she said honestly. "And you most of all."

She strode past him, hoping he'd call her back. Hoping he'd say something. Silence ensued. And his indifference said it all.

"You ready, cuz?" Bryan asked, grabbing her duffel bag and opening the front door.

She stopped and turned around, looking into Mac's cool dark eyes one last time. "I'm ready. Let's go home."

Eleven
<u></u>

"You okay?" Bryan asked as he drove along the private road leading to The Tides, Patrick Elliott's Hamptons estate. Bridget peered out the car window, noting the manicured gardens, the long circular driveway leading up to the estate and the house itself, understated yet so grand. Salty sea air from the Atlantic just below the bluff brought back memories of happier times, when she would run and play in the sand along the beach with her brothers and cousins.

Bridget remembered it all. The familiarity didn't bring her comfort, though. Her mind and heart were still fixed on a cozy Colorado house and a small-town sheriff who had embedded himself in her soul. "I will be, once

I see Mom. You said she was okay, right? It's been two weeks since I've seen her."

Bryan nodded. "She's been worried about you, Bridget."

"I'm so sorry about that." Bridget hated to worry her mother, but she hadn't planned on losing her memory. She hadn't planned on falling in love, either. Even now, as she thought back on her time with Mac, she couldn't honestly say that she'd change anything. Knowing him and loving him had brought a greater wealth to her life than anything her grandfather might fathom. But Mac couldn't understand why Bridget had to change things in her family.

"Mom's got enough to deal with right now." Four months ago Karen Elliott had undergone a double mastectomy. Ever since then she'd spent a lot of time at her in-laws' Hamptons estate.

"She's a tough cookie. Never lets on when she's down. But I know she'll be thrilled to see you."

Bryan stopped the car just outside the front doors. "I can't come in. I've got pressing business. Give Aunt Karen my love, will you?"

"I sure will. And that 'pressing business' has to do with the restaurant, right, cuz?"

Bryan slanted her a look. "What else?"

"Right," Bridget said, slanting him a look right back. She wondered if Mac's instincts were right about Bryan. Could her cousin be more than he appeared?

Bridget exited the car, giving him a big hug when he came around to her side to hand her the duffel bag.

"Thanks again for finding me. I don't know when or how I might have gotten my memory back without you."

Bryan kissed her cheek. "All in a day's work," he said. Right before hopping back into the driver's seat, he added, "For a second or two back in Colorado, I wondered if you really wanted your memory back."

"Another story for another day, Bryan." She waved in farewell, watching him leave, before climbing the steps to her grandfather's home. And when she opened the door, the scent of grandeur filled the air, from the lavish Italian marble beneath her feet to the rich antiques lining the wall of the regal foyer.

Always understated. Always elegant. Her grandmom Maeve had decorated the estate in the same manner that she'd carried herself.

Minutes later, Bridget found her mother sitting peacefully in the solarium, looking out at the ocean. The water took on a soft glow as the sunlight began to fade. Bridget watched her for a long moment before announcing herself, noting her pale complexion, a sign that the chemotherapy was sapping her strength. The colorful satin scarf around her head was just another reminder of what her mother had gone through recently.

"Hi, Mom."

Her mother turned at the sound of her voice. "Bridget, honey." She stood and her smile lit her face with renewed energy. Bridget ran into her mother's warm and loving arms. "I'm so glad you're all right. Any complications from the fall or the amnesia?"

She shook her head, breathing in her mother's

familiar flowery scent. "No, nothing. I'm fine, but I've been worried about you."

"I'm recuperating. It's a slow process, but I'm going to be okay."

The embrace lasted a long time, Bridget finding it hard to let her mother go. When they finally broke apart to take their seats facing the incredible Atlantic waves, Bridget spilled her heart to her mother about her time in Winchester with Mac and her confusion about writing her book.

Karen Elliott gave her a good piece of advice. "There's only one person who knows what's right for you, honey."

"I've set out to do something, Mom. I've never been a quitter."

Her mother smiled warmly, her green eyes bright and honest. "Sometimes we get exactly what we want, only to find out it's not what we wanted at all. Take some time, honey. Think what's most important to you."

"That's all I have been thinking about since leaving Colorado."

"Well, then, let me give you something else to think about. Your father and I are going to be grandparents. Gannon and Erika have just announced that they are expecting a baby."

"Really? Oh, Mom, that's great news."

"Yes, and I plan on being healthy enough to babysit my new grandchild."

"You will be, Mom." Bridget sighed, thinking about her one time jet-setting brother. "Just think, my big brother is going to be a father."

Karen chuckled. "Hard to believe, but yes. I think he finally met his match with Erika. They're very happy."

"Well, I'm happy for them."

Her mother reached for her hands, taking them in hers and applying gentle pressure. "That's all I want for my children, honey. Happiness. Sometimes it's not that hard to find, if you look in the right place."

Bridget's loft in SoHo was spacious and stylish but certainly didn't offer the same type of elegance her grandparents' home in the Hamptons did. She smiled as she roamed around, surrounded by furnishings and artwork that depicted her personality. Casual, contemporary and all the things a young twenty-eight-year-old woman might enjoy. But as she'd driven home this morning down Broadway, after spending the night at The Tides, she realized she'd never considered how cluttered the avenues were, how busy, the streets lined with shops, restaurants and brick buildings that looked as though they'd been here from the beginning of time.

All familiar.

Yet nothing so far had seemed quite right.

She would simply have to readjust. After her ordeal in Colorado, she supposed it was natural to feel a little "off" and out of tune with her normal way of life.

Bridget clicked on the radio and turned the dial, finding the station she wanted, tapping her toes to the music, killing time until her visitor arrived. When the knock came Bridget sighed with relief and strode quickly to the door, unlocking and sliding the heavy panel open.

"I brought wedding pictures," her new cousin Misty announced, lifting a white photo album in the air.

Bridget glanced at Misty's five-months-pregnant belly. In two weeks it seemed as though she'd grown another dress size, but Bridget wouldn't dare share those thoughts with her. Misty looked happy and pregnant pretty.

"Misty, I'm so glad you came to visit. Come in. Did you get your pictures back already?"

"Just the proofs. We'll get to that later." Misty gave her a good looking over, and once she seemed satisfied, she said, "You had us all worried sick. My maid of honor disappears right after our wedding reception and no one knows a thing! You didn't tell a soul where you were going. It's a good thing Bryan knew how to find you."

"My mistake. I'll never do anything like that again. Next time I'll be sure to let someone know where I'm heading."

Misty's eyes grew wide and her expression left no room for doubt that she didn't approve. "Next time?"

Bridget couldn't hold back a laugh. "Sit down. Take a load off."

"Hey, watch it. I'm older than you, but I still have some moves."

Both sat down on Bridget's cream leather sofa in an area of the loft known as the great room. Three rooms collided into each other and this one was where she relaxed, read, watched television or simply stared out of the giant floor-to-ceiling windows to the street below.

"I thought you used up all your moves on Cullen."

Her belly rolled when she chuckled. "Bridget, thank God you're home."

"Yeah," she said quietly, biting her lip. "I'm home."

"Uh-oh, I know that look. What's wrong?"

Bridget lifted her shoulders, shrugging casually, but inside she felt weighted down by heartache and indecision. "Nothing much, really. Except that I fell in love with the man who probably saved my life. He took me in when I had nowhere to go. Sheriff Mac Riggs. He thinks I'm a spoiled rich socialite with nothing better to do than to cause trouble. He doesn't approve of what I'm trying to do."

"Oh, I see." Misty's green eyes positively gleamed. "Mmm, a sheriff, you say? Tall, handsome? I bet he looks real good in his uniform."

The recollection of Mac in his uniform and *out* of his uniform was never far from her mind. "You're not making this any easier."

"Then let me ask you this—if he's so awful, why bother?"

"Yeah, you're right. Why bother? He is awful. Awfully stubborn. Awfully demanding." And then she softened her voice to a mere whisper. "Awfully kind. Awfully generous. Awfully sexy. So awfully good-looking that my heart stopped every time he walked into the room."

"Wow," Misty said, with a shake of her head. "So what are you waiting for? You're obviously crazy about him. Go back to Colorado and change his mind about you."

Bridget stood up and walked over to the window, glancing down at the street below. Traffic had come to a halt where two drivers had collided in a fender bender. They faced each other on the street, eyes bulging, mouths flapping and fingers pointing. She could only guess at the kind of language they used. She turned back to Misty. "I don't think I can change his mind."

"For a time Cullen didn't think he could change my mind, either, but he did. I wasn't making it easy on him. Thank goodness I put aside my misgivings. We're very happy," she said, patting her growing belly, "with a little one on the way. Bridget, if it's even remotely possible for you to have that kind of happiness, then do whatever it takes to make it happen."

Bridget took a deep, steadying breath, absorbing Misty's advice. But she still had doubts. She'd made herself a promise to write the book that would expose Patrick Elliott. And what of her aunt Fin? Didn't she deserve some happiness, too? "I'm still not sure, Misty. But I'll think about it."

"Don't think too long, my friend. Sounds like this guy has hunk-eligibility status." She fell silent for a moment as the radio blasted out Gretchen Wilson singing about rednecked women. "Heck, this guy's got you listening to country music. That *has* to mean something, honey. Now, I didn't just come over here to check on you. You're the photo editor in the family. How about taking a look at my proofs? I need help picking out a hundred or so for our wedding album."

"Gee, Misty, only a hundred?" she said on a teasing note, happy to have something productive to do today.

Tomorrow, she planned to start back to work at *Charisma*.

Bridget walked the halls of *Charisma* as she'd done a thousand times before, greeted by her employees and co-workers with welcoming smiles and hellos. She stopped to speak with a few, briefly explaining about her absence in the simplest terms. The trip to Colorado and her bout of amnesia were still too raw, too personal to talk about in detail, other than to the very few people she truly trusted.

Aunt Fin fell into that category. Bridget had worked alongside her for years and during that time they'd formed a close bond. Aunt Fin babied *Charisma* as if it were her own child. Everyone knew it. Everyone under-stood the need behind the countless hours and the devotion she put into the magazine. There was a void in her aunt's life, and Bridget had hoped to remedy that by finding the daughter taken from her at birth.

"Morning," she said, popping her head in the doorway of Finola's office.

Aunt Fin, knee-deep in paperwork as usual, slowly lifted her head, taking her eyes off the layout she'd been studying on her desk. "Bridget!"

She stood and came around her desk, meeting Bridget halfway into the room. Aunt Fin wrapped her arms around her, giving her a big hug, then pulled back to look into her eyes. "Thank God. You look wonderful."

"I do?" Bridget hadn't gotten much sleep last night. Or the night before. Pale and weary, she hadn't spent too much time covering up with makeup, either, this morning. But Aunt Fin always had something nice to say to her.

"You do to me, Bridget. I was worried sick about you." She guided her to the comfy sofa her aunt often used as a makeshift bed when working through the night. "Have a seat and tell me all about it."

"Don't we have a deadline?"

"We do. It can wait. Besides, we're ahead of schedule right now. I want to hear it all."

Bridget sat down with her aunt and held nothing back. She told Aunt Fin everything, from the anonymous tip about Finola's child she'd received at Cullen and Misty's wedding to her falling in love with and eventual breaking up with Mac. Her aunt sat back and listened attentively, and when Bridget had finally had her say, Aunt Fin took hold of her hands.

"You're my niece, Bridget. You know that I love you dearly, but I can't have you ruining your life for me. I want to know my daughter. I've dreamed of it often, but I don't want to cause a disruption in her life. I realize that she might not want to know me, but if she does, I've managed to list myself in a worldwide database. All of my information is out there on an adoption Web site. I'm easy to find, if my daughter feels the need. I only hope and pray that she's had a good life. And when the time is right, we'll find each other. So, write that book if you absolutely must, but I'd advise not doing it, Bridget. It won't change anything. If you immerse yourself in anger and resentment, you'll lose something more important. Love. And nothing is more precious than that. Not a bestselling book. Not even a bestselling magazine," she said with a sad smile.

"But—"

"No buts, Bridget. My father did something that ruined my life, but don't let him ruin yours. Scandalizing Patrick Elliott won't give you a moment of satisfaction, and he'll still end up the winner, while you…you'll have lost the man you love. Is it worth the price?"

Bridget drew her lip in, contemplating. "I hadn't quite thought of it in those terms."

"How much is Mac's love worth to you, Bridget? If you can let go of the past, you could have a wonderful future."

"That's a big if."

"Well, I'll give you another if. If it were me, I'd be on the next jet back to Colorado."

Bridget took Aunt Fin's advice and the next jet back to Colorado. She stood outside the Winchester County Sheriff's Station, butterflies attacking her stomach, her heart pounding madly and her head spinning. It was nearly midnight and she'd learned from Lizzie that Mac had been putting in late hours at the station these days. Mac's sister had seemed surprised to see her on her doorstep at that late hour, but she hadn't flinched, merely told her where she could find Mac, giving her a nod of reassurance and a big hug.

Bridget had needed that extra bit of encouragement. She'd always met her battles head-on, but this time it was different. This time her future was at stake. She was taking a giant leap of faith here.

Bridget entered the station house and was greeted by a deputy sheriff who recognized her. "He's in his office. Maybe you could do something to put a smile on his face. He's crankier than my old water heater."

Bridget nearly lost her nerve, but she talked herself out of fleeing the scene. She had to play this out. If she didn't, then she'd never know whether she stood a chance with the only man she'd ever love. She took the steps necessary to reach his office door, and knocked softly.

"What?" he bellowed.

His bluster made her smile. He didn't scare her. He never had. Instead, the sound of his gruff voice reminded her of how much she loved him.

She opened his door and stepped inside. "Working kind of late, aren't you?"

Mac snapped his head up from his desk. Surprise registered on his face, and his eyes were unreadable, except for one quick flash of hope. Then, catching himself, he looked down at the papers he'd been working on. "If you're here about your aunt's child, I think I know how you might find her."

"No, that's not why I'm here, Mac. Aunt Fin doesn't need or want my help. I've given up that search. She's listed her name on an adoption database. If her daughter wants to find her, she can."

Mac pursed his lips and nodded, keeping his eyes downcast. "We found your rental car in the lake about a mile up from where the others were found. Found the boys responsible, too."

"That's good, Mac. I knew you'd find them."

"Your luggage wasn't in there. They'd disposed of it."

"It doesn't matter."

Mac lifted his eyes to hers finally, staring at her, then he shifted his gaze to her throat. Bridget fingered the silver necklace he'd given her, the necklace she had never removed.

"No, I suppose it wouldn't. So why are you here?"

Bridget smiled and walked over to the side of his desk. Mac leaned way back in his chair, putting space between them. He couldn't let his guard down. Not yet. Not until he knew why she'd come. She looked beautiful and elegant, even though she wore a pair of blue jeans. They weren't Levi's, but some designer label that probably cost five times more than they should. Over them she wore the T-shirt he'd once given her. She'd rolled up the sleeves and tied the shirt at her waist, the initials WCSD crossing over her breasts. Winchester County Sheriff's Department.

Ah, hell.

Bridget dug deep into her big black tote and came up with a white bag from Colorado Chuck's. "One for me and one for you," she said, setting two Pike's Peak burgers out in front of him. The sloppy chili and onion-filled burgers stunk up the place, but Mac didn't give a damn. A smile lifted the corners of his mouth.

"Aside from a good meal, I came here to file a missing person's report. Seems that Bridget Elliott is missing." She seated herself on top of Mac's desk and leaned in a bit. Mac breathed in her scent, gazed at her silky blond hair and looked into her big lavender-blue eyes.

"Is she?"

"Well, the cynical and ruthless part of her is missing. And I'm sure that part of her will never be found again. Gone for good."

"And what else should I put in this report?"

"Well, it seems that Bridget Elliott still wants to write a book."

Mac's eyebrows arched up and he cursed the hope he'd experienced the second she walked into his office. She hadn't changed. She still meant to write that mean-spirited book.

"A children's book. Seems Bridget loved reading to the little ones at the bookstore. She thinks she might have found her true calling, writing children's books. That's *all* she plans on writing, Mac." Bridget smiled and her eyes shone with light. "Jane and Bridget are one and the same. I can't deny who I am. Yes, I'm wealthy, and all my life I've had privileges most people don't dare to imagine. But I've changed, Mac. Living here with you opened my eyes and my heart to something more important. The only thing I want now is your love, if you'll have me."

Hope sprung up again at her admission. She'd given up her idea of writing that scandalous book about her family. Maybe she was more like his Jane Doe than she thought.

Mac rose from his seat and stood before her. He braced both hands on the desk, trapping her so close that only inches separated their bodies. "Are you saying you're willing to give up trips to Europe, designer clothes and a lifestyle that most women only dream about?"

Bridget wrapped both arms around his neck and nodded. "For a chance at a lifetime of Pike's Peak burgers, rides out at your ranch on Daisy Mae and waking up with you every morning, Sheriff Riggs? You bet."

Mac could hardly believe he'd heard right. Heart pounding, head ringing, he had to ask, "Are you sure?"

Bridget's smile faded and for a moment he thought he'd imagined it all. "Mac, my whole family's in New York. I love them. I'll need to be in New York sometimes."

"We can manage that."

"We can?" she said, a hopeful note in her voice.

"Hell, Bridget. Look at this." He opened his desk drawer and lifted out the ticket he had tucked away. He handed it to her.

"It's a ticket to New York," she said, slightly puzzled. Then her beautiful eyes flashed brightly. "You were coming to see me tomorrow?"

"Planning on making a fool out of myself. I'd hoped to talk some sense into you and bring you home."

Joy washed over Bridget's face and those twin dimples peeked out, deep and adorable. Mac had never known love this powerful before. He'd never known that he could love someone so different from himself. He and Bridget came from opposite worlds, yet here he was, so deeply in love that he'd set aside all his misgivings and doubts to take the greatest leap of faith he'd ever had to face. "I'm crazy about you, sweetheart."

Bridget tossed her head back, her eyes shining. "I'm crazy about you, too."

Mac dipped into his desk drawer one more time, coming up with a black velvet box. Bridget gasped when she noticed it.

"Well, I might as well make a fool of myself tonight," he muttered. "Bridget Elliott, I love you with all of my heart. Will you—"

Bridget grabbed the black box and opened it. "Yes, yes! Oh, it's beautiful, Mac. My answer is yes."

He chuckled and placed the diamond ring on her finger. "Marry me," he finished, but he already had his answer. "Be my wife."

"Oh, Mac. I love you so much," she breathed quietly, as much in awe as he was.

He bent and kissed his soon-to-be wife deeply, his heart filled with love and devotion. The kiss went longer and deeper than Mac had expected, their mouths and bodies hungry for each other. When Bridget leaned back on his desk, papers flew as Mac followed her down.

"Mac," she whispered in a raspy voice, "you think it's a crime to make love to the sheriff in his office?"

Mac lifted himself off of her. "Probably," he said, walking swiftly to his office door and locking it good and tight before returning to the desk. He covered her body with his and claimed her lips in a long, slow, sexy kiss.

"But it'd be more than a crime if we didn't, sweetheart. It'd be a damn shame."

* * * * *